Spirituality through Interreligious Experience

Festschrift in Honour of Dr. Sebastian Painadath, SJ

I0634528

Spirituality through Interreligious Experience

Festschrift in Honour of Dr. Sebastian Painadath, SJ

Editor
Xavier Tharamel, SJ

2019

Spirituality through Interreligious Experience: *Festschrift in Honour of Dr. Sebastian Painadath, SJ*— published by the Rev. Dr. Ashish Amos of the Indian Society for Promoting Christian Knowledge (ISPCK), Post Box 1585, Kashmere Gate, Delhi-110006.

© Editor, 2019

All rights reserved. No part of this book may be reproduced or transmitted in any form or by any means, electronic, mechanical, photocopying, recording, or by any information storage and retrieval system, without the prior permission in writing from the publisher.

The views expressed in the book are those of the contributors and the publisher takes no responsibility for any of the statements.

Online order: http://ispck.org.in/book.php

Also available on amazon.in

ISBN: 978-93-88945-28-8

Laser typeset by

ISPCK, Post Box 1585, 1654, Madarsa Road, Kashmere Gate, Delhi-110006
• *Tel:* 23866323

e-mail: ashish@ispck.org.in • ella@ispck.org.in
website: www.ispck.org.in

Dr. Sebastian Painadath, SJ

Contents

Part-2
... encountering the other ...

Part-3
... moving as spiritual co-pilgrims ...

Part-4
... epilogue ...

Preface

This much awaited volume to honour Dr Sebastain Painadath, SJ brings out a collection of excellent inter-cultural and inter-religious reflections across the borders. It gives a comprehensive picture of interreligious approach from eminent thinkers on religions. This volume is a fitting tribute to Sebastian Painadath because its scope does transcend borders and points to new horizons. He has been going beyond the borders for more than three decades in the process of communicating inner spiritual journey to encounter the Divine. In this new millennium humanity finds no other way to rise above contemporary 'deadlocks' than through an inner journey.

The mission of Sebastian Painadath has been to help many seekers across the border realize the Divine dwelling within oneself. He always believes that diversity is beauty and this has been an abiding insight all through his life. He perceives beauty-in-diversity not only in the cultural spheres of human existence, like languages, art forms, literature, ideologies, etc. but also on the sacred landscape of religions with their scriptures, symbols, sages, myths and mystics. This aspect is highlighted by Norbert Nagler in his introduction.

The Vedic axiom *ēkam sat viprā bahudhāh vadanti* (Reality / Truth is ONE, those who perceive it speak of it in diverse ways, Rig Veda, 1.164.46) and the Catholic principle *Deus semper major* (God is ever beyond) shaped his theology and spirituality all these years. Any sort of absolute claim in relation to religion and the consequent fundamentalist attitudes has been alien to him; for these do not promote a culture of harmony and peace. The principle of inter-religious harmony, for him, means respecting the diversity of religions and recognizing the unity in spirituality. The distinction between spirituality and religion has been a basic premise in his theological reflection.

Sameeksha, Centre for Indian Spirituality, the brainchild of Sebastian Painadath, gradually took shape in an āśram setting incorporating the sublime values of Indian and Christian spiritual heritage: simplicity of life-style, closeness to local people, harmony with nature, an atmosphere of silence and study, and above all genuine hospitality to seekers of different religions and cultures.

Over the years Sameeksha has become a place where people of different religions and cultures feel at home. Sebastian Painadath is against big projects running at this centre. His concern all these years has been mainly to promote a culture of inter-religious harmony. In view of this, the Sameeksha Centre has been organizing inter-religious meditation sessions and *satsangs*, study of the classics of different religions, retreats based on the Bible, Bhagavad Gita, Upanishads and Sufi mystics, seminars on issues related to dialogue, ecology and social justice, a certificate programme of theological formation of the laity, life orientation programmes and counseling for adolescents, involvement in the acute issues of migrant labourers and some social uplift projects for the poor of the locality. Spiritual seekers from all over India and from other countries do come and spend a few days here for silent retreat and focused study. Those who have been thus acquainted with Sameeksha say that their stay in this ashram opened their minds to the mystery of the Divine vibrating in all human hearts, through all religions. A lot of warm friendship between persons of diverse religions emerged through these spiritual encounters; this is actually the base and goal of a culture of inter-religious harmony. Genuine inter-religious dialogue takes place where hearts meet in spiritual communion. True harmony evolves where the religious otherness of the other is respected. Genuine spirituality unfolds where there is openness to the *Spirit that blows where it wills*.

The first section titled "open horizons" is a collection of articles exploring various perspectives in the theology of religions. Michael Amaladoss addresses a significant existential question on suffering that people, whether religious or non-religious, face the experience of suffering. Francis D'Sa dwells on the Trinitarian spirituality because it takes all the three dimensions of reality, cosmic, divine and human, seriously. Felix Wilfred considers *Nostra Aetate* as a turning point in the relationship of Christianity to other faiths. Double Belonging: A Hypostatic Union, raises a serious question through the words of Paul F. Knitter. While Anand Amaladoss thinks in terms of the philosophical foundation for the Jesuit Mission Today within an intercultural dialogical Perspective, Xavier Tharamel looks at the interreligious approach of Raimon Panikkar and its uniqueness in the theology of religions.

The second section "encountering the other" invites one to perceive the encounter with other religions. In his article Christian M. Rutishauser uses an exclusively Jewish term, Halakha, to take the readers into the depth of Jewish-Christian encounter. Francis Clooney thinks that theology is an uncharted ground and religious diversity dramatized in vivid poetic form yields the possibility of returning to prayer and contemplation. Since prayer and praise of the Divinity can have dualistic forms there seems to be an unbridgeable gap between the one who praises (*stotā*) and the Divine; this is indicated by Bettina Sharada Baeumer. Gispert Sauch reminds that the Upanishads represent a moment of the Indian reality that integrated many forms of philosophy and spirituality found in the Bhāratvarsha in the first millennium before BCE. AMA Samy highlights silence as the source and ground from which words spring forth: the Eternal Father is silence, dwelling in light inaccessible. Christian notions of forgiveness and reconciliation and their Buddhist homologues are the concerns of Aloysius Pieris' article. Stephen Chundanthadam gives a scan of Zoroastrianism, both in the academic and religious realms, to deepen an appreciation for this ancient religious tradition. Priyadarshana Jain offers a spirituality of ahimsa from the Jain perspective. Victor Edwin brings in Fethullah Gülen, an outstanding figure from today's Muslim world who engages passionately and creatively to give witness to his faith by engaging with all by breaking many walls of prejudice, thus building strong bridges of enduring friendship with others.

The third section is titled as "moving as spiritual co-pilgrims" because it has five papers with more personal aspects of experiences in interreligious dialogue as indicated by Georg Evers in his article. Christian Hackbarth-Johnson presents an Integral and Interreligious Spirituality by following a spiritual path between Christianity, Zen and Sri Aurobindo. According to Martin Kämpchen life-related dialogue between Christianity and Hinduism is needed in the contemporary world because dialogue has become a fashionable word than a serious engagement. Jojo M. Fung theologizes on his rich experience of more than two decades of journeying with the indigenous peoples like Lakota the Apache in US, the Semai of Perak and the Murut of Malaysia, the Boctoc and Ifugao of the Philippines, the Karen and Lahu of northern Thailand and the Kayah and Kayan of Myanmar. Henry Pattarumadathil has a short narrative, semi-autobiographical in nature, recalling some of his memories and experiences from his forty-year long relationship with Sebastian Painadath.

The epilogue of the book contains an excellent article by Sebastian Painadath and a long and exhaustive list of his publications to help researchers. In a special manner I am grateful to all the writers who contributed to this volume. Fr Valentine Ekka, SJ and Fr V.T. Jose, SJ helped in the process of reviewing the text and they are gratefully remembered. Thanks to Nithin Monteiro for the creative cover. This volume would not have seen the light of the day but for the encouragement of Fr E.P. Mathew, SJ, the Provincial of Kerala Jesuit Province. ISPCK has been gracious in accepting our request to publish this work.

Xavier Tharamel, SJ

Introduction

Sebastian Painadath, a Relentless Spiritual Seeker

Dr. Norbert Nagler, Missio, Aachen, Germany

Today, Monday after Pentecost 2013, as I am giving final touches to this essay, the Catholic community of Sankt Josef parish in Puchheim, Munich, is celebrating the 40th anniversary of the priestly ministry of Sebastian Painadath SJ. During his theological studies at the University of Innsbruck he was well acquainted with the Puchheim parish which later took pride in having his ordination there. Ever since he was keenly interested in the pastoral and theological formation programmes in the local Church of Germany.

Since 1983 Sebastian has been closely associated with *missio*, Aachen / München / Wien. For about 10-12 weeks every year he used to conduct meditation courses, dialogue seminars and theological discourses organized by *missio* in the German speaking countries of Europe. It was never a *job* that he did, nor did *missio* ever want to make a *job* out of his services. It was rather a beautiful form of collaboration between two local Churches, between India and Germany / Austria / Switzerland. For *missio* he has been an effective partner in the theological and spiritual formation projects; for the thousands of participants he has been a spiritual guide helping them to look at life differently and to discover new paths with the divine Spirit. He was engaged in this service with authenticity and commitment. The collaboration between *missio* and Sebastian has been characterised by mutual trust and spontaneity. It is with great gratitude and appreciation that *missio* esteems his services. We consider this collaboration as an enriching gift of partnership within the universal Church.

In all these *missio* programmes Sebastian has been sharing with the spiritual seekers of the West the authentic elements of the spiritual heritage of the East. He did this out of the resources of his own spiritual experience, study and exploration. His concern is not to import foreign elements of spirituality to Europe but to help the people here discover the depths of the mystical traditions of Christianity in dialogue with the East. Hence his meditation courses were not just techniques of introspection; rather he offers them on the basis of great spiritual classics / masters like the Gospel of John, Letters of Paul, Meister Eckhart, Bhagavad Gita, Upanishads and the Church Fathers. For the participants the 4-5 days of meditative inner journey meant a rediscovery of the indwelling presence of Christ. Through spiritual discourses in a clear and simple language and through the repeated practice of meditation every day the participants are helped to experience a new access to the depth of Christian spirituality. Through these programmes of the last thirty years in the German speaking local Churches Sebastian Painadath has been acclaimed as a bridge-builder between the East and the West.

Sebastian´s life has been a constant pilgrimage; he has been a relentless spiritual seeker, a wanderer between continents. From the young years of his formation in the Jesuit Society he has been constantly on the move, spiritually and spatially. The Ignatian ideal to be ever alert to the *more universal good* characterises his life and spirituality. He is a seeker between philosophies and religions, a wanderer between continents, a pilgrim exploring the horizons of the Spirit. What he shares with others seems to touch a deeper note in them. His theological explanations and spiritual insights evoke in them an enthusiasm for a culture of dialogue. As a Jesuit and representative of the World Church he conveys surprising interpretations and wider perspectives which open up a new way of looking at spirituality and religion. He has been widely recognized as a competent resource person in matters concerning the theology of inter-religious harmony.

While on the way with *missio* programmes in Europe he is constantly on the move with an enormous discipline and generous availability. He is easily on the move between villages and cities, between retreat houses and academies, between formation institutes and theological faculties, between Protestant *Kirchentag* and Catholic *Congress*. From one programme to another he goes with very little regeneration phase in between; but he can be totally present to the next group. God has blessed him with bodily resilience and mental flexibility.

"To be always on the move" – this is how Fr Eric Englert OSA, President, *missio*, Munich, characterized Sebastian´s life and thought, his theological paradigms and spiritual search, his research and meditation. (Talk at the seminar on the 25th anniversary of collaboration between *missio* and S.Painadath, Würzburg, 10.03.2007). This spiritual dynamism makes a person creative and explorative. We know that our knowledge is so very fragmentary and our understanding so limited. Encounter with other persons helps us overcome this deficit to some extent. Hence to be on the move with others adds to the quality of life. Faith can motivate us to be in solidarity with others. "Jesus Christ is not so much the answer to our questions, as the question on our preconceived answers. Christ invites us to be on the move towards the wider horizons of the Spirit" (S. Painadath SJ, *Christ in der Gegenwart*, 27/ 1998, p. 230). In encountering others, in dialogue with others, in searching and struggling with others, our convictions gain clarity and our insights get deepened, religious growth takes place and the very knowing process overcomes boundaries. Readiness to move with others, to explore and experiment with others, presupposes openness and willingness to dialogue with them. Through the other I come to know myself in depth; in the other I discover myself anew with all my strengths and limitations; with the other I explore surprising elements of wisdom and of faith as well. This is the basic paradigm for inter-cultural and inter-religious dialogue. Sebastian clarifies this on the background of his dialogue with Hindus in India: "Hindus help us Christians to read our Scripture with a mystical sensitivity and to interpret our symbols in tune with the cosmos. On the other hand, we Christians inspire Hindus with the prophetic dimension of spirituality and with the resultant social responsibility." (cited according to Georg Evers, "Sebastian Painadath SJ, Theologe aus Indien", in: *Forum Weltkirche*, 2/ 2008, p. 29).

The talent for spiritual exploration was almost a birth-gift in Sebastian´s life. He recalls his early childhood days: "I was brought up under the loving care of my maternal grandfather who was born of Hindu-brahmin parents in 1886. In 1893 the family came over to the Catholic Church. He kept up his intellectual heritage and became a professor for Sanskrit at the University. I remember him holding me on his lap and reciting Sanskrit slokas, which left an indelible mark in my psyche" ("Nachwort" in: Peter Schreiner, *Bhagavad-Gita, Wege und Wesiungen*, Benziger, Zürich, 1991, p. 189). At the age of 24 in 1966 Sebastian entered the Jesuit Society in Kerala. After his theological studies in Innsbruck he did the doctoral research under the guidance of Professor Walter Kasper (now Cardinal) and procured doctorate in Theology from the University of Tübingen in 1978. After his return to India he was engaged in spirituality seminars and dialogue sessions, which brought him in close contact with Hindus and Muslims. With this rich experience he founded in 1986 an aśram at Kalady, Kerala, to promote a culture of inter-religious harmony based on the converging lines of spirituality. He named it *Sameeksha*, which means integrated vision, meeting everyone in friendliness. The vision of the Jesuit province in starting this aśram was to create a space where seekers of different religions and cultures would feel accepted and respected. For about two decades young Jesuits were given in this aśram context the three-year long basic theological formation.

Everyone who comes in contact with the *priest* in Sebastian would be impressed by the modesty and humanness of the person. He understands his priestly ministry as a form of humble service. "A priest is not primarily an authority figure or a manager; rather he is a man *en route*, a pilgrim-brother ever moving with spiritual seekers. His role is not to keep the faithful bonded to the traditional images of God, but to free them, to explore and experience the Spirit of Christ, that transforms their life to the new being" (S. Painadath SJ, *Christ in der Gegenwart*, 27/ 1998, p. 230).

So we at *missio* hope and pray that with God´s grace he may be able to continue for many more years this great service of sharing the liberative and humanizing message of the Kingdom of God with personal credibility and theological competence. Wholeheartedly I thank Sebastian officially in the name of *missio* and on my personal behalf for his long-lasting service, for the humanly precious friendship, for the enriching theological discussions and for the competent collaboration in our local Church.

Part-1
... open to the horizons ...

Religions and Suffering:
The Questions

Michael Amaladoss SJ

One of the existential problems that people, religious or non-religious, face is the experience of suffering. The source of suffering could be a natural catastrophe like an earth quake, a tsunami, a heat wave. It can be physical like various types of illnesses or being victims of natural or human caused accidents. It can be mental when we are hurt by some remark or other unwelcome behavior on the part of others. Natural and physical sufferings too can cause mental stress. It can be psychological when it is caused by some psychic disorder. Some of these may even be unconscious, though with conscious effects. People expect and want to have a happy life. So when suffering intervenes the question often is: why me? We may be quite aware of the causes of the suffering. But our question is why an accident or illness should affect me. Why should I be the victim? A second question often follows this: What have I done to deserve this suffering? We almost take it for granted that suffering must be a punishment for some wrong doing. Based on such a supposition the problem can become acute when an innocent person – a child, for instance – is afflicted. We all know children born with various handicaps. What have they done to deserve this? For people who believe in God there is a third question. If God is good and powerful, why does God allow such suffering? So the dilemma: either

God is not good, if God does not bother or Godself may be the cause of it, or God is not powerful so that God cannot stop it, supposing that the suffering comes from elsewhere. The suffering of the innocent or unmerited suffering is also experienced as unjust. So one questions God's justice. Such questioning may lead some people to say that God does not exist or God does not bother. Others may affirm their faith in God, but see suffering as a mystery beyond their understanding. Some may satisfy themselves by saying that God is not punishing them, but just testing their loyalty and faith. Such people will also look for a reward. So if suffering is not a punishment, it must be oriented to a reward for acceptance and good behavior.

Sometimes people think that a good God cannot cause suffering. It is then seen as evil. Good and evil are not merely descriptive but moral terms. Since God is all good, evil can only be explained by an evil principle. Then the problem is how to reconcile a good God with an evil principle, which may even be personified as an evil spirit. For any believer in God, who does not believe in two origin principles of good and evil, evil can only be subordinate to the good. Then, how does God handle the evil spirit? Why does God need it in creation? So some people deny the evil spirit. Others assert that evil spirits are creatures who have become such by disobeying God. The story of creation in the Bible suggests that suffering and evil come into the world because of the humans who disobey God by misusing their freedom. But not wanting to put the whole blame on the humans, it is said that they are tempted by a serpent, who is obviously evil. Then the question is where did the serpent come from.

We see here two series of questions. The first series in the first paragraph talk about suffering. They are more experiential. The second series in the second paragraph rather talk about the cause of such suffering. These are more reflective or theological. By talking, not of suffering, but of evil, they add a moral dimension. People who talk about the "problem of evil" make it a moral and theological issue. The focus is more on God than on people who suffer. Without ignoring the second series of questions I would like to focus more on the first, because these are the questions that people usually ask. If these can be answered the second series of questions too will find a solution.

I am not adopting here a purely rational, philosophical approach. My orientation is theological. I take for granted a belief in God, though what this involves is kept open. At the same time, God is not a kind of stop-gap answer. We are open to God's mystery. But God will not be brought in to justify a refusal to look for an answer. The scholastics, following Augustine, considered evil as non-being. God is good. Beings created by God are good. Evil is only a privation – a sort of negative being. The Indians would have called it *maya*. These theologians ignore the real suffering that people experience. Others may invoke Jesus Christ's suffering and our need to be in solidarity with it. But suffering, including Christ's suffering, is taken as a punishment for sin. Of course, there is one book in the Bible that challenges this assumption: the book of Job. But this does not influence much of the discourse in the Bible. The Old Testament takes for granted that all suffering is a punishment from God for the sins of the people, mostly idolatry and disobedience. In the New Testament it is repeatedly asserted that Jesus Christ suffers and dies to make reparation or satisfaction or expiation for our sins. This link between suffering and sin will have to be questioned. Sin is evil, moral evil. But suffering is not evil, but a painful fact. Imposing it on someone may be evil, but not undergoing it. I shall also attempt to look at suffering as understood in the Indian – Hindu and Buddhist – tradition. I shall try to avoid a metaphysical approach to what is called 'the problem of evil'.

The phenomena of suffering: From nature

There are different kinds of suffering that humans endure in the world. The first kind is what happens when there are natural phenomena like tsunamis, floods, earthquakes, etc. Human habitations may collapse or flooded and people may lose their lives. We know that the earth is evolving for millions of years after the 'big bang'. The evolution is not over. Various earth plates are still moving, though slowly, and when they dash against each other there are earthquakes and tsunamis. There are unseasonal rains and floods. God could have created a clocklike universe, all ready-made, where there are no catastrophes. Then the world will not be what it is. God is not interfering either at every moment to direct the evolution of the universe. So accidents of nature are natural – if this is not tautological. We have to learn to live with it. We are part of it ourselves.

We are learning now that some of our actions can affect the earth and its functioning. We know that the earth is warming up because of the carbon dioxide, coming out of the various fuels that we are burning, being emitted into the atmosphere. This is making the sea warmer, melting the glaciers on the mountains and on the poles of the earth, affecting the monsoons, etc. We are also destroying various fauna and flora by our overuse or misuse. We are having acid rains. The earth may be slowly becoming uninhabitable. The slow destruction of the earth may also lead to other diseases. Therefore the suffering that comes to us from the earth are partly natural due to an evolving universe and partly human made because of the way we handle the goods of the earth, interfering with its natural sustainability and balance.

We humans are living in this universe. We have a body that has evolved from the earth. It is made of various material elements. There can be various imbalances in the system owing to heredity, the place where we live, the atmosphere, etc. There are all sorts of bacteria that infect us. Once again these are natural for a body that is an imperfect and growing organism, sensitive to its surroundings, to our way of life and our use of material goods. All of us are destined to die some time or other. The length of our lives and the time and kind of death are once again due to so many factors, beyond our control.

Some of the illnesses may be brought on by our style of life, by what we eat and drink, etc. People may smoke tobacco or use various other drugs or over-consume alcohol. These lead to various illnesses like cancer.

We have to live with these sufferings. They are part of our being human. We can blame ourselves and our style of life for part of it. We are free beings. We can change our habits of living. One of the problems is that we have to do it together. We know how difficult this is with the many international meetings to save the earth's atmosphere being ineffective. The rest is natural to an imperfect, evolving universe. Even without our intervention the earth may become a dry desert after millions of years or it may be destroyed by a star or a planet crashing into it. We do not know. As I said earlier, God could have created a different kind of universe and a different earth. God could have created us like robots in it without initiative and freedom. Whether we would have enjoyed living in a world like that is a question to reflect on. Anyway, as things are, we can only accept the earth as it is, learn to respect it, adjust our lives to be in harmony with it and enrich our own lives with creativity and freedom. This becomes a challenge if we become aware that we are not alone here, but are part of a community.

The phenomena of suffering: From the humans

Nature, or the earth and the universe, are not the only sources of our sufferings. Humans too can cause each other suffering. Humans are said to have their origin somewhere in Africa. They later spread over the earth. They settled down as groups in various geographical areas. Each group developed its own language and culture. They made use of the resources of nature for their needs. As different groups spread around the earth clashes between groups started. The reasons for such clashes would have been competition for control or possession of the earth's resources, differences in language, culture and religion that made one group see the other as different and threatening rather than friendly, and a love for power and domination that sought to dominate and exploit the others and their labour for one's own benefit. Similar reasons of egoism, desire and quest for power led also to individual or smaller group clashes within the same group. Sometimes it may simply be the desire of a hero for adventure. Great semi-historical epics like the Mahabharata and Ramayana, Iliad and Odyssey illustrate such conflicts. All the human emotions like self-love, envy, anger, jealousy, love for power, and cunning found expression in those conflicts. Violence led to violence and became a spiral with increasing intensity. Historical memory with the spirit of revenge continued those conflicts over centuries. When some people thought that they had been specially chosen by God, religion too became a cause of violence. Violent conflicts lead to a lot of suffering. Many people get killed. Families are broken, houses and fields are destroyed, groups of people become migrants and refugees. Similar causes also lead to conflicts between individuals. Conflicts like these, especially between individuals, cause not only physical violence, but also mental agony: hatred, fear, disappointment, stress, anger, a spirit of vengeance, a sense of defeat and loss, distrust and distress. There have been occasional peace makers like Francis of Assisi or Mahatma Gandhi. But their efforts hardly made a ripple in the stream of history though they did become signs of hope. Who is responsible for all these sufferings? The humans and their freedom. They can blame only themselves, not God.

Conflicts and struggles also bring out the best in the humans: the strength of character, courage, trust in oneself, imagination and creativity. People also go out of their way to help others who are suffering. Conflict is not the only reality that characterizes the human community. There is also compassion and mutual concern. The community builds itself up. This involves mutual love and service, structures of sharing and self-help. These qualities offset, and sometimes make up partially for the sufferings and make them meaningful. This is particularly so when suffering is the consequence of self-gift for a cause. Some people can choose to suffer on behalf of others.

I think that the kinds of sufferings I have listed above cover more or less all that the humans experience in the course of their lives. As we have seen, they are of two kinds. Some of them are natural to the cosmos and to the humans. This is the kind of imperfect, evolving universe, including humanity and other living beings, that God has made. Some people may not like to think about God. Anyway, the world is there.

Natural catastrophes and human illnesses and death are part of it. We too are part of it. We have to live through it. Modern scientists would say that we cannot do much to change it. There are, however, people who believe in miracles who think that God can intervene to change the course of nature temporarily. I have heard stories of miraculous healings from persons who experienced them and who have tested them medically. These are exceptions, in any case, and we need not go into that issue here.

There are other kinds of sufferings in which humans play a role through their freedom. This concerns the way in which they treat nature for their own presumed benefit and in the way that they treat each other. These sufferings become a moral issue, because they are the result of evil inclinations, to which individuals and groups freely choose to give expression. The morality may be thin when we are dealing with ecological issues, for example, because the people are also conditioned by culture. It is thick when it concerns the relations between human individuals and groups. Sufferings caused by humans, however, can be also reduced or even abolished by human free decision. The humans can collectively decide to avoid ecological destruction and to improve natural processes. Similarly, the humans can, individually and collectively, decide to avoid conflict and violence and love and serve each other more. Here too God can help the humans 'miraculously', enabling them to change their hearts.

One of the problems with philosophers and theologians is that this distinction between natural and moral is not often made. By talking about the 'problem of evil' all suffering is considered evil as opposed to good and is thus given a moral tone. This is not particularly helpful, as we shall see later. At the moment let us focus on how some of the religions face this issue of suffering.

Buddhism

The Buddha started with an affirmation that life is full of suffering. He said that the cause of suffering is desire. To get rid of suffering one must get rid of desire and desire can be got rid of by following the eightfold path. Buddha does not bring God into the picture. Buddha accepts the fact of suffering as given. But the suffering is not explained in terms of exterior causes but of interior dispositions. Suffering is unfulfilled desire. So one seeks not to escape suffering, but become free of the desire for the object that one does not have. Then one is at peace. One is not disturbed by pleasure or pain. They are accepted as facts of life. There is no talk of good and evil. One simply accepts the non-fulfillment of one's desire. One of the stories told about the Buddha is illustrative. A woman comes to the Buddha with a dead child asking that the child should be made alive again. Buddha asks her to go into the village and bring some rice from any house where no one has died. The woman makes the round and comes back empty handed. In the process she realizes that death is inevitable for the humans and she accepts that her child is no more and cannot be brought back to life. She goes in peace. Her desire to get her son back alive is not fulfilled. But realizing that death is inevitable for all she abandons her desire. Once she accepts the death of her son as inevitable the suffering disappears. So the lesson of the Buddha is that one should accept life as it comes, detached from any desire. Life is passing and is made up of a succession of mutually dependent events. We should let it pass without holding on to anything at any moment. We have to be like an observer who keeps watching an event taking place before his/her eyes without getting involved. Suffering is not denied but accepted and transcended. What is a limitation here, not evil in itself, is desire. It is said that during the process of his self-realization the Buddha was tempted by an evil spirit – Mara – who tried to provoke his desire. But he did not yield. The evil spirit was simply ignored.

Hinduism

Hinduism takes suffering seriously. But it supposes that suffering is a punishment for sin. If one has not sinned in the present life, one must have done so in a past life. This is the theory of *karma*, which means that every action, good or bad, will produce its appropriate fruit as pleasure or pain even if the effect is delayed till the next life. The need for the rebirth is indicated by the fact that one has to work out one's karma. This is *samsara* – the cycle of births. The Bhagavad Gita suggests two ways of getting rid of the *samsara* cycle. The first way is somewhat like the Buddhist way. You do what you have to do according to your karma but you stay detached from that action and its fruit. Then it is not credited to your account, so to speak. So the cycle is broken. The other way is that you surrender to God in loving devotion and God frees you from the cycle of births. The great Indian epics like the Ramayana and the Mahabharata are an intricate network of stories in which the karmas of the different actors work themselves out in mutual interaction. God oversees the operation of karma, but God can also free you from it if you have loving devotion to him. Suffering is not denied. But a way to escape in provided. Desireless action and devotion do not come naturally. It involves self-discipline. Part of this self-discipline is to get rid of the evil tendencies in you. So the context is one of struggle between good and evil in every person. But a victory with or without the help of God is possible. The real evil is not a spirit, but the evil tendencies in you. The evil spirit is a dispensable instrument. Shaivism, for instance, is very clear that the real evil in you is your own egoism. The spirits can tempt you. But you are the master.

Christianity

The Christian tradition is more complicated. Suffering is recognized as punishment for sin. The real evil is not suffering, but sin. But God created everything good, according to the Bible. (Cf. Gen 1:31) So where does evil come from? It is outsourced to an evil spirit, the serpent. Tempted by the serpent, Adam and Eve disobey God. Swift judgment and punishment follow. They are expelled from the garden of Eden. Suffering and hard work and finally death come as a consequence. (Gen 3:16-19) This sense that suffering is a punishment for sin continues in the Bible. But given the strict monotheism of the

Jewish tradition, the evil spirit is subordinated to God. The dualism of two equal principles, good and evil, which the Zoroastrians (and later Manicheans), acknowledged is denied. So we see Satan in the court of God in the story of Job, who 'tortures' Job only with the permission of God. (cf. Job 1:12; 2:5) But Job realizes that God is the true author of his sufferings and consoles himself saying, "Shall we receive the good from the hand of God, and not receive the bad?" (Job 2:10) But Job makes it very clear to his wife and to his friends that he has not done any wrong to deserve the suffering and he challenges God to prove him wrong. God does not directly respond to his challenge, but side steps it claiming his power to do what he pleases, being the Creator. (cf. Job 38-39) So the story of Job makes it clear that suffering need not be a punishment for sin, but only a test. But this idea linking sin and suffering will not be abandoned in the Bible.

When the disciples see a blind man they ask Jesus: "Rabbi, who sinned, this man or his parents, that he was born blind?" (Jn 9:2) Jesus denies their implication linking suffering to sin: "Neither this man nor his parents sinned; he was born blind so that God's work might be revealed in him." (Jn 9:3) So suffering need not be a punishment for sin, but may have another purpose in God's plan. When Jesus suffers and dies on the cross he does not attribute his suffering to any evil spirit nor to his own sins but to the Jews. He prays for them to be forgiven, while hanging on the cross. (cf. Lk 23:34) But trying to understand the meaning of the suffering and death of Jesus, the Apostles fall back on the sacrificial system of their own Jewish tradition and interpret the event as Jesus suffering for our sins. Jesus' suffering and death was a total self-gift (cf. Jn 15:13; also Phil 2:6-8). But the Christian tradition has not abandoned this idea of suffering, even Christ's suffering, as a punishment for sin. Even here, the real evil is not suffering, but sin.

The sufferings of Christ show us that they can be accepted and even welcomed for a good cause. Caught in a situation of conflict, suffering may be inevitable. But the conflict can be ended and even won by not retaliating. This is the strategy of non-violence. Christ manifests his love for us by standing up to the Jewish leaders in defense of the values he advocated: justice for the poor, sincerity and transparency in following God's law of love, sharing and service and a total commitment to love for God, shown precisely in the love of the neighbor. Jesus dies as a martyr for this cause. By raising him up, God sanctions his cause of universal, self-giving love. The sufferings of Christ will be meaningless without the resurrection, the new life that God gives and Jesus receives and shares with every one – the whole universe in fact. (cf. Rom 8; Eph 1:3-10; Col 1:15-20) The death and resurrection of Christ offers us a new insight into the meaning of suffering.

God's play

Suffering is often experienced as meaningless at the historical, phenomenological level. The suffering of the innocent is a case in point. But we believe that such suffering or even death is not the last word. Accepted, not merely passively and stoically or in the Buddhist manner, but as a surrender to the Lord, it leads to fuller life after death, not as a sort of reward, but as a generous expression of God's responding love which is as immeasurable as God's own self. Religions which believe in God accept that God is the lord and master – as did Job. We do not fully understand the kind of world that God has created and why. But we can understand and appreciate the values of creativity and freedom that are embodied in it. Freedom involves the possibility of mistakes and even misuse. God takes the risk. But God has the final word. And that final word is that "God will be all in all" (1 Cor 15:28) and that is what finally matters.

The Indian (Hindu) tradition speaks about God's play. Every play has rules. But we cannot predict how the play proceeds, since the players are free and creative. People may be hurt in the process. Accidents happen. What is really important is not who wins and who loses, but the joy of playing itself. Playing is its own reward and pain may be a part of it. God makes sure that all have a party after the game – the winners as well as the losers. The joy of playing and the party and togetherness after that is the important thing. All the rest is passing and 'part of the game'. For a person who loses it may be painful at the moment. That is because, s/he does not see the game, but only him/herself and his/her self interest. If the players forget their selves and simply play the game, they may appreciate the game and their own role in it, even when they lose. The game would not have been possible without them.

Suffering is not evil

We should not mix up suffering and evil. Suffering is part of life in the world as we know it. Suffering is not evil. Some suffering may be the consequence of evil. What is evil is not the suffering but the evil will that caused it. The possibility of being evil is part of being free. Do we need an evil spirit to promote evil in the world? I do not think so. I am not saying that there are no evil spirits in the world. I have heard some biblical scholars say so. I do not know. But I think that they are not necessary to explain the sufferings in the world. They need not be brought in to excuse God from being the author of suffering and to excuse the humans who are considered incapable of doing great harm. If suffering as such is not evil, a good God can be responsible for it. Sometimes people say that the evil is so great that it is beyond the capacity of an ordinary human. We do not realize the force of ideologies and the power of evil structures that almost take on a life of their own – a collective evil that is more powerful than all the individuals put together. If there are evil people in the world, God is certainly responsible for having created them and given them the freedom to become evil. But God also keeps calling them constantly to repent. And God can eventually bring good out of evil. Jesus is an illustration of this. He opposes evil by the power of love. This opposition is not a once for all event on Calvary. His death on Calvary is a symbolic action. It is an ongoing process, picked up by many martyrs and others, for whom the cross becomes a symbol. The resurrection is real and at the same time a symbol and the first fruits of an ongoing process of transformation. We may not be able to see this if we only look at individual cases. Respecting the solidarity of humanity we need a global, holistic outlook and vision. Perhaps this vision itself is eschatological. In the meantime we have faith, inspired by the event of the resurrection of Jesus. This faith can make us bear suffering, not merely with passive resignation, but with active acceptance, if not joy, precisely because we have faith and hope in the Lord. The faith and the hope can be inspired by the infinite love and mercy of God in which Christianity and the Bhakti traditions of Hinduism believe.

People accustomed to think of salvation as the expiation of the sins of humanity by Jesus who takes on himself the punishment – sufferings – due to them may have some difficulty with this point of view. The Greek Fathers spoke of salvation rather as a divinization of the humans. The Word became human in order to make the humans divine. Jesus passes through death to life. By his death Jesus identifies himself totally with humanity. It is an act of total surrender and self-gift. God raises him and Jesus shares his new life with all. The new life is an unmerited gift of God from God's abundant and merciful love. Human suffering too, when self-chosen or willingly accepted, can be a manifestation of love to which others and Godself will respond. Such suffering love can provoke conversion or change of heart in the other. Did not the centurion and those with him say: "Truly this man was God's Son"? (Mt 27:54).

An Indian scholar with a heavily handicapped child struggles with the problem of suffering. After exploring the answers provided by Hinduism, Christianity and Islam, he turns to a passive acceptance with a feeling of powerlessness.[1] I think that only hope in God who guarantees the future can help to develop a spirit of active acceptance and expectation, if not joy. The sufferings of the child need not be meaningless, either for itself or for us, because this life is not the last word.

I can conclude with a few affirmations. Sufferings are real. They are not non-being or *maya*. They are inevitable in an imperfect, evolving world, in which there are also free human beings. Much of the suffering is natural and some of it is human made. Suffering is not evil, but the human will that causes unjustified suffering is evil. I think that it is not necessary to evoke evil spirits to protect God's goodness, on the one hand, and the inability of the humans to cause grave harm, on the other. The weakness of an individual is made up by the strength of a group. Group psychology vouches for it. The idea of suffering as a punishment for sin in this or in a past life or as a source of merit for the future can and should be abandoned. This is a very human view. Suffering has meaning only in the light of a life after death and God's own great love and generosity. God will make all things new and bring everything to fulfillment.

Endnotes

[1] See Arun Shourie, *Does He Know a Mother's Heart? How Suffering Refutes Religions.* (New Delhi: Harper Collins, 2011).

Trinitarian Spirituality in the Time of Secularization[1]

Francis X. D'Sa SJ

Sebastian Painadath, to whom these reflections are dedicated as a sign of my appreciation and admiration, belongs to the rare species of spiritual masters who has consistently held the view that meditation is essential to human, to human living because it leads to integration and personal fulfillment. For decades Sebastian has been successfully conducting meditation courses for all kinds of people seeking meaning in life.

The background: A theology of the world

The title of the reflections that follow might give the impression that we are trying to know the known with the help of the unknown. Be that as it may, the title expresses something that is hardly discussed by theological colleagues. As a matter of fact, as everybody knows by now, secular is not the same as secularism or secularization though all three derive from *saeculum*. Saeculum refers to an epoch, age, era, time of the world, the world of space-and-time. Secularization is of relatively recent derivation and is meant to be a corrective to secularism that overstresses the saeculum ideologically. As such secularization highlights the importance of the saeculum in any cosmovision. Developing this aspect is an important part of this paper. However, that is not all. It also develops two other equally important themes: "Trinitarian Spirituality" and "in the Time of Secularization."

A theme that constitutes the backdrop for these reflections is *a theology of the world* that must be part of any cosmovision that claims to be relevant and holistic today. The reason for this is that our being and speaking and thinking presuppose the primordial experience of being-in-the-world. It has taken me years to realize the inescapable implications of this involvement. I shall put down here a sketch of how I see the role of the world in our experience and why it is important to thematize it.

The world of consciousness and consciousness of the world

Whatever we experience, we experience, to some extent at least, also the world of what we experience but not as a subject experiencing an object.[2] This is more than the geographical world, more than the physical world, more than the psychological world with which we are all familiar. It is the world of consciousness. This consciousness is neither consciousness *of* a world nor *of* an object. Rather it is a world-consciousness (subjective genitive) in which we share and of which we are a part. This consciousness is larger than the consciousness of an individual. Even individual consciousness is not a consciousness that an individual has. Here the language of be-ing is more appropriate than the language of having. When we speak of the language of be-ing (again a subjective genitive, i.e., the language that be-ing speaks, not an objective genitive about be-ing) it is be-ing that is conscious, or more precisely, it is conscious be-ing, or conscious-of-being-in-the-world.

Now individual consciousness is not separate from world-consciousness; the former participates in the latter. Without the latter we would not have the former. We are so used to subject-object consciousness that we overlook or ignore the primary and larger area called consciousness in which we live, move and have our be-ing.

At the level of be-ing (=the level of the real), be-ing and consciousness are one and the same or, to put it differently, they are two sides of the same coin. Be-ing is consciousness and consciousness is be-ing. Those who dismiss this as just playing with words may not be aware of the consequences of such a stance. To neglect the level of be-ing as empty speculation is to be estranged from the real. Experiencing being as be-ing is the basis of all spirituality as we shall see in what follows. Be-ing is the core of reality, that is, experiencing be-ing is the core of the real. Ultimately meditation efforts intend to make one aware of this level - through different paths.

Awareness has different stages: There is the ground stage of perception of the world around us, of the world in which we live, of the world we are. Even on this level most of us seem to be really superficial because we do not proceed further but get stuck at the surface level. That is why our perception of perception sounds and remains hollow and shallow. There is more to perception than meet the eye. On this level we mostly work with reason – almost exclusively, I think. Making use of reason is good and salutary but making it the final seat of wisdom can be our undoing.

Beyond perception there is understanding. Understanding takes us one step nearer to the person we understand, a little deeper into things that we need to understand and closer to the goal we want to reach. When we understand someone or something, we undergo change to the degree we understand. In this age of information highway and information technology we easily underestimate the significance of understanding vis à vis information. Understanding transforms us in that it modifies our approach to the Cosmic, the Human and the Divine.[3] To understand, says Panikkar, is to stand under the fascination of the person or thing understood. We need to revise our understanding of understanding. Perhaps we need to retrieve the element of fascination because it makes sense (*poēsis*) of our being human in this world. Person, her world and her understanding of world are all intimately interconnected. They all meet at the point we are talking about, namely, understanding.

Connected with but different from perception and understanding is believing (=faith). Believing is a different mode of consciousness. Faith is a kind of openness of our be-ing, open to anything that might come into our lives.[4] Panikkar distinguishes between faith as experience and faith as expression (belief).[5] To this I add "doctrine" which is a sort of popular systematization of beliefs in a particular age and culture as is attested in the credos of the first councils of the early Church.[6]

These distinctions are important. Whatever has to do with language is historically conditioned. Everyday language and much more the language of faith is not like the fixed formulae of mathematical language. Instead we have here the language of symbol and metaphor. The special characteristic of such language is that it is open to interpretation depending on the time, place and culture of the interpreter. Language, among other things, is like a glass window that lets us see through to the world outside. It is also like a mirror that mirrors what or who stands in front of it. These features of a text are important. But language does not get frozen in spite of human efforts. The moment a text emerges from the writer, there is no way that the writer can control it. This is one major difference between discourse and text.[7] Human intentionality cannot control a text for long. Semantic autonomy comes into its own, when discourse is transformed into a text.[8]

This eminently suits the requirements of the phenomenon of believing. Believers also stand in a tradition which shapes their "preunderstanding" which is different from the preunderstanding of the early Church. This has very little to do with competence or beliefs or good-will of the persons concerned. However, it has much to do with the phenomena of text, history and faith.[9]

Add to these factors the complexities that different cultures bring in. We know this from the way experience of faith is understood and expressed in different cultures and different periods of history. The divide that extremists on the right and on the left create is unnecessary.[10] If only they would sit down and share their cultural differences first and work out how other differences like differences in formulation of beliefs emerge from here.[11]

The world of symbol and the language of metaphor

In the process of deepening awareness, it will help if we also acquaint ourselves with the world of symbol and the language of metaphor.[12]

Hindu Traditions tell us that we are unable to see reality as it is because we are blinded by the tempestuous and obdurate nature of our likes and dislikes (*rāga-dveṣa*). Because of this we are unable to plumb the depths of a symbol and so we reduce it to an object, a thing. We treat symbols as something depending on our imagination. We need to retrieve their originary potential if we are to do justice to them. Symbols are not a way of looking at reality; they are a mode of being.

Similarly, we are unable to gauge the length and breadth of a metaphor as it were and so we treat it as a figure of speech. For such minds, metaphors are just a way of speaking, not ways of pointing to the depth-dimension of reality, to the symbolic nature of reality.[13]

Symbol is firstly, a way of being and secondly, a way of understanding being. Its task is to reveal the nature of reality by symbolizing, that is, by making the symbolized reality present.[14] Presence, presencing, is of the essence of a symbol.[15] Let me illustrate this with two examples.

(a) A smile as symbol

Let us take a smile, preferably the smile of a child. A smile cannot be reduced to a certain movement of the facial muscles. The "facial" smile is not what we usually refer to as smile. It is only the first dimension of the smile, as it were. Essentially a smile is the joy in our heart that reveals itself in and through the facial smile. The facial smile is the symbol, a real symbol, which makes present the joy in our heart that is the symbolized reality.

(b) The human body as symbol

The other example of symbol is our body. It symbolizes the person we are. The body makes our person present. Those who love us do so because of the person we are. They do not get stuck to the body as those, who do not know us and do not love us, do. Moreover, authentic symbols are born, not created. Only a real personal relationship enables us to see through the body and reach the person. For the others we are just bodies, living bodies without the depth-dimension which alone can make life live-able, love-able and enlightening because the Mystery of reality manifests itself as Life, Love and Light.

This is the unmistakable characteristic of a real symbol. Though symbol and symbolized reality are intimately bound together, they are not identical. There is the symbolic difference between them. To overlook the symbolic difference is to reduce the symbol to an object.

This is the stage where we all find ourselves in. We have become blind to the depth-dimension of reality (however we may call it). Reality is now taken to be a collection of objects. There is no symbol reality far and wide. All that we have now are only objects we can manipulate at will. What this means is that our way of experiencing reality has turned out to be one-sided and defective. The mystery has disappeared. As far as we are concerned there is no mystery left in reality. We only have things that are dead. At all levels of reality, we have only objects. The world of symbols has disappeared long ago. Our world has been reduced to a world of objects.

To experience any being fully there is need of a "symbolizer," who is the discoverer, not the creator, of a symbol. But to be the discoverer of the world of symbol one needs a special antenna. Our likes and dislikes as basic motivation for our behaviour have blinded us. As spiritually blind people we are not in a position to experience the symbolic dimension of reality. A spirituality worth the name has to lead to a cure.

Our language of reality is basically descriptive and informative because we (who are spiritually blind) can only perceive the perceptible dimension, not the depth-dimension. The antenna we have as people who have been blinded by our own likes and dislikes is not sensitive enough to locate the depth-dimension.

It is people like poets and prophets who can sensitize us to the wholeness of reality. Their language is basically the language of metaphor and parable, not the language of information. Through the language of information metaphor transports us to a higher level of transformation. Essentially our Scriptures speak a metaphor language.[16] Symbol is the world of reality and metaphor is the language of reality. One who experiences the world of symbols speaks the language of reality. A spirituality that leads us to the world of symbol is the need of the hour. The world of symbols is a world of wholeness.

Trinitarian or cosmotheandric nature of reality

As Panikkar has repeatedly pointed out, reality is trinitarian, i.e. cosmotheandric.[17] We experience it as constituted by the cosmic, human and divine dimensions. More precisely, we experience it as a whole but we can locate three constitutive dimensions in it. In every experience we can distinguish the objective (i.e. cosmic) dimension, the objectifying (i.e. human) dimension and the depth-dimension (or the divine dimension). Because of the depth-dimension the cosmic dimension can be endlessly objectified. Similarly, the human dimension can go on objectifying endlessly. This endlessness that is inherent in reality should give us pause to reflect. Reality is not just material, spiritual and divine. This would be to introduce separations. The fact is that one flows into the other without separating them. Reality is a totality without separations. One can stress it either from the material (cosmic) or human (consciousness) or depth- or divine dimension.[18]

The endlessness is not a separate trait. It animates and enlivens the other two dimensions "from within" in order to reach its full potential. But it does this in such a way that in spite of the constantly changing nature of the cosmic and the finite nature of human existence both of them display something that assures us that matter is more than matter and that finitude is the threshold of infinity.[19] Actually reality is a mystery. However, we need to speak of it but in a manner that "makes sense" to us. That is the point in calling it the "divine" dimension. For heuristic purposes however we speak of three dimensions.[20] It makes sense, but we cannot make it make sense.[21]

William Blake's poem (see footnote 13) has anticipated our discussion on trinitarian spirituality. Poetry is not entertainment in the normal sense of the word. It opens our eyes, and our senses, broadens our horizons and deepens our understanding. Blake's poem is a fairly convincing illustration of what we mean by "trinitarian spirituality". We are deliberately using the hallowed word trinitarian. We are primarily referring to the trinitarian or cosmotheandric nature of reality. Our spirituality has to do with the three dimensions of reality. For a human being to be is to be natural, spiritual, and holistic. There is no need of adding anything extraneous. Natural because it deals with the nature of reality. Spiritual because it is life-giving. Furthermore, the material flows into the spiritual and the spiritual into the material. Holistic because it leaves out nothing of the real.

Trinitarian spirituality in the time of secularization

What does trinitarian spirituality imply?[22] Trinitarian spirituality takes all the three dimensions of reality seriously. That is, it takes seriously the life-giving dynamics of each of the three dimensions. Without objectifying them it highlights the potentiality of each of them. In Blake's lines the sense of "seeing" is heightened: "To see a world in a grain of sand and [to see] a Heaven in a wild flower." For most of us a grain of sand is as good as useless and means nothing. The same is the case with a wild flower. But it is in this "uselessness" and "nothingness" that the revelation of "world" and "Heaven" takes place. It reminds us obliquely that it is we who by objectifying reality render it useless and rob reality of its mystery and in the process witness to our blindness. Its nothingness derives not from the grain of sand or from the wild flower but from our propensity to objectify them.

Blake then turns to the sense of holding and feeling infinity in the finite palm of our hand and then the sense of being touched and gripped by [beholding] Eternity in an hour. Here too Blake has anticipated what Panikkar has called "tempiternity", that is, in and through time to sense eternity.[23] Panikkar insists, it is not time now and eternity later. It is tempiternity. Alas, our touch has been transmogrified into grasping - literally and metaphorically.

Tempiternity may be a new word but through it Panikkar draws attention to an experience that everyone goes through without knowing that they are going through such an experience. When we see a baby smiling, we are gripped by that smile, we forget at that moment everything else because we enter into a new world. Our Lord must have had a similar experience when he saw the widow putting all her fortune into the temple money-box or when he held a child before his disciples and declared "of such is the kingdom of God". The experience of the disciples on the way to Emmaus couldn't have been very different as they confessed "Weren't our hearts burning within us as he expounded the Scriptures on the way to Jerusalem?"

True, these are sporadic experiences and we are not inclined to take them seriously and dwell on them. In our alienated scheme of things they are nothing more than mere memories. We are ignorant of their dynamics and their enriching potentiality. It is here that we have to deepen our awareness of the profound potentiality of such experiences.

Trinitarian spirituality consists in responding to the dynamics of reality, that is, the dynamics of the Cosmic, the Human and the Divine. The dynamics of the Cosmic refer to the physical dimension and its characteristics of "holding and beholding". Our holding should not turn into a possessive attitude. Such an attitude does not respect the dynamics of the cosmic dimension. Attachment to the things of this world is not conducive to internal freedom. Objectification destroys the sense of belonging and solidarity that we need to discover. We come from the earth and to the earth our body will return. This should give rise to a deep sense of solidarity that we share with Mother Earth. We weaken or even destroy this relationship of solidarity when we reduce it to a collection of objects. Detachment from the things of this world will lead to openness to the Divine.[24]

The poet Gerald Manley Hopkins discovered: "The world is charged with the grandeur of God."[25] The physical world is the bearer of the charge that helps to switch on the light of God's grandeur. It is the dynamics of the human dimension to sing of the wonder and mystery of this phenomenon. At the basis of this attitude is our beholding, contemplating creation. Contemplation helps us discover not only our solidarity with the world, but also especially the world of our body. There is danger today of making a cult of the body which cannot accept aging and the various signs accompanying aging. We need to concentrate on that aspect in us that does not age, that aspect which *anima*-tes us and transforms us from an individual into a person. An individual is like an island, not so a person. A person is a veritable network of relationships. The more we discover our relationships within the cosmos the more we grow in depth and breadth as persons and begin to relate to the diverse members of the cosmic family. With that our familiarity with the depth-dimension deepens and our awareness of the "symbol-dimension" comes into its own.

The dynamics of the divine or depth-dimension are of an altogether different kind. The depth-dimension confers endlessness on the cosmic and the human dimensions. The cosmic dimension is endlessly objectifiable. And the human dimension can go on objectifying the cosmos endlessly.[26] The dynamics of the two dimensions are correlative. From this one might get the impression: That is all! This however is not the case since there has to be a reason for their correlatedness. That reason is this. The depth-dimension is at work in the cosmic and the human dimensions. Let me explain this with an example.

In the phenomenon of attraction, we have three aspects: Attraction, attractive, and being attracted. Now (1) attraction is at work both in the one (2) who is attractive, and (3) in the one who is being attracted. The attraction comes through us but not from us! If it had come through us we would be able to switch it on and off as we wanted. This however is not possible. In this context attraction is not manipulable because it derives from the depth-dimension of reality. Here we need to deepen our awareness. Reasoning can prepare us for this step as we have been doing here up to now. But the focus has to be on deepening awareness.

If we look closely at the level of person (the holistic level) a threefold relationship makes eminent sense. E.g., Love, loving-loveable,[27] loved, (rather than love-loved only). We find love not by itself alone but along with and in loving/loveable and in being loved. Love is real-ized and encountered in the person who is loving/loveable and in the person, who is being loved.

The point of our discussion is simply this: The trinitarian nature of reality demands a trinitarian spirituality. In other words, we respond differently to the different dynamics of the Cosmic, the Human and the Divine.

The time of secularization

R. Panikkar has been one of the very few thinkers who see a positive contribution in the secularizing trend in history. As long ago as 1973 Panikkar published an insightful book *Worship and Secular Man* (New York: Orbis, 1973) with the subtitle: An essay on the liturgical nature of man, considering Secularization as a major phenomenon of our time and Worship as an apparent fact of all times. A study towards an integral anthropology.

For Panikkar, "The *saeculum* is not simply the world, and certainly not the *kosmos*, but rather its temporal aspect..."[28] Panikkar is aware of the complexity of the phenomenon of secularization.

> Secular means, therefore, the temporal world, the temporal aspect of reality. Now, the different meanings and evaluations of the secular will depend on the particular conception of time that is being expressed.[29]

> In a word, the process of secularization is connected with ever increasing importance being given to time and the temporal.[30]

Panikkar distinguishes briefly between the various attitudes to time.[31] The new attitude refers to the transhistorical consciousness. Here the secular is sacred and symbolizes the mode of spirituality that is emerging. Time is not the whole of reality, it is an aspect of reality, hence it is real, and not a mere means to the real. [32]: In another place time for Panikkar is not an accident to Being. On the contrary he asserts that "Temporality is an intrinsic and essential feature of all beings and of Being itself."[33]

But Panikkar warns us that "Historicity should not be confounded with temporality."[34] Temporality cannot be reduced to "a mere succession of events" because it is 'a peculiar mode of existence', an inner movement of things, which not only gathers together the past but transports it into the present. It is that which makes possible the life-span of things.[35] In the very heart of a thing it keeps it going. It ensures the rhythm of every being. Temporality is also an ultimate feature because without temporality Man and world would not be; they would cease to be. To *be* then is to *be in time* because time is constitutive of reality.

Panikkar distinguishes between nonhistorical consciousness, historical consciousness and transhistorical consciousness. The world of historical consciousness is coming to an end and transhistorical consciousness is emerging. "It is both (and together) the *ex* and the *sistence* which constitute our being. This is why only by in-sisting on the ex-sistence are we saved. And this is the experience of contemplatives. They live the present in all its in-tensity and in this tension discover the in-tentionality and in-tegrity of life, the tempiternal, ineffable core which is full in every authentic moment."[36]

Transhistorical consciousness means not merely living in the present. It is much more; it is realizing that the present is the only real moment. True, the past is rarely fully past; somehow it is at work in the present. And the future is never totally in the future. It too is somehow at work in the present. Past and future have their operative reality in the present.

Living in the present implies not being oppressed by tragedies of the past und paralyzed by the terrors of the future. It implies harnessing these energies not for the small world of the illusory Ego but for the welfare of all.[37] But above all and through all, it implies coming in touch with timelessness through time, coming in touch through time with eternity, *tempiternity*!

Time is important in this secular age not so much because today time is money or because time is passing[38] but because the full awareness of time leads to the fullness of time (past and future meet in the present), which is tempiternity. "May I call this transhistorical consciousness, the mystical awareness? It is a consciousness which supercedes time – or rather which reaches the fullness of time, since the three times are simultaneously experienced."[39] It is not for nothing that Panikkar calls this age *sacred secularity*. The sacred and the secular are not opposed. Secularity has its own specific kind of sacredness, and consequently its own kind of spirituality, which we urgently need to discover.

For Panikkar, "this spirituality would heal another open wound for modern Man: the chasm between the material and the spiritual and, with this, between the secular and the sacred, the inner and the outer, the temporal and the eternal."[40]

Endnotes

[1] *Love in the Time of Cholera* is the only novel I have read of Nobel laureate Gabriel José de la Concordia García Márquez who died on 17th April 2014.

[2] Martin Heidegger drew our attention to the way we relate to the world much before we are aware of it. We never relate to some individual or thing as such: what we experience is a panoramic whole in which we encounter persons and things. *Being and Time*, Translated by J Macquarrie & E. Robinson (Oxford: Basil Blackwell, 1978), 78ff and 182ff.

[3] See Panikkar, "The End of History. The Threefold Structure of Human Time-Consciousness" in, Scott Eastham (Ed.), *The Cosmotheandric Experience. Emerging Religious Consciousness* (Maryknoll: Orbis, 1993), 79-133.

[4] R. Panikkar, "Faith as a Constitutive Human Dimension", in: *Myth, Faith and Hermeneutics. Cross-Cultural Studies* (New York/Ramsey/Toronto: Paulist Press, 1979), 188-229.

[5] Panikkar, "Faith and Belief", in: *Intrareligious Dialogue* (New York: Paulist, 1978), 40-61.

[6] See my, "Die verschiedenen Glaubenswelten der Religionen am Beispiel von Christentum und Hinduismus", in: Bernard Nitsche (Hg.), *Gottesdenken in*

interreligiöser Perspektive. Raimon Panikkars Trinitätstheologie in der Diskussion (Frankfurt-Paderborn, 2005), 68-77.

[7] Paul Ricoeur, *"What is a Text? Explanation and Understanding",* in his *Hermeneutics and the Human Sciences. Essays on language, action and interpretation.* Edited, translated and introduced by John B. Thompson (Cambridge, Cambridge University Press, 1985), 145-164. Also, Panikkar, "The Texture of a Text: In Response to Paul Ricoeur", in: *Point of Contact* II:1 (New York, 1978), 51-64.

[8] See my "The Re-Membering of Text and Tradition. Some Reflections on Gerhard Oberhammer's Hermeneutics of Encounter", in: F. X. D'Sa/R. Mesquita (Eds.), *Hermeneutics of Encounter.* Essays in Honour of Gerhard Oberhammer on the Occasion of his 65th Birthday (Vienna: Indologisches Institut der Universität Wien, 1994), ix-l.

[9] Cfr, my "Tradition of Texts and Texts of Tradition. A Hermeneutic Reflection on Text and Tradition", in: Anand Amaladass (Ed.), *Christian Contribution to Indian Philosophy* (Madras: Christian Literature Society, 1995), 69-112.

[10] Philip Hughes, *The Church in Crisis. A History of the Twenty Great Councils* (London: Burns & Oats, 1961), 55: "From the beginning, to instance one major theological complication, the party of Eutyches claimed to be nothing more than loyal disciples of St Cyril, one of whose favourite theological dicta became, as it were their watchword and (for them) the touchstone of orthodox belief about the Incarnation of the Divine Word: "There is only one *physis*, since the incarnation of the Divine Word"; where (for St Cyril) the Greek word in italics stands for what the Latins called person; but - the old trouble all over again - to a vast number of the Greek-speaking theologians of his time, the word meant not person but nature, Cyril himself, in the settlement of 433, had recognized that the Antiochean way of expressing the doctrine - that spoke of two *physes* - seemingly the contradictory of his own, was just as orthodox as his: that the other side was using he same word to mean something else, But, to the men who claimed to be carrying on Cyril's work, the Antiocheans held the heresy that there were two *persons* in the Word Incarnate."

[11] Philip Hughes, *The Church in Crisis,* 60, Footnote 19: "The accounts of what happened in the church are conflicting. According to one story Flavian was set upon by Dioscoros himself and the monk Barsumas. At the ensuing Council of Chalcedon, Dioscoros was greeted with shouts of 'Murderer!'" For a brief account of the linguistic confusion prevalent at the time see Leo Donald Lewis, *The First Seven Ecumenical Councils (325-787): Their History and Theology* (Collegeville/Minnesota: Liturgical Press, Reprint 1990).

[12] See F. X. D'Sa, "Re-Searching the Divine. The World of Symbol and the Language of Metaphor", in: Job Kozhamthadam (Ed.), *Interrelations and Interpretation.* Philosophical Reflections on Science, Religion and Hermeneutics in Honour of Richard De Smet, S.J. and Jean de Marneffe, S.J. (New Delhi: Intercultural Publications, 1997), 141-173.

[13] The language of religion is neither dead nor neutral like the language of information. It has an eminently transformative function. When the language of religion is authentic it is contagious like the smile of a child.

[14] R. Panikkar, *The Rhythm of Being, The Gifford Lectures* (Maryknoll, New York: Orbis, 2010), 197: "The concept demands understanding, the symbol participation."

[15] We are not employing the expression "symbol" in the sense of a flag being the symbol of a nation. The reason: there is no real presence involved in such an approach.

[16] Here are some simple examples from the New Testament (Mt 5:1-16 RSV): 1 Seeing the crowds, he went up on the mountain, and when he sat down his disciples came to him. 2 And he opened his mouth and taught them, saying: 3 Blessed are the poor in spirit, for theirs is the kingdom of heaven. 4 Blessed are those who mourn, for they shall be comforted. 5 Blessed are the meek, for they shall inherit the earth. 6 Blessed are those who hunger and thirst for righteousness, for they shall be satisfied. 7 Blessed are the merciful, for they shall obtain mercy. 8 Blessed are the pure in heart, for they shall see God. 9 Blessed are the peacemakers, for they shall be called sons of God. 10 Blessed are those who are persecuted for righteousness' sake, for theirs is the kingdom of heaven. 11 Blessed are you when men revile you and persecute you and utter all kinds of evil against you falsely on my account. 12 Rejoice and be glad, for your reward is great in heaven, for so men persecuted the prophets who were before you. 13 You are the salt of the earth; but if salt has lost its taste, how shall its saltiness be restored? It is no longer good for anything except to be thrown out and trodden under foot by men. 14 You are the light of the world. A city set on a hill cannot be hid. 15 Nor do men light a lamp and put it under a bushel, but on a stand, and it gives light to all in the house. 16 Let your light so shine before men, that they may see your good works and give glory to your Father who is in heaven.

An example from the Bhagavadgita (R.C. Zaehner, *The Bhagavad-Gītā* [London, etc.: Oxford University Press, 1969] ,7.8-11 : In water I am the flavour, in sun and moon the light, in all the Vedas [the sacred syllable] OA, in space [I am] sound, in men [their] manliness am I. Pure fragrance in the earth am I, flame's onset in the fire: [and] life am I in all contingent beings, in ascetics [their] fierce austerity. Know that I am the primeval seed of all contingent beings: insight in men of insight, glory in the glorious am I. Power in the powerful am I, - [such power] as knows neither desire nor passion: desire am I in contingent beings, [but such desire as] does not conflict with righteousness.

[17] See Panikkar, Chapter V The Triadic Myth: *Advaita* and Trinity, *The Rhythm of Being*. The Gifford Lectures (Maryknoll/New York: Orbis, 2010), 212-262. See also F. X. D'Sa, "How Trinitarian is Panikkar's Trinity?", in: Proceedings, George Mason University, Fairfax, 2011 (US.VA) 2011, CIRPIT REVIEW n.3, 2012 Supplement, 33-49.

[18] See Panikkar's *The Cosmotheandric Experience. Emerging Religious Consciousness* edited by Scot Eastham (New York: Orbis, 1993).

[19] See, for example, Blake's simple but exalted verses in: "Auguries of Innocence", in: *A Treasury of Great Poems English and American*. Vol. 1 from Chaucer to Burns. With Lives of the Poets and Historical settings selected and integrated by Louis Untermeyer (New York: Simon & Schuster 1964 Reprint), 608.

To see a world in a grain of sand

And a Heaven in a wild flower,

Hold Infinity in the palm of your hand

And Eternity in an hour.

[20] See Francis X. D'Sa, "How Trinitarian is Panikkar's Trinity?", in: *Rhythm and Vision. Conference in Memory of Raimon Panikkar*. Proceedings, George Mason University, Fairfax, U.S.A. 2011, CIRPIT REVIEW n.3, 2012 Supplement, 33-49.

[21] The functional equivalent for "making sense" (*poēsis* of the Greek tradition) is *apauruceya* (originlessness) of the PūrvamīmāCsā school. See F. X. D'Sa, *Śabdaprāmāyam in Śabara and Kumārila*. Towards a Study of the MīmāCsā Experience of Language (Vienna: De Nobili Research Library Vol. VII, University of Vienna, 1980), especially 105-108 and 192-200.

[22] Margaret Chatterjee, *The Concept of Spirituality* (Ahmedabad, etc.: Allied Publishers, 1989), vii: "The term 'Spirituality' exerts a certain seductiveness among those who write on religions these days. It is often used as we all know what it means. And yet the uses are so various that there seems to be a question mark set against any such assumption, for often there is not even a family resemblance between the various uses we come across."

[23] Panikkar, "The Destiny of Being", *The Rhythm of Being*, 98: "Being ist *act*. An entity is an entity insofar as it *is* Being. If an entity is, it is. This *is*, the *is* of Being and Becoming is neither merely temporal nor solely eternal; it is *tempiternal*. Time seems to be intrinsic to Becoming and eternity to Being. If Being and Becoming belong together in an *advaitic* relationship, this entails that time and eternity are the two faces, as it were, of what I call *tempiternity*." And again, "The Triadic Myth", *The Rhythm of Being*, p. 226: "The tempiternal being is sustained in existence by an eternal Being. Eternity is the very ground of temporality. The Creator is not 'outside'. Eternity is co-eternal with time, just as time is co-temporal with eternity. Time is temporal - it exists because it has its 'backing' in eternity. Eternity is eternal, it exists because it is (and not only manifests itself) in time."

[24] See the Bhagavadgita 7:1. Attach your mind to Me: engaging [still] in spiritual exercise put your trust in Me: [this doing] listen how you may come to know Me in my entirety, all doubt dispelled.

[25] Here one is reminded of the poem "God's Grandeur" by the English Jesuit Poet Gerald Manley Hopkins (1844-1889): "THE WORLD is charged with the grandeur of God!" http://www.bartleby.com/122/7.html (23rd April 2014).

[26] Here the expressions "objectifiable" and "objectifying" stand for functions in discourse, not metaphysical entities. In discourse one can assert, "This is a table" but this need not be interpreted metaphysically.

[27] A loving person is a loveable, love-able, person.

[28] *Worship and Secular Man*, 10.

[29] *Worship and Secular Man*, 10.

[30] *Worship and Secular Man*, 11.

[31] Ibid. 12: "In our days a new attitude is emerging: this considers time to be both positive and definitive, good and final, not a means that one can manipulate or a period which one has to go through, but an end in itself and the only real mode of existence. It is not by chance that today only mystics can understand the language of the secular."

[32] Ibid., 140: "The *saeculum*, i.e., the temporal world, is the real universe. The World is temporal, and temporality is its ultimate character."

[33] Panikkar, "Time and Sacrifice-the Sacrifice of Time and the Ritual of Modernity", in: J.T.Fraser (Ed.), *The Study of Time* (New York: Springer, 1978), 708.

[34] "Methodological Reflection", *The Cosmotheandric Experience,* 85.

[35] Panikkar, "A Self-Critical Dialogue", *The Intercultural Challenge of Raimon Panikkar,* 287.

[36] "Transhistorical consciousness", *The Cosmotheandric Experience*, 124-125.

[36] The Bhagavadgītā 5:25 and 12:4 have an extraordinary phrase which I also encountered in the Mokcadharma section of the Mahābhārata: *sarva-bhūta-hite ratā%*, taking passionate delight in the welfare of all beings! Not just the welfare of all human beings but of all beings (*sarva-bhūta, sarvāGi bhūtāni*).

[37] This is an euphemism. Time is not passing; it is we who are passing!

[38] Panikkar, "Transhistorical consciousness", *The Cosmotheandric Experience*, 132-133.

[39] Panikkar, *The Cosmotheandric Experience*, 151-152.

Nostra Aetate of Vatican II - An Asian Re-reading after Fifty Years and the Way Forward

Felix Wilfred

Nostra Aetate was a turning point in the relationship of Christianity to other faiths. Indeed, it is the *Magna Carta* of dialogue for our times. Seen against the general hostile attitude of Christian theologians and missionaries to other religions throughout history, *Nostra Aetate* was a revolution. It was a landmark in the two thousand years of Christian doctrinal history when an Ecumenical Council accepted positively other religions and their validity. Even more, *Nostra Aetate* could be considered as signifying the *conversion* of the Church to the religiously other. Instead of a blanket "no" to other religions on the assumption that to be Christian is a state of possessing all truth and wisdom, *Nostra Aetate* signifies the historic moment when the official Church looked straight into the eyes of the religiously other. It read on the face of the religiously other, things which it never cared for. What comes out is a humble recognition of the value and richness the faiths of others signify.

"The Catholic Church rejects nothing that is true and holy in these religions. She regards with sincere reverence those ways of conduct and of life, those precepts and teachings which, though differing in many aspects from the ones she holds and sets forth, nonetheless often reflect a ray of that Truth which enlightens all" (NA 2).

We realize the depth and significance of this statement if we compare it with so many other statements and practices through Christian history which rejected outright other religions. A glaring example is the statement of the Council of Florence which states,

> [The Holy Roman church]… firmly believes, professes and preaches that "no one remaining outside the Catholic Church, not only pagans," but also Jews, heretics or schismatics, can become partakers of eternal life; but they will go to the "eternal fire prepared for the devil and his angels" (Matt 25:41), unless before the end of their life they are received into it.[1]

This revolution of *Nostra Aetate* was strongly supported by *a new theological vision* which the document outlines in a very concise manner. It speaks of the universal salvific will of God, the common origin and destiny of humankind, and the presence of the Spirit in human history. Here the traditional soteriology and pneumatology undergo a transformation. These are all important elements in the new theological vision which paved the way for a positive relationship with other religions.[2]

Nostra Aetate has taken to its logical conclusion the ecclesiology of *Lumen Gentium* which extricates itself from the understanding of the Church as *societas perfecta* (perfect society) with closed doors. Instead, it characterizes itself as a "sign and sacrament of communion with God as well as of the unity of the human family" (LG 1), and thus tries to reach out to others (LG 16). What have we to make out of the spiritual legacy of the one human family of which all of us are part, is what *Nostra Aetate* sets out to do. That we cannot settle down with a realized eschatology, but need to look forward to a futuristic eschatology has become clear from the orientation of the Council and its different documents. This became evident particularly in considering the Jewish faith in relation to Christian faith, as worked out in *Nostra Aetate*.

I would like to also highlight here that *Nostra Aetate* and *Gaudium et Spes* have the same theological axis and they complement each other. In *Nostra Aetate* we see a Church blinded by its own closed claims of the past open its eyes to see the marvels of God blooming in innumerable spiritual gardens of humanity, whereas in *Gaudium et Spes* we see a Church closed on itself by insulating from the world, reaching out to the wonders of temporal realities, thanks to a fresh reinterpretation of theology of creation. In both cases the mutual relationship is fostered by continuous dialogue. To be able to understand in depth the dialogue with peoples of other faiths advocated by *Nostra Aetate*, we need to relate also to the Conciliar document on Divine Revelation (*Dei Verbum*). If *Lumen Gentium* paved the way for an open ecclesiology pointing to the entire humanity, the document on revelation provided the grammar for dialogue. It sees God's self-revelation itself having taken place through a process of *conversation or dialogue*. In *Dei Verbum* we could hear the echo of the words of *Ecclesiam Suam* of Pope Paul VI which imbued Vatican II with the spirit of dialogue. It states,

> Revelation too, that supernatural link which God has established with man, can likewise be looked upon as a dialogue. In the incarnation and in the Gospel it is God's Word that speaks to us...the whole history of man's salvation is one long, varied dialogue, which marvellously begins with God and which he prolongs with men in so many different ways.[3]

All this has rooted *Nostra Aetate* even more firmly in the field of inter-religious dialogue.

Confirmation of Asian initiatives and practices

Even before *Nostra Aetate*, the necessity of dialogue was keenly felt in Asia, especially in India as numerous initiatives pre-dating Vatican II show. Dialogue was already an experiential reality in Asia. The initiatives to explore the riches of other religious traditions and experience the Christian mystery in dialogue with the experience and spirituality of Hinduism took the form of *ashrams*. Pioneering works in dialogue was done by these ashrams, thanks to Brahmabandhab Upadhyay, Jules Monchanin, Swami Abhishiktananda, Bede Griffiths and others. At a time when such initiatives were looked upon by many as unorthodox and even heretical, *Nostra Aetate* came to confirm that such works of dialogue taking place in Asia are in keeping with Christian faith, and even more that such initiatives need encouragement and further expansion. Hence, under the inspiration of *Nostra Aetate*, further new initiatives were taken, centres of dialogue were created, and also commissions for inter-religious dialogue were established at national, regional and diocesan levels in different parts of Asia. FABC took the vision of *Nostra Aetate* one step further when it stated in its very First Plenary Assembly in Taipei as follows:

> In this dialogue we accept them as significant and positive elements in the economy of God's design of salvation. In them we recognize and respect profound spiritual and ethical meanings and values. Over many centuries they have been the treasury of the religious experience of our ancestors, from which our contemporaries do not cease to draw light and strength. They have been (and continue to be) the authentic expression of the noblest longings of their hearts and the home of their contemplation and prayer. They have helped to give shape to the histories and cultures of our nations.[4]

These words bring to mind millennial Asian practice of living together of peoples of different religious traditions in harmony and mutual respect. Daily life in Asia bears out that people go about respectfully with the religious experience, sacred places and religious teachings of others. This is something inherent in the Asian way of life and daily existence. Hence we could look at *Nostra Aetate* as a confirmation as well of the traditional Asian approach to other religions in the spirit of harmony and understanding.

Dialogue - A new culture and a new process

How do we put into practice this new vision about other religions? It is here that the general spirit of all-round dialogue initiated by Vatican II finds its application vis-à-vis other religious traditions. Even before the close of the Council, Pope Paul VI gave a fillip to the Council by highlighting in his *Ecclesiam Suam* (1964): dialogue as the new way of being Church. Dialogue became a key concept that inspired the

entire corpus of Vatican II documents. What *Nostra Aetate* did was to
set in motion a new culture and a process of dialogue with peoples of
other faiths. It implied a *change of attitude* towards other religions as
it viewed them in a completely different light. Dialogue involves also
a process of learning.[5]

The spirit and orientation of *Nostra Aetate* was sustained through
the several official documents of the Church, such as the encyclical
Redemptor Hominis which spoke of the presence of the Spirit outside
the confines of the Church (RH. 16) in the various religious traditions;
so too *Redemptoris Missio*, where the role of the Spirit outside the
bounds of the Church gets even more deeply acknowledged and stated.
According to it, the Spirit is present in "individuals...society and history,
peoples, cultures and religions" and it goes on to add "the Spirit is at
the origin of the noble ideals and undertakings which benefit humanity
on its journey through history" (RM 28).[6]

From a theological point of view, if we start from *pneumatology* we
will understand the mystery of Jesus Christ more deeply, and it is the
same pneumatology which opens the doors for us to understand the
religious experience and traditions of our neighbours of other faiths.
Hence, one need not be preoccupied that acknowledging the presence
of the Spirit in other religions would water down the mystery of Jesus
Christ. Rather when we start from pneumatological considerations
we will be able to relate harmoniously our faith in Jesus Christ with
the recognition of God's grace and the presence of the Spirit in other
religious traditions.

Closer spiritual affinity

The landmark event of Pope John Paul II praying with leaders of other
religious traditions in Assisi in October 1986 is but a logical consequence
of the grand vision of *Nostra Aetate*.[7] The realization of one common
humanity and the experience of sharing in one and the same ultimate
mystery in which "we live, move and have our being ..." (Acts 17:28),
cannot but naturally lead us to invoke together the same mystery in

prayer. This was exactly what the event in Assisi was. When Pope John Paul II made his concluding address at the event, one could hear the echo of *Nostra Aetate*. He said,

> We hope that this pilgrimage to Assisi has taught us anew to be aware of the common origin and common destiny of humanity. Let us see in it an anticipation of what God would like the developing history of mankind to be: a fraternal journey in which we accompany one another towards the transcendent goal, which He sets for us.[8]

The bold initiative of praying with others, made rumbles in certain quarters of the Church, including several ecclesial leaders. The pope defended the legitimacy of a common prayer with others when he spoke to the Roman Curia in December, 1986. He said, "We can indeed maintain that every authentic prayer is called forth by the Holy Spirit, who is mysteriously present in the heart of every person... every man and woman is capable of... submitting oneself totally to God."[9]

Humanistic import of *Nostra Aetate*

The times of *Nostra Aetate* did not witness the kind and scale of violence, religious fundamentalism and chauvinism we are experiencing today. The developing situation in the world is a crisis of great magnitude. Peace and understanding among religions have become an imperative necessity for the future of humanity. The challenges of the hour globally and in Asia, make dialogue no more an option but a necessity. This shows why relationship of Christianity with other religions should not be treated as a matter of Christian doctrine alone; one has to critically look at the claimed doctrine whether it contributes to peace and harmony among religions and peoples, or whether it becomes a threat to these ideals all of humanity is called upon to pursue relentlessly. In other words, we have to take into account the humanistic and political implications of Christian doctrines, especially when it touches upon the delicate question of inter-religious relationships, which has become so very crucial for peace in the world. Further, increasing migration of peoples from one geographic region to another, from one cultural and religious setting to another has brought about also intriguing issues of co-existence and tolerance, identity, recognition and respect.

Even though *Nostra Aetate* did not envisage such issues and situations, nevertheless, if we do a re-reading of it, what we would find is that it is a document not only about a new theology of religion, but also a more basic document about peace and inter-religious understanding on the basis of a larger vision of humanity. As such, *Nostra Aetate* continues to be an inspiration even as we face new and increasingly complex questions bearing upon religions and religious beliefs. Today we are in a position to draw the implications of *Nostra Aetate* in terms of its humanistic import.

An intermezzo – Asia on the procrustean bed

When *Dominus Iesus* (2000)[10] appeared, many in Asia were wondering how to reconcile it with *Nostra Aetate* and many other documents that followed which corroborated the vision of this Conciliar document. For many Asians, *Dominus Iesus* was an embarrassment, and it appeared to be the case of one step forward and two steps backwards![11] The language of power, suspicion, intimidation and threat go back to pre-Vatican II times.[12] Many Asians were asking themselves whether such a regression has taken place. For, the document seemed to speak a different language and set a different tone from *Nostra Aetate*. It says, "objectively speaking they [other religions] are in a gravely deficient situation in comparison with those who, in the Church have the fullness of salvation" (no. 22). It was difficult to see for Asians, for that matter anyone who makes a comparative study of texts, how *Dominus Iesus* could square with *Nostra Aetate* which is imbued with the spirit of dialogue and *Lumen Genitum* which has an inclusive approach. Dialogue takes place when we try to understand peoples of other faiths the way they would like to be understood. We close the doors of dialogue when we are prejudiced, become judgmental and want to reduce the other within our scheme of things.

Moreover, Asians saw in *Dominus Iesus* a document written primarily from a doctrinal preoccupation, and intended to serve as a caveat. The question of dialogue was approached through neo-scholastic method and in its spirit. Any essentialist philosophy like neo-scholasticism sees identities as fixated, clearly defined and demarcated. In actual life, however, identity is not defined by isolation but in relationship. One needs to avoid carefully binary like "we" and "they", "inside" and "outside." In the dominant Western theological tradition, however, there is an obsessive preoccupation and inquietude to know clearly who is in and who is out. This is what I would call *theology of "Noah's ark"*. Either you are inside or you are outside the ark. It is difficult to apply this philosophy, and this kind of image in the realm of mystery, which is the case when we deal with the sacred realm of religious experience. It is a grey zone. Totalitarianism is not only political. It has also a religious version. When we want to create out of Christianity a system of thought, similar to the philosophical system of Kant and Hegel, Christianity is emptied of the sense of mystery, and one seeks to place everything in a particular slot or pigeonhole of the overarching grand system of thought. The religious traditions of our neighbours get truncated when they are forced into our system of thought and belief, reminding us of the Procrustean bed.[13] Moreover, such an approach does not vibrate with the Asian ethos either, which sees the reality organically interrelated; it tries to connect things rather than demarcate and circumscribe one from the other.

Asian theology has been under a cloud of suspicion of not proclaiming the uniqueness of Christ and of having fallen into relativism. To be able to gauge such suspicious attitudes, we need to remember that the pastorally oriented Asian theology is read and interpreted through Western systems of thought, categories and preoccupations. Asia is not understood in its context and cultural setting. Generally, when relativism is spoken about, one understands it to mean that "there are many truths which vary according to the subjects who hold different opinions of reality."[14] This is not the way we approach truth in Asia. Instead Asian spiritual traditions tell us that *truth is not many but one*. This was expressed laconically in Rig Veda, "*ēkam sat viprāh bahudhāh vadanti*" (Truth is one, the sages have called it by many names).[15] The one mystery appears differently in relation to the diverse experience of people which is very important and crucial. Far from a dilution of truth, as being feared, it is an enrichment of truth. If this is applied to the understanding of the mystery of Christ, we arrive not at any indifferent relativism, but an engaging and enriching pluralism.[16] The mystery of Jesus Christ is richly illuminated through a plurality of experiences. The rich pluralism which Asian theology is trying to highlight is being misunderstood through the Western understanding of relativism, so much so the attack on Asian theology often amounts to a shadow-boxing. Is it not a case of mistaken identity? To fathom the depth of Asian theology of religions, especially the mystery of Jesus Christ in its multifaceted nature, one needs to study closely the statements of FABC, in particular, those of the Office of Ecumenical and Interreligious Affairs (OEIA).[17]

Moving ahead with the spirit of *Nostra Aetate* in Asia

Thanks to *Nostra Aetate* and the many dialogical efforts preceding Vatican II, Asia moved ahead to new horizons in developing a theology of religions and practiced inter-religious dialogue which all became an issue of highest priority, given the fact that Christians in this continent live amidst great masses of peoples who are Buddhists, Hindus, Daoists, Confucianists, Muslims, Sikhs, Parsis and peoples of primeval religious traditions.

The Roman Synod on Asia saw the theological and pastoral prowess of Asian bishops, under the influence of FABC. That notwithstanding, the end-result of the Asian Synod in Rome in the form of *Ecclesia in Asia* would have left many bishops wondering, whether this was what they really tried to say at the synod. Two months after the Asian Synod, FABC Plenary Assembly gathered in Thailand in January 2000, and its theme has another focus than doctrinal Christology of *Ecclesia in Asia*. The theme is "*Renewal of Church in Asia: The Mission of Love and Service*". The doctrinal approach of proclamation, gives place to an evangelization of love and service in the spirit of the Gospel. Here one hears another language which the Asian bishops could say authentically their own, and not filtered. Their language is not one of other religions waiting to be fulfilled by Christ, rather one of solidarity and partnership. The poor of Asia become the focus of this partnership:

> As we face the needs of the 21st century, we do so with Asian hearts, in solidarity with the poor and the marginalized, in union with all our Christian brothers and sisters and by joining hands with all men and women of Asia of many different faiths.[18]

When the house is on fire, we need to pay attention to save the essentials, and there is no point in disputing who should do the work of saving. Everyone is called today to the mission of saving humanity and nature from the critical situation. Our neighbours of other religious traditions become brothers and sisters in a common task of justice, and in the defense of the dignity and rights of human beings – be it the question of the marginalized, women, indigenous people or migrants and refugees. Therefore, simply *missio ad gentes* is not enough; nor *missio inter-gentes*. We need *missio cum gentibus*. This presupposes a theology of mission and a theology of dialogue from the perspective of the *Kingdom of God*.

That inter-religious dialogue should not be conditioned by doctrinal preoccupations was clearly brought out by the Japanese Bishops' Conference already in the context of Asian Synod. Reacting to a *lineamenta* overly preoccupied with the proclamation of Jesus as the unique Saviour, the Japanese bishops responded saying,

> Jesus Christ is the Way, the Truth, and the Life, but in Asia, before stressing that Jesus Christ is the Truth, we must search much more deeply into how he is the Way and the Life. If we stress too much that "Jesus Christ is the One and Only Saviour", we can have no dialogue, common living, or solidarity with other religions. The Church, learning from the *kenosis* of Jesus Christ, should be humble and open its heart to other religions to deepen its understanding of the Mystery of Christ.[19]

The thought of Pope Francis, his statements and many symbolic gestures confirm the position of Japanese bishops and the vision of FABC in general.

New trajectories of dialogue in Asia

I would like to present a few thoughts which will help the future of theology of religions and praxis of dialogue in Asia.

To be on the way

We need to move away from theological disputes to inter-religious collective praxis and transformation. This is what the papacy of Pope Francis beckons us to do. Issues like uniqueness of Christ, the relationship between dialogue and proclamation, which were the centres of attention and hotly debated a few years ago,[20] are receding to the background, as Pope foregrounds the common engagement of all religions to respond to the plight of humanity and of nature. We hardly hear him speaking about those hot theological debates of the past. In his address in Turkey,[21] for example, he pointed out areas of common concern which religions need to respond to urgently. The message is the same when he met religious leaders in Sri Lanka and elsewhere. He has articulated it clearly in his *Evangelii Gaudium* (EG).

> We can then join one another in taking up the duty of serving justice and peace, which should become a basic principle of all our exchanges. A dialogue which seeks social peace and justice is in itself, beyond all merely practical considerations, an *ethical commitment* which brings about a new social situation. Efforts made in dealing with a specific theme can become a process in which, by mutual listening, both parts can be purified and enriched. These efforts, therefore, can also express love for truth (EG 250).

There are two clear indications in the theology of Francis which will be helpful for our project of inter-religious dialogue in Asia. In the vision of Francis, *to be Christian is to be on the way, to be on a journey with others* – religious, secular – for the transformation of humanity and the flourishing of nature. The orientation of the pope confirms our own vision and practice in Asia. In fact, in 1987 there was a consultation between FABC and the Christian Conference of Asia (CCA) on the question of dialogue with peoples of other religions. It was titled: "*Living and working with Brothers and Sisters of Other Faiths*". FABC general assembly in 1986 in Tokyo, Japan meaningfully captioned its final statement as "*Journeying together toward the Third Millennium*". . Journey and pilgrimage are very dear imageries in Asia. The motif of journey re-appears again and again in the thought of Pope Francis, his speeches and documents, including *Evangelii Gaudium*.

Mercy and compassion

A second theme which is very helpful for our dialogue in Asia is that of *mercy and compassion. Mercy is the key word to characterize the pontificate of Pope Francis.*[22] It is the *mainspring* of the praxis of Francis. This for him is *the hermeneutical key to read the entire Scriptures and the life and teachings of Jesus.* It is the jewel of the Sermon on the Mount. "Be merciful as your heavenly Father is merciful" (Lk 6:36). In the narration of the Last Judgment too (Mt 25: 31-46), mercy and compassion are the criteria by which human beings are ultimately judged. If this is the case, then mercy and compassion should also get reflected in our relationship with peoples of other faiths. Instead of claims of superiority or absolute possession of truth which, unfortunately, have contributed to create a gulf between Christians and others in Asia, we need to encounter the other with a lot of love and respect for what they hold and practice as sacred. With this approach, we could join peoples of other faiths to transform the world and society more just and compassionate. In fact, Pope Francis during his visit to Turkey spoke of the need of religions joining together in the struggle against terrorism and fundamentalism. He said, "interreligious and intercultural dialogue can make an important contribution to attaining this lofty and urgent goal, so that there will be an end to all forms of fundamentalism and terrorism which gravely demean the dignity of every man and woman and exploit religion".[23] Against skeptics on the role of religion in the modern world, pope speaks of the collaboration among religions to contribute to the life of the world. In the words of Cardinal Walter Kasper,

> For Francis it is not only a matter of dialogue about the common as well as different cultural and religious traditions, but also about a common contribution to the well-being of the poor, the weak, and the suffering; it is about common service to justice, reconciliation.[24]

Dialogue and evangelization

We do admit that evangelization and dialogue are inter-related, and they are a mutual enrichment. However, in the past in Asia we had difficulties to accept the way evangelization and dialogue were related, especially when dialogue was converted into a means for evangelization. We raised in Asia critical questions regarding this position, and it came out very clearly in the joint FABC-CCA meeting held in Singapore, way back in 1987. It stated,

> We affirm that dialogue and mission have their own integrity and freedom. They are distinct but not unrelated. Dialogue is not a tool or instrument for mission and evangelization, but it does influence the way the Church perceives and practices mission in a pluralistic world. ...Dialogue offers opportunities for Christian witness.[25]

Today we can confidently revisit the question of dialogue and proclamation, if we take mercy and compassion as the key point of reference, since they reflect the heart of the Gospel. For, under the inspiration of Pope Francis, there is a fresh approach to mission, evangelization and dialogue. Evangelization is not seen as an *occasion or opportunity* to justify the doctrinal claims of Christianity. There is a great spiritual depth in Pope Francis in that he sees proclamation not only related to truth but also to *mercy and love.* The way he thinks of proclaiming the Gospel and especially the manner he does it makes us realize that we can indeed bring together both these realities harmoniously into Christian life and praxis. If we proclaim God's love and mercy in Jesus Christ, who will be against such an evangelization in Asia? After all, the message of compassion will vibrate with Asians, seasoned in the Buddhist religious and cultural tradition with focus on *karuna* or compassion. The moment Christians raise their pitch and start proclaiming doctrines from a high pedestal making many unique claims above the head of the people, they will put themselves in a position of not being heard, and even could be perceived, instead of being messengers of love, peace and divine compassion, as a threat to societal harmony.

Ecology and inter-religious dialogue

Ecology has become a new and important motive for interreligious dialogue. Integral cosmic vision is characteristic of Hindu, Buddhist, Daoist, Shintoist and primaeval traditions in Asia.[26] But if we are to dialogue with them, we need to revisit our traditional Anselmian soteriology - *Cur Deus Homo?* The dominant Christological discourse is associated with a particular and limited conception of salvation. There is need to rethink salvation in new terms closer to the Gospel. The Gospels tell us that Jesus was concerned about human suffering and privations rather than about *sin*. Unfortunately, Christian soteriology came to be constructed around sin and not on the most important aspects of Jesus' praxis for the wellbeing (*salus*) of human beings and of communities.

We have in *Laudato Si* an attempt to re-conceptualize the traditional understanding of salvation. Salvation – *salus* or wellbeing - is extended to the whole of creation and nature.[27] The new anthropology and soteriology implied in *Laudato Si* brings us closer to Asian religious traditions than ever before. This new and refreshing opening to nature and creation, together with recognition of the universal reach of God's salvation and the presence of the Holy Spirit offer a new theological basis to dialogue with neighbours of other faiths. By affirming nature as an integral aspect of Christian theological vision, *Laudato Si* leads us also to rethink present forms of Christian worship excessively centered on the word and preaching, whereas these religious traditions have worship close to the elements of nature – earth, water, fire, air, ether (the *mahāpanchabhūta*). We could look at *Laudato Si* as a document that leads *Nostra Aetate* to new horizons.

The challenge of praxis

Asia, perhaps, is the continent in which this shortest and highly significant Conciliar document *Nostra Aetate* found most reception. The contribution of FABC to inter-religious dialogue, inspired by *Nostra Aetate*, is universally recognized. Through the years, FABC has developed a grand vision, and an impressive theology of religions and dialogue. What is missing, however, is *realization* of this theology and its implementation in concrete praxis. The opposition to dialogue and skepticism about it is not only from without, but from within too. This is in great part due to lack of an *adult faith*. Infantile faith, nurtured by all kinds of sanctimonious practices and pious devotions, will not find it easy to accept a new theology of dialogue. The conclusion is that we need to cultivate pastorally an adult faith among the believers in Asia for theology of religions and inter-religious dialogue to gain acceptance and bear fruit. The dissonance and asymmetry between infantile faith and inter-religious dialogue need to be overcome with appropriate pedagogical means.

Religious cosmopolitanism

One of the important pastoral means is to include in Christian catechesis a chapter presenting positively other religious traditions and their spiritual experience. For some, this may sound provocative. But I think this should be normal, if we take seriously the grand vision of *Nostra Aetate* on humanity and its quest for God. If *Nostra Aetate* is one of the sixteen documents of the Council, forming integral part of its teaching, what prevents us making other religions integral part of Christian catechism? Further, the numerous educational and other institutions run by the Church need to impart the students, including Christian students, knowledge about other religions which will lead to respect and appreciation for them.

Living everyday in the midst of the religious world of our neighbours, Christians in Asia will acquire not only the skills to dialogue with them, but also feel at home in their religious places like pagodas, mosques, gurudwaras, temples, etc. This is what I would call *religious cosmopolitanism*.[28] Pope Francis not only visited the Great Synagogue of Rome,[29] but also mosques, and a Buddhist temple in Sri Lanka. Were he to visit India one day, we can surmise, he will visit also a Hindu temple. He has no doctrinal inhibitions when it comes to respecting the sacredness of the religious experience of peoples of other faiths.

Religious cosmopolitanism is the ability to enter into the religious universe of the other, without losing one's identity. It requires a lot of openness. "Men and women do not have to forsake their identity, whether ethnic or religious, in order to live in harmony with their brothers and sisters," Francis said in his address to the religious leaders in Sri Lanka during his visit in January, 2015.[30] Religious cosmopolitanism requires an adult faith, and unconditional openness to the infinite mystery. It calls for a new catechesis and faith-education in Asia.

Collaborative-partnership model

We noted how important this model of partnership is for Asia, faced with many socio-political and ethical challenges. Today, the realization is growing about the importance of religion in public life and its potentials to create peace and harmony. The issue is not merely that of peace among religions for social harmony. Rather religious resources are increasingly in demand for the creation of peace and justice in the world, and for upholding dignity of human beings and their rights. Besides, at the global level, events like 9/11 have brought to the consciousness of humanity the importance of religion in international affairs. Mere secular pursuits may not be able to create a world of equality, justice and peace. To save the human, religions pointing to something beyond seem to be very necessary. This is well expressed by Jürgen Habermas when he states, "Among modern societies, only those that are able to introduce into the secular domain the essential elements of their religious traditions which point beyond the merely human realm will also be able to rescue the substance of the human."[31] Given this overriding importance of religion for harmony, social cohesion and for saving the human, interreligious dialogue on the model of partnership could substantially contribute to the transformation of the world and societies. Hence in Asia we are challenged to be *partners* with our neighbours. However, there is more to the joint working of peoples of different faiths than social action or involvement. Religions could bring to our contemporary social and political life a necessary *mystical* dimension of seeing everything interconnected and interdependent. It is not a mysticism of closed eyes; it is a "mysticism of open eyes."[32]

Particularly important would be the working together of religions for peace. "Interreligious dialogue is a necessary condition for peace in the world, and so it is a duty of Christians as well as of other religious communities," (EG 250) reminds us Pope Francis. United Nations and its various bodies, especially UNESCO have proposed inter-religious dialogue as an important means for peace. We need to strengthen the efforts of humanity for peace by promoting inter-religious understanding. The global world rightly awaits a significant contribution from Asia on this question. This challenge takes the Asian Church beyond the walls of the minority Christian communities to the larger agenda of the entire humanity.

Endnotes

[1] Council of Florence, from the Decree for the Jacobites (1442) – For the English translation of the text see, J. Neuner – J. Dupuis, *The Christian Faith in the Doctrinal Documents of the Catholic Church* (Bangalore: Theological Publications in India, 1973): 265.

[2] Viewed from Asia, this looks to be the abiding significance of Vatican II. This is different from the view of Rahner, who saw the enduring significance of Vatican II in that the Church got actualized for the first time as universal and Catholic. For critical comments on Rahner's position seen from an Asian perspective, see Felix Wilfred, "Vatican II and the Agency of Asian Christians", in Elochukwu E. Uzukwu ed., *Mission and Diversity: Exploring Christian Mission in the Contemporary World* (Zürich: LIT Verlag, 2015): 99-111.

[3] *Ecclesiasm Suam,* No. 70.

[4] Statement of the First Plenary Assembly of FABC, no. 14 (Taipei, Taiwan: 1974); for the text, see *For All the Peoples of Asia: Federation of Asian Bishops' Conferences,*

Documents from 1970-1991, Gaudencio Rosales – C.G. Arevalo, eds. (Quezon City: Claretian Publications, 1992): 11ff.

[5] As *Ad Gentes* puts it, "through sincere and patient dialogue they [Christians] themselves might learn of the riches which a generous God has distributed among the nations" (AG no. 11).

[6] When I served as the secretary of the Office of Theological Concerns (OTC), a long document (almost 100 pages) on "The Spirit in Asia" was prepared which brings out more concretely how the Spirit is operative in other religious traditions and in various other forms in the life and heritage of Asia. For the text of the document see, *For All the Peoples of Asia: Federation of Asian Bishops' Conferences Documents from 1997-2001*, Franz-Josef Eilers, ed. (Quezon City: Claretian Publications, 2002): 237-327.

[7] For an overview of the statements and gestures of Pope John Paul II, see *John Paul II and Interreligious Dialogue*, Byron L. Sherwin – Harold Kasimow, eds. (Maryknoll: Orbis Books, 1999).

[8] *L'Osservatore Romano*, weekly English edition (3 November, 1986): 3.

[9] Pope John Paul II, "Address to the Cardinals and the Roman Curia, 22 December 1986", in *Assisi: World Day of Prayer for Peace*, 27 October 1986 (Pontifical Council for Justice and Peace: Vatican Polyglot Press, 1987): 146.

[10] *Dominus Iesus: On the Unicity and Salvific Universality of Jesus Christ and the Church* (2000). This declaration was issued by the Congregation of the Doctrine of the Faith. Text of this document as well as other documents relating to dialogue and evangelization are readily available online at the official websites of Vatican as well of different congregations and offices of Vatican.

[11] To understand how *Dominus Iesus* came across to Asians, see the special issue of *Jeevadhara*, vol. 31, no. 183 (2001). This issue contains the contribution of several Asian theologians - Francis X. D' Sa, Michael Amaladoss, Edmund Chia, Rui de Menezes, José de Mesa, Jacob Parapally, Sebastian Painadath. For reporting, see, "Japanese indifferent to Dominus Iesus", in Union of Catholic Asian News UCAN, 5 October 2000; "Dominus Iesus Brings Cultural Tension for Vietnam Catholics", UCAN, 18 September 2000; "Indians of Various Religions Shocked over 'unnecessary' Vatican Document", UCAN, 19 September 2000; "Theology Institute Initiates Public Discussion on Dominus Iesus", UCAN 29 December 2000; "Media Say Vatican Document Threatens Dialogue: Communal Peace", UCAN 3 October 2000; "Bishops Note Room for 'Theological Inquiry' in Toning Down Dominus Iesus, UCAN 3 May 2001.

[12] Cf. John O' Malley, et al., *Vatican II: Did Anything Happen?* (New York: Bloomsbury, 2007); see also ID., John O'Malley, "Trent and Vatican II: Two Styles of Church", in *From Trent to Vatican II: Historical and Theological Investigations*, Raymond F. Bulman and Frederick J. Parrella, eds. (Oxford: Oxford University Press, 2006).

[13] Procrustean refers to Procrustes, a Greek mythical figure who attacked people and stretched them on an iron bed, and then cut off their legs so that they could fit into the size of the bed!

[14] The Office of Theological Concerns (OTC) of FABC is of the view that such a position is a misunderstanding. It clarifies how Asia offers space to look at one truth from different perspectives. See OTC document on "Methodology: Asian Christian Theology: Doing Theology in Asia Today", in Vimal Tirimanna, ed., *Sprouts of Theology from Asian Soil: Collection of ATC and OTC Documents [1987-2007]* (Bangalore: Claretian Publication): 255- 343, 258.

[15] *Rig Veda* 1:164.46.

[16] Cf. Felix Wilfred, "In Praise of Christian Relativism", in *The New Pontification: A Time For Change, Concilium 2006/1* (London: SCM Press, 2006): 86-94.

[17] An excellent doctoral research work was done by Edmund Chia on the contribution of FABC to interreligious dialogue by analyzing its numerous documents. See Edmund Chia, *Towards a Theology of Dialogue*, (Nijmegen, 2003); see also Preman Niles, *The Lotus and the Sun: Asian Theological Engagement with Plurality and Power* (Barton ACT: Barton Books, 2013):150 ff.

[18] Final Statement of VII FABC Plenary Assembly – for the text see, *For All the Peoples of Asia: Federation of Asian Bishops' Conferences, Documents from 1997-2001*, vol. 3, Franz-Josef Eilers, ed. (Quezon City: Claretian Publications, 2002): 8.

[19] Peter Phan, ed., *The Asian Synod: Texts and Commentaries* (Maryknoll: Orbis Books, 2002): 30.

[20] This question led to the issuing of a few official documents by the Church trying to clarify the relationship between dialogue and evangelization. The Pontifical Council for Interreligious Dialogue (then known as Secretariat for Non-Christians) issued a document called *Reflections and Orientations on Dialogue and Mission* (1984). The Congregation of Evangelization of Peoples and the Pontifical Council for Interreligious Dialogue jointly brought out a document entitled: *Dialogue and Proclamation: Reflections and Orientations on Interreligious Dialogue and the Proclamation of the Gospel of Jesus Christ* (1991).

[21] See http://www.bbc.com/news/p. 104-105. world-europe-30250098 accessed on 10 February 2016.

[22] In fact, the Episcopal motto of Jorge Mario Bergoglio was "*Miserando atque eligendo.*"

[23] See www.bbc.com/news/world-europe-30250098 accessed on 10 February 2016.

[24] Walter Kasper, *Pope Francis' Revolution of Tenderness and Love* (New York: Paulist Press, 2015): 63- 64.

[25] For the text of the statement, see *Living and Working Together with Sisters and Brothers of Other Faiths in Asia: An Ecumenical Consultation, Singapore, July, 5-10,*

1987 (Singapore: CCA-FABC, 1989): 104-105. This way of relating evangelization and dialogue is very different from considering interreligious dialogue as "part of the Church's evangelizing mission" (*Dominus Iesus* no. 2), which does not seem to recognize the validity of dialogue in itself. One would defeat the spirit of dialogue if it is made simply an instrument for something else, and not a value in itself.

[26] Western theologians may leaf through the pages of their philosophers – Kant and Hegel, Paschal and Kierkagaard, Haberms and Foucault, Lyotard and Levinas - , and they will find in none of them the kind of cosmic and integral vision of reality we note in Hinduism, Buddhism, Confucianism, Daoim and Shintonism. Hence, the message of Pope Francis in *Laudato Si* cannot be interpreted in the light of these philosophers. Rather here is a call to go to those traditions which have embedded in them a cosmic vision of reality which enlightens us also on the mystery of God, world and the human, avoiding all kinds of dangerous dualism. In the West itself, there are instances of individuals who have fostered integral vision of reality like St Francis of Assisi, from whose canticle Pope Francis has culled out the title of his encyclical – *Laudato Si*. However the tradition St Francis represents is a marginal and neglected one in Western history.

[27] Cf. Felix Wilfred, "Theological Significance of Laudato Si: An Asian Reading" in *Vidyajyoti Journal of Theological Reflections* vol.79 (September 2015): 645-661.

[28] See my lecture on this topic at a conference at the University of Louvain, held in November, 2014, entitled "Christianity and Religious Cosmopolitanism". This text will be published shortly by the Oxford University Press, Oxford: *The Past, Present and Future of Theologies of Inter-religious Dialogue*, ed. by Terrence Merrigan.

[29] See *L'Osservatore Romano*, Weekly edition in English (22 January, 2016).

[30] http://www.news.va/en/news/pope-highlights-importance-of-interfaith-dialogue accessed on 10 February 2016.

[31] As quoted in Michael Reader and Josef Schmidt "Habermas and Religion", in *Awareness of what is Missing: Faith and Reason in a Post-secular Age* (Cambridge: Polity Press, 2010): 5-6.

[32] John Baptist Metz, *Mistica degli occhi aperti: Per una spiritualità concreta e responsabile* (Brescia: Queriniana, 2013).

Double Belonging:
A Hypostatic Union?

Paul F. Knitter

This is going to be an exceptionally personal presentation. But I think that is appropriate since it is also an expression of my personal and long-time friendship with Sebastian Painadath S.J. and of my great esteem for both his scholarship and his own deep, personal faith. He has been an example and an inspiration for me as I have trod, together with him, the path of exploring how an engagement with other religious teachings and spiritualities can challenge, even transform, our own understanding of, and commitment to, Jesus and the Gospel.

My topic is one that is dear to Sebastian's heart: spirituality based on Christology. I would like to explore the question whether the much-discussed phenomenon of "double religious belonging" can be understood through an analogous comparison with Chalcedon's hypostatic union of two natures and one person in Jesus? But in order to do that, I am going to do a theological reflection on my own experience.

So, first let me offer a bird's eye, and therefore limited, view of my two-faced identity: I was born into a traditional, not very critical, Catholic family in the Chicago of 73 years ago. At 13, I decided (against my parents wishes) to enter a minor seminary in order to become a priest and went through the whole 14 years of training. For the last four years of that training I had the profoundly good fortune to be sent to Rome, arriving there in 1962, two weeks before over 2000 bishops marched into St. Peter's Basilica to start the Second Vatican Council. Ordained a priest in 1966 and animated with Vatican II's new openness to other religions, I did a dissertation at the University of Marburg, Germany, on Christian theologies of religions. When I returned to the States in 1972, I taught theology at Catholic Theological Union in Chicago, and when I decided to leave the Catholic priesthood in 1975, I moved to Xavier University in Cincinnati where I continued teaching theology for some 28 years.

It was during those years, in 1980s, that I began not only to teach courses on Buddhism but also to practice daily Zen meditation. Gradually, I came to realize that Buddhism, its theory and practice, was seeping into and coloring the way I understood and practiced my Christian creed – to the point that, in 2007 I took refuge in the Tibetan Dzogchen tradition and since then have been under the guidance of my teacher, Lama John Makransky. It was around this time that I faced the need to figure out just what or who I was – a Buddhist Christian or a Christian Buddhist. So, typical academic that I am, I wrote a book.

In *Without Buddha I Could Not Be a Christian*,[1] I declared and defended my primary identity as a Christian who was thoroughly drenched in Buddhism. But when I recently read Rose Drew's penetrating analysis of the various ways of blending dual religious belonging in her *Christian or Buddhist? An Exploration of Dual Religious Belonging*,[2] I started to wonder. From her ethnographic study of actual dual-belongers, she found that some a) have a primary religious identity (the group I thought I belonged to), b) alternate between both primary identities, c) cannot attribute primacy to either or any identity, and d) are too bewildered by it all to say anything.[3] As I pondered Drew's description and analysis of her interviewees' meanderings back and forth across religious lines, I had to admit that I wasn't sure where I belonged. In this brief presentation, I'm trying to figure things out.

An inappropriate analogy

My problem is that as my Christian and Buddhist practices have continued over these recent five to ten years, more and more, I can't keep them apart. They remain clearly distinct, but unlike Roger Corless, of blessed memory, I have not been able to honor their distinct identities by practicing them, as Roger apparently did, separately: being a Buddhist from Monday to Thursday, and a Christian from Friday to Sunday (and then waiting to see what would happen). Rather, for me, when I'm at Mass, I hear the words of the Scripture readings or of the sermon (though I usually resort to Zen mindfulness of my breath during most sermons) with Buddhist ears. I feel the powerful symbols of the Eucharistic liturgy with Buddhist sensitivity. And when I'm on my cushion meditating, my awareness of the breath feels like awareness of the Spirit. When encouraged to sit like the Buddha I find myself also sitting like the Christ. In the guided meditations that are part of our Tibetan practice, I drift between both Buddhist and Christian images.

I can't keep my two practices apart, and yet they remain distinctly identifiable. I suspect I really belong to Drew's third category – those double belongers for whom one can't speak of primacy. But then how to understand or speak about such a blended dual practice? In pondering that question, I found myself resorting to a perhaps inappropriate analogy that came to me from my past.

In the course titled *De Verbo Incarnato* that I took with Bernard Lonergan, S.J. at the Pontifical Gregorian University back in 1964, I spent many an exciting but also frustrating hour trying to follow his analysis of the Council of Chalcedon (451). The language and the images have become part of my theological *modus operandi* ever since. It returned to my awareness as I pondered what was "double" in my religious belonging. The actual, ancient language that the bishops finally formulated, and which has been kept alive down through the centuries through debates about its meaning, actually seems to fit and clarify what double religious belonging might mean:

… two natures not confused, nor changed, nor divided, nor separated (*inconfuse, immutabiliter, indivise, inseparabiliter*), at no point is the difference between the natures taken away through the union, but rather the property of both natures is preserved and comes together into a single hypostasis. (DS 302)

If we take the classical understanding of *natura (*or in Greek, *ousia)* as the "*principium operandi,*" the operational principle or source of the kind of activity of any entity, and if we hold to the conciliar understanding of *hypostasis* as the actual personal being expressing this activity, then maybe these concepts or images might be just as helpful in throwing light on the mystery of dual religious belonging as they are for trying to express the mystery of the hypostatic union in Jesus (maybe even more helpful for the former than the latter!).

In the spiritual life of one double-belonging human being, two very different spiritual "operational principles" "come together in a single hypostasis or person" – but without being "confused or changed or divided or separated," for "the property of each is preserved." – These images and philosophical distinctions of the fourth and fifth centuries might help explain how one person can be both Buddhist and Christian at the same time. Just as doctrine construes Jesus of Nazareth as one person who is acting both humanly and divinely, so too a double belonger can be understood as one person acting both Buddhistically and Christianly.

The helpfulness of these categories increased for me when I did my analogy with a group of doctoral students at Union Theological Seminary a couple of months ago. One of the students, Mr. Kyeongil Jung, astutely observed that the "hypostasis" or self in which these two activities commingle can be understood from a Buddhist perspective as a "not-self." Then the hypostasis of a double belonger (including the hypostasis of Jesus) is all the more engagingly imaged as an empty space in which the dual practices become indivisibly one without losing their distinction.

A non-dual union: Buddhist ontology and Christian particularity

But more needs to be said. If, as Chalcedon puts it, "the property of both natures is preserved," how might I describe these differing properties? What is distinctively Buddhist and distinctively Christian about my practice? Or, how might I describe, broadly, what each brings to the empty space of my not-self hypostasis?

In the hypostatic union of my Buddhist and Christian practices, I've come to realize that Buddha supplies the "big picture," while Christ supplies the living color. Or, Buddha describes the broad energy field and Christ is a revealing instantiation of what happens when that energy takes form. Or, Buddhism provides the ontology and Christianity provides the particularity. Buddha makes clear *what's* going on. Christ shows *how* it goes on.

Buddhist ontology: Essentially, I'm talking about Mahayana's and especially Madyamaka's understanding of the nonduality between Form and Emptiness, Nirvana and Samsara. All finite or relative reality is grounded in the groundlessness of Emptiness or open Spaciousness. Everything, absolutely everything, is contained in or gives expression to what is described, especially in Tibetan traditions, as vast, aware, and compassionate Spaciousness or Emptiness. Absolute reality and Relative reality are distinct, but they are not separable. They co-exist by co-inhering. They dance together, distinct but both essential for the Dance. In this Dance, the relative forms are real. But Emptiness or Spaciousness is, in a sense, more real. The forms dance on into impermanence. Emptiness is the abiding music. This is a thoroughly non-dual understanding and perception of the relation between finite and Infinite. They're not two. But neither are they one. – That's the big picture.

Such a nondual big picture translated into the relation between God and creation, is generally not evident in popular Christian practice and awareness, but it is not at all foreign to the experience and teachings of followers of Jesus. I mean, of course, Christian mystics – Eckhart,

Theresa of Avila, John of the Cross, Julian of Norwich. But not just mystics. Also, in theologians and spiritual writers there are analogous attempts at trying to articulate or gesture to this inexpressible co-inhering of God – especially symbolized as Spirit – and all of creation. Two of my own teachers and mentors have played pivotal roles in my life in alerting me to the nondual unity of the Divine and finite long before Buddhism entered my life.

Karl Rahner's notion of the supernatural existential is a Christian attempt to point to the co-existing of divine and human life. Every nook and cranny of our *existence*, he taught us, is *supernatural.* All is pervaded by grace, by God's self-giving. There is, he pressed his case, no such thing as *natura pura* – nature all by itself.[4] Divine activity, or self-communicating Spirit, is everywhere and therefore is always available. Raimon Panikkar pushed this even further with his image of all reality as *cosmotheandric.* What is really going on at every moment of personal existence is a threefold interplay (again, the symbol of "dance" applies) between *theos* or divinity, *cosmos* or material reality, and *aner* or humanity. Each is different. Each is essential. Remove any one of them and the dance stops.[5]

But if this big picture of nonduality is present on the Christian stage, it is found, for the most part, in the mystical and theological wings. In the Buddhism I practice, it plays center-stage. The ineffable experience of co-inherence or oneness between Emptiness and Form – or as Lama John Makransky puts it, between vast space and our inner space – is at the heart of my Buddhist practice. Or in more philosophical terms, what might be called a nondual ontology is present much more centrally, clearly, effectively in Buddhism than, I think I can say, in Christianity.

So as far as this "big picture" is concerned, I'm primarily a Buddhist. Buddhism for me gets the big picture right much more lucidly and coherently than Christianity does. In fact, if someone were really to prove to me that this nondual Buddhist picture were incompatible with Christian experience and teaching (that hasn't happened and I don't think it can), I would have to abandon Christianity for Buddhism.

Christian particularity: But in order to know and feel what can happen – indeed, what needs to happen – to a human being in order to wake up to this nondual big picture taught so centrally and clearly in Buddhism, I have found that Jesus of Nazareth is not only helpful but vital. For me, Jesus the Christ is the embodiment, the instantiation, the realization of this nonduality between Form and Emptiness, divinity and humanity. He makes it real for me. I see it in him. I feel it through him. He embodies both how one needs to live in order to grow into the realization of nonduality or "oneness with the Father," and how one will carry out one's life after having awakened to this oneness. He is both the *way* that leads to the experience of co-inhering with the Divine and also the *life* that results as this experience deepens and becomes more real. Thanks to Buddha, Jesus as "the way, the truth, and the life" (John 14:6) has taken on added meaning and power for me.

When I say that Jesus embodies or incarnates the nonduality between Emptiness and form, or between Abba and us, I'm talking about Jesus *of Nazareth.* I'm relating to Jesus in all his particularity, his historical concreteness as a Jew, a prophet, a victim of Roman imperial oppression, as crucified, as living on within his followers. This historical particularity is powerfully important for me in understanding and living into the "big picture" that Buddha makes so clear. The embodiment of Emptiness or Holy Mystery in the particularity of Jesus is for me a genuine revelation. By that I mean that it's not just expressing what I already know. It's making clear, or revealing, to me the kind of *forms* that Emptiness *can take* in the relative world because it *has taken* this form in Jesus. But – and here I speak primarily out of my Christian conditioning – Jesus represents a form that Emptiness or Spaciousness *needs to,* or *intends to,* take in the finite, relative order.

I'm not implying that what happened in this Jesus of Nazareth, and what continues to happen through him, is in any way *exclusive* of what has happened in other spiritual figures who have "awakened" or "been called." But I am saying – and I'm saying it because I'm feeling it – that what we see in this Jesus, or in this particular Form that

Emptiness has taken – is important also for others. While it is central and most effective for me as a Christian, it is also relevant and maybe even urgent for others.

But so is Buddha relevant for others who are not Buddhists and who don't intend to be Buddhists.   Particularities matter. If Buddha and Jesus are both "forms" in which Emptiness or Spirit is particularly and powerfully present, and if they are very different forms, then they are important not just for their own followers but also for the followers of each other. In my own dual-belonging and in my Christian language, I know that Jesus "has what it takes" to "save" me; but my practice and study of Buddhism have also made clear that something is missing in this Jesus, or in how he has been understood. (And I make bold to ask whether Buddhists might say the same thing about Buddha).

Coming together of two in one

So, if Buddha, in his particularity, provides the big picture and Jesus, a particular living out of that big picture, how do they, in the language of Chalcedon, "come together into a single hypostasis" that is a double-belonger? Certainly, there is no one way to understand or describe such a hypostatic union of dual-practices and visions. It will be experienced and known differently "according to the mode of the knower" – that is, according to the "causes and conditions" (or "social-construction") of the person and community doing the interpreting. But also, what Catholic theologians call "the signs of the times" – or the state of the world – will provide (or should provide) a hermeneutical guiding light in trying to understand what a Buddhist-Christian identity means. So, given my own and my Christian community's conditioning after two generations of liberation theology, and given a world in which incredible injustice promotes incredible violence, I have identified the real but complementary differences between Buddha and Jesus in the difference between "Being Peace" and "Making Peace" -- or more analytically, between "experiencing *prajna*" and "enacting *agape*." (Here I bow in grateful indebtedness to Thich Nhat Hanh and Aloysius Pieris, S.J.).[6]

Buddhist Being Peace: I have found in my practice and study that Buddha teaches and embodies the path to *being* peace. In his teaching and analysis, Buddha offers me the possibility and the methodology for transforming my sense of who I am. If we will never be able to comprehend and put into words what Nirvana or Enlightenment is, we certainly can describe and identify what it looks like in others and feels like in ourselves. The "waking up" is a transformation of the self – a transformation in which we experience that what we really are is not what we think we are: what we are is both non-substantial and incessantly impermanent. If it's impossible to define what this "not-self" is, it is fairly easy, again, to state how we feel when we live as an *anatta:* peace and freedom. There is a peacefulness that can sustain us no matter what happens and that becomes the ground out of which we confront or embrace all the events and the beings that make up our lives.

Buddhist teachers such as Thich Nhat Han and Lama John Makransky stress that such "being peace" must be the pre-condition, as it were, for all our efforts at making peace.[7] Or in Pieris's perspective, while *prajna* and *karuna,* wisdom and compassion, make up the two sides of one enlightened coin, *prajna,* for Buddhists, has a certain, perhaps we can say pragmatic, priority. While compassion is really nothing but the living out of the wisdom of interbeing – so that really, they are two manifestations of one reality – still, if we are not actively nurturing our wisdom, our capacities for compassion are going to dwindle. Thus, Thich Nhat Hanh's thundering admonition to all activists: you need to *be peace* in order to *make peace.* Unless there is some level of waking up to our not-self reality, our ego-self is going to keep getting in the way of our activism and peace-making. Whether it is clinging to our own plans, or wearing out when those plans don't materialize, or hating those who stand in the way of our plans – ego, or the lack of wisdom, can often make a bigger mess than the one we are trying to clean up.

This, then, is what I have experienced to be an essential, and an indispensable, ingredient in Buddha's particularity. In giving the big picture of nonduality, he announces the universally important message that we have to experience or realize our identities as not-selves within this big picture if we are going to be able to confront and remove the sufferings of sentient beings.

Christian "Making Peace": But if the particularity of Buddha reminds us that making peace must flow from being peace, the particularity of Jesus makes clear just what the job of making peace is going to require. If Buddha provides the *ability* to make peace, Jesus clarifies how *to do* it. If earlier I suggested that Jesus shows us how one lives after experiencing the nonduality between Emptiness/Form or Abba/Self, now we're filling in the picture of what such a life entail.

Because of his Jewishness, because of his participation in a tradition of socially engaged prophets, and especially because he lived and taught and experienced Abba at a time when the Roman Empire was brutally oppressing his people, Jesus' *mystical* experience of Abba was at the same time a *social* experience of the reality he called the *Basileia tou Theou – the Reign of God*. For Jesus, the two were much like the Buddhist understanding of wisdom and compassion: you can't have one without the other. A God without the *Basileia* of God – or an experience of Abba without an experience of the need for *Basileia* – was, for Jesus, an experience of a false God. As Aloysius Pieris sees it, if Buddha assigned what I've called a "pragmatic priority" to waking up to *prajna*, Jesus seemed to place a pragmatic priority on the *agape* of struggling to realize the *Basileia*. If you're going to the temple to pray and realize that you are in a rift with your brother, fix the rift before going to the temple (Matthew 5:23-25).

More particularly, or more concretely, the *Basileia* of God requires not only the transformation of the self but also the transformation of society; and that means social, political, military structures. What was the case at the time of Jesus is the case throughout history: empires keep taking shape; some nations or classes of people (they're usually led by males) take advantage of and oppress others. The life and teachings of Jesus call all enlightened people to confront and seek to change such oppressive structures. The awareness of oppression – or the preferential concern for the oppressed – was a pivotal part of how Jesus experienced and lived out his oneness with Abba. So, Jesus would remind Buddhists that the three poisons of ignorance, greed, and hatred are not just internal to the person; they are also embodied in social, political, and economic structures. And once so embodied, they take on an existence of their own, independent of their existence in the hearts of humans.

Therefore, while the transformation of the self into *being peace* is absolutely essential, it is not enough. *Being peace* will not, as it were, automatically or seamlessly *make peace*. To truly *make peace*, oppressive structures, and those who hold them in place, have to be confronted. This renders *making peace* a further step after *being peace*, a step that can be more complex and dangerous than *being peace*. It requires taking on what St. Paul called the powers and principalities. (Rom. 3:38; Eph. 6:12) This is what led to Jesus' crucifixion and to Paul's beheading.

So, I'm a Buddhist Christian but also a Christian Buddhist – one person with two religious natures or "principles of operation." Buddha provides the most compelling and transforming teaching and illustration of the nondual big picture which enables me to *be peace*; Jesus offers the most compelling and transforming incarnation of how living in the big picture calls for *making peace* within this world.   To have one without the other is to have neither.

Endnotes

[1] Oxford, Oneworld Publications, 2009.

[2] New York: Routledge, 2011.

[3] Ibid., 7-13.

[4] Karl Rahner, *Foundations of Christian Faith* (NY: Seabury Press, 1978), 116-33.

[5] Raimon Panikkar, *The Cosmotheandric Experience: Emerging Religious Consciousness* (Maryknoll: Orbis Books, 1993).

[6] Thich Nhat Hanh, *Being Peace* (Berkeley: Parallax Press, 1987); Aloysius Pieris, *Love Meets Wisdom: A Christian Experience of Buddhism* (Maryknoll: Orbis Books, 1988), 110-36.

[7] Thich Nhat Hanh, op cit.   John Makransky, "How Contemporary Buddhist Practice Meets the Secular World in Its Search for a Deeper Grounding for Service and Social Action," published in the on-line journal, *Dharma World*, March 2012.

A Philosophical Foundation for the Jesuit Mission Today: An Intercultural Dialogical Perspective

Anand Amaladoss SJ

Philosophy or theology has to begin with experience. Every movement, every reformer or founder begins with a fundamental experience. It is said that Western philosophy began with the experience of wonder and the Indian philosophy began with suffering, meaninglessness (*duhkh*a), or impermanence of things. One begins to reflect on this phenomenon and responds to it.

Jesus calls for an experience of conversion acknowledging one's unworthiness to enter into the Kingdom of God ("Repent and enter into the Kingdom of God" Mk.1,15). The Jesuit mission began with the experience of the situation in the Church of that time. Ignatius and his companions felt the need of the time and responded by placing themselves at the service of the Pope. The first missionary who came to India saw the situation in India and began his ministry among the poor people.

What is experience then? In the Indian tradition, it is not merely an intellectual grasp of things, giving information. It is *anubhava*, *anubhūti*, that is, becoming new, a knowledge that changes, a new state of being leading to action, it is transformative as a result of that coming in contact with the given situation. In fact Karl Rahner uses faith experience in this sense of transformation which comes closer to the Indian understanding of experience. But this notion was not properly understood in the early days of modernism and so Pope Pius X condemned it in his Encyclical *Pascendi Dominici Gregis* (1907).

This experience took three fundamental forms in Indian history of philosophy:

a. An experience of the impermanence of all things and the question was how to overcome that suffering and to reach the transcendence. One way would be: behind all the experiential statements we make, there is the "is-ness" of things that remains. Sankara bases on this is-ness judgment we make and goes to the experience of identity (*abhēdavāda*);

b. But the is-ness is not the same in all things. Each one is different from the others. Things are not one, but there is a difference in themselves. The devotees (bhaktas) of India insisted on the alterity. If identical, there is no bhakti, love for other beings;

c. Between these two extreme views there is another view, namely, experience is primarily complementary, essential in every experience of human being, man/woman, nature/man. This experience is not absolute identity or difference, but a complementarity of different reality. This is the view of Bhaskara, Nimbarka and others. *Bheda* (difference) and *abheda* (identity) are experienced simultaneously. But this idea was not developed in the Indian tradition further for various reasons.

It is significant that the Vatican Document *Fides et Ratio* (1988) for the first time perhaps has given a special place for India. "In India particularly, it is the duty of the Christians now to draw from this rich heritage the elements compatible with their faith, in order to enrich Christian thought" (no. 72).

On the other hand, Pope Benedict XVI's recent remark on the Greek philosophy becoming integral part of the Christian tradition has much to say on the debate about the inculturation of the Christian message. One has to take into account the historical process of growth of a particular faith tradition which has assimilated within itself several elements from various traditions down the centuries. In other words, one cannot today completely de-hellenize, de-europeanize and de-hebrewize Christ's message, as if one gets the Jesus' message straight from the mouth of the Apostles and transplants it in the Indian soil, for example, as in a flower-pot from Jerusalem, so that it blossoms into an Indian Christian theology.[1]

This is said in view of the title of this paper where an Indian perspective is proposed which has to be taken within the total context of the Jesuit heritage down the centuries.

Part I

Jesuit Concerns in their ministries.

Brief historical sketch of Jesuit experience in India

Before speaking about the Jesuit mission India, it may be worthwhile to sketch briefly how the mission of the Jesuits in India began and the main goals of the early missionary period. One can point out three areas of concern: a.) conversion and founding of the new communities; b.) adaptation and the rite controversy and c.) dialogue of religions.

Right from the beginning of the Jesuit Order, India was the first missionary land for the Jesuit: Francis Xavier, the first Jesuit missionary, came to India in 1542 even Society was formally approved on 27 September 1540. There were conversions in India all along the Coasts of India - Goa, Mangalore, Malabar, Tuticorin etc. That happened not always without force and violence. So much so the first Council of Goa in 1567 had to speak against the 'violent mission'.

About adaptation the question was whether one should condemn and demonize the customs and cultural practices of the people, which go together in some way or other with religion or one should consider them much more as the soil on which the seed of the Gospel should be sown. The question may sound theoretical, but a fight arose out of this question (the so-called the rite-controversy), which has moved the minds of all missionary orders. This historical episode is mentioned here, since the basic question of adaptation is in no way a settled one and the inculturation of the Gospels is yet to find its fullness in India.

In the great dialogue of religions in Agra the Jesuits were not the initiators; rather they were more pre-occupied with coverting the royal family. Much more the emperor Akbar the Great invited the representatives of all religions for a dialogue and the Jesuits from Goa were also invited. Akbar's attempt at a unified religion for the whole kingdom did not materialize. But the necessity of dialogue between great religions of humanity becomes increasingly more important and urgent.

After the first period of mission followed the process of decline coinciding with the suppression of the Society in 1774. After the restoration of the Society in 1814 the Jesuit mission in India gained more significance. The French Jesuits came to Tamilnadu, the Italians to Kerala and Karnataka and the Belgians to Bengal, Bihar and Madhya Pradesh.

There were great Jesuit missionaries who contributed significantly to Indian mission: Francis Xavier, Thomas Stephan (1549-1619), Roberto De Nobili (1577-1656), Constanso Joseph Beschi (1680-1747), Johann Hoffmann (1857-1928) to mention only a few.

Option for the poor and the Jesuits

Poverty has been one of the great challenges to the religious orders in the Church. In the history of the Church there have been significant movements to follow the poor Christ by living a life of a beggar- especially in the 11th and 12th centuries. St. Ignatius of Loyola wanted to make a contribution to the spiritual renaissance according to the model of Francis of Assisi and St. Dominic. But there is a difference in the way the Society of Jesus went about its mission. The very geographical location of Jesuit presence in Rome reflects the psychology of their approach to spirituality. St. Benedict wanted to be away from the city atmosphere on Monte Casino in prayer. The Franciscans went outside the city, but not so distanced as on the mountain top. But the Jesuits took their position in the very heart of the city of Rome.

Recent research in the field of economics has highlighted how the Spanish Jesuit philosophers towards the end of 16th century have contributed to the economic questions besides their theological concerns. Luis Molina (1535-1600) is mentioned as a leading figure in this regard. According to him the discussion about the "just price" can result only when the market avoids every kind of monopoly and cheating. Molina places the accent not on fixing the content, what justice in economics is or could be, but much more on the institutional conditions out of which the just results could be seen.[2] Another example from the Jesuit history is the well-known experiment of "Reductions" at Paraguay in the 17th century, where the American Indians maintained their own State. Much less known is perhaps the attempt of the Jesuits like Constant Lievens (1856-1893) and John Baptist Hoffmann (1857-1928) in Bihar, North India, where they initiated the process of the *Chotanagpur Tenancy Act* in 1908 and *Credit Cooperative Society, to rescue* the people of Chotanagpur from the clutches of money-lenders, *to educate* the people in thrift by spreading the habit of saving from the little surpluses they have and *to educate* the people in the self-management and self-help, "that spirit of manly and sound independence and activity which is so highly rational and Christian."[3]

The present situation

The Jesuit mission has been defined and elaborated in several documents from the beginning of its existence. The Decree 4 of the GC 32 is the key Document which affirms the commitment for the poor as integral part of the Jesuit apostolate and this was ratified by the following General Congregations in 1983 and 1995. The option goes back again to the Gospels where Jesus reveals himself in the form of the poor, discriminated, suffering people (Mt. 25, 31-46). Therefore the option for the poor is a fundamental decision which is spiritual as well as a political.

But in the recent past, the focus has been sharpened more and more as a response to the world situation around. In a globalized world of affluence wealthy players could frame the rules of the game and reap the gains of market economy and the poor would have no place in their world. There is no face of compassion for the under-privileged. Hence the Christian mission gains greater significance in this scenario.

The Jesuit apostolate in particular concentrates itself on option for the poor which includes, the *dalits* (in India) who are discriminated because of their birth, descent and occupation, and also the women and the refugees. From this perspective one has to see the faith and justice dimension. With increasing culture-wars on the horizons, the world is truncated into ethnic groups, religious fundamentalist sects, linguistic factions and peace is not given any chance. Hence promotion of intercultural/ interfaith dialogue becomes the urgent task. The concern for the poor leads to the apostolate of education, giving them the basic knowledge to be aware of their human dignity. Whether one is busy with educating the people or working for interfaith harmony, the main concern is the welfare of the other which is to be rooted in love.

Source of inspiration for this mission

The Jesuit mission takes its inspiration from the call of Jesus Christ, his vision of the *anawim, the poor.* God has created us out of love and the love of God is manifested in and through Jesus Christ. His mission and message could be summed up in three Biblical metaphors: "washing of the feet", that means service; the "breaking of bread" which means sharing of what one is and has with the others, and the "pentacost" which implies building communities of love and brotherhood crossing the borders. If any one of these is left out, then Christ's message is not complete. The followers of Jesus are expected to live according these values.

Expression of this concern for the poor is also found in other religious traditions like Hinduism, Buddhism, Sikhism in India. Buddha's notion of community, the notion of *karuna* (compassion) and *maitri* (love) are expression of this concern. The concept of *lokasangraha* ('coherence of the whole' and thus comes to mean "cosmic welfare") in the Bhagavadgita is basic to the Hindu thought and the liberated person or a saint is defined in the Gita as one who takes delight in the welfare of all beings (*sarvabhūta hitē ratāh*, BG, 5,25) and Lord Krishna's discourse to Arjuna explicitly speaks of personal love. The Saivite saints like Tayumanavar (1608-1664), Ramalinga Swami –alias Vallalar (1823-1874) and others express their concern for the poor sharing the pain of the people.

Part II

Philosophical foundation

Jesuit concerns are not outside the human concerns and the concerns of the Gospels. Jesus' preferential love for the poor is the starting point here and the Christian mission is based on our faith in Jesus Christ. This faith assumption does not take us away from the philosophical way of reflection. Faith is rooted in nature and the destiny of human beings.

We are created human beings. God is the author of life and all of us are brothers/sisters to one another, since each one is equally a creature of God. We love our brothers/sisters because we have the same destiny. We must lift them up by being in dialogue with them. Human life is nothing but dialogue, dialogue with God and dialogue with one another.

The Indian seers had an insight into the reality and we too are inspired by the faith of other religions: to be in contact with the pluralistic world. We come from a common source and that is the insight of Indian sages. They have gone deeper into this mystery: we are one with the Supreme and others spoke of the difference. But we both are one with and different from God. The Hindus have seen this aspect of it. Expressions of it may be defective due to the substantialistic way of thinking in the Indian traditions.

Modern psychologists and anthropologists brought in another reason into this dialogue, one of complementarity: men/women, cultures and societies. Even in economics one talks of the developed countries going to the developing countries in order that they too may in turn find their growth process. No science can develop by itself in isolation.

The Hindu expression for all these aspects of love, development, etc. is *bheda-abheda* – difference and identity. Dialogue is not a means, but an end in itself, in the sense that it becomes a way of life. The goal is not to make others like myself but allow him/her to grow in her/his own way recognizing the complementarities. Dialogue is a constitutive dimension of human being, not simply an instrument. It is not the luxury of the privileged few nor is it an optional extra. To be authentically human requires being in dialogue, without which one remains in isolation and ignorance, becoming indifferent and contemptuous of others.

Why are we concerned with these issues? What is the rationale behind these apostolic considerations? One can argue from the religious consideration and be motivated in order to be involved in this humanitarian task. In fact people do work for the poor out of their faith conviction taking inspiration from their sacred texts like the Bible, Quran, Gita, etc.

As human beings there is also a search for meaning based on reason. Even when one believes, that faith seeks understanding, one looks for a rational foundation for that faith. That urge is quite human and that goes by the name philosophy. Hence an attempt is made to find a philosophical framework for the pursuit of justice, love for the poor, dialogue, etc. in the following pages from the Indian tradition.

If love is the source and starting point of all service, it presupposes identity and difference. One loves the other because he/she is part of the other person. There is similarity, but still dissimilar. If the other is completely different, one cannot love the other, and if one completely is identical, love does not mean anything. There is difference and identity, a complementarity.

"God created us out of love" means in the Christian tradition that he deigns to share his own life, his being, his intelligence with the creatures. Christianity insists on the self-gift of God. This love is gratuitous, yet his love makes us similar to him but never reaches the identity with him. In the Hindu tradition it is said that God creates the world out of free will, out of love, without any compulsion. It is explained through a metaphor of dance (*lila*).

Identity cannot produce love. Similarity is the root of love. This similarity and dissimilarity is the foundation for anything that we do for others. The poor are myself and yet different. It is my duty to make them happy, for they are myself. Even this identity and difference are God's gift.

In the same way all religions are similar and dissimilar- *bhēda* and *abhēda*. Man and woman are similar and dissimilar. One cannot be without the other. The notion of dialogue also stems from this foundation. Life is one of dialogue, not an extra option. Dialogue between cultures, between different religions, between man and woman and is a way to life and a way to grow.

This notion of love presupposes the notion of reality itself, how one understands God, world and man and how these three are interrelated. In the Indian philosophical tradition there is a foundation for this sort of understanding reality, which is called *bhēda-abhēda-vāda*, relation of difference and non-difference.

Some Indian approaches

1.   Nimbarka and his philosophy

The great philosopher Nimbarka who was a Bhagavata Vaisnava Vedantin and lived between the second half of the 5th Century and the first half of the 6th Century AD, (this is the traditional date, though other historians place him in 14th Century AD) has propounded a theory of *bhēda-abhēda* relation, between Brahman and the world and the humans, namely, the difference and identity.[4] It avoids the absolute identity and the absolute difference between Brahman and the created world. According to Nimbarka, Brahman is the only entity (*sat*) and we all share in his ontological existence. Being the supportive cause of the created reality, Brahman not only pulsates within the entire creation in so far as the created world is co-substantial with him, but also transcends them all and ever remains as the Other, the Ultimate, the One, the Infinite, the Absolute and the Beyond.

Nimbarka denies that there is an absolute difference or an absolute non-difference between Brahman and the living beings. Brahman is not out of all relationships. He is the ground of all relationships, for he sustains all things. It is he who gives meaning to the finite. In the realm of *being* there is the One, the Infinite, the Absolute Brahman, while in the world of *becoming* there are the many, the finite, the relative, the living beings and the world. *Becoming* is as real as the *Being*.

Nimbarka explains the relation between Brahman and the living beings and the world not only in terms of the cause and its effects, but also through other analogies and similes such as the ocean and its waves, the sun and its luster, a substratum of power and its power, the whole and the parts, the snake and its coils etc. These analogies and symbolic expressions point out both the difference and the non-difference between Brahman and the living beings and the world. One can infer from this that the world and the living beings have also the difference and non-difference among themselves just as the pot and the plate, which are the effects of clay. In other words, these analogies point out that there is the absolute independence and transcendence of Brahman and so there is difference between Brahman and the world of the human beings.

Secondly there is the total dependence of the created world of living beings on Brahman for their existence and activity. Brahman is the ontological primus of the relative existence. The Absolute constitutes the relative. Yet the relation between the One and the many is one of co-existence and not of contradiction. The many participate in the existence (*sat*) of the One. In this sense there is the relation of non-difference between Brahman and the world of living beings.

2.   Ramanuja's vision of reality

Another great philosopher from South India is Ramanuja of the Vaishnava tradition (1017-1137 traditional date). His vision of reality consists of God-world-Man as a well-knit organism: *cit* (Conscious Being), *acit* (Matter) and *Isvara* (Divine). He conceives reality as a totality where the material and human dimensions are metaphorically explained as the body of the Divine. The *Isvara* or the Divine is the soul that animates and sustains and supports the body, which is distinct and real. The interrelationship between these three realities is described, not as pantheism as it is sometimes wrongly interpreted, but as "pan-en-theism", that is, "the view that deity is... distinguishable from and independent of any and all relative items and yet, taken as an actual whole, includes all relative items."[5]

This body-soul analogy suggests that materiality is a potential vehicle of spiritual nature. This is remarkable, for no other system in the Indian tradition was able to give such a positive role to the body in relation to the soul and hence to the whole universe in relation to the Supreme Self.[6] This metaphor of body-soul also indicates the inseparable relationship between God and the universe *(aprthak-siddhi-sambandha)*. This inseparable relationship is not reciprocal, i.e., the body is dependent and God is not dependent on the soul and the world. Ramanuja develops this idea in three sub-metaphors, like, the supporter/thing-supported (ādhara-ādheya) relationship, Controller/thing-controlled (*niyantra-niyanya*) relationship; and principal (*śeshin*) / accessory (*śesha*) relationship.

After all, in Christian tradition, there is a precedent of a kind for body-talk in a divine context, in the doctrine of the mystical body. The New Testament epistles also are not hesitant to use body imagery in connection with the believers' relationship to Christ. The stress on the utter derivativeness of the world from God, both as to existence and intelligibility distinctively through the notion of the 'substrative cause', the insight into the Lord as absolute controller of the world or individual, and the emphasis on the Lord's being the crowning glory of creation, counter-balanced from the microcosmic view point, by the finite atman's being in its own right a support, controller and principle of its body, both challenge and echo Christian thought. This theological method of Ramanuja deals with the *mysterium tremendum et fascinans* par excellence. God is experienced as the ground of our being, 'in whom we live and move and have our being'; yet we also experience our own substantial realities. God is experienced as the sole *raison d'etre* for our existence; yet we experience the inalienable ends-that-we-are-in-ourselves. Here the paradox of human moral autonomy and God's universal causality is not dissolved, but one acknowledges the paradox for its true value as Ramanuja has attempted.[7]

Indian thinking is substantialistic and inclusivistic

Some European indologists have pointed out that the Indian way of thinking is substantialistic, quantifying everything, unlike the Thomistic existentialistic approach. One has to be aware of this also, when one speaks of God's love from the Christian point of view.

According to Hegel the inherent and distinctive principle of the Indian stage of thought is the principle of "substantiality" or "substanceness", i.e., of the unity and ultimacy of one underlying "substance". The religions of India see God as ultimate "Substance", pure, abstract being-in-itself, which contains all finite and particular beings, as non-essential modifications, leaving them without any identity and dignity of their own.[8] Indian philosophy is inseparable from religion and the principle of substantiality applies to philosophy and religion.

Pure substance means indeterminate being-in-itself. It is the one out of which everything arises, and in which it vanishes again; it is ultimately nothing but abstract unity, "substance without subjectivity." Brahman is formless and indeterminate, unspeakable and unthinkable. Any attempt to describe it would lead away from it to the particular and non-essential.

The Indian mind has thus found its way to the One and the Universal, but it has not found its way back to the concrete particularity of the world. It has not brought about the mediation and reconciliation of the universal and the particular, the one and the many. The undivided unity of Brahman and the multiplicity of the world do not and cannot affect or permeate each other. Regardless of all abstract assertions to the contrary, they are related to one another in un-reconciled negation and exclusion.[9]

Halbfass refers to some curious analogies between Hegel's notion of "substantialism" and Hacker's inclusivism as the basic principles of Indian thought. But Hegel's system of universal historical inclusion and "suspension" ("Aufhebung") is the most dynamic inclusivism in the West. How does this systematic and historical "superceding" relate to Indian inclusivism? All other doctrines and traditions appear as preliminary and subordinate stages, to be included in and superceded by the context of European thought and specifically Hegel's own system. Nothing remains "outside"; here everything finds its historical completion and fulfillment. It is the historical dimension which distinguished Hegel's system most significantly from the Indian schemes of inclusion in which time and history seem to be *a priori* discarded or superceded. This remains true in spite of the fact that one very important manifestation of inclusivistic thought in India is the "retrospective" inclusion of earlier layers of the tradition by its later developments; for example in the Vaishnava doctrine the *Bhāgavatapurāna* encompasses and somehow supercedes the Vedas.

Hacker cites the *Bhagavadgita*, its presentation of Krishna as the hidden and implicit goal of all forms of religious devotion and the ultimate identification of all other deities with Krishna, as an exemplary case of inclusivism. For Hegel, on the other hand, this represents "substantialism", that is, the absorption of all individual differences and all particularity by the one indefinite absolute, the substance which is pure being-in-itself and "the night in which all cows are black". In making such statements Hegel asserts the historical superiority of Europe and its commitment to being-for-itself, individuality and historical development.[10]

Hacker never referred to Hegel, since he despised in general German idealism. But Hacker also talks about the substantive way of thinking in the early Indian thought.[11] According to Hacker, substance is that which has an existence, which stands by itself independently. Characteristics are attributes of a substance, they do not exist independently, but they have the substance as basis. Events are either realized or caused by the substance and they have therefore the substance as the base. The Vedantins describe Brahman as being-consciousness-bliss (*sat-cit-ānanda*). These three characteristics are not understood as attributes or qualities of the Absolute. The Vedantins explain that each of the three characteristics describes the whole of the Absolute. This sort of thinking is substantialism, that is, a substantial identity of the three characteristics of the Brahman, there is an essential identity between being, consciousness and bliss in the Absolute.[12]

3.   Cosmotheandric vision of Panikkar

Another great thinker, Raimon Panikkar (1918-2010), has been drawing our attention on how our truncated vision of reality is the cause for all the malaise in the world. According to him, the "primordial" form of human consciousness is the trinitarian awareness. Every culture, he says, from the dawn of time has envisioned reality holistically, but in terms of three primordial worlds: the world of gods, the world of humans and the world of things or a material world;heaven, earth, underworld;the sky, the earth and the in-between;past, present, future;a metaphysical or transcendent aspect, a noetic or conscious or thinking factor and an empirical or physical or material element etc. Whatever may be the expression, there is no doubt it manifests a triadic bearing.

In other words, for Panikkar reality is all that *is*, and *all* that *is* is inter-related and in this interrelationship one observes a trinitarian principle. First of all, there is the material world (cosmos, universe) we live in and without which we cannot be. This world is the background of our very existence. Secondly, there are the humans, who inhabit this world, who are conscious of their own existence and the existence of the world around them. Thirdly, there is an all-pervading *Mystery* present in the universe which grasps us, before which we stand in awe and which sustains and satiates our thirst for Meaning, for the Infinite. There exists nothing outside these three fundamental invariants. None can make sense all by itself. None is independent of the other. The world is meaningless without the humans and the humans cannot exist without the world. God cannot be known and experienced without the humans and the world. There is an existential link, an ontological relationship between these three: God, World and Humans. If something goes wrong with one, all three are affected, because they are mutually interdependent and irreducible to the others.[13]

In Panikkar's vision of reality there is unity in diversity and identity in difference. These three dimensions (cosmic, human and depth) are three dynamic centres each equally unique and mutually irreducible. There is a link uniting all the three: there are "super-human urges" in man, "creative power" in the cosmos, and the "humanizing bent" in the divine. "Every real existence is a unique knot in this threefold net. Here the cosmotheandric vision of reality stands for a holistic and integral insight in to the nature of all that there is."[14]

4.   Interrelatedness and responsibility

Nowadays one hears of interrelatedness of things, relationality and responsibility. "Whatever exists co-exists and everything that co-exists, pre-exists. And everything that co-exists and pre-exists subsists by means of an infinite web of all-inclusive relations. Nothing exists outside relationship".[15] In other words, the is-ness implies the otherness and nothing exists for itself.

In that connection one is becoming aware of the interculturality even in the midst of culture-divide that is taking the centre stage in socio-economic-political debates. Interculturality is not so much dealing with disciplines, which is the case with inter-disciplinary studies, as with cultures, and cultures are the much-discussed human nature, which is always expressed according to the categories of a particular culture. Hence the intercultural challenge is solely related to the monopoly of only one culture as universal heritage of all humankind. "Intercultural dialogue is realized in the conversation between people and not only individuals, since it is not only an individual dialogue between two human beings released from their own substrate and histories, but an osmosis between two visions of the reality, better between two worlds represented, so to say, by two people bringing with them all the weight (histories) of their own culture."[16]

Interculturality also means transcending one's own point of view. To evaluate the point of view of the other requires knowledge of his/her culture and that is possible only with love or at least sympathy. Interculturality invites us to discover the universal in the deepening of the concrete. As a matter of fact all the wisdom traditions have been articulating this notion of interculturality in different ways. It is this: everything is related to everything else. *Sarvam sarvātmakam* is an ancient statement of the Mallavadins in India.[17] The Buddhist notion of *pratitya-samutpada*, dependent origination, or the Hindu understanding of *karma* are different expression of the interculturality.

If it is true that everything is related to everything else, Panikkar argues further, it is as much truer that every part of the whole is different, as all men are different among themselves. Each one is a person, i.e., a unique knot in the network of relationships that constitute the reality.

When this knot breaks the threads connecting it with other knots, when tension becomes so tense to allow no more the freedom constitutive of the inter-dependence between knots and, ultimately with the reality, there individualism is born and such an individualism upsets the harmony and brings about a person's death, causing the loss of his own identity. In other words, human differences are also cultural. As the human personality of each one must be respected so that the network of human relationship does not break, so the warp must be kept flexible, according to the needs, in order that the body of humanity or of cosmos does not break. Hence interculturality is indispensable for not falling into monolithic vision of things that may lead to fanaticism.

III

Jesus' vision of social order

Hindu thinkers did not develop a social theory and Hindu society is a sacred, hierarchical society willed by Purusha. But the Neo-Vedantins have argued that this supposed shortcoming actually hides a rich potential of untapped positive possibilities and that the *advaita Vēdānta* in particular has direct relevance for the social and political problems of our time. It is true that the social themes have occasionally been taken up within the context of philosophical discourse and philosophical terms and perspectives have been applied to social matters. The significance of these references cannot be assessed on a quantitative basis and yet to be worked out in the intercultural dialogue.[18]

But Buddha thought differently than the Hindu thinkers of his time. He criticized the hierarchical society and thought of a freer society, with a vision of working for the other. The notion of Sangha sums up Buddha's understanding of community. Sakhyamuni visited the people of the city of Vajjis and praised the people of the city for their community organization. He adapted seven conditions of their community organization for Buddhist sangha. The Buddhist order was in its origins clearly one of the religious groups composed of *sramana,* but in its administration it is said to have followed the example of the representative system of the town of Vesali of the Vajjis which constituted a model samgha-polity.

Sakhyamuni then predicted that if the Buddhist order were to observe the seven principles, it too would prosper far into the future.

1. The monks should hold frequent assemblies;

2. They should assemble in unanimity, make decisions in unanimity, and dispose of matters relating to the order in unanimity;

3. They should honour, revere, and serve their elders, seniors and leaders, and heed what they say;

4. Even if passion should arise, they should strive not to succumb to it;

5. They should have preference for living in secluded places (avoiding association with secular authority).

6. They should devote themselves to their practice, so that seeing this others of potentiality may be drawn to join the order and those who have already joined may remain their in spiritual comfort.

The characteristics of the Buddhist Sangha are also compared to the ocean. For example, when the rivers enter the ocean, they all lose their names and become part of the ocean, likewise, when one enters the Sangha one renounces one's social class, position and name, and all alike are addressed as "ascetic belonging to the son of the Sakhyas." This simile represents the advocacy of equality of castes. This declaration also means that the Buddhist Sangha was acknowledged as a seat of power within Indian society standing outside the jurisdiction of royal authority. This was because the Buddhist Sangha was recognized by the world at large as something supra-mundane, a spiritual community existing on a plane different from that of normal society and because it was also regarded as a model of morality.[19]

Jesus' vision of society

Jesus' vision goes in a parallel line. Human beings must be free and find the will of God by prayer and meditation. This idea disappeared slowly after the Constantine era and the Roman society became the model for the Church. When the missionaries brought Christianity to India with the hierarchical notion of the Church it fitted well with the Hindu worldview of the sacred society. Those who were closer to the missionaries became the rulers later on.[20]

What is the Church according to the mind of Jesus Christ? It is a free and non-hierarchical society, where human dignity and freedom are the leading values. The equality that characterizes in the discipleship of equals in the communities of Jesus Christ is not an anarchy. Power is an issue whenever two or more persons engage in social interaction. What we do with it makes it function creatively or destructively. Christian community is no exception. There will always be in Christian community some structural way power and leadership function. While Jesus gives no precise structure, he proposes three images for how power is to function among his disciples: *Steward, Shepherd and Servant.*

The steward image affirms that the community does not belong to the leader. The community is God's people and the leader has temporary responsibility on God's behalf. The shepherd metaphor also emphasizes that the leader does not own the community, but Jesus picks out two further characteristics of the shepherd that are displayed in his own life as well: inclusivity and care for the stray. Jesus shocked his contemporaries by his table fellowship with sinners as well as saints. The shepherd metaphor discloses why the sinner can sit with Jesus. The servant metaphor reminds the community leader that his or her agenda comes from the community and it is not imposed by the designated leader. Rank and privilege and caste are only inappropriate for power operations in the communities of Jesus Christ.[21] There are differences that are God-willed like the difference between man and woman, but other differences are man-made like the difference between rich and the poor.

That all will find their fulfillment in Jesus Christ is globalization – the *pleroma* "that ... he might gather together in one all things in Christ both which are in heaven and which are on earth"(Eph.1,10). There are other types of globalization based on economics and political power. Too much insistence on social upliftment does not do justice to the universality of human fulfillment, but the upliftment of human beings according to God's will which is Jesus Christ.

The Jesuits have the task of giving a new orientation to their ministries by taking into account their past heritage, even critically looking at some of their past missionary approaches. The guiding principle is always Jesus' understanding of the Kingdom and his concern for the poor. This does not confine itself merely to the social uplift through developmental projects, but to work for a society where the values of Jesus' Kingdom will be realized. For the contribution of the Jesuit philosophers and theologians it will be good to provide a philosophical and theological framework, to clarify and question, if necessary, the key concepts that are operative in the ruling powers of the day.

In other words, one has to ask the basic question: what is it to be a Christian and a Jesuit in today's context. One could say that it is a committed interaction with the world as 'protest dimension', an element of contradiction, which characterized Christianity down the centuries. Without this element there will be a passive pragmatic world where no one will dare for the impossible or there will be new concentration of power, as we have experienced in the modern totalitarian regimes. Christian presence is not meant here as the solution for all the puzzles of the world. Obviously it is also not simply a principle of progress, a socio-political therapeutics. Christianity is the measuring yard, the yardstick for the Christians anyway, a testing ground. Hence the Christian presence cannot remain passive, it has to get involved in human situations. And that is its mission on which its loyalty to God has to be measured and on which will measure its dealing with the world.[22]

Endnotes

[1] In the context of finding European identity one hears of such statements as: "Europa wurde mit, gegen und ohne das Christentum. Ohne Christentum aber ist Europa nicht denkbar. Das Christentum wurde mit, gegen und ohne Europe. Ohne Europa ist mithin auch das Chrsitentum nicht denkbar. Wer aber benötigt wen stärker im dritten Millenium?" Ludger Kühnhardt, Europas Identität und die Kraft des Christentums. Gedanken zum Jahr 2000 nach Christus. ZEI – Zentrum für Europäische Integrationsforschung. Bonn, 2000.

[2] Luis Molina, *De justitia et de jure*, 2. Bd., Koeln 1594, disp. 348, Nr. 3.

[3] Michael V. d. Bogaert, "Hoffmann's Credit Cooperative Society: Its Originality", in *The Munda World*. Hoffmann Commemorative Volume, edited by P. Ponette. Ranchi: Catholic Press, 1978, 53-67.

[4] There is an excellent study on the philosophy of Nimbarka by Joseph Satyanand to which I am indebted for writing this paper. *Nimbarka. A Pre-Sankara Vedantin and His Philosophy*. Vishwa Jyoti Gurukul, Varanasi, India, 1994.

[5] Robinson, *Exploration into God*, London 1967, 91.

[6] Eric Lott, *God and the Universe in the Vedantic Theology of Ramanuja*, Ramanuja Research Society, Madras, 1976; Julius Lipner, *The Face of Truth*, Albany: State University of New York Press, 1986.

[7] Julius Lipner, "The World as God's Body: In Pursuit of Dialogue with Ramanuja", *Religious Studies*, NO. 20, 145-161.

[8] Cf. W. Halbfass, *India and Europe*. Albany: State University of New York Press, 1988, 88.

[9] Halbfass, 89.

[10] Cf. W. Halbfass, *India and Europe*, 1988, 418.

[11] Paul Hacker, *Grundlagen indischer Dichtung und indischen Denkens*, Wien, 1985, 108ff.

[12] Hacker, 109.

[13] Raimon Panikkar, "The Cosmotheandric Intuition", in *Jeevadhara* XVI 79 (1984) 29-30.

[14] R. Panikkar, "Colligite Fragmenta; For an Integration of Reality," in: F.A. Eigo, (Ed.) *From Alienation to At-one-ness*, Proceedings of the Theology Institute of Villanova University, The Villanova University Press, 1977, 19-91, 75.

[15] Leonard Boff, *Ecology and Liberation. A New Paradigm*. Orbis Book, New York, 1995, 7.

[16] Raimon Panikkar, *Pace e Interculturalita. Una Riflessione Filosofica*. Jaca Book, Milano, 2002.

[17] Cf. A. Wezler, "Studien zum Dvadasaranayacakra des Svetambara Mallavadin", in *Studien zum Jainismus und Buddhismus.* Gedenkschrift für Ludwig Alsdorf. (Hrg.) Klaus Bruhn und Albrecht Wezler. Franz Steiner Verlag, Wiesbaden, 1981, 358-408.

[18] Cf. Wilhelm Halbfass, *Tradition and Reflection. Exploration in Indian Thought.* Especially Chapter 10, " Homo Hierarchicus: The Conceptualization of the Varna System in Indian Thought." Albany: State University of New York Press, 1991.

[19] Cf. Takaski Jidiko, *An Introduction to Buddhism.* Translated by Rolf W. Giebel, The Toho Gakkai, Tokyo, 1991, 247-249.

[20] Cf. Joseph Thekkadath, *Indian Church History* Vol. II. on the Protuguese idea of church organization.

[21] Bernard J. Lee, "Community", in *The New Dictionary of Catholic Spirituality,* edited by Michael Downey, Minnesota: The Liturgical Press, Collegeville, 1993.

[22] Hans Maier, *Welt Ohne Christentum - Was wäre anders?* Herder, 1999.

Theologizing with Panikkar: Towards a Relational Pluralism

Xavier Tharamel SJ

...It is a circle dance, three circles interweaving, people from distant lands holding hands, discovering each other as they learn how to dance together.[1]

Raimon Panikkar (1918-2010) is mostly considered a theologian advocating pluralism which marks an entirely new approach in the theology of religions. Panikkar's attitude and the methodological stance to the issue of religious pluralism are famously expressed in his autobiographical statement, "I started as a Christian, I discovered I was a Hindu and returned as a Buddhist without ever having ceased to be a Christian."[2] Panikkar's birth itself, as a child of an Indian (Hindu) father and a Spanish (Roman Catholic) mother suggests his multi-religious context. What does it mean to be a Christian, a Hindu and a Buddhist simultaneously? Therefore, the fundamental questions I have considered in this paper are: (i) where can we precisely locate Panikkar's complex pluralistic vision within the pluralistic theology of religions? (ii) what is "the actual" pluralistic paradigm which Panikkar is proposing to incorporate the dichotomy of the one and the many? (iii) how does Panikkar respond to the question of the undeniable experience of multiplicity within a non-dualistic framework?

The methodology I have adopted in this study is to locate Panikkar by briefly presenting three significant pluralistic thinkers namely, John

Hick, S. Mark Heim and Stanley Samartha. These pluralistic thinkers represent not only three different traditions, but also characterize fresh understandings of religious pluralism, which seem to be appropriate in this exchange. In the light of the above mentioned three thinkers, I will be comparing Panikkar's pluralistic vision.

A comparative overview

As a prolific British thinker and theologian, John Hick   presented a radical pluralistic vision by challenging the traditional and contemporary Western Christian theology.[3] In his critical paper "The reconstruction of Christian belief for today and tomorrow" Hick pointed out that the exclusive idea of the divine revelation, creation *ex nihilo,* the virgin birth and the resurrection had to be reinterpreted with a fresh understanding as the traditional theology was outdated.[4] Religious pluralism means, according to Hick, various responses to the Real (God) through different "...human concepts, images, and experiences of..."[5] that same God. He quotes the 13th century Persian mystic poet Jalalu'l-Din Rumi to show how religions are differently experiencing the same God (the Real) in various forms: "The lamps are different, but the Light is the same."[6] Furthermore, it implies that transcendent reality or God is at the centre and religions rotate around it. Thus, Hick criticises the idea of the one single religious tradition that is more significant than other religious traditions. The question that can arise at this point is whether Hick is emphasizing a universal religious scheme which would regulate and bring in different religions around "the Ultimate Reality" and a single system. Secondly, he seems to propose a reinterpretation of the Christian doctrines that would dismiss the traditional faith perspectives. For instance, Hick does not accede to the Christian faith about the incarnation of Jesus Christ.[7] In other words, Hick proposes a universal pluralistic system that is theocentric and different religions are regarded as valid paths leading towards this final goal.

The second thinker I would like to look at is S. Mark Heim, an evangelical theologian from the United States. As Veli-Matti Kärkkäinen observes, Mark Heim is perhaps "…the most innovative…"[8] theologian to discuss varying religious goals. His works titled *Salvations* and *The Depth of the Riches: A Trinitarian Theology of Religious Ends* have presented a totally different understanding of religious pluralism. He suggests that different religions have different ends or goals in God.[9] Unlike Hick, Heim works from the Christian trinitarian God concept (God as the Father, the Son and the Holy Spirit) and his approach implies neither liberal nor conservative characteristics but an affirmation of the possibility of religious diversity and diverse religious ends.[10] While Hick's approach is not limited to any particular religious tradition, Heim's approach includes "…both biblical and historical Christian traditions…"[11] which limits the scope of his pluralistic thinking. Although Heim creates a space for different religions in his method, unlike Hick and Panikkar, he does not move out of the Christian framework to explore the possibility of having an interreligious dialogue. For this reason, Veli-Matti Kärkkäinen thinks that Heim is an inclusivist rather than a pluralist.[12] I would prefer to call him a "Christian pluralist" rather than an inclusivist.

Another Christian theologian who argued for a theocentric approach from within the Christocentric framework is Stanley Samartha. As an Indian, he adopts a dialogical method[13] in order to address the question of religious pluralism which is quite similar to Panikkar's approach. Although Samartha argued for a theocentric engagement akin to John Hick, he does not reject or wish to reinterpret the Christian doctrine to accommodate other religions. For instance, Samartha's theocentric vision is inextricably related to Jesus Christ. According to him, God's involvement with human beings transcends religious boundaries because Jesus' engagement with different persons exemplifies God's openness to the entirety of humanity.[14] Samartha justifies his Christian approach to pluralism in his work titled *Courage for Dialogue*: "To acknowledge the fact of religious pluralism means that one cannot take shelter in neutral or objective ground. There is no theological helicopter that can help us to rise above all religions and look down…Our stand point… has to be Christian; but by same token our neighbours are also free to have their particular stand points."[15]

Having briefly sketched out the key ideas of the three leading pluralists, the task is to locate Panikkar within these conversations. Does Panikkar fit in with these pluralistic conversations at all? I think that one cannot easily categorise Panikkar's pluralistic stance under a single schema. The following discussion will hopefully shed light into the "complex" nature of Panikkar's pluralistic vision. It is suggested by Gerald James Larson in his well annotated article[16] that Panikkar's method embodies the theoretical pluralism which is not satisfied with mere discussion of pluralism but the very concerns with philosophical foundation of pluralism. Although Larson thinks that "Panikkar has succeeded...in constructing a formulation of the notion of pluralism that is conceptually tight, reasonably consistent, properly differentiated from other positions..."[17], he strangely concludes his essay by stating that the Panikkarian theoretical pluralism breaks down on the basis of multi-valued judgements. In contrast, Beverly J. Lanzetta points out in his article "The Mystical Basis of Panikkar's Thought" that Panikkar devoted more than thirty years to a systematic and rigorous mystical approach to interreligious dialogue.[18] According to Beverly, Panikkar's pluralistic approach is mystical and rooted in the inner dynamism of the Trinitarian God because the trinitarian life symbolises plurality in oneness, or unity in diversity. The Trinity denotes a radical relationality between the Father, the Son and the Holy Spirit. In Panikkar's view, the trinitarian model (unity of three persons) expresses unity in diversity as we see in the God-World-Man relationship which I shall later expand on.[19] The Trinity stands for an essential harmony of reality which is multi-faceted. As Veli-Matti Kärkkäinen observes Panikkar's trinitarian vision perhaps expresses the radical theological imagination of relating the Christian concept of the Trinitarian God to otherworld religions.[20] As a result, Kärkkäinen thinks that Panikkar differs "...from Hick and most other pluralists."[21] Although Paul Knitter in *Introducing Theologies of Religions* specifies that the fundamental basis of Panikkar's theology of religions is a personal mystical experience,[22] Knitter's earlier article titled "Cosmic Confidence or Preferential Option?"[23] suggests that Panikkar is a radical pluralist. Dr. Francis D'Sa, one of the renowned experts on Panikkar, has suggested in his recent article that Panikkar is a relational pluralist as the ground of his pluralistic theology is an organic interconnectedness.[24] Whether Panikkar is appreciated as a mystical, theoretical, radical or relational pluralist within the pluralist or so called 'post-pluralist' circles,[25] Panikkar offers a consistent paradigm across cultures and religions based on the principle of relational advaita which is pure relationality. For that reason, although Panikkar's paradigm appears similar to that of Hick and Heim, his pluralism operates as relationality. Undoubtedly, Samartha shares more with Panikkar's dialogical method. However, like Heim, Samartha's pluralism seems to be limited by his commitment to the Christian tradition. This does not mean that Panikkar concurs with Hick in rejecting the traditional Christian doctrines but shapes a fresh understanding. In this article my focus is to expose and to understand Panikkar within a unique non-dualistic concept, which I would call "relational advaita." Before we proceed to discuss his pluralistic vision, we should explore the background in which this notion of relational advaita emerged.

Influence of Indian thought on Panikkar's pluralistic vision

In order to understand the framework of Panikkar's relational advaitic thought, it will be significant to highlight the basic characteristics of the Indian approach to any philosophical-theological question. Unlike in Western thought, one may not be able to talk about the beginning or the end of something in Indian thought, such as the creation of the world.[26] The western mind from the outset has been struggling with the question of foundation and starting point. However, it is not relevant to speak about a starting point of anything in Indian philosophy. In the same way, one cannot say that the Vedas have authors or Hinduism has founders like Christianity. "…Hinduism is more an existence than an essence…not doctrinal but existential."[27] Again, when speaking about the Brahman (the Absolute Reality), it is not only unknowable, it does not know as well. Nevertheless, Indian philosophy is concerned with the goal, the end point of everything. The goal is concerned about the Whole and that Whole is moreover present also. Fundamentally, the idea of the Whole is not a reflective one, but it is an awareness of the totality. Since, the entire reality is holistic, there is no subject-object dichotomy. There is neither knowing subject, nor an object to be known. Panikkar elucidates the notion of holistic vision:

> ...the holistic attempt tries to "reach" the Whole not by a dialectical synthesis but by means of an immediate contact with the Whole, defying the dualistic subject/object epistemology...the holistic attempt can only be an insight from the Whole; it is the *svayamprakāśa*...or the self-illumination of so many spiritual schools in the Buddhist, Christian, Sufi traditions, etc.[28]

In short, Indian thought offers a holistic vision which overcomes the dichotomy between subject and object. Furthermore, unlike the Western approach, there cannot be a clear-cut division between theology and philosophy, sociology and anthropology etc. Ultimately, one has to overcome duality whenever it emerges in life. It is significant to point out that in a dualistic or pluralistic system in the Indian philosophical perspective dualism or pluralism is not numerical but indicative of the Whole. Panikkar's vision points towards a holistic vision in which, - the cosmos, God and human beings together make up a fragmented Whole. The cosmos is a symbol of God, an expression of the Whole and vice versa. It means that reality in its entirety is represented in every microcosm. However, the genius of Panikkar has been that he could address the undeniable experience of multiplicity within a holistic system. His cosmotheandric vision proffers an effective account of the experience of multiplicity which I shall explain later in this article.

In accordance with Indian tradition, the term religion is used by Panikkar as a "way of life"[29] rather than a system. As a way of life, religion belongs to the realm of existences which can have many forms and many values. Thus, according to Panikkar, religion does not rest on either the intellectual or the value plane but on an indescribable existence. Panikkar strongly emphasises the ultimate existential character of religion. I would like to specify, how this aspect of religion is significant in the Indian approach to religion. In India, the entire approach in philosophy/theology has been a search for identity. "'Who am I?'"-*kōaham*- this is the existential question that vibrates through all the Upanishads."[30] This search is inexhaustible as it is a search for Atman. The true identity is found when one can equate Atman with Brahman. Since Brahman is present in the entire universe and in the core of one's subjectivity, there cannot be an individual identity but only an identity of existence as a whole. "...*Atman is Brahman*: what one experiences 'deep within the cave of the heart' and 'in the infinite space of the 'universe' is one and the same absolute reality(Tait.Up 2:1; Chand. Up. 8.1.3)."[31] Multiplicity lies only in the realm of thought. The decisive point is that there lies a power of synthesis in Indian thought: the power of synthesis that can provide an insight into a holistic or harmonious way. A harmonious view is more valued and emphasised in the Indian way of thinking. This harmony is sought between transcendence and immanence without seeing these as two different aspects. That means the goal is not 'something beyond' or temporal but a combination of these dimensions what Panikkar would call "tempiternity", "...that is, temporal and eternal in one and the same time in a non-dualistic relation."[32] As a result, one may not strive to achieve a goal that would give a sense of 'fulfilment in time'. Fulfilment is not a result of the achievement of a particular goal in time but arises from overcoming the desires of achievement by intensively realizing every moment. Thus, it is through freeing oneself from needs or by overcoming desires, that one attains fulfilment in life. Furthermore, this stage is reached not at an individual level, but by participating in the totality. Thus, Panikkar elucidates:

> The "end of Man" is not individual happiness but full participation in the realization of the universe –in which one finds one's as well "own" joy.... You need not worry about your own salvation or even perfection.[33]

My argument is that the fundamental structure of Panikkar's thought has been "inherently pluralistic". His world view has been thoroughly pluralistic (here pluralism implies 'relational advaita') where multiplicity is stressed without dismissing individuality. Thus, Panikkar's pluralism gives an account for the multiplicity without reducing the Whole to fragments. In order to interpret the *Whole* within a western framework, he chooses the term *perichoresis*.[34] In classical Christian theology, the term *perichoresis* defines the relationship in God where the Father, the Son and the Holy Spirit share the identity of the same Godhead without losing their distinction. This inter-relationality within the Godhead indicates how individuality and multiplicity can concomitantly form a relationship.

> The main insight of the doctrine of the Trinity is simple. Ultimate reality is neither One (Being, or anything real) with three modes, nor Three (substances, beings) within a single abstract oneness—*neti- neti*. The Trinity is pure relationship...if the Divine is infinite relationship, this relationship also enters all creatures and Man in a special way.[35]

However, Panikkar is not applying the classical Christian theological term to account for the multiplicity. The term is used to explain non-dualism (*advaita*) that is not familiar to the Western mind. According to Panikkar, the "...Trinity amounts to *advaita*."[36] This does not any way mean that Panikkar is equating the concept of Trinity with advaita. As he points out; "...It should be clear that I do not intend to mix up Christian Trinity and vedāntic *advaita* as theological belief systems."[37] According to Panikkar, these two concepts represent two different human experiences. Panikkar would call this "the homeomorphic equivalents" which implies functional similarity. It is not a notional equivalent "... but a functional equivalent...that is equivalent to that exercised by the original notion in the corresponding cosmovision."[38] The trinitarian character of the harmony of reality is seen as a constituent aspect of every bit of reality. The three-foldness accounted for the Whole by manifesting inter-dependent and inter-independent relationship.[39] Thus, monism and dualism are overcome through relationality expressed in the triune structure. In other words, relationality shapes the Panikkarian pluralistic thought. The relationality in plurality would synthesis inherent difference in religions and cultures. As I mentioned above, Panikkar's cosmovision is the ground of this relational pluralism. According to him, God, human beings and the world are three dimensions that indicate relational pluralism at a fundamental level. Panikkar calls this relationality the Cosmotheandric Vision.[40] This term is a combination of three Greek words: cosmos (world), *aner* or *anthropos* (human beings), and *theos* (God). According to Panikkar, these aspects or dimensions constitute reality.

As I stated above, the fundamental structure of Panikkar's theology is relationality which he draws from *advaita*. It is significant to survey the characteristics of Panikkar's approach to *advaita* and how it is different from classical *advaita*. The basic question raised in Śaṅkara's *advaita* (absolute idealism) Vedanta is how the eternal is related to the temporal. Although the question is about the relationship between Brahman, the individual soul and the world, the *advaita* Vedānta of Śaṅkara lays stress on the principle of identity. Brahman is considered as the pure identity and the rest of reality is subtracted as mere appearance. Thus, Śaṅkara emphasizes:

> …the reality of the unconditioned and unqualified Brahman…regards God (īsvara), the individual souls (jīva) and the world (jagat) as appearances due to an indefinable principle called Māyā (cosmic nescience) which is neither real, nor unreal, nor both, nor neither…Brahman is one, eternal, pure, transcendental consciousness.[41]

This means, according to the Advaita Vedānta of Śaṅkara, the individual souls and the world stand only for practical purposes. The ontological reality of Brahman is maintained as the only identity. Consequently, Śaṅkara thinks that it is by realizing real identity that one attains liberation. The knowledge (jñāna) of Brahman will help one to transcend the duality of subject and object. As a result, Śaṅkara's non-dualism does not account for the multiplicity. In order to answer this question in a relatively different way, Panikkar moved away from the acosmic (*negation of the objective reality of the individual souls and the world*) Advaita of Śankara, by stressing the relationality between Absolute Reality and the temporal world. Panikkar's paradigm is a combination of dualism and non-dualism where the multiplicity is accounted for without dismissing the individuality. This is possible because Panikkar emphasises the relationship between the Absolute Reality or Brahman, the individual souls and the world. Here, the non-dualism is seen within the relationship between these three dimensions but not in downplaying the identity of the temporal world. In other words, everything is real, and nothing is unreal as far as things are related to the each other. The relationality implies that within the non-dual nature of reality, a personal relationship with Absolute Reality is plausible. According to Panikkar, Absolute Reality can only exist in relation with the temporal world. Panikkar elucidates:

> ...it means to discover me, image of the entire reality, at the meeting place of the real, at the crossroads of Being, at the very centre. But the centre would be unreal if there were not the sphere (or what not) for which it is the centre. The image would be mere hallucination if the original were not real.[42]

This means, the world is real only in relationship with God and human beings and vice versa. Every existence is possible only within interrelatedness. Panikkar further expounds this aspect of interrelatedness:

> ...between them Heaven (*God*) and Earth support all other beings and their tension is relational so that one cannot be without the other. There is no earth without heaven and heaven would be devoid of meaning if it were not perpetuated by the dwellers on earth.... There is no God without Man and the World. There is no Man without God and the World. There is no World without God and Man.[43]

Panikkar goes further to the extent that "...beings themselves are nothing but relations."[44] This relational ontology is the foundation of Panikkar's *advaita*. For that reason, I think that Panikkar's cosmotheandric vision is best described as a "relational advaita."

Pluralistic genre of Panikkar

In the light of his relational advaita, I think that Panikkar's pluralism has to be seen as a state of inescapable relationship of multiplicities. According to him the very nature of truth is pluralistic but not plural.[45]There are three important points to highlight in order to define Panikkar's pluralism. Firstly, as every religion has emerged within a particular context, there are divergent cosmo visions which are entirely different from those found in other traditions. That would mean, no religion can be pluralistic in nature. Secondly, "...pluralism is not a supersystem, a meta-language, a referee in the human disputes, an intellectual panacea. Pluralism is an open, human attitude, which therefore entails an intellectual dimension that overcomes any kind of solipsism..."[46] or absolutism. Finally, every system whether it is philosophy or religion, or beliefs is open to criticism. Thus, no one religious system or thought is pluralistic. In Panikkar's view pluralism is an attitude which subsumes every religious system but does not subscribe to a universal theory of religion.[47] Pluralism is a fundamental awareness "...that the world of objects has no existence of its own..."[48] and it recognizes the fact that there could be several centres of intelligibility in the truth. As it indicates in such a comprehensive relational attitude, his pluralism can be seen as a radically relational pluralism. Accordingly, Panikkar's pluralism in the genuine sense of the word means, being ready to accept and tolerate the ways that are not recognizable, as different ways leading to diverse goals. In Panikkar's words, it is a "...*fundamental human attitude* which is critically aware both of the factual irreducibility...of different human systems purporting to render reality intelligible, and of the radical non-necessity of reducing reality to one single centre of intelligibility, making thus unnecessary an *absolute* decision in favour of a particular human system with universal validity-or even one Supreme Being."[49] Thus he affirms that not only are there various ways and different goals, but he asks that the idea of a single Supreme Being may be questioned. Consequently, Panikkar rejects any idea of parallelism as well. For him, the nature of religions is so dynamic that any model emphasizing ways as parallels does not satisfy him. This does not mean that Panikkar rules out the possibility of similar meeting points in diverse traditions. There are homoeomorphic equivalents which have similar functions in respective traditions. His pluralism undoubtedly speaks of the existence of corresponding meeting points as it may be possible that one walks on different roads during the journey. The metaphor of rivers elucidates the possible way of meeting points:

...the rivers of the earth do not actually meet each other not even in the oceans, nor do they need to meet in order to be truly life-giving rivers. But "they" do meet: they meet in the skies-that is, in heaven. The rivers do not meet, not even as water. "They" meet in the form of clouds, once they have suffered transformation into vapor, which eventually will pour down again into the valleys of mortals to feed the rivers of the earth... My metaphor does not stand for a transcendent unity of all religions in an unqualified way.[50]

It is really significant to point out that Panikkar does not see any need of meeting of organized religions. In fact, there is no meeting point of religions as such but only the convergence of a transformed form of religions which is similar to a circular dance. Panikkar thinks that there is no convergence of religions in their 'visible' forms, but it takes place in the radically transcendent dimension. It is at a spiritual level where doctrinal or ritualistic aspects are reformed as spirituality. At the spiritual level, the convergence happens as a mutual dance and interpenetration. That means one cannot understand the meeting of religions as utter parallelism or essentialism. Panikkar envisages and insists on relational form of encounter which goes beyond simple peaceful co-existence. In such a relational form of encounter, one is compelled to meet the other as participants in a mutual dance. "I am not for a pantheon of religious symbols in peaceful co-existence. I am for the *perichoresis*, for the *circumincessio*, for the mutual dance and interpenetration..."[51]"It is a circle dance, three circles interweaving, people from distant lands holding hands, discovering each other as they learn how to dance together."[52] In Panikkarian vision, convergence of religions means dancing together to experience the rhythm of life. The dance with others is a learning procedure as this provides one with a specific space to chip into a circular movement. Thus, Panikkar envisages the meeting of religions as participatory convergence; in other words, religions participate at a spiritual level without defining a common goal in advance. In other words, Panikkar does not accede to any kind of universal theory of religion or promote a pluralistic theology of religion. According to him, religions are different ways towards perfection, or the way which leads to *the* ultimate goal is religion. As I mentioned above, there is no common goal but the idea of perfection in various traditions may share similarities.

I have identified three important aspects of Panikkar's pluralism namely; (i) reality in its entirety is pluralistic (ii) *relational advaita* is the epistemology (iii) participatory model is the praxis rather than a universalistic model. Primarily, the question of pluralism that Panikkar addresses is not restricted to the theology of religions but it explores the inextricable nature of relationship. As every reality is pluralistic, it cannot escape relationality. In other words, pluralism as the very building block of everything, is independent and inter-dependent simultaneously. It means that any idea of convergence or meeting of religions indicates a participatory interaction rather than isolated feat. This is the first point of departure for Panikkar from the three pluralists (Hick, Heim and Samartha) whom we briefly encountered at the outset. Secondly, A new interpretation of *advaita* (what I call "relational advaita") is the foundation of his pluralism. "*Advaita* was usually translated as "nonduality," because the dialectical mind of the European Indologists…interpreted the *a* as a negative article. In fact, the *a* of the advaita intuition does not connote a dialectical negation, rather, here the *a* is a primitive prefix pointing to an "absence of duality."[53] The advaita experience cannot refer to either one or two or more, but rather a relationality that connects everything. This relationality stands above everything that can be tallied.[54] "We could provisionally call it the *unifying myth* and note its thrust toward overcoming the epistemological subject-object dichotomy…"[55] Reality in its foundation is relational and therefore one cannot perceive anything as isolated reality. Thus, relational *advaita* accounts both for the unity and the diversity of religions

Finally, according to Panikkar, one should not seek for a universal model for pluralism. In a universal model of pluralism, one will have a common goal through different paths. As the way is different so the goal also is quite different. For the pilgrim, there is always only one way, and that is "*the* Way."[56] The different ways do not meet or need not meet as the goal is completely different as well. "We must accept that some religious traditions are mutually incommensurable."[57] Then what can unity and dialogue mean? As indicated above, plurality is the groundwork of every reality. Every religious tradition reflects in a quite different way the understanding of life; at the same time there could be some kind of similarity as well. The idea of unity is not possible without having plurality of religions. That means if the religions are different in themselves, then the Ultimate Reality or God cannot be reached from the same view point as God or the Divine itself is multifaceted. "...It is not that this reality [the Ultimate Mystery] *has* many names and each name is a new aspect..."[58] but this multidimensional aspect of God or the Divine cannot be comprehended in a universalistic model. That will be an act of curtailing or reducing the many-sided reality into a single reality.

> Pluralism [that is the diversity of religions or the Divine] does not allow for a universal system. A pluralistic system would be a contradiction in terms. The incommensurability of ultimate system is unbridgeable. This incommensurability is not a lesser evil...but a revelation of the nature or reality.[59]

Panikkar thinks that developing a system of pluralism is not the way to approach the pluralistic theology of religions. As Paul Knitter observes Panikkar reminds John Hick and other pluralists not to get stuck with "pluralism of religions".[60] We cannot build bridges between religions as if they had some kind of common goal. When religions are bridged, then we are creating a system that is implausible. These different paths are absolutely new ways of understanding multidimensional reality. There is no possibility of asking a question as to whether someone is moving towards the same goal.

Again, when he refers to a holistic or *advaitic* approach to pluralism, it means many things. Firstly, holistic approach would mean a cosmotheandric religion. This vision emerges from a fundamental religiosity that is present in every human being. Such a religiosity means the desire to have fulfilment or realization or to be liberated from something that is bondage. As human beings are unfinished, they strive to reach perfection not only through the self but through something that also includes but the cosmic and the divine. Cosmotheandric religion forms a three-fold structure of reality consisting of human, cosmic and divine dimensions. The relationality between these aspects which is invariant to every culture grounds the religion. For Panikkar, this is a concept of totality that can help us to achieve full realization or perfection. Thus, cosmotheandric religion becomes cosmotheandric spirituality. In other words, religion in its true sense is one's personal spirituality.[61] However, Panikkar speaks of religion from three levels. At the first level, religion operates from the cultural dimensions intertwined with regulations. Religion is sacramental and ritualistic at the second level. Here all the religions are complementary to each other. At the third level, all religions reach the dimension of mystery.[62] It is at this level, that Panikkar sees the possibility of a religious synthesis. He envisages a synthesis in a spiral form by avoiding such notion as centripetalism and centrifugalism. "We must not flee from the existent religious denominations nor break with them in order to find true religion, and yet, we cannot remain on a static centre of one of them."[63] As mentioned elsewhere, Panikkar rules out the prerequisite of some kind of external fusion of existing religions, although a fusion of religions may lead to a peaceful coexistence, but not to the level participation. Thus, Panikkar would lay stress on a hidden unity and the undeniable plurality of religions towards an inherent convergence. Therefore, the meeting of religions should spring from the awareness that pluralism is not a system but a fundamental reality enabling us to discover deeper harmony and unity. The goal of every religion should not be presumed as God; acknowledging unity and plurality means that religions strive towards different forms of perfection where there is no uniformity and homogeneity but an all-embracing wholeness.[64] In order to speak about the idea of the "all-embracing wholeness", Panikkar points towards the human invariants of the divine, the human and the cosmic dimensions. This forms the ground for his cosmotheandric vision which as I pointed out is relational *advaita*.

Relevance of Panikkar's relational pluralistic vision

Such ideas lead us to a fresh understanding of the idea of pluralism. By fresh understanding I mean that Panikkar is pointing towards a relational model of pluralistic awareness. The question of pluralism here is not an impasse presented by religions or cultures. It is a compelling question that emerges in the presence of the other religions, cultures, people etc to engage, to understand and to live in within differences. Essentially, the differences engender conflicts within the diverse context. Often the question of pluralism is raised to tackle differences and to peacefully co-exist or to seek out survival. However, I think the issue is to discover the differences themselves. Perhaps, the pluralism (differences) becomes a problem because the effort is taken to have a peaceful co-existence or survival but not to uncover the differences as such. Certainly, isolation is not possible in today's world. Thus the 'issue' of pluralism has been an everyday experience rather than some theoretical topic for schoolwork.[65] However, if pluralism is a question of subsistence, (religions, cultures, people etc) will become problems to resolve and would need to find a common platform to exist together. In this case, the concern for our discussion will be 'the other as problematic' one. Again, if the other is a problem, then that has to be resolved to ensure world survival. Hence, the next question is about tolerance, a term much used and abused in a multi-religious context. If tolerance indicates broad-mindedness or open-mindedness, then it is a term implying a conflicting situation. However, I think that it is not an appropriate expression in a multi-religious context as it always implies survival. When tolerance becomes an ideology, one is "...forced to tolerate what it cannot yet extirpate."[66] Thus the understanding of pluralism I am proposing does not depend on tolerance. The pluralism indicated here is the fundamental human attitude of recognizing the presence of the other who is different and at the same time rediscovering the inextricable relationality with this individual. In the context of religious pluralism, it is obvious that a believer has to recognize the presence of God or the Supreme Reality who is the 'other'. This is a significant step towards unveiling the relationship between God and human beings. Similarly, it is extremely significant to critically evaluate our fundamental attitude towards differences.

As mentioned above, the primary task is to be familiar with a fundamental attitude towards diversity within oneself. To recognize pluralism does not mean becoming aware of plurality. By plurality I mean that difference on the surface level. It is all about the quantifiable aspect of life. This can also be considered as a multiplicity of differences. Perhaps, this multiplicity of differences could be seen as a qualitative one. However, I am pointing towards pluralism as a fundamental human attitude. It is an attitude of recognizing the presence of the other in the world. This is a fundamental attitude that cannot be eliminated from the human consciousness. It is not a learnt attitude but is inherent in the fundamental nature of human awareness. If pluralism is a learnt attitude, then it is based on some kind of concept or a universal theory. Recognizing the presence of the other is not a thought but an awareness of someone different from oneself. It implies becoming mindful of a subject that transcends the objective dimension. This is because a subject demands a response as it is incomprehensible. The response is always inextricably intertwined with prejudice that debars us from effectively recognizing the "otherness" of the other. As Panikkar would say, it is not possible to have a so called "phenomenological epoche" to respond effectively to the other.[67] If it were possible, the question of pluralism would not have arisen in a multi-religious or multi-cultural context. Recognizing someone or something is one of the basic values of pluralism. To discover or rediscover an underpinning relationality is another fundamental human attitude. Thus, discovering relationality is the first step towards encountering the other with open-mindedness. Whenever contradictions emerge within a context, we seek for relationships to resolve conflicts. Relationality can be one-sided if one has not yet recognized the other that means the "otherness of the other". The fundamental nature of relationality is to create space for the other as it recognizes that "…there may be several centres of intelligibility…"[68] Again, it is a realisation that a different point of view is as important as a particular dominating view point. This is possible only when constituent relationality is unveiled. This process is prompted within human interactions when limitations of human rationality are accepted, and the individual learns to live in the presence of the totally other.

My conclusion is that Panikkar treats pluralism as an essential human attitude rather than a theoretical structure. When Hick, Heim and Samartha construct/ uphold their respective pluralistic stances by placing an *absolute* (God/Real/Trinity etc) at the center, Panikkar's pluralism operates without a centre while every reality is a centre. Since his pluralism operates as relationality between irreducible differences, it does not need to 'revolve' around an 'isolated' centre. In other words, Panikkarian pluralism is "relationship in operation." That is why I think that Panikkar's pluralistic genre is unique within the pluralistic theology of religions.

Endnotes

[1] Scott Eastham. "Introduction" *in the Cosmotheandric Experience: Emerging Religious Consciousness* by Raimon Panikkar (Maryknoll, New York: Orbis Books, 1993), viii.

[2] As quoted by Keith D'Souza, "In Praise of A Cosmotheandric Mystic", *in Raimon Panikkar: Being Beyond Borders. A Commemorative Volume.* ed by Johnson J. Puthenpurackal (Bangalore: ACPI, 2012), 17.

[3] Harold Howard, *Pluralism: Challenges to World Religions* (Maryknoll, New York: Orbis Books, 1985), 29.

[4] Veli-Matti KÓrkkÓinen, *Trinity and Religious Pluralism: The Doctrine of the Trinity in Christian Theology of Religions* (England, USA: Ashgate, 2004), 109.

[5] Ibid.,110.

[6] As quoted by John Hick in *An Interpretation of Religion: Human Responses to the Transcendent. Second Edition* (New Haven and London: Yale University Press, 2004), 233.

[7] Ibid.,116.

[8] Ibid.,134.

[9] Cf. Veli-Matti KÓrkkÓinen, *Trinity and Religious Pluralism: The Doctrine of the Trinity in Christian Theology of Religions*,134

[10] Cf. Ibid.,135.

[11] Cf. Ibid.,143.

[12] Cf. Ibid.,151.

[13] Harold Howard, *Pluralism: Challenges to World Religions*, 39.

[14] Stanley J. Samartha, *Courage for Dialogue* (Maryknoll, N.Y.: Orbis Books, 1981), 40.

[15] Ibid.,40.

[16] Gerald James Larson, "Contra Pluralism" in *The Intercultural Challenge of Raimon Panikkar*. ed. Joseph Prabhu (Maryknoll, NY: Orbis, 1996), 71-87.

[17] Ibid.,78.

[18] Beverley J. Lanzetta, "The Mystical Basis of Panikkar's Thought" in *The Intercultural Challenge of Raimon Panikkar*. ed. Joseph Prabhu, 71-87, Maryknoll, NY: Orbis, 1996.

[19] Cf. Raimon Panikkar. *The Rhythm of Being: The Gifford Lectures* (Maryknoll, New York: Orbis Books, 2010), 171.

[20] Veli-Matti Kȯrkkȯinen, *Trinity and Religious Pluralism: The Doctrine of the Trinity in Christian Theology of Religions* (England, USA: Ashgate, 2004), 128.

[21] Ibid.,121.

[22] Paul Knitter, *Introducing Theologies of Religions* (Maryknoll, New York: Orbis, 2002), 126-129.

[23] Paul Knitter, "Cosmic Confidence or Preferential Option?" in *The Intercultural Challenge of Raimon Panikkar*. ed. Joseph Prabhu, 177-191, Maryknoll, NY: Orbis, 1996.

[24] Francis X. D'Sa, "Relevance of Raimon Panikkar: A Preview of His Thought" in *Raimon Panikkar: Being Beyond Borders. A Commemorative Volume*. ed. by Johnson Puthenpurackal (Bangalore: National Printing Press), 40-60.

[25] Jyri Komulainen, *An Emerging Cosmotheandric Religion? Raimon Panikkar's pluralistic Theology of Religions* (Leiden. Boston: Brill, 2005), 10.

[26] Cf. John Hick in *An Interpretation of Religion: Human Responses to the Transcendent. Second Editio*, 362.

[27] Raimundo Panikkar. *The Vedic Experience: Mantramañjarī. An Anthology of the Vedas for Modern Man and Contemporary Celebration (Pondicherry*: All India Books, 1977), 15.

[28] *The Rhythm of Being*, 17-18.

[29] Cf. Ahlstrand, Kajsa. *Fundamental Openness. An Enquiry into Raimundo Panikkar's Theological Vision and its Presuppositions*, 183.

[30] S. Painadath SJ, *We Are Co-Pilgrims: Towards a Culture of Inter-religious Harmony* (Delhi: ISPCK, 2006), 16.

[31] Ibid.,16.

[32] Panikkar, "Alternative a la Culutre Moderne (Texte II Dialogue)," *Interculture 15* (October-December 1982), 25.

[33] Panikkar, *The Cosmotheandric* Experience, 132.

[34] Cf. Ahlstrand, Kajsa. *Fundamental Openness. An Enquiry into Raimundo Panikkar's Theological Vision and its Presuppositions* Studia Missionalia Upsaliensia LVII. Diss (Uppsala: The Swedish Institute for Missionary Research, 1993), 184.

[35] Panikkar. *The Rhythm of Being: The Gifford Lectures,* 225.

[36] Ibid., 224.

[37] Ibid., 224.

[38] Raimon Panikkar, "Religion, Philosophy and Culture: inaugural address of the Congress of Intercultural Philosophy in Mexico, 1995" in *InterCulture,* Issue, 135.

[39] Cf. Panikkar, Intra-religious Dialogue, 31.

[40] Panikkar, *the Cosmotheandric* Experience,17.

[41] Jadunatha Sinha, *Indian Philosophy.* Volume II (Delhi: Motilal Banarsidass Publishers Private Limited, 1999), 461-462.

[42] R. Panikkar. *Myth, Faith and Hermeneutics: Cross-Cultural Studies* (New York: Paulist Press, 1979), .282.

[43] Panikkar, Vedic experience, p. 496; Panikkar, *The Cosmotheandric Experience: Emerging religious consciousness.* Edited with Introduction by Scott Eastham (Maryknoll, New York: Orbis Books, 1993), 75.

[44] Raimundo Panikkar. *Worship and Secular Man: An essay on the liturgical nature of man, considering Secularization as a major phenomenon of our time and Worship as an apparent fact of all times. A study towards an integral anthropology* (Maryknoll, New York: Orbis Books and London Darton, Longman and Todd, 1973), 1.

[45] Cf. Raimon Panikkar. "A Self-Critical Dialogue" in *The Intercultural Challenge of Raimon Panikkar.* ed. Joseph Prabhu (Maryknoll, NY: Orbis, 1996),227-243.

[46] Ibid, 227-243.

[47] Ibid.,227-243.

[48] Ibid.,227-243.

[49] Ibid.,227-243.

[50] Raimon Panikkar, "The Jordan, the Tiber and the Ganges: Three Kairological Moments of Christic Self-Consciousness" in *The Myth of Christian Uniqueness: Towards a Pluralistic Theology of Religions.* Eds. John Hick and Paul F. Knitter (Maryknoll, New York: Orbis Books, 1987),.92.

[51] Abraham Koothottil, "Man and Religion" a Dialogue with Panikkar," *Jeevadhara,* Vol.XI, No. 61(1980), 5.

[52] Scott Eastham. "Introduction" *in the Cosmotheandric Experience: Emerging Religious Consciousness* by Raimon Panikkar, viii.

[53] Raimon Panikkar. *The Rhythm of Being: The Gifford Lectures* (Maryknoll, New York: Orbis Books, 2010), 216.

[54] Cf. Panikkar. *Myth, Faith and Hermeneutics: Cross-Cultural Studies,* 282.

[55] Panikkar, *the Cosmotheandric* Experience, 17.

[56] Raimundo Panikkar. *The Unknown Christ of Hinduism: Towards an Ecumenical Christophany. Completely Revised and Enlarged Edition* (Maryknoll, New York: Orbis Books, 1981), 24-25.

[57] Raimon Panikkar, "God of Life, Idols of Death," *Monastic Studies* 7 (1986), 105.

[58] Panikkar, *The Unknown Christ of Hinduism*, 19-24.

[59] Raimon Panikkar, "The Jordan, the Tiber and the Ganges. Three Kairological Moments of Christic Self-Consciousness" in *The Myth of Christian Uniqueness. Towards a Pluralistic Theology of Religions*. Eds. John Hick and Paul F. Knitter (Maryknoll, New York: Orbis Books, 1987), 89-116.

[60] Paul Knitter, *Introducing Theologies of Religions*, 129.

[61] Dominic Veliath. *Theological Approach and Understanding of Religions. Jean Daniélou and Raimundo Panikkar: A Study in Contrast. Instead of a Forward: An Open Letter by Raimundo Panikkar* (Bangalore: Kristu Jyoti College, 1988), 154.

[62] Abraham Koothottil, "Man and Religion" a Dialogue with Panikkar," *Jeevadhara*, Vol.XI, No. 61(1980), 16.

[63] Dankfied Reetz. "Raimon Panikkar's Theology of Religions," *Religion and Society* (Bangalore: The Christian institute for the Study of Religion and Society, Vol.XV, No.3 (Sept.1968), 41.

[64] Ibid.,36.

[65] Cf. Panikkar, *Invisible Harmony, Essays on Contemplation and Responsibility*. Ed. Harry James Cargas. (Minneapolis: Fortress Press.1995), p.57.

[66] Panikkar, Myth, Faith and Hermeneutics, 25.

[67] Panikkar, *Intra-religious Dialogue* (New York, NY: Paulist Press, 1976), 79.

[68] Raimon Panikkar. "A Self-Critical Dialogue" in *The Intercultural Challenge of Raimon Panikkar*. ed. Joseph Prabhu, 252.

Part-2
... encountering the other ...

Halakha for Christians

Christian M. Rutishauser SJ

"**H**alakha for Christians" is the title I have chosen for my contribution to this *Festschrift*. I don't know what kind of associations it would evoke. Halakha is certainly not a common term in Christian theology and interreligious dialogue. It is exclusively Jewish term. It designates the body of the Jewish religious law. A large part of the oral Torah, the Mishna for example, is Halakha. The five Books of Moses, the Pentateuch, contain large sections of Halakha, of law texts. That is why the Old Testament is sometimes referred to simply as "The Law", a *pars pro toto* term. So, what could Halakha for Christians mean? Is it about what Christians could learn from the Jewish law in an interreligious dialogue? Or could the title suggest a religious body of law for Christians? 'Law and being a Christian' is quite a hot issue. Ever since Martin Luther and the Protestant theologians radically contrasted Law and Grace, many believe that the Gospel and Law are no longer compatible. In addition, law and spirituality seem to be exclusive of each other too. Putting an exclamation mark behind the title "Halakha for Christians!" seems to be a form of provocation. Is that the way it should be? Or would you prefer a question mark, as "Halakha for Christians?" Wouldn't it be a rather rhetorical question? Let's leave the punctuation open for the time being – we will come back to it at the end.

Experience on a pilgrimage

Let me begin with a personal experience. In 2011 I undertook a pilgrimage on foot from Switzerland to Jerusalem. 2796 miles in all, across the Alps, through the Balkans to Istanbul, through Turkey and Syria to Israel. We spent seven months on the road, three friends and me. It was a deep spiritual journey. I'd had enough of journey to Israel, to Jerusalem time and again by plane. I wanted to approach the centre of my faith, in a spiritual and existential sense, as a pilgrim.[1] When we were in Turkey and people asked us where we were going, we simply answered: "We're on the Hajj to Jerusalem." *Hajj* is the Muslim word for the pilgrimage to Mecca. So, the people immediately understood that we were on the Hajj to Jerusalem, just as they go to Mecca. When I told a young Muslim in Edirne that we were doing a Hajj to Jerusalem,[2] he was surprised and said: "I didn't know that Christians also had to go on the Hajj. I thought the rule only applied to Muslims." I replied: "We Christians do not *have to* undertake a Hajj to Jerusalem." "Why on earth are you going then?" the young man asked. I had to laugh. Although both of us were talking about the pilgrimage anchored in our respective religious traditions, the notions behind it were completely different. The Hajj in Islam is a religious duty. The young Turk seemed to understand his religion predominantly in the form of obligations, of law. For Christians, there is no religious law compelling us to go to Jerusalem on a pilgrimage. Doing so is a spiritual exercise, a freely chosen form of devotion. By the way, a lot of Jewish friends also followed our pilgrimage project with interest. The Israeli cameraman on the film crew that accompanied us said: "What you are doing is *alijabarägäl*, like in Biblical times." He was excited about the fact that we were walking to Jerusalem. While the Temple was still standing, Jews, too, were bound by religious law to make this journey three times a year: for Passover, *Schavuot* and *Sukkot*, the Feast of Tabernacle. (Deut. 16/16f) But since the destruction of the Temple in 70 A.D., Jews are no longer obliged to undertake pilgrimages to Jerusalem.

Some Christians might jump to conclusions here. You see, they'd say, Islam is an externalised religion that simply compels its adherents to follow a set of rules. And so is Judaism. Christianity, on the other hand, is an internalised spiritual faith. Jews and Muslims are primarily guided by rules and religious laws, without attaching a deeper or spiritual meaning to them. We Christians, on the other hand, act autonomously, from the heart, taking responsibility ourselves. We don't need religious law. Naturally, such a verdict is far too simple, too much dictated by prejudices and clichés. It's never just one or the other. Catholics are well aware of the ecclesiastic law. Protestant Churches also have their rules for the faithful. It comes down to balancing law and internalised faith, religious prescriptions and inner freedom, commandment and charisma. This intrinsic tension has always fascinated me. I was never satisfied by the Reformation age theology that looked at Law and Gospel as opposed to each other. Much of the Catholic theology of the 1970s and 1980s that, infused with the spirit of 1968, over-emphasises individual freedom and rebels against any form of ecclesiastic order seems to me to be naive. Perhaps that is the one reason why, as a young man, I felt attracted to the Orthodox Judaism. I felt that new meaning needed to be found in religious law, and its due place in relation with freedom, charisma and individual calling. I wanted to explore this question in the context of Judaism. So, when I entered the Jesuit Order after completing my Theological studies, I was guided by the intuition that the Jesuits are the Rabbis of the Catholic Church. In fact, research over the past decades has in some ways confirmed this view. Nearly over twenty percent of the Jesuits in the 16th century were Spanish "Conversos" or converts, i.e. men of Jewish origin. And there are texts from around 1580 in which the Jesuit Order is called the "Hebrew Synagogue within the Church."[3]

The Halakhic person

During my doctoral studies, I happened to come across the works of Rabbi Joseph Dov Soloveitchik. From the early 1930s on, he lived in Boston, taught Philosophy, dealt with Talmudic Studies at the Yeshiva University in New York, Manhattan, and became one of the charismatic leaders of what is known as *Modern Jewish Orthodoxy.*[4] He wrote his key philosophic works mainly in the early 1940s, one of them called *The Halakhic Man.*[5] It was this book that presented me with a theology and a spirituality of the Halakha. Soloveitchik paints an ideal picture of a Halakhic personality. It is someone who is creative, who embraces all areas of human life, who studies, weighs and integrates them in his or her religious world view. In particular, such a person is constantly trying to find the right form of conduct in relationship with things and situations of the world. Thus, a Halakhic person, familiar with and inspired by the traditional Halakha, constantly creates new "laws" in accordance with new situations. Such persons can deal creatively with existing religious rules and adapt them to unforeseen situations. In so doing, the Orthodox Jew sanctifies his or her environment by appropriate behaviour. Soloveitchik, in line with the spirit of his times, trusted in scientific progress for the good of mankind. He therefore saw mathematicians and scientists as role models of a Halakhic way of life. Just as scientists measure, order and explain the world with their instruments, Orthodox Jews are to approach modern reality with the help of Halakha, its distinctions, categories and methods, in order to act appropriately. Religious law is not seen as something cast in stone, to be followed come what may, without sensibility towards given circumstances. Instead, law, in the moment of its coming into being and in the moment of its application, is considered a tool that brings about order and provides awareness of the sacred dimension in all situations. David Hartmann called Soloveitchik the poet of the law, who, for inspiration, draws on the best living and orally transmitted tradition of Orthodox Judaism.[6]

Soloveitchik distinguishes between *Halakhic man* and *homo religiosus.* The latter, in Soloveitchik's view, is someone who lives out of a religious feeling, a feeling of absolute dependency, as described by Friedrich Schleiermacher and others in the 19th century.[7] Soloveitchik disliked the subjective and romantic element in this, the emphasis on sentiment and mystical experience. He saw the threat of individualisation in such a personalised spirituality. Religion for him does not mean transcending nature and the natural world. He rejects any Platonic model of the purely spiritual, of leaving the world of scientifically established reality behind. In his view, this represents paganism. It turns religion into an anthropological phenomenon. It creates a yearning to transcend the technical, rational and functional world of everyday life, wrapped in a protective layer of religious feeling. Soloveitchik repudiates the *homo religious* model. By so doing, he repudiates Christianity, because his Christian counterparts in the early years were liberal, bourgeois Protestants in Germany. And these were, for him, the embodiment of *homo religiosus*.

The Gospel's logic as formal principle

Soloveitchik was a dialectic and occasionally a polemic thinker. Not afraid of typecasting, he strictly contrasts *Halakhic man*, represented by Orthodox Jews, with *homo religiosus*, represented by Protestant Christians. In my paper on Soloveitchik, I showed how he had been influenced in this juxtaposition by the dialectic theology of Karl Barth. Barth worked on the contrast between religion and faith.[8] Religion was, for him, a negative term, as it represented a purely human striving for transcendence, whereas faith builds on the revelation of God in Jesus Christ. Soloveitchik's arguments are structured in a similar way. A Jew should turn to the revealed body of law, the Halakha, and not, like *homo religious*, strive to escape the world by seeking the purely spiritual. These distinctions, religion versus faith in the one case, and *homo religiosus* versus Halakha in the other, have given us a tool that has proved useful to this day. We may weigh the two sides as we see fit but should not lose sight of the distinction.

So, what can we Catholics learn from this today? Faith also involves a lot of religion.[9] The Church, too, encompasses a lot of natural religiosity. Religiosity and spirituality are characterised by a feeling of dependency. If believers want to base everything on their personal experience, if they speak of energy fields and spiritual power centres, when they rely on the forces of nature for health, they remain on the level of natural religiosity. Subjective perception and sentiment are the foundation. Even though such a stance should not be seen as negatively as Karl Barth did, believers should not remain at this level. Classical neo-scholastic theology taught: *Gratia supponet naturam et perficiteat*, Grace presupposes nature and brings it to fulfilment. Christ himself should not be considered just another source of energy for such an experience. Religious experience is estimated but challenged by Christ who wants to bring it to fulfilment. The point is to radically expose oneself to the revelation of Scripture and of Christ. God's call to us should be the foundation, whether I feel called myself at this moment or not. The Gospel is to Christians what the Halakha is to Jews. In the Gospel of St. John, Jesus says: "I am the way and the truth and the life" (John 14:6). In Hebrew, one could translate this as "Anihahalacha, haemetvehacchaiim." Christ is the way, *däräch*, or indeed *Halakha*, by which we are guided.[10] He is, for us, the Halakhic man, who approached reality creatively and appropriately in every situation. This means he always acted fully in accordance with the spirit of the Law. The two elements, which Barth and Soloveitchik pitted one against the other, should be brought to a balance in the life of a Catholic. In cases of doubt, however, the revelation of the Gospel, of the law, should take precedence over the personal religious experience. To put it in a nutshell: The principle and the form-giving source of Jewish existence is the Halakha. And for Christians, it is the logic of the Gospel. Christina Busta, an Austrian poet of the 20th century, once said: "I am a Pagan broken by Christianity, and for this breaking I am grateful." The logic of the Gospel is ultimately the decisive factor, not any subjective sentiment, however much this sentiment might be expressed in Christian terms. Neither Christianity nor Judaism is a result of the human quest for the transcendent. Both should take this human quest seriously. But ultimately it is enveloped by God's quest for man.[11]

Spirituality has become a buzzword of our age. It is used in a trans-religious fashion.[12] Even the secularly minded people speak freely of spirituality. Their point of reference is *spiritus*, a spirit, the human spirit that blasts open the narrow reality of empiricism and positivism. In the modern era, the scientific approach came to dominate the world, but it has left humanity locked in its worldliness, its lack of transcendence. Spirituality has cracked this lock. Christian spirituality, however, just like Jewish spirituality, takes the divine spirit, the *Spiritus Sanctus* as its foundation, not the human spirit. This distinction between divine spirit and human spirit is grounded in the belief in creation. But it also implies that God's spirit is reflected in human spirit. Ultimately, however, the *Spiritus Sanctus* is embodied in the Halakha and in the spirit of the Gospel. Only through these can it be recognised by the human spirit. No truly Christian life is without the spirituality of the Gospel. No being Jewish is without the poetry of the Halakha. Faith means putting your trust in them. In fact, it takes this trust, it takes willingness to let your life be determined by the Halakha or the Gospel, for Jewish or Christian spirituality to arise in the first place.

From religious law to religious ethics

The Halakha is at the heart of the gift that is the Torah. Religious law is explicit, concrete, revealed. The Christian New Testament contains hardly any legal texts. In Christian tradition, however, the Gospel has been specified in the form of dogma, rules and ecclesiastical law. This is legitimate and necessary. If I am pleading the case of the Gospel as the form-giving principle, I would also like to add dogma and law as points of reference. Downright rejection seems to me rather a juvenile attitude. Still, Christian life is not legalistic. It's not about blind obedience to religious duties and regulations. Enough damage has been done to the Church by dogmatic and legalistic fundamentalism. Especially in our postmodern world, where life has become so complex, the lure of fundamentalism has made a comeback. On the other hand, dogma and ecclesiastic law alone can never be the foundation of faith.

In the case of Soloveitchik, we saw how the Halakha as religious law became less rigid and more fluid. Soloveitchik presented Halakha in its moment of appearance, or in the moment of its application, as part of the flow of life. Such turning of law and dogma into something fluid is the very essence of the messianic movement around Jesus of Nazareth. The Sermon on the Mount in St. Matthew begins with such a programmatic statement: "Do not think that I have come to abolish the Law or the Prophets. I have not come to abolish, but to fulfil them. For truly I say to you, until heaven and earth pass away, not an iota, not a dot, will pass from the Law until all is accomplished" (5:17-18). And then follow what are known as the antitheses, which show in an exemplary fashion how creatively Jesus operated out of the spirit of the law. Soloveitchik's work with objective Halakhic law leads him to Halakhic humans and their freedom of action. The ecclesiastic law and dogma must be rooted in Christ. It is the spirit of the Gospel that is decisive.

The Christ of the Gospel must not be reduced to a subjective human projection. It is not romantic religious sentiment that makes us transcend our petty ego on the way to becoming truly human. Christ is the way and the embodiment of the Halakha. He is the Law in action. The law outlines his way of life. Therefore, the Gospel and Letters of St. John speak of Christ as love in action. It is fitting to quote again from the Gospel of St. John: "I have loved you, as the Father has loved me; abide in my love. If you keep my commandments, you will abide in My love and live on in it, just as I have obeyed my Father's commandments and live on in His love" (15:9-10). This definition of love as action, as implementation of the law, is a truly Jewish element in the Gospels. The German author Erich Kästner puts it quite simply: "There is nothing good unless you do it."

Since modern states have the monopoly of legislation, both Jewish religious law and ecclesiastic law have become extremely relativized. In many cases, religious law has been pushed aside entirely. Rabbis have been shifted from the legal arena to the pastoral field. Specialists in canon law have been side-lined by priests and pastors. Jewish and Christian Church authorities have only partial jurisdiction over their respective religious laws. For many Christians, the Church law has become totally irrelevant, because there are no sanctions against breaches. The realm of sexuality seems to be the only exception. Since the 19th century, ethics and morals have replaced religious law in both Christianity and Judaism. Ethical and moral concerns, not legal concerns, impact the everyday choices of believers. Ethics and morals are less stable, less easily graspable, than the prescriptions of law. This is the context in which the philosophy of German Idealism blossomed in Europe. Many Jews and Christians built their lives on a sense of universal and humanistic ethics. Ritual and liturgical rules were separated from this body of ethics and relegated in significance. Being a good Christian or a good Jew was equated with an ethical or a moral way of life. Since the 19th century, there have, however, also been counter-tendencies. The First Vatican Council is a case in point. By promulgating the infallibility of the Pope, the Catholic Church tried to salvage at least its spiritual authority. The Jewish neo-orthodox movement started in Germany with R. Samson Raphael Hirsch in mid-19th century, fighting against dissolving Judaism into the history of a nation.[13] Soloveitchik fought with his modern orthodoxy against dissolving it in individualistic and subjective religiosity. He, as we have seen, worked on behalf of Orthodoxy and against Reform Judaism by placing the Halakha in all its manifestations at the heart of his philosophy of religion. In an open, globalized world and a postmodern society, we have come to realize that ethics alone is not enough. Religions need rituals and liturgical identity markers. These are ultimately governed by religious rules. No faith can survive entirely without law. Because faith is not a purely individual matter but is nurtured by a community that has been carried through history by the Halakha in the case of the Jews and by the Gospel in the case of Christianity. So, spirituality and spiritual practices always have to be in a healthy tension and balance with rules and laws. Whether interpreted in a more ethical or more legalistic way, the key fact remains that faith means acting out of the source of a tradition to which one belongs.

Spirituality of action

Soloveitchik, when propagating his Halakhic Man, was primarily concerned with a spirituality of action. In the first half of the 20th century, when the Orthodox Jews were a minority among Jews in

Western Europe and North America, when they were in danger of being eclipsed by the Reform Judaism, Soloveitchik needed to create a new foundation for Halakhic life.[14] He did not turn to the Cabbalistic tradition for this. It is not from metaphysical speculation that the individual commandments were to gain new meaning.[15] Soloveitchik did not ascribe acting in accordance with the law to any alignment with cosmic forces. He was very much a Modernist who looked at the world with the eyes of a philosopher and saw the Orthodox Jew as the creator and designer of a down-to-earth – not transcendent – world. The Halakha provided him with the tools he worked with, just as a secular thinker works with the tools of philosophic tradition. The spirit of oral and written Jewish tradition was the foundation of his worldly, orthodox spirituality of life in action.

In the Catholic Church, as mentioned before, the Jesuit tradition is the one closest to the Jewish Rabbinic tradition. The numerous converts from Judaism in Spain had a strong impact on the Jesuit Order in the 16th century and led to some fierce internal disputes. In 1598 the 5th General Congregation of the Society of Jesus decided – in contrast to the original spirit of the movement – that no more Jews would be admitted.[16] But the Jewish tradition had left its mark. In the 17th century, the Jesuits developed a legal and moral school tradition of their own. They became the main representatives of the so-called Probabilism. In due course, the casuistry of the Jesuits became proverbial. But to this day, the spirituality of the Jesuit Order has been one of action. It is founded on the Spiritual Exercises, the meditative path laid out by the order's founder, St. Ignatius of Loyola. The Exercises do not follow the three-step road that is often described in Christian mysticism: *via purgativa, via illuminative* and *via unitiva*. True, the *via purgative* is also at the start of the Spiritual Exercises, but it is here entirely focused on the attainment of inner freedom. "Indifference" is the term Ignatius used for this aimed-at inner state. This is not the same as in the modern usage of the word 'indifference'. In the sense of St. Ignatius, it means a softening and cleansing of all our psychological, emotional, mental and judgmental patterns and attachments, of being freed up from them. And this enables our inner and outer life to be redirected. 'Freedom from' is followed by 'freedom for'. In the second phase of the Spiritual Exercises, the goal is to use this new-found freedom to put our life in the service of God, of Christ, and thereby in the service of the world. Both the phase should be permeated by Divine illumination and unity.[17] The *via purgative* is followed by the way of succession, by becoming a follower of Christ, and being guided by the example of Christ's action in the world. The mystical path of the Spiritual Exercises does not consist in drawing ever closer to God. This part of the journey is only necessary for the purification process and the redirection of one's life. It is the *conditio sine qua non*. The journey then turns and Christians let themselves be sent out into the world by God, with Jesus as their guiding light. This movement towards God and then back into the world is the characteristic feature of the Spiritual Exercises.

Soloveitchik reminds us that the Jews have been given the Halakha as a set of tools. St. Ignatius tells his followers who have undergone the spiritual exercises to become followers of Christ, who "works within the world".[18] He has endowed the Jesuits and all those who live in the spirit of his exercises with a theological grounding and with tools for meditation and reflection, among them the "discernment of spirits". Guided by the Gospel and spiritual knowledge, Christians are called to act in an ethical way by deciding what is appropriate in each specific situation. This becomes an ongoing process, increasingly bringing the sacred into the realm of the mundane (or sanctifying the environment by appropriate behaviour, as Soloveitchik had propagated for his Halakhic man), and thus inching the world closer to the Kingdom of God. This is a process of sanctification, underpinned by a spirituality of mission and action.[19]

St. Ignatius of Loyola has been called a pilgrim on behalf of the will of God. Both the Ignatian spirituality and Rabbinic thought are geared towards identifying God's will anew in each situation and then putting it into practice. In Christian terms, it is about acting in a way that is permeated by the logic of the Gospel and flows out of the personal relationship with Jesus Christ. I don't know whether Soloveitchik was aware of the proximity and the structural parallels between the Halakhic and the Jesuit thought. In any case, he participated in programmes in the 1960s that were launched by Loyola University in Chicago.[20] Halakha for Christians – Should there be a question mark at the end? Or an exclamation mark? Or just a dot? At the end of these reflections, I'll leave the decision to the reader.

Endnotes

[1] Rutishauser Christian, Zu Fuss nach Jerusalem. Mein Pilgerweg für Dialog und Frieden, Patmos 2013. Movie with English subtitles: Die Schrittweisen. Zu Fuss nach Jerusalem, Loyola Productions, Munich: 2012.

[2] Ibid., 101.

[3] Maryks Robert, *The Jesuit Order As a Synagogue of Jews. Jesuits of Jewish Ancestry and Purity-of-Blood Laws in the Early Society of Jesus*, Brill, Leiden: 2010; Rastoin Jean-Marc, Du même sang que Notre Seigneur. Juifs et jésuites aux débuts de la compagnie de Jésus, Bayard, Paris : 2011.

[4] On his biography: Rutishauser Christian, *The Human Condition and the Thought of Rabbi Josef B. Soloveitchik*, katv Publishing House, New Jersey: 2013, 1-27.

[5] Soloveitchik Josef B., *Halakhic Man*, Philadelphia: 1983.

[6] Hartman David, *The Breakdown of Tradition and the Quest for Renewal. Reflections on Three Jewish Responses to Modernity*, Forum Nr. 37/38/39, 13.

[7] Schleiermacher Friedrich, *Der christliche Glaube nach der Grundsätzen der evangelischen Kirche im Zusammenhange dargestellt*, 2/1830/31, ed. by Schäfer Rolf, Berlin: 2003, 38.

[8] Barth Karl, *Die kirchliche Dogmatik*, Bd. I/2, Munich / Zürich 1932-1967, 305-335.

[9] The development of the term *religion* see: Henrici Peter, *The Concept of Religion from Cicero to Schleiermacher. Origins, History, and Problems with the Term*, in: Becker Karl J./Moralillara, *Catholic Engagement with World Religions. A Comprehensive Study* (Faith Meets Faith), Orbis Books, New York: 2010, 1-20.

[10] Cf. Pope Benedict who describes Jesus as the embodiment of the word of God, of the Tora, in: Ratziner Josef, *Jesus von Nazareth*, Teil 1, Herder, Freiburg, Basel, Wien: 2007, 142f.

[11] Cf. Heschel Abraham Joshua, *God in Search of Man. A Philosophy of Judaism*, Farer Straus Giroux, New York: 1976.

[12] On the term *spirituality* and its use today see: Peng-Keller Simon, *Einführung in die Theologie der Spiritualität, Wissenschaftliche Buchgesellschaft*, Darmstadt: 2010, 9-28.

[13] Liberles Robert, *Champion of Orthodoxy. The Emergence of Samson Raphael Hirsch as Religious Leader*, Association for Jewish Studies Review Nr. 6/1984, S. 42-60.

[14] Rutishauser Christian, The Human Condition and the Thought of Rabbi Josef B. Soloveitchik, katv Publishing House, New Jersey: 2013, 12f.

[15] Rav Kook redefined Halakha in the 20th century by Cabbala, see: Linets Olga, *Modern Orthodox* oderreligiöser Antifundamentalismus von Rav Abraham IsaakhaKohenKuk, Grin Verlag, München: 2012.

[16] Colombo Emanuele, "The Watershed of Conversion: Antonio Possevino, New Christians, and Jews," in Bernauer James, Maryks Robert (Ed.), *The Tragic Couple. Encounters between Jews and Jesuits*, Brill, Leiden: 2014, 25-42.

[17] On the structure and theology of the Exercises, see: Köster Peter, *Zur Freiheitbefähigen. Kleiner Kommentar zu den grossen Exerzitien*, Benno, Leipzig: 3/2004; Lefrank Alex, *Umwandlung in Christus. Die Dynamik des Exerzitienprozesses*, Echter, Würzburg: 2010.

[18] Spiritual Exercises No. 236.

[19] Cf. Rutishauser Christian, "The Goal of the Ignatian Exercises and Soloveitchik's Halakhic Spirituality," in Michel Thomas (Ed.), *Friends on the Way. Jesuits Encounter Contemporary Judaism*, Fordham University Press, New York: 2007, 38-56.

[20] His most famous work grew out of the associated lectures: Soloveitchik Josef B., *The Lonely Man of Faith*, New York: 1992.

An Instance of
Interreligious Contemplative Reading:
In the Absence of the Beloved

Francis X. Clooney SJ

In light of the theme of this volume, "Spirituality through Interreligious Experience" and Sebastian Painadath SJ's lifelong commitment to that very goal, I offer this reflection on my most recent book, *His Hiding Place Is Darkness* (2013),[1] which is devoted to an interreligious reading that opens on the one side into the light and dark places of experiencing God, and on the other into a theology which hopes to be truly open to God's mystery in Christ.

The Beloved and yet also the absence of the Beloved are realities central to religious experience, and many a great poet and saint has taken up the topic. My book was a venture into this territory, first of all by a reading of the Biblical *Song of Songs* (*Shir ha-Shirim*) and then too the Srivaisnava Hindu *Holy Word of Mouth* (*Tiruvāymoli*), the most important of the works of the mystic poets of 8th-9th century South India known as the alvars. Each body of poetry is large, deep, and full of many possible meanings; as the title of the book implies, I focus in it on the theme of absence, a Beloved who is seen and felt all the more intensely in times of absence. The book's title echoes a quote from Psalm 18, itself imbedded in a passage by John of Ford (1140–1244), the Cistercian monk who wrote sermons on the last four chapters of the *Song*: "He has made darkness His hiding place." I wanted, in the book, to explore the reality and centrality of God precisely in those moments when God has seemed most absent, noticed in longing rather than presence.

In preparing the book, I studied the *Song* (in English, in Latin, but not in the Hebrew), paying particular attention to the situation of the woman at those moments when her Beloved is absent, when she seeks him but only sometimes finds him again. To read the text was a case of *lectio divina*, the contemplative, prayerful reading so well known in Christian tradition. In this reading, I was guided by a single medieval Christian tradition of good reading, that of Bernard of Clairvaux and Gilbert of Hoyland and John of Ford. These were three Cistercian Catholic monks who over many years produced a complete series of sermons on the *Song*, each beginning where the previous had left off. One could spend a very long time learning from these deep and passionate sermons.

But I knew also that it was time to read more widely, in another tradition too. So, I read also the songs of another woman in love, similarly bereft of her Beloved, in the *Holy Word*. Out of the 100 songs in this work, as many as 27 are in the voice of a young woman in love – or that of her mother or friend – and express her suffering in separation from her Beloved in poetic form, and in the drama of searching, seemingly to no avail. Here too, I was guided by medieval interpreters, particularly Nanjiyar and Nampillai. These revered teachers taught the text with great devotion, exploring the direct and subtle meanings of every word of it.

Each tradition of reading opens up poetic and spiritual possibilities in an unanticipated yet deeply engaging way, and all the more so by the double reading itself, as the poetry, read together, coheres as it were into a still greater Text. Yet too, each work, the *Song* and the *Holy Word*, invites us to enter its world and stay just there. Each shines inward, creating and illumining a spiritual world that needs no other. For centuries readers of each have taken their images and dramatic scenes to be complete and compelling bodies of poetry for reflection and for guidance along the spiritual path, without need of supplement from other religions. The larger theological meanings arising in relation to these texts, even if ever deferential to the poetry and the underlying mysteries of love, were taken to be more or less settled inside and for the respective traditions. It is God and the soul told *here*, Christ and his Church, Krishna and everyone loving him. The *Song* and the *Holy Word* do not in any obvious way need one other. Readers might well spend a lifetime with either of them, seeking no further.

But they certainly can be read together and in a certain harmony. These holy poems have no entirely fixed boundaries, and in their beauty and allure excite rather than close off the play of imagination. His *Hiding Place Is Darkness* arises from meditating on these texts together. It a work that I call theopoetic and theodramatic, allowing room for necessary spiritual and humane precedents to theology as we ordinarily think of it.

As already mentioned, I attended especially to the absence of the Beloved as this has been imagined, suffered, and turned into presence-in-absence, light-in-dark, in several strands of Hindu and Christian tradition. I did this in order to write about a real God who can really be present, but therefore also absent, whose absence makes life seemingly impossible and yet prepares the way for still deeper life.

Six times over, I constructed and worked through parallel readings, not so much for the sake of an exterior comparison, but in order to allow them to "sit together" and affect one another:

Song 1.1-7, and *Holy Word* I.4: initial doubts

Song 2.16-3.1 and *Holy Word* V.4: alone in the night

Song 3.2-4 and *Holy Word* V.9: searching and finding (or not)

Song 5.2-6 and *Holy Word* VII.3: on not finding the Beloved

Song 5.7-6.4 and *Holy Word* IX.6: dazzling but fragile, temporary moments of encounter, lost and remembered

Song 8.13-14 and *Holy Word* X.3: the final ambiguity: does the Beloved come? go?

The book was thus entirely in the debt of Biblical and Hindu poetry and proceeded as reflection more particularly on the experience of a woman whose Beloved has not returned and seems nowhere to be found. For the sake of this reading, and to give the reader maximum freedom, I first and without comment gave the texts side by side, on parallel pages, under the title, "for meditation." Only thereafter did I offer my own reading of the particular songs under consideration. My hope was that an interreligious reading and experience would accumulate and intensify throughout the book. None of the paired texts is exactly the same as that with which it is paired, of course, but the resemblances and harmonies are notable. Reading them together is conducive to intensifying what each in its own way has expressed, because as readers we are made to imagine and feel the experience in each way and then twice over. This double reading of love and absence, manifest in more than one culture, would, I hoped, show something of the nature of God encountered in our own tradition and yet too beyond its seeming borders.

If we have read well across religious boundaries, then even as we focus on this Beloved, images and scenes from Hindu poetry flood the Christian's imaginations; taking to heart the *Holy Word* and its medieval Hindu readers, we wander off a straight Christian path only to find Krishna intimately, passionately nearby—not our Beloved, but very close by. A Hindu reader given over to Krishna may find Jesus, the other Beloved, likewise unpredictably nearby. But in reading together the *Song* and the *Holy Word*, we multiply possibilities and accentuate the challenges facing readers who honor the theological and literary dimensions of both sacred texts and their traditions. We do so without betraying the love with which we begin and to which we return. Jesus is the Beloved, even if we cannot fail to remember that Krishna is for the woman in the *Holy Word*, and for millions of others, the Beloved. In our reading, we travel both ways, getting lost in each body of poetry and its drama of loss and search, in the loves intensified in the hiding. Like the woman, we may find ourselves uncertain where to go next. Our faith seeks to understand, but first finds itself carried away by love, for the moment possessed of no sure, guiding words. Studying and remembering the *Song* and the *Holy Word* together ideally made it impossible, for author or reader, to revert to a thinking that neatly separates the Hindu and the Christian, this love and that love, God this way and that. We have new memories that aid and vex us in seeking after a God who should not have to be sought after, who now visits the expected places only occasionally, and who returns just when we think this beloved can never be found. Because we do remember, we still have with us our own traditions, but cannot rely exclusively on how they have spoken of God. We find ourselves in the open space of powerful yet discontinuous insights, suspended between two works of poetry, in the gap where no one set of rules applies. In these songs of absence, the reader would, I hoped, encounter over and again realities all too familiar from ordinary life: we are alone, we are searching, and even in our successes we fail to say what we mean.

But a caution is required here. It is not as if the poems want to be read together. Each invites us to enter its world and stay only there; each shines inward, a world tolerating no other. Nor do Bernard and Gilbert, Nanjiyar and Nampillai, need anything more than what they find in the texts right in front of them. And yet, with respect and care, we do read them together, and my book grew out of that improper, impossible project. Faced with this necessity, we are where we need to be, implicated, obliged to more than we could up to now handle. Our situation is now more difficult and intense than before we had studied these texts together. And thus, we are better off.

So where does this contemplative reading leave us? So, what is the theology that arises from this reading, these meditations on two poetic traditions of the Beloved who hides from us? And what is a Christian theology that is truly Christian yet does not do injustice to each body of poetry and its drama? (I ask my Hindu readers to write the necessary

Hindu theology to follow from such meditations, and in a way that is open to Christian sensitivities.) How are we to manage to write a proper theology — as a theo-logy, still theo-poetic, still theo-dramatic — across two traditions, at home where we are at home, yet without too calmly forgetting or too blithely presuming to find the Beloved, while yet saying something of theological substance?

In its last sections *His Hiding Place Is Darkness* took on a more formal theological character, but it remained important not to reduce these songs' meaning to a mere list of similarities and differences, as if the goal were to prove or disprove something about religion or poetry. But writing theology after contemplative poetry is itself something of an art. There is always the danger of saying too little or too much, and of killing poetry by prose. Nor could the theological conclusion be of the sort that might have been written before the double reading even took place. The practice of contemplative reading—slowly, plodding, erring, but still moving forward and back—has at its best entangled us in the images and emotions of two traditions, each in its own way powerfully evoking her loss. At such a moment, if we have done well, we are without the comfort of simple solutions, no longer able to draw on just one tradition's devotion with a purity that bans or keeps at a distance other love.

In the end, though, it is still the case that even after my double reading, truth, and even the Christian Truth, is not lost or endlessly deferred. Rather, it is received over and again in acts of the imagination. It is nurtured, even if hidden in unruly poetic and dramatic forms that never quite add up to doctrinal clarity. Theology reemerges in a certain manner, without any escape from the unsettled poetic and dramatic contemplation of God's absence we worked hard to produce by the double readings of the poems together. There is no reason to rule out further substantive theological reflection entirely focused on Jesus (or, for the devout Hindu, Krishna). Indeed, our readings open up those very poetic and dramatic possibilities which better Christian theologies presuppose, and which that theology can later on study with a certain reverence, without abandoning the rhythms of the poetic and dramatic.

In the book, I drew at both beginning and end on the great trilogy of Han Urs von Balthasar, his aesthetics (*The Glory of the Lord*, what I would term his "*theo-poetics*"), dramatics (*theo-drama*) and finally, afterwards, theology (*theo-logic*). In these works, with care and due caution, he shows us how to leave room within a Christian narrative for uncertain and undigested moments of poetic and dramatic import: stepping aside from his examples, I focused on the union and separation of the *Song's* lovers and of Krishna and the woman who loves him beyond despair. Nearby book's end, I turned to volume V of the *Theo-Drama* and volumes II and III of the *Theo-Logic*,[2] to show a way back to Christian theology. I followed his teaching on language, reformulated—uttered and heard differently, anew— and traced out in terms of spirit, searching, and silence. This triple disposition offered insights into the human condition before God, and helped map out, in a preliminary way, a certain manner of theology, such as might follow upon the exercises at which I (and my readers) had labored throughout the book. The goal, in the final pages of the book but also after it in essays such as this, has been something as simple and difficult as a spiritual, searching, and silent theology.

The required brevity of this essay does not allow me to report fully on my study of *Spirit, search,* and *silence* in Balthasar, so by way of example I will illustrate the process by speaking of the *search* that is intrinsic to an authentic Christian theology, even as we are led by the Spirit and preparing to enter God's silence. The woman has spoken over and again of her search for the Beloved, her Jesus, her Krishna. In the search and its passing successes and failures she gave flesh-and-blood evidence of the crisis that was his departure and her inability to be satisfied by anything but his return. The Beloved, intimately close in the past, now seems to be in hiding, as if available only to those ready to seek. But it is not clear whether a proper search is possible.

But after it all, what is the meaning of this "search"? At the end of volume V of *Theo-Drama*, when meditating on "the creature in God," gets at the mystery of searching for an already present God by first summarizing three points made earlier in the same volume. First, there is "the fullness of life within the Godhead" that contains in itself what is still, among created beings, "permeated by potentiality"; there is always more, not yet realized, beyond any given moment of seeming completeness. Second, the world itself remains a pilgrim, ever stepping beyond itself toward "an ultimate, though unimaginable, state 'with' God," who is the origin but also the goal not yet reached. It is as if all of reality is searching for the Beloved. Third, although it is finite and imperfect and needy, the world is never really outside of God, for "this locus, in its finitude, must be always embraced and surpassed by the infinite distinction between the Divine Persons" (*Theo-Drama* V, 394-395).

Indeed, the search must be understood in a certain way, if the experience and the theology are both to be respected. As Srivaishnava Hindus can attest, there is never some other place to which we must go, even in those moments— or endless ages—when we find ourselves apart from God. To seek God merely in a literal sense would require that we step outside of reality as we experience it, in God. And yet we search for God. In the second volume of his *Theo-Logic*, Balthasar encapsulates this curious dynamic with reference to the "biblical formula" of the two paths, beginning with an "a priori certainty that what is sought is 'beyond' (*via eminentiae*)." We seek out what is not God in order then to pass beyond it, "negating everything finite, definable, and non-divine (*via negativa*) only in order to strive unswervingly toward the object of the search." (*Theo-Logic* II, 97) Like the woman possessed by a love that settles for nothing but God, we wander, seeking the Beloved in the wrong places, where he had been in the past; yet we make progress because we can recollect how the Beloved had indeed been in those places and still dwells there in our remembering. In the end, though, we must also be ready *not* to find God in those expected places.

One cannot seek after God, as if this Beloved were in a particular place, here, there, or somewhere else. Balthasar finds that Anselm catches the dynamic well: "Lord, if you are not here, where can I seek you, absent? But if you are everywhere, why do I not see you, present?" (*Theo-Drama* V, 395: [My translation of Balthasar's citation of the Latin]. One does not move from outside of God to inside of God. How the unbounded God is present to limited human beings is best imagined, says Balthasar, by parsing the asymmetries of heaven and earth as spiritual states: "There is no distance between heaven and earth—if by earth we mean freedom in its pilgrim state and by heaven we mean freedom's ultimate state, the ratification of its positive fundamental choice by the One it has chosen, namely, God, who can now openly entrust himself to this freedom." (V, 395) To traverse the small, difficult space of this singular freedom, however, we must conceive of God "in dialectical terms," since the most intense presence is what is "beyond all that we can grasp." (V, 396) Because we cannot plumb the depths of God, the deeper we fall into God, the less likely we are ever done with searching. And all of this always retains a poetic and dramatic form, ever resistant to firm conclusions: as we shall mark in Act Three, the *Song* has no definitive ending, and neither does the yearning of the woman in the *Holy Word*: "in God there is eternal life and hence 'eternal surprise,'" (Ruysbroeck, quoted by Balthasar, V, 400) and we shall never be done with our amazement.

When our love has to do with God, it cannot easily escape the prospect of a divided consciousness: "Though we live wholly in God and wholly in ourselves, yet it is but one life; but it is twofold and opposite according to our feeling." (Ruysbroeck, quoted by Balthasar, V, 400). We cannot become God or live entirely for ourselves apart from God; for us there is only an in-between space where "we find nothing else but the grace of God and the exercise of our love." (V, 400) We plunge into the now of God's nearness, but that moment keeps passing us by as well. Searching then is a necessary fiction that helps us to endure the "passing by," in order that we might better be overtaken by the God who hides right here, in front of us, behind us. This in-between space and this passing-by create the spiritual reality of searching.

It is this searching, I suggested in the book, that takes poetic and dramatic form in the *Song* and in the *Holy Word*, and doubly so in our reading of them together, as we open up an uncertain space unpredicted by either tradition. In the unfinished drama of our times, we are always stepping away from the certainties of faith, even if we return a moment later, steadfast again until the Beloved departs once more. We expect one love to put aside all others, but we also come to see that the intensity of one love does not of itself diminish the intensity of the other. Thus, we come to stand, in our best theology, onto admittedly uncharted ground. Religious diversity, dramatized in vivid poetic form, keeps yielding the possibility that we might be surprised yet again by this Beloved, and so we return to prayer and contemplation, at home and abroad, in and yet also after the poetry.

This reflection is already overly long, and here I must stop. I hope that this contribution to the art and prayer of interreligious contemplative reading — illustrated at length in *His Hiding Place Is Darkness* but only briefly here – will honor, in my own way, the deep and enduring commitment to wisdom, love, and contemplation that has marked the life and work of Sebastian Painadath, S.J.

Endnotes

[1] *His Hiding Place Is Darkness: A Hindu-Catholic Theopoetics of Divine Absence* (Stanford University Press, 2013). Several passages from the book have been borrowed and rewritten for the sake of this essay.

[2] All references to the English translations: *Theo-Drama: Theological Dramatic Theory*. 5 vols. Translated by Graham Harrison. San Francisco: Ignatius Press, 1988-98; *Theo-Logic: Theological Literary Theory*. 3 vols. Translated by Adrian J. Walker. San Francisco: Ignatius Press, 2000-2005.

Stuti:
Praise in a Non-dualist Context[1]

Bettina Sharada Bäumer

tvatstutau yadi yaco mama
tvadbhāvanāmayam sampannam
If I utter praise to you,
may it be perfect
as the contemplation of
my union with you.
Kṣemarāja comm. on
Stavacintāmaṇi v.119

Prayer and praise of the Divinity can have such dualistic forms that
there seems to be an unbridgeable gap between the one who praises
(*stotā*) and the Divine. The non-dualist tradition of Kashmir Śaivism
– also called Trika (the triadic school) or Pratyabhijñā (the school of
divine Recognition) – has been conscious of an apparent contradiction
between the dualism implied in praise (*stuti*) and the ultimate nondualism
of the soul (*aṇu* or *nara*) and the Divine (Śiva, Bhairava, Parameśvara
etc.). It is precisely this tradition which is extremely rich in hymnical
or Stotra literature, not only in praise of Śiva,[2] but also of the Goddess[3]
and even of the Divine Sun (Sūrya).[4] Recitation of these hymns is very
much part of the religious practice of Kashmiri Śaivites until today.

How did the *stotrakāras* (hymnologists) and their learned commentators, steeped in the non-dualist philosophy of the school of Pratyabhijñā, deal with the problem of overcoming a sense of duality implied in the division (*bheda*) between the singer of praise, the praise itself, and the divine object of praise, corresponding to the threefold nature of knowledge : *pramātā, pramāṇa, prameya*?

This is a vast subject on which I can only throw light on the basis of some selected texts: the Śivastotrāvalī of Utpaladeva (late 9th – early 10th century), the *Stavacintāmaṇi* of Bhaṭṭa Nārāyaṇa (about the same time), and the *Sāmbapañcāśikā*, ending with a *stotra* fragment by the great Abhinavagupta. Fortunately, the commentator to all these texts is Kṣemarāja, disciple of Abhinavagupta and great commentator of the Tantras. Being a master of Pratyabhijñā, his constant endeavour is to lead the implied duality back into the experience of oneness with the Divine. But the approaches differ in the different Stotras, as we shall see.

The spiritual approach of the tradition emphasizes sudden enlightenment over gradual progress on the spiritual path. A classical verse in Bhaṭṭa Nārāyaṇa's *Stavacintāmaṇi* expresses the conscious relationship of the ways the devotee is related to the Divine. Kṣemarāja, the commentator, in the introductory sentence to this verse already expresses the precaution of a non-dualist:

"One who is filled with devotion is established in the non-dual Consciousness of the Lord in all states. Keeping this in mind the author states:

namaḥ stutau smṛtau dhyāne

darśane sparśane tathā |

prāptau cānandvṛndāya

dayitāya kapardine ||

Stavacintāmaṇi v.36

Salutation to the dearest Ascetic,[5]

an abundance of bliss

present in every act of praise, remembrance,

meditation, vision, direct experience,

and attainment of identity.

The starting point is praise (*namaḥ* and *stuti*), and the following acts represent an ascending order in the experience of the devotee, leading him or her stage by stage from duality to nondual union with the Divine. "Attainment" (*prāpti*) is explained by the commentator as "consisting in a state of perfect repose in one's essential (i.e. divine) nature." And in the case of the Lord, unlike in human relationships, "such a state is ever fully present and does not know any more or less."

The most common form of praise in Śaivism is contained in the mantra (*oṃ*) *nama śivāya*. The same author praises the devotees who experience the power of this mantra (v.20). Not only the commentator, the *stotrakāra* himself is conscious of the universally present nature of the Lord. He therefore exclaims,

> *kaḥ panthā yena na prāpyaḥ*
>
> *kā ca vāṅnocyase yayā* |
>
> *kiṃ dhyānaṃ yena na dhyeyaḥ*
>
> *kiṃ vā kiṃ nāsi yatprabho* ||
>
> v.21
>
> By which path are you not attained?
>
> which word is there that does not express you?
>
> What meditation is there by which you are not meditated upon?
>
> Is there anything, O Lord, what you are not?

The commentator unfolds this universality:

> What is not accomplished by reflection on *mantra*, such as *namo namaḥ* Śivāya? What is that which lacks the nature of Your unlimited Light? Nothing, not even the smallest thing. Therefore, what path (or activity) belonging to embodied beings could exist that doesn't lead to You? Furthermore, the whole of speech has You as its content; even meditation,

which is of the nature of ideation, has You as its support (ālambana). Therefore, we are, always and without any effort, identical with you.

(B. Marianovic, transl. modified, p. 151)[6]

The very next verse makes it clear that the motive for the overflowing streams of praise is love for the Lord. This is a love which finds expression in praise, but flows over into all activities of life, as Kṣemarāja emphasizes:

> All of my daily activities, whether physical, mental, or on the level of speech, are permanently established in the Lord. Therefore, that Lord, who is the supreme Reality in the form of Consciousness, shines in all the states (of consciousness) as 'this and that' and is thus worshipped, meditated on, and is pleased. In this context, the word *rasa* means 'love' or 'devotion' (*abhiniveśa*). Therefore, let my love, which exists for You, multiply in thousands of currents.
>
> p. 152, comm.

At the end the author makes it clear that the state of permanent union with the Lord is the result of grace, and does not depend on the devotee's effort:

> *prasanne manasi svāmin kiṃ tvaṃ niviśase kimu |*
>
> *tvatpraveśātprasīdet taditi dolāyate janaḥ ||*
>
> *niścayaḥ punareṣo'tra tvadadhiṣṭhānameva hi |*
>
> *prasādo manasaḥ svāmin sā siddhistatparaṃ padam ||*
>
> *Stavacintāmaṇi* vv. 117-118
>
> People are doubtful O Lord: whether you enter one's mind when it is already purified, or does the mind become purified when you enter it?
>
> This is our conclusion: it is the descent of your grace that is the placidity of the mind; this alone is perfection and the supreme abode. (vv. 117-18)
>
> (tr. p. 271)

At the very end of the *Cintāmaṇi*, Bhaṭṭa Nārāyaṇa comes back to the all-embracing presence of the Lord but expressed in the form of a prayer. The commentator introduces the verse as follows:

Having praised the very essence of the Lord with various verses in different styles, the author expresses his desire that his identity with the Lord becomes permanently established in all states and under all conditions.

vacaścetaśca kāryaṃ ca śarīraṃ mama yatprabho |

tvatprasādena tadbhūyād bhavadbhāvaikabhūṣaṇam ||

v. 119

By your grace, O Lord, let my verbal, mental and physical activities possess only one decoration – that of identity with you. (tr. p. 275)

(Comm.:)

If I speak in praise of You, let that always happen in the form of a contemplation on You. Speech always follows mind and mind is based in the body. Thus, if any act, such as speech, thinking, or movement (*parispandana*) is to be 'effected' by the organs of speech, mind, and body, then let all of that, O Lord - 'through Your grace' (*tvatprasādena*); that is, by bringing Your purity into prominence and minimizing the function of Your hiding nature — possess only one ornament (*ekaṃ bhūṣaṇam*), which is identity with You. (tr. p. 276.)

I want to draw the next examples for this theme from a mystical hymn to the Sun-God from Kashmir, the *Sāmbapañcāśikā*, which has been integrated in the non-dualist Trika.[7] I have suggested that it may belong to the same age as the Mārtaṇḍa Sūrya Temple in South Kashmir, which is dated to the 8th century. The commentary by Kṣemarāja, disciple of Abhinavagupta, proves its inclusion in the Kashmir Śaiva nondualism latest in the 11th century. One of the reasons for this inclusion was the conscious theory of speech (*vāc*) and its four levels, as is already evident in verse 4.[8] Primarily, the Divine Sun (*paramāditya*) is identified by Kṣemarāja with the Sun of Consciousness (*cidbhānu, cidarka* etc.). The Hymn displays a clear awareness of the dualistic implications of praise. We may analyze this reflection in three verses.

tvāṃ stoṣyāmi stutibhiriti me yastu bhedagraho'yam

saivāvidyā tadapi sutarām tadvināśāya yuktaḥ |

staumyevāhaṃ trividhamuditaṃ sthūlasūkṣmaṃ paraṃ vā

vidyopāyaḥ para iti budhair gīyate khalvavidyā ||

v.11

If I say "I will praise you with hymns", this is a sign of duality; it is my ignorance. But this (kind of ignorance) is more appropriate to eradicate itself.

Verily, I praise (you) who are manifest in three ways: gross, subtle and supreme. (For) the wise have said that the means to attain wisdom is (actually) ignorance.

The duality or difference (*bheda*) which is the most obvious sign of ignorance is the duality of the one who praises and the object of praise. The *stotrakāra* defends his composing such a hymn by stating that he is using this kind of ignorance in order to overcome it. Kṣemarāja comments on this that "ignorance consists in the non-realization of the nondual nature of Consciousness" leading to a sense of difference (*bheda*). But in order to destroy or uproot it, "I praise you by submerging my individuality consisting of identification with the body (vital energy, mind etc.)" (*tvāṃ staumyeva dehādipramātṛtā-nimajjanena*). And he clarifies who is that "object" of praise: "I praise You, the Sun of Consciousness" (*tvām eva cidarkaṃ staumi*).

Praise is thus a means (*upāya*) to eradicate the limited individual consciousness and merge it in the unlimited universal Consciousness.[9]

In verse 15 the author (supposed to be Sāmba) comes back to the theme by making a statement of non-duality, and again justifying his act of praise:

stotā stutyaḥ stutiriti bhavān   kartṛkarmakriyātmā

krīḍatyekastava nutividhāv-asvatantrastatoham |

yadvā vacmi praṇayasubhagaṃ gopate tacca tathyaṃ

tvatto hyanyat kimiva jagatāṃ vidyate tanmṛṣā syāt ||

You are the one who praises,

you are the object of praise

and you are the praise itself –

being one (only), you play (the roles of) doer, action and its result.

Therefore, I am not able to offer praises to you.

But, O Sun,[10] my love for you makes my prayer auspicious and real.

For what is there in this world other than You?

(If there were anything else) it would be unreal.

Kṣemarāja in his commentary paraphrases Gopati, a name of the Sun, by "the Lord of the circle of the rays of Consciousness" (cinmarīcicakreśvara), and he bases the entire interpretation on his non-dual philosophy of Consciousness. He ends with the statement: "Thus praise is nothing but the essence of non-duality with You applied as a method" (itham yuktitatvadabhedasāraiva stutiḥ). This is the closest nondual definition of stuti !

Another conscious reflection on the act of praise is contained in verse 48:

kiṃ tannāmoccaratī vacasaṃ yasya noccārakastavaṃ

kiṃ tadvācyaṃ sakalavacasāṃ viśvamūrte na yattvam |

tasmāduktaṃ yadapi tadapi tvannutau bhaktiyogād

asmābhistad bhavatu bhagavaṃstvaprasādena dhanyam||

O You of universal form:

Is there any word uttered whose speaker you are not?

Is there any object of any word that you are not?

Therefore, whatever we utter for your praise out of the union of devotion (to you), may that be a blessing to us, O Lord, by your grace!

The creative tension is clearly one between bhakti and advaita, which are not contrary to each other but supporting or intensifying each other.

Kṣemarāja stresses the fact that the Sun is here called viśvamūrti, implying that he embraces the word and its object (vācyavācaka).

At the end (v.52) the Stotra is called "one that contains within it the spiritual secret" (*stotramadhyātmagarbham*), also in the sense that it leads to the overcoming of all pairs of opposites or dichotomies (e.g. in v. 25).

In Utpaladeva's Śivastotrāvalī we do not find so much a reflection on language and a justification of praise, as in the two examples given earlier. Being in the same philosophical tradition of the unity of Consciousness, the author addresses Śiva as "the essence of consciousness.[11] He expresses the contradictory nature of the Divine that is overcome in an ecstatic experience. He praises the one who is beyond description:

samastalakṣaṇāyoga eva yasyopalakṣaṇam |

tasmai namo'stu devāya kasmaicidapi śambhave ||

May the Lord be glorified,

the mysterious Śambhu,

whose only characteristic is

that he is devoid of all characteristics.

ŚSt II.6

The second Stotra is full of such praises of the Lord as the 'coincidence of opposites', to borrow an expression of Nicolaus Cusanus. The extreme example of these opposites is the world of *saṃsāra* and its transcendence:

saṃsāraikanimittāya saṃsāraika-virodhine |

namaḥ saṃsārarūpāya niḥsaṃsārāya śambhave ||

ŚSt II.8

Glory be to Śambhu

the sole cause of the world

and its only destroyer,

who has taken the form of the world

and who transcends the world.

Such praises demonstrate the limitation of language in approaching the Divine.

Not only the opposite characteristics of the Divine, also the opposite emotions experienced by the *bhakta* are both, included and transcended by praising, in an ecstatic state.

rudanto vā hasanto vā tvām uccaiḥ pralapantyāmī |

bhaktā stutipadoccāropacāraḥ pṛthageva te ||

ŚSt 15.3

Whether weeping or laughing,

they address you in loud delirious speech,

uttering hymns of praise, the devoted

are truly unique attendants.

(transl. Bailly)

Praise or invocation often comes in an ecstatic state, such as:

bhakti kṣīvo'pi kupyeyam bhavāyānuśayiya ca |

tathā haseyaṃ rudyāṃ ca raṭeyaṃ ca śivetyalam ||

ŚST 16.7

Let me be enraged and yet

compassionate toward the world.

And thus in the madness of devotion

may I laugh and weep and chant

Śiva, thunderously. (tr. Bailly)

However, in one verse Utpaladeva is fully conscious of the requirement for praise:

nirvikalpa mahānandapūrṇo yadvadbhavāmstathā |

bhavatstutikarī bhūyād-anurūpaiva vāṅmama ||

ŚSt 6.4

May my speech which utters praises to you

be completely conform to you:

just as you are beyond thought,

and filled with the highest bliss.

Praise is not worthy of its object, the Divine, unless it conforms to it
(*anurūpa*), and hence it already requires a transformation of the one
who praises into the divine nature. How can praise be *nirvikalpa* if it has
to use words and concepts? Both divine characteristics again point at
an ecstatic experience of the mystic struggling to utter in words what is
really inexpressible. Kṣemarāja paraphrases *nirvikalpa* by śuddhacidrūpa,
"of the nature of pure consciousness" (comm. on 6.4).

One last example will illustrate the complete nonduality of the
experience even though he still utters a praise to Śiva:

antarbhakticamatkāra-carvaṇāmīlitekṣaṇaḥ |

namo mahyaṃ śiyāyeti pūjayan syāṃ tṛṇānyapi ||

ŚSt. 5.15

With my eyes closed

relishing the wonder of innermost Love,

may I worship even the blades of grass thus:

'glory to Śiva, to my own Self!'

The most common mantra of praise *Oṃ namaḥ* Śivāya is here applied
in a state of complete non-duality to Śiva, to the Self of the *bhakta*, and
to the whole of creation, represented by blades of grass. Ecstatically,
any possible dichotomy between the worshipper, the Divine, and the
whole of reality is overcome.

In the end we may look at a *stotra* fragment by the great Abhinavagupta
in which he himself analyses the implications of praise. Not by chance
he gives the title of the entire hymn, which unfortunately has not come
down to us, as Śivaśaktyavinābhāvastotra, "the Hymn in praise of the

undivided union of Śiva and Śakti". He quotes the fragment in his commentary on the *Bhagavad Gītā*, an early work.[12]

tava ca kācana na stutirambika

sakalaśabdamayī kila te tanuḥ |

nilkhilamūrtiṣu me bhavadanvayo

manasijāsu bahiṣprasarāsu ca ||

iti vicintya śive Śamitāśive

jagati jātamayatnavaśād idam |

stutijapārcanacintanavarjitā

na khalu kācana kālakalāpi me ||

O Mother! who does not sing your praise

for your body is consisting of all the words!

In all forms, whether mental on manifested externally,

I find my connection with you.

Reflecting thus, a Graceful One (Śivā)

who pacifies all that is inauspicious,

in this world there is not a single moment

that is not spontaneously[13] filled with your praise,

recitation of your name, your worship

and meditation on You.

This quote comes in the context of Abhinavagupta's commentary on *Bhagavad Gītā* 15.19:

He who thus knows Me free from delusion

as the Supreme Person (*puruṣottama*),

he becomes all-knowing and shares in Me

in all states, O Bhārata.

Translating *bhajati* literally as 'having a share or communion' shows the Gītā's approach of *bhakti*, which Abhinavagupta transforms into a nondual interpretation, based on the theory of speech (*Vāc*). In the Trika philosophy all components of speech and sound (śabda implies both) are the body of the divine Energy, and hence at the level of divine recognition ("who know Me") every word uttered is a praise of the Divine. This is obviously a comment on the "in all states" (*sarvabhāvena*) of the verse. The emphasis is on the effortlessness, which is in agreement with the nondualist path of recognition.

In conclusion, the examples presented from the Stotra literature of Kashmir show a dynamic relationship between the duality implied in praise and the ultimate nondualist realization, implying the dynamics of *bhakti* and *advaita*.

Endnotes

[1] This reflection is a heartfelt homage to Fr. Sebastian Painadath, with whom I have a deep and long lasting fraternal connection. We have been travelling a similar path, trying to integrate the mystical treasures of India into Christian spirituality. We have been sharing and teaching fundamental texts such as the Upanishads, and once Utpaladeva's *Úivastotrâvalî*.

[2] The most important being Utpaladeva's *Úivastotrâvalî* and Bhamma NârâyaGa's *StavacintâmaGi*.

[3] Cf. the highly poetical and very popular five hymns of the *Pañcastavî* to the Devî.

[4] The *Sâmbapañcâúikâ* had been integrated into Kashmiri Śaivism when the Sun cult (Saura) vanished as a separate tradition.

[5] Śiva is called here Kapardin.

[6] Wherever the translation by B. Marjanovic is quoted, the page numbers refer to his edition (see References).

[7] Cf. Bettina Bäumer, Sűrya in a Úaiva Perspective: The Sâmbapañcâúikâ, A Mystical Hymn of Kashmir and its Commentary by Kcemarâja, in : Sah[daya, Studies in Indian and South East Asiam Art in Honour of Dr. R. Nagaswamy, ed. by B. Bäumer, R.N. Msra, Chirapat Prapandvidya, D. Handa, Chennai (Tamil Arts Academy), 2006, 1-28.

[8] This verse seems to rely on Bhart[hari's *Vâkyapadîya*, since it mentions only *paúyantî, madhyamâ* and *vaikharî*.

[9] See also the last part of the commentary.

[10] Gopati means also the lord of speech (a Vedic concept).

[11] E.g. 2.1.

[12] See references.

[13] Literally "effortlessly."

The Spirituality of the Upanishads

G. Gispert-Sauch SJ

I feel much honoured to be asked to contribute to a Festschrift in honour of Sebastian Painadath, who today is surely one of the most outstanding Christian scholars of interreligious dialogue and of Indian spiritual traditions. Through his writings, conversations, teaching, research centre and above all through his own personality he has initiated many Christians as well as other seekers into the wealth of Indian spirituality, not only in our country but also abroad. I am particularly happy to accept the request made as he has been extremely kind and supportive of my efforts to think theologically from an Indian perspective. Through this contribution I hope to pay part of my debt to him and also myself learn about the interesting topic assigned to me.

I have been asked to write on "The Spirituality of the Upanishads." The area is vast, but I am given freedom to handle it in the way I think best. I must begin by reminding myself that the Upanishads represent a moment of the Indian reality that integrated many forms of philosophy and spirituality found in the Bhāratvarsha in the lively half millennium before what is for us the common era. Reviewing a book published in 1993 on the Upanishads, the guru of many students, Richard De Smet SJ, regretted that the author had restricted himself to exposing the Upanishads exclusively from the perspective of Sankaracharya: "This may be regrettable, he wrote, since the Upanishads are not a unified system but a corpus of chronologically disparate though allied texts and they would have deserved to be exposed in their own right" (ITS 30/2 (1993) 175, reproduced in Coelho 448).[1]

In fact the Upanishads are a kind of literature that collects reflections on our ancient ancestors elsewhere in Asia around the theme of the sacrificial system, which they brought to the South Asian subcontinent and where it was transformed into the treasure trove of Indian wisdom, even if it is true that at that time this area was not yet called India but Bhāratvarsha. The Upanishads are a literary genre of both integration of the past and transition into a new culture. Established in the subcontinent, the ancient Aryans opened their traditions to different trends of spirituality and reflection they found in India, thus fusing north and south, Aryan and Dravidian, yoga and śaktism, sun worship and the sacred mountain, and whatever they find valuable also in tribal or popular traditions.

It is not too fanciful to see them as emerging in a world similar to ours, where conflicting trends meet in the spiritual agora of the world and influence one another. We too have rich traditions fashioned in East and West, but ours is a new cultural world, a world where geographic borders have softened and a new kind of pluralism emerges, hastened by the digital revolution. Even as collections of ancient texts, the Upanishads are not closed books. Though the oldest and most authoritative ones are those on which the great acharyas commented, there is no clear-cut tradition about their number. We have collections of 'principal Upanishads' that give us the text and/or translations of 12, 13, 14, 18 texts, and in mediaeval traditions we have also 101 Upanishads, appropriate for the vaishnavas, śaivas, śāktas and other trends of India. I am told, but I have never seen, that there is even an Upanishad of Queen Victoria! It is not surprising therefore that the Gujarati spiritual convert to Methodist Christianity, Dhonjibhai Fakirbhai, should have published his meditations of the meaning of his new faith as a *Khristōpanishad,* published fifty years ago in Bangalore (CISRS, 1965). Clearly the Upanishads are really open texts, inviting dialogue.

They are also texts that integrate and fuse many trends. This exercise of opening ourselves to other traditions and enriching ourselves through them, while we share what we have with the 'other', is the characteristic of 'dialogue'. In this sense the traditional Upanishads are eclectic and dialogal. They offer a synthesis of many trends, a synthesis which may be more or less successful. Not surprisingly, therefore, they are today one of the main sources for reflections on east and south Asian thought, not only in India but also in other continents. We could perhaps say that what the Upanishads are for India the later Platonic dialogues are for the European culture. It has been said with much exaggeration that western philosophy is a footnote to Plato: shall we one day discover that the world thought is a footnote to the Upanishads?

The Upanishads emerged from the "Vedas"

I take two starting points for this reflection. First the *terminus a quo* of the Upanishads. De Smet shows well that one aspect of the newness of the Upanishads consists in adopting and establishing a change of perspective regarding *time*. The early pre-Indian speculations had been in great part rooted in the Vedic sacrifice. But unlike the older text, the Brahmanas and the Upanishads were not interested in the ritual performances. Those earlier speculations had interpreted the *sacrificial performance* in ways that went beyond the explanations implicit or explicit of the sacrificial prayers and rituals. These had made clear by whom, to whom and what offerings were made for what purpose. In their explanations the Brahmanas interpreted the rituals by interpreting those rituals and prayers as symbols. Symbols implied interpretation more or less appropriate, and often created new ideas. The concept of time as duration was an important innovation.

In the earliest perception the Aryans had seen time as a frightening, dark foreshadowing of death, *kāla*. Time consisted of a succession of instants each of which could contradict the others and cause mental chaos and anguish. Over twenty years ago de Smet published a brilliant essay with a long title, "Fleeting Time and sacrificially produced continuity in

Vedic Brahmanism and in Early Christianity" (ITS 19/2 [1982] 119-144). Acknowledging his indebtedness to the masterful work of Lilian Silburn, *Instant et cause* (Paris: Vrin, 1955) de Smet shows convincingly, I think, how the sacrifice domesticated the monster of time by introduction the idea of *duration and renewal*. Time now had consistency. If the sun was linked to the perception of time, as it must have been because it marked the succession of morning, noon and evening, and after its demise in the western horizon showed itself renewed and strengthened in the east, the succession of moments had now unity and meaning. The sacrifice followed the rhythm of the sun and of time, with morning, noon and evening oblations, and showed it to be meaningful for human beings as a means to commune with the gods through offering of gifts, in expressions of gratitude, and in an awareness that the gap between their lives and ours could be filled up with proper attitudes. De Smet summarizes his article in his introductory paragraph:

> In the Vedas and Brahmanas, the conception of time is intimately bound to the conception of causality. It begins with ordinary time, time as natural (*prākrta*) and given to us in its fugacious, unorganized and fleeting multiplicity of instants, and therefore as a source of anxiety. But then, through a discovery that shakes off this anxiety, it conceives of constructed (*samskrta*) duration in which discontinuous time is made (*krta*) into a cohesive and continuous totality by the exact concatenation of sacrificial rites. It is only through organizing, constructive (*abhi+sam+kr-*) activities that temporal (and spatial) continuities arise and through many converging and concentrating acts that the datum of scattered, untied time is constituted into a stable and continuous duration. But what engenders synthesizing and purposive acts is thought (*manas*). And it is because duration proceeds from the activity of thought that it transcends organic life and tends in Vedism to culminate into the unlimited untemporality of thought itself (p. 119).

The sacrifice brought to the awareness of the thinkers of that time that the traditional and the innovative personal axes had to be integrated to have a satisfactory outcome. We find in the early sacrificial sutras of that era the mention of the *kratvartha* and *purushārtha*, both concepts important for later Indian thought.

The *kratvartha* tells us that there is an intrinsic purpose inbuilt in the sacrifice: *svarga-kāmo yajeta*, "the one who wants liberation should sacrifice" is the oft-repeated slogan of the Mimamsakas. 'Svarga' etymologically means the 'journey into the light or the sun." In the 9th century Vachaspati Mishra defined *svarga* thus in his *Sāmkhya-Tattva-Kaumudī* ("The moonlight of the Truth of Sāmkhya") 2: *Svargaś ca yan na duhkhēna sambhinnam na ca grastam anantaram / abhilāshopanītam ca tat sukham svahpadāspadam iti / duhkhavirodhī ca sukhaviśeshaś ca svargah //* ("Svarga is the place or state of light where there is a special pleasure obtained just by desiring it and is not mixed with any pain and no interruption is perceived: the very opposite of pain.") I think that this comes close to the idea of St Thomas, based on Aristotle, according to which every creature desire and seeks '*beatitudo*' or happiness and therefore has a right to it as the goal of its existence inset in it by the Creator. Svarga could therefore be translated just as pure 'happiness'.

The *kratvartha* is the purpose (*artha*) for which the 'powerful' sacrifice or offering (*kratu*) exists. It is the intrinsic goal of the institution. The *purusartha* is the purpose for which a person offers the sacrifice. It is proper of the *yajamāna*, the principal offerer, to specify this intention during the sacrifice itself but they will be integrated into intrinsic sacrificial purpose. I believe that the famous prayer *asatō mā sad gamaya, tamasō ma jyōtir gamaya, mrtyōr ma'mrtam gamaya*, mentioned in the Brihad Aranyaka Upanishad 1.3.28 was an expression of this total sacrificial intention of the sacrifices:

> Now next, the praying of the purificatory formulas (*pavamana*).

The Prastotri priest (Praiser), verily begins to praise with the chant (*sāman*). When he begins to praise, let (the sacrifice) mutter the following:

> From the unreal lead me to the Real!
>
> From darkness leand me to Light!
>
> From death lead me to Immortality!

When he says, 'From the unreal lead me to the Real!', —the unreal, verily, is death, the Real is Immortality. 'From death lead me to immortality. Make me immortal!'—that is what he says.

'From darkness lead me to light'—the darkness, verily is death, the Light is immortality. 'From death lead me to Immortality! Make me Immortal'— that is what he says.

'From death lead me to Immortality'—there is nothing there that seems obscure.

In the later tradition this expression of the purushartha was called the *sankalpa* and became more important. In the bhakti tradition sankalpa was applied to the divine will to bring salvation to the one capable of receiving it. One can consult on this the long and tedious, but highly theological mediaeval mystery play composed by Vedanta Desika the *Sankalpa Suryoday*, ("The Sunrise of the Divine-Will [to save]"). One may find a basic information about this text in my article "Grace in the Viśishtādvaita Tradition: The Sankalpa-Suryodayam" in *Divine Grace and Human Response*, ed. by C.M. Vadakkekara. Bangalore: Arisvanam Benedictine Monastery, 1981, pp. 17-50.

I would suggest that this prayer may be interpreted as summing up the need and value of tradition in the struggle for liberation. Individualism is not enough. One needs to count on society and the structures it has evolved, in this case the sacrifice (*kratu*) itself. But the sacrifice is performed by individual persons living in specific times and places. There are therefore specific aims and needs for which people perform the sacrifice. The main function of the yajamana, the Principal Sacrificer, normally not a priest, is to articulate these desires on behalf of the community he (with his wife, often) represents. (See my "Purushārtha and Kratvartha: Freedom and Structure in Ancient India," in Francis D'Sa (ed.), *The Dharma of Jesus: Interdisciplinary Essays in Memory of Fr George Soares-Prabhu, S.J.*, Anand: GSP 1997, 392-407).

Following the trend to a spiritualization of the sacrificial wisdom found already in the Brahmanas, the Upanishads re-read the sacrificial theology as a metaphysical key which was also an anthropological theology. The key word of the Upanishadic thought may be said to be *ānanda*, usually translated as bliss or joy. In the old thinking the sacrifice led us through the regions of the cosmos above the earth (symbolized in the various layers of the sacrificial altar) to the heavenly region where there was ineffable bliss. The older Vedic tradition had visualized joy and happiness in the uppermost region of the Universe, where the sacrifice, like a huge śyena ("falcon") bird flies up with the Sacrificer. The Upanishads placed *ānanda* in the deepest layer of the human being where one could enter the absolute bliss of Brahman. Later the bliss was said to be the fruit of an integration of all the inner drives of the human person: there is a sign of it in the deep sleep, unperturbed by fleeting dreams, when the deepest unity and peace is experienced. It was compared in the Upanishads to the ecstasy at the acme of the integration of man and woman in the sexual union.

In this respect the Upanishads may be seen to offer a spirituality of hope and fulfillment: the beatitude, bliss eternal, is the human destiny and it is available, not really in ritual practices but in spiritual awareness through meditation which presupposes the various yamas and niyamas, personal and cultural 'controls' prescribed in the first two stages of Yoga. I think that these are beautifully prescribed in the book of Sebastian Painadath, *The Power of Silence* (ISPCK, Delhi). Probably this power of integration and of elevating us to the divine realm found in the Upanishads created the faith in the power of *mantras*, the Vedic short sentences that the guru imparts to each disciple individually as a help to grow in the spiritual path towards enlightenment.

The Upanishads point to the Gita

I would like in this last part to look at the Upanishads from the other end, not from their roots in the *older* Vedic lore but in their influence in the later formation of what we now call the Hindu tradition. And I may perhaps look at them primarily in their reference to the Bhagavad Gita, which Sebastian Painadath has made one of the most significant pillars of his life's mission.

Let me begin with the allegory recorded in the *Gītādhyānam*, often printed as introduction in the popular editions of the Gita: "All the Upanisads are cows, milked by the joyous Krishna. Arjuna is the calf. The wise enjoy the milk which is the Immortal nectar of the Gita" (*sarvōpanishadō gāvō, dōgdhā gōpālanandanah / pārtho vatsah sudhīr-bhōktā gītāmrtam mahat*). This metaphor finds its justification in the very name of the *Gītā* which, as we know, forms part of the Mahabharata. In the popular editions of this text each of its 18 chapters ends with a colophon like the following: "This is the first chapter called 'the yoga of the despondency of Arjuna', (found) in the dialogue between the Lord Krishna and Arjuna, (which is) a spiritual treatise (*yoga-śāstra*) in *the upanishads sung* by the Supreme Lord .... in the holy Mahabharata." Unlike what many people may think, the word *Gītā* was originally not a noun, but a feminine past passive participle of the verb to *gai*, to sing, and it agrees with the word *upanishad* which in Sanskrit is a feminine noun. The Gita is thus presented (i) as one among the Upanishads, (ii) as a dialogue and spiritual treatise, and (iii) as 'sung' by the Lord Krishna. It is therefore a divine 'revelation' even if it is a dialogue of several participants: the blind Grandfather Dhritarashtra who only recites the introductory stanza, Sanjaya, the chronicler who connects the various parts of the conversation, the disciple and main hero of the Pandavas, Arjuna, and finally the Lord Krishna who is the speaker in most of the text and the supreme apocalyptic revelation in chapter XI.

The Gita surely shares some of the characteristics in form and concepts found especially in the middle and later Upanishads: it is on the whole theistic, although often read through the advaita lens of Sankara. It stresses the three main paths of salvation of the Indian tradition, the path of action (*karma*), which it explains in an innovative way, the path of knowledge (*jñāna*) that is generally theistically interpreted, and the path of loving devotion (*bhakti*), which it made popular as foundation of the religion for the 'new' India emerging out of Vedism. Bhakti had certainly been found in the old Samhitas and more clearly in a few late Upanishads. But the main stress then had been the sacrificial action and metaphysical knowledge respectively. Now a new form of spirituality was emerging. The Upanishadic tradition opened the gates for the new era. In this it marked a spiritual revolution which would actually take a form which is post-upanishadic.

The spirituality of the Gita is one of *prapatti* as we find in the heart of the theology of Ramanuja. Prapatti literally means the action of coming near, arriving, taking refuse, entering into and obtaining. It comes to mean total surrender to the saving will of God, going beyond the question of our fulfilling of the divine will. The mystery play Sankalpa-suryodaya mentioned earlier is an exposition of the value of the act of pure faith. Its classical mantra is the humble prayer of Arjuna to the Lord Krishna in the Gita 2.7: *sishyas te'ham sādhi mām tvām-prapannam* ("I am your disciple: teach me surrendered to you").

Knowledge and bliss

Before I conclude this short homage to Sebastian, I want to mention two important theological insights which I found in the Upanishads and which I think are fruitful for any theology, certainly for a theology that would incorporate the traditions of our country. First is the awareness of kinds or degrees of knowledge. The human problem is basically one of wrong perception. The original sin is seen as an avidyā that has to be overcome by a deeper perception that can only emerge out of a different experience of the Absolute Mystery. This could eventually lead much of the Indian theological speculation to speak of basically three forms of perceptions: perceptions that are merely sensitive without an inner connection, as we find in our dreams. Though these can cause anxiety and fleeting joys, they obviously do not respond to the reality of the world. By themselves they cannot lead to true moksha. Their negative traits are healed by simply awakening. This puts us with a world we know to be real because it is lasting.

This leaves us with two other degrees, which in the Upanishads are at time called vidyā and avidyā, wisdom and non-wisdom, or at times higher and lower (*parā* and *aparā*) wisdom. Eventually they will develop as pāramārthika and vyāvahārika truths or ways of perception. The Upanishads lead us to seek a new and holistic way of looking at the world, seeing it as one, in spite of the diversity of perceptions. We need to overcome dualities with a higher sense of the unity not only of the human family, not only of the cosmic reality, but even between the Transcendent Absolute or Brahman and the creaturely existence. This new insight would hopefully be the spirituality of the future. I have tried to sketch a comparison of this double truth with the Christian theological concepts of 'eschatological and historical truth' founded on the New Testament's deepest sense of eschatology as seen clearly in St John's writings. (See "Eschatological or Pāramārthika? Challenges and Prospects in the Mission of the Church," in *Seeking New Horizons*, ed. by Leonard Fernando, S.J. Delhi: ISPCK & VIEWS, 2002, pp. 288-302).

More important for me is another theme found also in the Upanishads, the theme of bliss or joy. This may seem surprising to many, as the Upanishads do not seem to produce that sense of euphoria, exaltation or optimism that we find in some forms of bhakti and other trends of spirituality. Have not the Upanishad a rather somber atmosphere, full of anxiety because we have not yet realized the truth of the Self? This may seem to be the case. But the theme of ānanda normally translated as bliss, is an important teaching not only of the Taittirīya Upanishad but also in earlier Upanishads like the Brhadaranyaka Up. See my *Bliss in the Upanishads: An Analytical Study of the Origin and Growth of the Vedic Concept of Ānanda*. New Delhi: Oriental Publishers & Distributors, 1977.

I have at the beginning touched on the theme of *svarga* or 'heaven' found in the Samhitas and the Brahmanas. That heaven is where we hoped to ascend through the sacrificial offerings and songs, or through their substitutes, the inner meditation. What is the characteristic of the Upanishads is that they make of ānanda an essential characteristic of the eternal Brahman and since Brahman is found in the innermost root from which our existence grows, bliss has to be discovered inside us. We have it, we have to bring it to consciousness, because Brahman *is* bliss. This simple idea eventually produced the invocation of the divine as *Sac-cid-ānanda*, popular in India from the middle ages. Naturally many have compared it with the Christian sense of the Divine Trinity. Though there is no equivalence between the two 'trinities' there is a certain analogy between the two, as theologians, both Hindu and Christians, have often shown.

The one that expressed it most beautifully is Brahmabandhab Upadhyay (1869-1907), the Bengali convert that has been considered the father of an Indian Catholic theology. His Christian "Ode to the Trinity," in Sanskrit easily understood by speakers of north-Indian languages, has been often commented upon in several languages and is still in use in Catholic worship. What interests me more is the discovery that the Spirit is God's own and eternal Bliss. I developed more fully this *bandhutā* or 'correspondence' in "Ānanda, Hedonê and the Holy Spirit" in *Indica* (Mumbai) 16, pp. 82-102. Three of the great theologians in the New Testament give witness to a special relation of the Holy Spirit and joy: Luke, of course, but also Paul and John. I cannot summarise here the evidence, but what comes out of it is that the Spirit, precisely because She is the mutual Love of Father and Son, is also the Eternal Bliss of God. It is into this Bliss that the Lord invites the servants, high or low, to "enter into the joy of the master" (*eiselthe eis tên charan tou kyriou sou*) (Mt 25:21.23). I would think that in the same chapter Matthew hints that this joyful outcome of the human undertaking is the result of not only 'understanding' the unity of being, but of living it effectively by sharing of what we have with the hungry, the thirsty, the naked, the lonely and in general the needy. Bliss is the fruit of love lived in truth. We may find here solid ground for an Indian theology of liberation. In the measure in which we are *one with* humanity, especially the marginalized in history, in that measure we discover ourselves as carriers of a divine bliss. In the Vedic sources bliss is seen as the innermost core or *kośa* of the human reality, when it is in touch with the divine and has achieved total spiritual and physical integration. Now we realize that this is not merely a matter of personal unity, but of the oneness with the cosmos by a realistic love that excludes no one. Bliss leads us to love the other, love leads to the ultimate Ānanda.

Endnotes

[1] Ivo Coelho, ed., *Understandking Sankara.* Delhi: Motilal Banarsidass Publ. 2013.

"Be still and know that I am God"
(Psalm 46:10)

AMA Samy SJ

Silence is the source and ground from which words spring forth. The Eternal Father is silence, dwelling in light inaccessible. The Word leaps forth from the silence of the Father into the world. Actually, silence and word are the front and the back of reality; they are not-two and not-one. Christianity, however, is said to be a religion of word, whereas Buddhism is said to be centered on silence. The Buddhist meditation, as well as the Zen meditation, is grounded in silence and mindfulness.

There is a story of a non-Buddhist philosopher asking the Buddha, "I do not ask for words; I do not ask for non-words." The World-honoured One remained silent for a while. The philosopher said admiringly, "The World-honoured One, in his great mercy, has blown away the clouds of my illusion and enabled me to enter the Way."[1]

The Buddha is famous for his refusal to answer metaphysical questions. These ten are said to be not answered by the Buddha.[2]

1. The world is eternal.

2. The world is not eternal.

3. The world is (spatially) infinite.

4. The world is not (spatially) infinite.

5. The soul (*jiva*) is identical with the body.

6. The soul is not identical with the body.

7. The Tathagata (a perfectly enlightened being) exists after death.

8. The Tathagata does not exist after death.

9. The Tathagata both exists and does not exist after death.

10. The Tathagata neither exists nor does not exist after death.

The Buddha said that he taught only what was conducive to liberation and *nibbana*, and not what would lead to vain speculation: "As the great ocean has only one taste, the taste of salt, so my teachings have only one flavour, the flavour of emancipation."

St. Paul writes after his ecstasy: "No eye has seen, nor ear heard, nor the heart of man conceived" (I Cor. 2:9). In Christian theology and spirituality there is from the beginning the apophatic way which points to the ineffable and incomprehensible mystery of God which transcends the human mind and can be approached only by silent love of the heart. It is said of the great theologian Thomas Aquinas that when celebrating Mass, he received a revelation that so affected him that he wrote and dictated no more, leaving his great work the *Summa Theologiae* unfinished. When Brother Reginald requested him to return to writing, Aquinas said, "I can write no more. I have seen things that make my writings like straw."

Karl Rahner is a theologian who articulated his theology on the basis of the incomprehensible mystery of God. "…our theological assertions descend into the silent incomprehensibility of God's very self. Our theoretical statements then share the same existential destiny as we do, namely, that of a loving, trusting self-surrender to the unfathomable reign of God, to God's merciful judgment and sacred incomprehensibility."[3]

The Zen meditation is grounded in silence and stillness. It is the silence in the face of the incomprehensible mystery of self and of reality. Zen is not against words, language and thought. Actually, there is no zen without language! Words and silence go together; they are like the flesh and bones of what it is to be human. But one has to go beyond words and language and thus discourse freely in language and words. What zen abhors is making idols of the images of reality and of self and worshipping at their altars. Zen abhors the vain attempts to formulate, explain, comprehend and try to fix reality and self. Such attempts are nothing but idolatrous craving for self-identity and security. Silence is often the renunciation of such craving. Silence bares one's skin, bones, flesh and marrow. Bodhidharma, the Indian Patriarch who is said to be the founder of zen in China, meditated in utter silence for nine years. In the following story, Bodhidharma tests, as well as confirms, the enlightenment of his four disciples. It seems that the silence of Hui-k'o (Eno in Japanese) shows the highest attainment:

Nine years had passed and Bodhidharma now wished to return westward to India. He called his disciples and said: "The time has now come. Why doesn't each of you say what you have attained?" Then the disciple Tao-fu replied: "As I see it, the truth neither adheres to words or letters, nor is it apart from them. It functions as the Way." The master said: "You have attained my skin." A nun Tsung-chi'ih said: "As I understand it, the truth is like the auspicious glimpse of the Buddha land of Akshobhya; it is seen once, but not a second time." The master said: "You have attained my flesh." Tao-yu said: "The four great elements are originally empty; the five skandhas have no existence. As I believe, no Dharma can be grasped." The master said: "You have attained my bones." Finally, there was Hui-k'o. He bowed respectfully and stood silent. The master said: "You have attained my marrow."[4]

There are many kinds of silence—silence before the incomprehensible mystery of reality, silence of voluntary asceticism, silence of ignorance, silence of anger and resentment, etc. The saving silence is silence in the face of mystery. Gabriel Marcel makes the distinction between mystery and problem. Problems can be solved; at least they are amenable to a solution; mystery by its nature cannot be solved by reason. God and self are mysteries; they will remain a mystery all the time. Reality is mystery, mystery that is graciousness. It is by participation in this mystery that the self attains salvation. The Zen meditation is in terms of abiding in this mystery that is graciousness. In facing the mystery in silence, the self is transformed, liberated and redeemed. True silence is being without egoism; it is being selfless; and it lets the other be other, and lets self be self. It is utter simplicity and openness of compassion.

Authentic and true silence is to abide in one's own home-ground of the Self which is the Mystery of the Buddha-Mind:

"The eighteenth patriarch was Venerable Gayashata. He served the Venerable Sanghanandi. One time, he heard the sound of the wind blowing the bronze bells in the temple. The Venerable Sanghanandi asked the master, "Are the bells ringing or is the wind ringing?" The master replied, "It is neither the bells nor the wind; it is my Mind that is ringing." The Venerable Sanghanandi asked, "And who is the Mind?" The master replied, "Because both are silent. "The Venerable Sanghanandi said, "Excellent, excellent! Who but you will succeed to my Way?"[5]

To the question, "What is the Buddha?" one master asked in reply, "Who are you?" The question about ultimate reality or God or Buddha is about oneself. The question probes one's own heart and exposes one's desires and passions and intents. One faces oneself, is thrown upon oneself. The questioner comes to a crisis, the question has become the questioner. Yet in our relationships as well as in our search for truth, we are more often than not caught in endless games and manipulations- in argumentativeness, defensiveness, blaming, excusing, explaining away, stonewalling, resenting, double-speak, evasions, etc.- it is all about the "games people play." Our silences can be part of this game-silence out of resentment, anger, fear, ignorance, cowardice, manipulation and so on. However, sticking too much to clarity is another ego game. And we can be caught in and carried away by beliefs, pre-judgments, views, ideas or ideologies. These become matters of our identity and security. But life is full of ambiguities and uncertainties. We cannot have certitudes as regards the ultimate reality, but we can have insight and understanding; and freedom and peace; and compassion. We attain to this so-called 'second innocence' after our old worlds have been shattered and our ego selves are silenced and we are born anew from true silence, from Emptiness, as zen proclaims. Silence born of love and wisdom is creative and life-giving; it falls as gentle rain and flowers bloom, children smile, and earth becomes fragrant; such silence is divine.

There is a touching story by a rabbi and psychotherapist, Howard Cooper narrated in the article, "The Therapist and the Suffering Servant."[6] In the story, the therapist is confronted by the profound silence of the 'patient,' which probes his heart and exposes his nakedness, strips him of his rationalizations and manipulations, lets him fall into a dark abyss, and thus leads him to release and liberation. Let me quote parts of the story, though in this fashion it may lose its beauty:

> The therapist opens the door of his office in order to leave; there he finds a gaunt, tall man standing and waiting for him. "But now, that first time, he just stood there, passively, waiting. Waiting for me, it seemed. How long had he been there? What did he want? How could I get rid of him? These were my first thoughts. Later I asked another question, simpler still: who was he?" The man provoked disgust in the therapist. But perhaps he was a poor devil, lost and suffering intolerably. Well, the therapist will have pity on him, help him, save him from his misery. He brought him in, had him seated, and sat there facing him for long, waiting for some words from the man. For so long there wasno words. "Silence. No words. No movement. No restlessness. No nervousness. Nothing. Just his look, steadily piercing me through. I felt uncomfortable. This was strange. I didn't understand why I couldn't look at him, but I felt that if I looked something terrible might happen—a glass shattering into a thousand pieces. I knew he was looking at me. I felt I was being observed from a great distance, and at the same time he was much too close for comfort. I shrank into my chair, hugging its sides, wanting to disappear. I was being seen. I began to feel I was being seen through." The therapist was becoming restless, feeling helpless, inadequate, useless. "It must be hard," he said to the man, "to have come here for help, to talk, yet be unable to speak." Nothing. Silence.

> The therapist formed many hypotheses in order to understand the man. Perhaps it was pure defiance; fear of rejection; passive-aggressivity, and so on and on. And then the therapist began getting angry, wanted to hurt the man, attack him, throw him out. But he was the therapist to help people out. "In my head I shouted at him: 'What do you want with me?

For God's sake tell me what's wrong. You're suffering. I can feel it. I can feel your suffering. You're in pain. Admit it. You're a joke, a sick joke. God must have been looking the other way when he made you, friend.'" Still silence. It was becoming unbearable. The therapist was confused, not knowing even his own role and identity, scared witless. "He was here with me—and forever beyond my grasp. Unreachable. All I had was his silent presence. And out of the midst of his silence he was looking at me and I was seeing my suffering and my pain. And my lack of worth. As if he was a mirror. In him I saw myself: weighed down with suffering, burdened with pain. H was carrying them for me.'"

The therapist reviews how he usually goes through the lives of the patients with them. He can usually relive his own wounds and get healed; and help heal the wounds of the patient. But no, the therapist is not now thinking of healing the pain of the man. "I felt his silence was oppressing me, almost attacking me, inviting me to add to his humiliation, crush him even further, like an insect, like a vermin. It felt that, perversely, this *untermensch* actually wanted my aggression…Silence was his way of showing me my own darker instincts, my own hatred and violence, my own wish to destroy, to murder, to annihilate him." Still silence. "The session must come to an end. There is no hope here. This one is beyond help. I too am beyond help. We are all beyond help…this had to end now. He had to go. Then I wouldn't have to answer any more questions. I had been destroyed. It was not that I had failed him. It was much worse: I was a failure. I was faced with the meaninglessness of everything I had believed. I was faced with my own helplessness. I could do nothing. There was not even an 'I'. There was just the hurt.'"

"Suddenly the ground seemed to give way beneath me, and I was being buried alive. I found myself in quite another region. The loneliness of the human soul is unendurable…I understood that it was not that he was sick, but me. His silence had come to make me whole. The pain and the suffering I saw in him could heal me. His refusal to make verbal contact with me was deeper form of communication than I had realized. He was saying that in human relations one should penetrate to the core of loneliness in each person and speak to that." And for the first time, the therapist saw the man as he was. He had projected onto him everything. He had come to show the therapist his inner horrors, loneliness, powerlessness, darkness, destructiveness, shame and worthlessness. "And they were his story, his suffering. But they were also my story, our text, our suffering. We face our darkness if we dare."

"I looked away toward the window. Everything had suddenly changed. The window was wide open. There were no bars on it. This room, this world, was no prison.... A pair of swallows were feeding their young. It was a miracle of beauty: real, eternal and simple."

In response to the monk Vaccagotta's question about the after-death existence of the Arhat (saint) the Buddha rejects as inapplicable the entire range of possible answers in terms of which the question was posed:

"The saint, O Vaccha, who has been released, is deep, immeasurable, unfathomable, like the mighty ocean. To say that he is reborn would not fit the case. To say that he is not reborn would not fit the case. To say that he is both reborn and not reborn would not fit the case. To say that he is neither reborn nor not reborn would not fit the case."[7]

Vaccha then expresses his bewilderment and disappointment, and the Buddha responds, 'You ought to be at a loss, Vaccha, you ought to be bewildered. For Vaccha, this dhamma is deep, difficult to see, difficult to understand, peaceful, excellent, beyond dialectics, subtle, intelligible to the wise...' It is misleading to say that after death the Tathagata-that is, the fully enlightened individual that we know in this life-exists, or does not exist, or both exists and does not exist, or neither exists nor non-exists beyond this life. The Buddha then illustrates the idea of a question which is so put that it has no answer by speaking of a flame that has been quenched. In which direction has the flame gone-east, west, north or south? None of the permitted answers applies. Likewise, what happens after the bodily death of a Tathagata cannot be expressed in our available categories of thought. For the analogy of the quenched flame is not intended to indicate one particular answer, namely nonexistence. For 'Freed from denotation by consciousness', Gautama says, "is the Tathagata, Vaccha, he is deep, immeasurable, unfathomable as is the great ocean."[8]

The ultimate reality we are seeking, and questing cannot be comprehended in concepts and ideas. Silence is the doorway into the mystery of the ultimate reality and its realization. Awakening to the ultimate reality is realization; it is not some vision or feeling or experience. Once awakened, one comes to abide in the mystery:

> Thus, have I heard: The Exalted One was once staying near Savatthi, in the Deer Park. Then the Venerable Radha came to the Exalted One. Having done so, he saluted the Exalted One and sat down to one side. So seated, the Venerable Radha thus addressed the Exalted One:
>
> "They say, 'Mara! Mara!' Lord. Pray, Lord, how far is there Mara?"
>
> "Where a body is, Radha, there would be Mara or things like Mara, or at any rate what is perishing. Therefore, Radha, regard the body as Mara; regard it as of the nature of Mara; regard it as perishing, as an imposthume, as a dart, as pain, as a source of pain. They who regard it thus rightly regard it. And the same is to be said of feeling, perception, the activities and consciousness."
>
> "But rightly regarding, Lord, for what purpose?"
>
> "Rightly regarding, Radha, for the sake of disgust."
>
> "Disgust, Lord, for what purpose is it?"
>
> "Disgust, Radha, is to bring about dispassion."
>
> "But dispassion, Lord, for what purpose is it?"
>
> "Dispassion, Radha, is to get release."
>
> "But release, Lord, what is it for?"
>
> "Release, Radha, means Nibbana."
>
> "But Nibbana, Lord, what is the aim of that?"
>
> "This question, Radha, goes too far. You can grasp no limit to the question.
>
> Rooted in Nibbana, Radha, the holy life is lived. Nibbana is its goal. Nibbana is its end."[9]

The Buddha tells Radha, 'This question, Radha, goes too far. You can grasp no limit to the question.' The question reaches its limit and falls into silence. However, the question is not false or absurd. We question truly only when the mysterious has stirred within our bosoms. The question leads one to be touched and wounded by the mysterious and the unknowable. The Absolute breaks open our finite hearts and minds and the questioning mind vanishes into silence, humility, wonder and reverence. The Biblical Job, after his long struggle and questioning God, finally comes to the confession: "I have dealt with great things I do not understand; things too wonderful for me, which I cannot know. I had heard of you by word of mouth, but now my eye has seen you. Therefore, I disown what I have said, and repent in dust and ashes." (Job 42: 3-6)

Thomas Merton had an awakening when he saw the faces of the Buddha at Polonnaruwa, Sri Lanka. He captures in words something of the Wisdom of the Buddha, of the Prajna Paramita, 'the wisdom that has gone beyond': "Then the silence of the extraordinary faces. The great smiles. Huge and yet subtle, filled with every possibility, questioning nothing, knowing everything, rejecting nothing, the peace not of emotional resignation but of Madhyamika, of sunyata, that has seen through every question without trying to discredit anyone or anything-without refutation, without establishing some other argument."[10]

When the future Zen master Fa-Yen felt driven into a *sackgasse* and implored Master Wanshi Shogaku to show him a way out, the master said, "The Reality has no definite aspect of its own; it reveals itself in accordance with things. The Wisdom has no definite knowledge of its own; it illumines in response to situations. Look! The green bamboo is so serenely green; the yellow flower so profusely yellow! Just pick up anything you like and see! In everything It is so nakedly manifested."[11](Izutsu)

It is said that during the Buddha's forty-five years of preaching, he uttered not a single word: it means that all his preaching welled up selflessly from the depths of his silence out of compassion. The hallmark of emancipation and the true attainment of non-duality will be a life of compassion. The layman and bodhisattva Vimalakirti are lying sick and when asked why he is sick, he says: "Because all living beings are sick, therefore I am sick. If all living beings are relieved of sickness, then my sickness will be mended. Why? Because the bodhisattva for the sake of living beings enters the realm of birth and death, and because he/she is in the realm of birth and death, he/she suffers illness. If living beings can gain release from illness, then the bodhisattva will no longer be ill."

Setcho's verse to the case (84) of Vimalakirti in Blue Cliff Record reads:

> You foolish Vimalakirti
>
> Sorrowful for sentient beings,
>
> You lie sick in Vaishali,
>
> Your body all withered up.

In the silent practice of zazen we enter into the Mystery that is graciousness; entering into the Mystery, our heart-mind is awakened and transformed into the heart-mind of compassion.

Endnotes

[1] Blue Cliff Records, Case No. 65

[2] Suttas 63 and 72 of the Majjhima Nikaya.

[3] *Cambridge Companion to Karl Rahner*, .299.

[4] Henrich Dumoulin , *Zen Buddhism*, Vol.I, New York: Macmillan, 1988.

[5] Dojun Cook, (trans) *Zen Master Keizan's Denkoroku*, Wisdom Publications, 2003.

[6] *Cross Currents*, (Winter 1992-93). It is also the process of zen meditation in silence as well as in interaction with the zen master.

[7] Majjhima Nikaya: Aggivacchagotta Sutta

[8] John Hick, "The Buddha's 'Undetermined Questions" and the Religions, http://www.johnhick.org.uk/article8.html

[9] Samyutta Nikaya: Radhasamyutta Sutta

[10] The Asian journal of Thomas.

[11] Izutsu, *Towards a Philosophy of Zen Buddhism*, Shambala.

Christian Notions of Forgiveness and Reconciliation and their Buddhist Homologues

Aloysius Pieris SJ

It is claimed that reconciliation and forgiveness are Christian inventions and have no Buddhist parallels. We grant that there are distinctive words which a particular religion invents and which are not easily admissible or translatable in another. Religions constitute distinctive *paradigms* and certain words do not mean the same when transferred from one paradigm to another. In football we do not score runs and in cricket we do not kick goals. But runs and goals fulfill a similar purpose in both games. Thus kicking goals is the soccer player's *homologue* for the cricketer's scoring runs. Similarly there are *homologues* (as opposed to 'equivalents') to be recognized in any inter-religious discourse that respects the non-negotiable differences between religions.

For instance "conscience" is thought to have no equivalent in Buddhism. *Hṛdayasak@iya* is regarded as a neologism created by Christian missionaries. Buddhists do, however, speak of *hiri-otappa* in Pali, translated into Sinhala as *lajjā-bhaya*. Lajjā is a sense of shame that prevents us from doing wrong and *bhaya* is the fear of social censure which too could act as a deterrent. The Buddha refers to them as the two *loka-pālakā*, literally "world-rulers" and idiomatically "the censors of human behaviour". Here *hiri* or *lajjā* (in its restrictive sense of "internal censor" as explained above) could be a Buddhist *homologue* for what Christians mean by conscience. I am grateful to Prof. Dr Asangha Tillekeratna for suggesting a much closer Buddhist homologue for "conscience" in the Pali phrase *attānuvāda-bhaya* (the fear of one's own reproach).

Christians should apply this principle also to the notions of "forgiveness" and "reconciliation" and look for their *homologues* in Buddhism. The *purpose* of such a search is to foster an inter-religious praxis in the resolution of social conflicts that occur and have occurred in our pluralistic society. The theoretical clarification offered here is only a small initial step on that long road to peace.

Revenge: The opposite of forgiveness

The Christian notion of forgiveness sharpens its contours when contrasted with *vengeance,* which is its opposite. For there are cultures in which vengeance is justified. In feudal societies a member of the nobility, whose feudal pride is hurt by another, challenges the latter to a duel that necessarily ends up in the death of one's of them. This is known as "avenging one's honour" —a euphemism for revenge.

But the Law of Retaliation (*lex talionis*), which the Bible has borrowed from Middle Eastern cultures of the time, does not come under that category. The ancient principle of love and justice revealed in the OT (in the "The Law and the Prophets", as Jesus puts it), namely "Treat others the way you want others to treat you" (Mt 7:12), seems to have been operative in the law that stipulates "eye for an eye, tooth for a tooth… life for life… etc."(Ex 21:23-25). He who plucks someone else's eye would have to endure what he had inflicted on the other. This law was not only a deterrent against violent anti-social behavior but also a preventive measure taken against inflicting a punishment that *exceeds* the damage incurred by the victim; furthermore, it was a time-honoured custom not to allow the victim to indulge in a personal vendetta but have justice done through *a court of law* —not unlike the *lex talionis* ("life for a life"!) applied in the case of capital punishment in our own times. But there seems to be no evidence that the law of retaliation was advocated as the dominant principle of justice among the ancient Jews; the very opposite prevailed in the teachings of the OT, as I am about to demonstrate.

The OT of the Bible reveals that the Oppressed (who are God's covenant partners) when deprived of *justice and equity* consider themselves entitled to appeal to their Divine Ally for intervention! Thus more than 40 of the 150 psalms in the Bible register the helpless victims of injustice venting their grievances before *their* God, calling for divine 'vengeance' upon their oppressors. But the Hebrew verbal form *nqm*, often over-translated as vengeance, actually points to God's *just intervention* as required by God's defense pact with all the oppressed of the earth. The Bible, therefore, repeats with great frequency and consistency that vengeance or more accurately, retribution is *not our business* (Det. 32:35; Prov. 20:22; 24:29; cf. Rom 12:19) *but what God does in God's good time* (Gen 4:15;Prov. 6:34; Is 34:8, 35:4, 63:4; Jer. 11:20; 50:15,28; 51:6;56:11; Ezek 25:17; Nah1:2). Hence God's People are explicitly forbidden to take revenge on one's enemy (Lev.19: 16-18) but are exhorted to treat even the enemy's ox and donkey with kindness (Ex 23:4-5)!

In the NT, Jesus Christ builds on these OT teachings, and demands that we put no limits to love. The Law of Retaliation, even as a mere legal safeguard makes no sense to him:- "You have heard it said [in popular lore, not in OT] 'love your neighbor and hate your enemy.' But I say to you, love your enemies and pray for those who persecute you, so that you may be children of your Father in heaven" who lovingly takes care of the good and wicked alike (Mt 5:43-45). "God's forgiveness" (a Christian synonym for "salvation") is not possible for those who cannot forgive others who have sinned against them (Mt. 6:14). Hence the salvific imperative of loving one's neighbor necessarily includes *forgiveness of and reconciliation with one's enemies*, which moreover is the hallmark of Christian discipleship (Mt 5:46-48).

Forgiveness in Christianity and Buddhism

"Forgiveness" is such a common human experience that it is very strange to hear it said that it has no parallel in the Buddhist vocabulary. On the other hand there could be some basis for this negative view because Christians believe that God can forgive sins that we commit against others (i.e., humans) because God, as revealed in the person of Jesus Christ, identifies God-self with all humans, specially the victims of neglect and oppression, who are, therefore, declared to be His "Me", or *His own body,* which means in the Hebrew idiom, *His own person*; hence all sins we commit against our neighbours are sins against Christ's own divine Self. This view of divinity and divine forgiveness is not only absent but is outright rejected in Buddhism. But forgiveness sought and given among humans falls into quite another category and it is this notion of forgiveness that we are discussing here.

In popular Buddhism we have the concept of *abhaya-dāna.* The literal meaning of *abhaya* is "no fear"; *dāna* means "giving". Hence *abhaya-dāna* means "offering amnesty". The offended party tells the offender not to live in fear of being avenged. It is an act of reconciliation consisting of the suspension of a penalty due to a crime. Note, however, that the cancellation of a penalty is not necessarily a cancellation of the guilt; for the criminal is not, thereby, exempt from *karma-vipāka* (suffering the consequence of sin in this or the next life). Hence the *abhaya-mudrā* ("fear-not gesture") of the Buddha does not mean that he is forgiving people's sins (as often misinterpreted by some Christians); rather, it is his declaration, "Fear not (*a-bhaya*) because I have found the escape from this dreadful existence".

Another word for forgiveness is *samāva,* directly derived from Sanskrit *kṣamā* (root *kṣam-*) which denotes "tolerance", "patience", "endurance" and "forbearance"; and it is the notion of *forbearance* that allows *kṣamā* to be employed as a synonym for "forgiveness". In fact, the causative of this same verb, i.e., *kṣāmayati* — "cause [the offended one] to forgive [the offender]" is the Sanskrit term for "asking for forgiveness". It is from this same Sanskrit root *kṣam-* the we derive the noun *kṣānti* which stands for one of the ten perfections (*pāramitā*) practiced by a Bodhisattva, namely, the perfection of extreme patience or forbearance.

While *kṣamā* would come close to forgiveness as understood by Christians, its cognate noun *kṣanti* seems to connote stoic indifference to pain as practiced by a Bodhisattva, a candidate to Buddhahood. Hence the true Buddhist homologue for forgiveness is not *kṣanti* but the state of *adosa* (*adveṣa* in Sanskrit or *avera* (*avaira* in Sanskrit), which constitutes the Nirvanic freedom of a Buddha. For Nirvana is referred to as *arāga, adosa and amoha*. Here again *adosa (avera)* is *the offended person's total freedom from hatred even towards his or her own offenders*. It is the Buddhist homologue of Christianity's forgiving love.

But there is a snag here. Though Buddhists and Christians could come to some agreement about the "notion of forgiveness", as demonstrated above, there is, however, a huge difference in the "doctrine of forgiveness" that each religion upholds and teaches. As already explained, Theravada Buddhism insists that one's *akusala-karma-vipāka* (consequences one's sins) cannot be cancelled by the one who forgives the perpetrator of such sins, even if the forgiver is the Buddha. One may forgive my sins, but despite my sincere repentance, I am bound to expiate them in this or another life. Even when I forgive my enemy, it is I who do a meritorious deed and gain some footage in the Samsaric roaming; not the other, who has to pay for his or her crime either here or hereafter. Hence in Theravada Buddhism a sin that is forgiven is not necessarily a sin that is expiated. In Christianity, by contrast, forgiveness given by the offended person is forgiveness received by a *repentant* offender; that is to say, I can absolve the sin of my enemy by forgiving him or her unconditionally on my part, though on his or her part *repentance* is a pre-requisite.

Hence this conclusion:- Despite the aforementioned doctrinal difference, forgiveness, in both religions, constitute "a state of non-hatred" (*avera, adosa*), which, as suggested above, is the Buddhist homologue of Christianity's "forgiving love." In both religions it is regarded as a salvific experience.

In the Ubuntu tribe as well as in Christianity in South Africa, the offended party's forgiveness would relieve the offender of his or her sin provided the offender confessed it and expressed repentance. Non-forgiven sins even among two members of a community are regarded as a cancer damaging both tribal and Christian societies. This is the principle operative in the Truth and Reconciliation Commission. It was not a blanket pardon offered to criminals, for that would have had a disruptive effect on civil society. Rather it was an effective agent of *reconciliation* between the offender, who acknowledges his or her sin in a mood of repentance, and the offended one who responds with unstinted forgiveness. If forgiveness must be given even when unasked, as taught in both religions, how can it be refused when a repentant offender pleads for it?

There is post-script to this discussion: In our culture too *abhayadāna* as well as *kṣamā* or *adosa* (*adveṣa*) is usually an initiative of the offended person. A problem arises, however, from the fact that the offended party who offers amnesty (*abhaya, kṣam*) is usually a powerful person such as a King. What if the offended party is powerless? What if the Whites had come to power in South Africa? The answer to this question is vital for anyone engaged in the the mission of reconciliation.

Reconciliation in Christianity and Buddhism

"Reconciliation" seems at first sight an elusive word even in Christianity. It occurs about four times in the Second Book of Maccabees (an apocryphal or deutero-canonical book of the Old testament, not accepted as an inspired book by many Churches); there, it points to a *removal of estrangement between two parties*, in this case, between God (the offended) and sinner (the offender). But in these texts ((2 Mac. 1:5; 5:20; 7:33; 9:20) the human *offenders* take the initiative by making reconciliatory acts (such as, for instance, prayers, fasts, sacrifices and other forms of worship) to win back God's favour. This theory, though occurring in a biblical source accepted as canonical by some Churches, would seem heretical (or anti-biblical) to Orthodox Jews and Christians in general, who taught and believed that offenders or sinners cannot *ritually* manipulate, or bribe God into reconciliation —as was the custom among the so-called "gentiles" (those who did not recognize the God of Israel). Hence in the New Testament this 'heresy' of the Macabees —that sinners could reconcile themselves with God through acts of ritual worship, prayers and penances— is corrected by Paul who reiterates that God, the offended Person, is the one who forgives and thus reconciles the offenders with Godself, and does so gratuitously, i.e., with no conditions laid on the offenders except genuine *repentance* (Rom 5:10-11; 11:15; 2 C 5: 18-20; Col 1:20-22; Eph 2:16). Penances such as sack cloths and fasts are only a *sign of repentance* and *not the cause of forgiveness* (Ezra 10:1; 2K 22:19; Jonah 3:6-10).

In fact the Biblical God (YHWH) refuses to be reconciled by rites and rituals, and instead demands *justice to the victims of oppression* as the only true *worship* that pleases the Divine Self. This is stated with clarity and frequency in the Prophetic literature of the Bible ((Is 1:11-17; Jer. 7:1-15; Amos 5:21-24). For the God of the Bible, so to say, 'defines' God-self as the [only ?] God who joins the oppressed slaves in their struggle for freedom from slavery and oppression: "I am the God who delivered you from the house of [Egyptian] bondage, and therefore have no other gods before me" (Ex. 20:3). Therefore any person or a political system (such as the empires of Egypt, Babylon. Assyria) that flourished on the exploited labour of slaves became the target of God's severe criticism and ruthless intervention. For God is revealed in the Bible as the One who has signed a covenant (i.e. a defense pact, so to say) with the oppressed and the victims of injustice. Therefore authentic worship of *God,* as Jesus proved by life and example, requires that those rejected and marginalized be *re-integrated to* (i.e., "reconciled" with) the society. Hence *inter-human* reconciliation is demanded by Jesus as a pre-requisite for authentic worship of God, for he has emphatically declared that without reconciling oneself with the estranged person, one should not take part in divine worship (Mt 5:23-24). Without inter-human reconciliation there can never be a worship acceptable to the God of the Bible.

Among the believers, who are exhorted by Jesus to be "as merciful as" God (Lk 6:46), the divine example of the offended person taking the initiative in reconciliation must become the norm. It goes without saying that an offender's request for forgiveness makes it even easier for the offended person to effect a reconciliation. It is pre-requisite for salvation. Buddhism teaches that *adosa* or *avera* (total absence or eradication of ill-will even towards enemies) is a state of ultimate liberation, which, I repeat, is imperative on Christians too as a means of final salvation. The same, however, cannot be said in the case of *paṭisāraṇīya* in the Vinaya, (as some scholars have mistakenly suggested); for it is an ecclesiastical or canonical imposition by which a monk is made to ask pardon from a layperson whom he (the monk) had offended. But *adosa* / *avera*, on the other hand, is not a submission to a legal injunction but the experience of Nirvana. The former should not be confused with the latter.

Jesus was misunderstood and even criticized for reconciling a certain category of people who were *socially stigmatized as public sinners*. For such "sinners" were themselves victims of sinful (socio-economic and politico-religious) structures. Here reconciliation assumes a socio-political guise, since the target of Jesus' reformative discourse are those unjust structures as well those responsible for creating them. For instance,

(a) *Women prostitutes* in general belong to this category. Jesus, who opposed the patriarchal society that ostracized them, would convert them and reconcile them back to the new society of love ("Reign of God") which he was inaugurating as an alternative to the unjust "system" that would first *create* such public sinners and then *condemn* them !

(b) So were the *tax-collectors* or "publicans" who were hated by Jesus' contemporaries because, as the employees of the Temple Authorities, they extracted heavy levies from the masses. Jesus knew that the Romans obliged the Temple Administration (which was Israel's judiciary, its legislature, the executive and the Central Bank all in one!) to collect the taxes for the Romans. The temple in its turn wanted the tax-collectors to help in raising that money due to their Roman masters *plus* the revenue for the Temple. The tax collectors had to earn their own living by collecting more than what the Temple extracted through their services. So the ordinary folk saw villains in the Tax-Collectors, who had to earn their own living over and above what they had to collect for the Temple. Jesus saw the villain in the Temple Administration, which was the unjust system that made the Tax-collectors extract such huge levies and occasioned their dishonest activities. Jesus accepted the publicans (as the tax-collectors were known to be) into his company and attacked the evil system established by the politico- religious leadership; he did so not only by denouncing the system verbally but also physically driving out those who were doing business in the Temple.

(c) Some criminals, too, are creations of a *socially unjust economic system*, such as for instance, the repentant bandit whom Jesus, even while being murdered on the cross, reconciled to himself by offering forgiveness. The society or a country which witnesses an escalation of uncontrolled violence constitutes an unjust socio-political system that manufactures bandits. Jesus' compassionate and *reconciliatory* approach to the victims of a nefarious socio-political system —such victims as prostitutes, tax-collectors and that murderous bandit— and his uncompromisingly condemnatory posture taken towards the sinful social structure that produces anti-social elements was continuous with the consistent policy of the God of Jewish scriptures.

Hence it follows that the Biblico-Christian teaching on reconciliation imposes on the Christians the obligation to struggle non-violently for the transformation of unjust social structures.

Debt Cancellation

"Debt Cancellation" is another Biblical synonym for reconciliation and forgiveness. Originally it was the Sabbath law demanding that all debts be cancelled periodically to prevent some becoming richer and thus creating a pyramidal society. It was a device against class-stratification and against the genesis of the slavery-based 'empire model' of governance. Jesus while using the old Jewish idiom teaches his disciples (in the *Our Father,* the prayer he taught them) to ask God to "forgive us as we cancel the debts of others [who are indebted to us]". Now there are two kinds of "indebtedness" which clamour for cancellation, one on the part of our enemies and the other from our friends:-

· do not let your enemies be *indebted to you* by your demanding apologies or compensation for the wrongs THEY have done to you.

· do not let your friends be *indebted to you* by your demanding gratitude for the favours YOU have done to them;

Christians recognize in Buddhism the above mentioned two practices of what Christianity understands as supreme and salvific love :

· the first is *adosa,* (homologue of Christianity's *forgiving love*);

· the second is *alobha,* (homologue of Christianity's *non-possessive love*).

These last mentioned terms are synonyms for the final release from all bondage, or Nirvana. To a Christian, they are a negative formulation of what Jesus meant by forgiveness (*adosa,* non-hatred even towards enemies) which presupposes selflessness, greedlessness or non-possessiveness (*alobha*). They constitutes salvation in both religions, despite the doctrinal differences mentioned above.

To sum up: Forgiving the offender is demanded as a *conditio sine qua non for salvation* in both Buddhism and Christianity. The doctrinal difference is not about the obligatory nature of reconciliation (about which there is agreement between the two religions) but about the *beneficiary of salvation*. In Buddhism, the one who forgives unconditionally is saved; in Christianity both are on the path to salvation. But this doctrinal difference does not excuse the offended ones, be they Buddhists or Christians, from offering reconciliation, nor are the offenders, be they Christians or a Buddhists, excused from graciously accepting it through genuine repentance.

Zoroastrianism:
Prophetic and Ethical Implications

Stephen Chundamthadam SJ

Zoroastrianism,[1] also known as Parsee religion in India, is one of the most ancient surviving religions of the world. Zoroaster (628-551),[2] who is the founder of the religion, lived in ancient Persia at a time when polytheism[3] was slowly giving way to monotheism. Moses[4] in the Hebrew tradition was the first one to advocate monotheism in the history of religions. "Then God spoke these words. I am Yahweh your God who brought you out of Egypt, where you lived as slaves. You shall have no other gods to rival me."[5] Zoroaster vehemently opposed other gods and strictly propagated monotheism, *i.e.* the belief in only one God: Ahura Mazda. An analytical study of Zoroastrianism will help us to understand the influence it had on Judaism,[6] Christianity, and Islam as well as on prophetic and ethical teachings. Though, at present, the number of the followers of this religion is insignificant, it continues to exercise a tremendous influence on other religions and cultures. Along with monotheism, they stressed the importance of the role of prophets, ethical living and concern for nature and creation.

A close interaction with Zoroastrianism, both in the academic and religious realms, deepened my understanding and appreciation for this ancient religious tradition. Hence this paper is an attempt to explore the prophetic dimension and the influence of Zoroastrianism on other religions[7] along with their focus on ethical and sociological issues. Zoroaster, being chosen by God, had a prophetic role to play in the religion and in the social transformation.

Prophet in the Jewish tradition

The common Hebrew term for prophet is *nabi* and the Greek term is *prophetes* which means one who is 'commissioned or called'. In this sense a prophet is considered as the spokesperson of God either to communicate the will of God or to challenge the people about their evil doings or even to communicate a message of hope and deliverance. The Lord said to Moses:

> I have indeed seen the misery of my people in Egypt. I have heard them crying for help on account of their taskmasters. Yes, I am well aware of their sufferings. And I have come down to rescue them from the clutches of the Egyptians. So now I am sending you to Pharaoh, for you to bring my people the Israelites out of Egypt. *Exodus* 3:6-10 (*New Jerusalem Bible*).

Moses[8] and most of the prophets in the Old Testament were concerned about social justice, peace, love and concern for the poor and the marginalized. Prophets gave a high priority to liberation and leading the people on the path of God.

Appeal for a liberator

The settled agrarian community during the time of Zoroaster was oppressed and severely exploited. *Yasna* 29.1-5 highlight the agony of the creation represented by ox and the appeal for a liberator. In response to this appeal, The Wise Lord commissioned Zoroaster to protect the oppressed and destroy the wicked. *Y.*29.6. In the Bhagavad Gita, Lord Krishna tells Arjuna, "Whenever unrighteousness takes precedence over righteousness; and to uphold righteousness, to protect the good people and to punish the evil ones I take birth in each *yuga*." (BG. 4.7-8) Zoroaster's role as a prophet is a unique event in the Aryan tradition and something unheard of in the Vedic or Upanishadic tradition.

The position of no other founder of religion resembles so much the genuine Semitic conception of a Prophet, as that of Zoroaster. He is the man honoured by God with a personal intercourse, like Moses and Mohammad; what he promulgates is not his works, but the word of God communicated to him directly and letter by letter by God. Even the name of the Supreme Iranian God expresses manifestly the very same ideas as does that of the God of the Hebrews.[9]

Zoroaster was more like a prophet in the Jewish tradition like Moses, Amos, Isaiah, etc. There were great people both in the Jewish and Aryan tradition, who responded to the call of God in collaborating with his plan for humankind.[10]

Zoroaster in the history

During the time of Zoroaster, there were two prominent groups of people, *i.e.* the settled peace-loving agrarian community which took care of the cattle and was in peace with nature; and the invading tribes which used to attack the settled community, destroy their possessions including cattle and oxen. The former were known as *Ahuras* and the latter *Daevas*. The word used in the *Avesta* to represent the invading tribes is *aeshma* which means violence, fury, aggression, etc. As we read in the above passage there were constant fights between these two communities. Their social life, ethical values, worship of gods, relationship with nature, etc., were determined by this dialectic. Ahuras were considered as good people; the people of Zoroaster and Daevas were considered as evil people, the followers of Ahriman were leader of the devil. There was a reversal of roles in the Aryan tradition in India, i.e. *devas* were good people and *asuras* bad people.

Our knowledge about Zoroaster and pre-Zoroastrian religions is limited to the *Gathas* in the Yasna.[11] In the Yasna we read:

> They rush, they run away, the wicked, evil-doing Daevas; they run away with shouts, the wicked, evil-doing Daevas; they run away casting the evil eye, the wicked, evil doing Daevas: Let us gather together at the head of Aresurs!

For he is just born, the holy Zoroaster, in the house of Pourushaspa. How can we procure his death? He is the weapon that fells the friends; he is a Druj to the Druj! Vanished are the Daeva-worshipers, the Nasu made by the Daevas, the false speaking lie.[12]

The evil doers (*daevas*) were determined to destroy the new born baby whom they considered a threat to their wickedness.

The prophet: A friend of God

Zoroaster was the prophet chosen by God Y. 44.11, so he is the friend of Ahura Y. 44.2; 46.2 and the prophet in turn chose him as his friend. The prophet qualifies himself as a friend of truth and an enemy of lie:

> To the wicked (would that I could be) in very truth a strong tormentor and avenger, but to the righteous may I be a mighty help and joy, since to preparations for Thy Kingdom, and in desire (for its approach), I would devote myself so long as to Thee, O Mazda! I may praise and weave my song.[13]

In the context of many religions and gods, Zoroaster had to face stiff opposition from his own people in propagating the new faith but through political patronage and perseverance he succeeded in spreading the new religion. Zoroaster was deeply disturbed by the evil that existed in the society. Evil in the form of animal sacrifice Y. 29.1, invasion and cruelty inflicted on settled agrarian community and their oxen. Zoroaster had several years of wandering in agony seeking answers to religious questions and existence of evil in the society. Finally, he encountered the Good Mind (*Vohu Manah*) who took him to the true God, *i.e Ahura Mazda* (the Wise Lord).

The prophet commissioned by Ahura

Zoroaster was commissioned by the supreme Lord to preach the new religion, a religion which was against animal sacrifice, rituals and worship of many gods. Ethical living *i.e.* good thoughts, good words and good deeds and ecological concerns were the most important aspects of the new faith. "Make thy own self pure, O righteous man! Anyone in the world here below can win purity for his own self, namely, when he cleanses his own self with good thoughts, words, and deeds." (*Vendidad*, 10,19) The prophet in proclaiming the new religion severely criticised the traditional religions and their unhealthy practices. "And therefore, will I drive from hence the Karpans' and Kavis' disciples". Y. 32.15. In that process he antagonized the leaders of their communities *kavi* and their priests *karapan* . Soon Zoroaster had to flee from his people:

> To what land to turn; whither turning shall I go? On the part of a kinsman (prince), or allied peer, none, to conciliate, give (offerings) to me (to help my cause), nor yet the throngs of labour, (not) even such as these, nor yet (still less) the evil tyrants of the province. How then shall I (establish well the Faith, and thus) conciliate Thy grace), O Lord? Therefore, I cry to Thee; behold it, Lord! Desiring helpful grace for me, as friend bestows on friend (*Yasna* 46.1, 2).[14]

Zoroaster took refuge in a northern kingdom ruled by Vishtaspa (Y. 46.14, 15-16), continued his fight against the evil doers and encouraged his followers to do the same. (Y. 31.18) He worked against the animal sacrifice which was common in the traditional religions. (Y. 32.12, 14; 44.20; 48.10) In course of time king Vistaspa and his entire kingdom accepted the new faith as their religion. Political patronage, charismatic personality of the prophet and committed followers helped the new religion to spread far and wide.

Harmony in God and in the creation

Unlike the prophets chosen by God in the Old Testament, Zoroaster had the freedom to say 'no' to the call by Ahura Mazda; he accepted the mission entrusted to him by the Lord and in return acknowledged Ahura Mazda as the true God. After having chosen Ahura as his God he considers himself as a friend of God. (Y.34.1) For him the supreme Lord is represented by six aspects: the Holy Immortals (*Amesha-Spenta*) of which three possess masculine names and the other three feminine names.[15] As in the case of the concept of *Yin* (the dark side) and *Yang* (the light) in Taoism, a perfect balancing of the opposites which controls everything in nature and leads one to Tao, the ultimate principle; equal number of the holy immortals forms a perfect balance between the masculine and feminine aspects of the Supreme Lord. The same principle is seen in the dualistic principles Ahura Mazda and Angra Mainyu, the two aspects of life in the world. Besides the six holy immortals there are the *Yazata* (Adorable Ones) who serve the Lord like multitudes of angels. Among the adorable ones Mithra, Sraosha and Rashnu are prominent in their role as judges in the last judgement and caretakers of humanity.

Human freedom and ethical living in Zoroastrianism

The underlying theme of the Zoroastrian ethics is the fight between the settled peace-loving agrarian community and the nomadic aggressors represented by two fundamental principles, *i.e.* Truth (*asha*) and Lie (*druj*). Though human beings are created free, good and evil in the world are the result of human choice. (Y. 30.3-4) Like the primeval twins,[16] humans in their life can choose good or evil.[17] Those who choose good will be the followers of Ahura and those who follow evil will be the supporters of Ahriman.

> Ahura Mazda "the Wise Lord cannot be considered responsible for the appearance of Evil. On the other hand, Ahura Mazda, in his omniscience, knew from the beginning what choice the Destroying Spirit would make and nevertheless did not prevent it; this may mean either that God transcends all kinds of contradictions or that the existence of evil constitutes the preliminary condition for human freedom.[18]

The supreme Lord was extremely generous to humans by giving three blessings of Immortality, Righteous Order and the Kingdom of Welfare. (Y. 34.1) So humans in return through good thoughts (*humata*), good words (*hukta*) and good deeds (*hvarshta*) are expected to express their gratitude to the Lord and lead an ethical life in this world. (Y.34.2; 45.8) Like theology, ethics in Zoroastrianism also was elaborated during the Sassanian period with the help of Magi. The essence of Zoroastrian ethics 'do in holiness anything you will' places the responsibility of actions on each one. Eternal reward or punishment after death is determined by one's actions in this world;[19] souls of the good people will pass through the bridge of *Chinavat* and enter the House of Song (heaven), (*Y.* 51.15); whereas, the souls of the wicked people will be condemned to the House of Lie (hell), (*Y.* 49.11, 51.14). So, Zoroastrians give high priority to ethical living[20] and moderation in life. Ethical values in personal life were closely connected with an ideal social life as envisioned in the *Avesta* where there was no oppression, injustice and cruelty even to animals:

> "Good life in rich pastures and security against the blood-thirsty men of lies;" "the luck –bringing cow was created for man, not to be neglected, but to graze upon peaceful pastures." The aristocrats are the hereditary foes of the peasants, and they are also the prophet's opponents. Zarathustra fights for the cause of the oppressed peasant class; and this social reform-which is at the same time the transition from the way of life of the nomad to that of the agrarian and thus of the settler- is carried out in the name of the God, Ahura Mazda, who will not violence, robbery, and suppression by the nobility but justice and hence a proper ordering of the society."[21]

Social change

The prophet's concern was to liberate his people who were oppressed and exploited by the invading wicked people. He asks, "What is the award for him who prepares the throne for the evil, for the evil doer, O Ahura!" (Y. 31.15); When shall I in verity discern if you indeed have power over aught, O Lord! (Y. 48.9) In pain Zoroaster asks the Lord, when shall they drive from hence, the soil of this (polluted) drunken joy, whereby the Karpans with (their) angry zeal would crush us, and by whose inspiration the tyrants of the provinces hold on to their evil rule. (Y. 48.10) These emotional expressions by Zoroaster clearly articulate the anger and resentment against the evil that was going on in society which was perpetrated by the traditional religions and their gods. Prophets in the Old Testament severely criticized evil structures and practices in the society.... John the Baptist exhorted the people of his time to deviate from the path of evil. The main theme of Jesus' ministry was to establish the kingdom of God as articulated in his manifesto, Lk 4: 18-19; Mk 1:15.

Formation of human communities

There are individuals and organizations in the modern world, who fight against evil structures and unhealthy practices in the society in order to build up human communities based on ethical values and principles. These evil structures and practices can be in the name of political parties, religions, oppressive class discriminations, etc. Mahatma Gandhi and Nelson Mandela fought against exploitative political structures whereas Buddha, Jesus, Zoroaster, etc. fought against the evil and unhealthy practices in society in the name of religions and gods. Martin Luther King and Ambedkar dedicated their lives for the upliftment of the weaker sections of society who were discriminated in the name of caste, colour or division in the community. Each individual is called to make a choice in life either to join the evil forces or to join the good people. One who joins the evil forces will get all kinds of worldly achievements but will not get lasting peace and happiness; whereas the one who joins the good people will have to go through suffering and pain. But such a person may experience lasting peace and harmony and also may positively contribute to the building up of communities based on ethical values.

Concern for nature and creation

Good people, those who work for building human communities based on ethical values, cannot ignore the basic elements of nature: air, fire, water, earth, animals and other creatures which Zoroastrianism stressed so much. These elements are the creation of God and they are holy in the Zoroastrian tradition. They have an important role to play in the final liberation of all. The world according to Zoroaster is only a temporary abode of humans, a stage to prepare themselves for liberation through good thoughts, good words and good deeds. Hindus in general believe that the world is the place of repeated births and deaths of a soul (*samsāra*) before which it is completely liberated. The world is the cause of enslavement and attachment which one has to diligently avoid. Jews and Christians believe that the world and body are a hindrance to the salvation of soul; so, the world and body are to be conquered. The conquering aspect is very much reflected in the Western worldview and value system.

Ethics of moderation

Ahura created everything through thought out of nothing (*ex nihilo*) and the creation is holy like the creator. So, Zoroastrians take extreme care not to pollute any of these elements and whoever pollutes any of these elements will be subjected to severe punishments at the last judgement. They don't bury their dead for fear of polluting the earth, air, fire and water. Jains' respect for nature and material objects is based on the belief that there is soul even in material objects. They practise ethics of moderation, *i.e.* making use of material objects for leading a happy and ethical life. For Ignatius of Loyola, created things are for the salvation of souls. "The other things on the face of the earth are created for the human beings, to help them in the pursuit of the end for which they are created. From this it follows that we ought to use these things to the extent that they help us toward our end and free ourselves from them to the extent that they hinder us from it."[22] Zoroastrians worship fire because it represents Ahura Mazda; they respect water, earth and air because they are created by Ahura Mazda and they are holy. (Y. 17.10-18; 38.1)

Violence, terrorism, religious fundamentalism, consumerist culture, exploitation of the earth and natural resources are common in the modern world. These are destructive evil forces in the society which represent the *Haoma* sacrifice[23] during the time of Zoroaster. Opposite to this there are life promoting forces like good thoughts, good words and good deeds; ethics of moderation, love and respect for the other including nature and creation, gentlemanliness, etc. The fight between good and evil continues in the modern world in different ways and forms. In this fight, Zoroaster's prophetic call to join the good spirit to fight against the evil forces is still relevant. There are, in every age, prophets who responded to the call of God to fight against evil in society. Either one has to join the good spirit or the evil spirit, there is no neutral stand. To take a neutral stand is equal to encouraging the evil forces and running away from one's responsibility. Anyone who takes a stand against the evil forces will have to suffer like Zoroaster or like the prophets in the Old Testament. So, people are reluctant to take a stand against evil in the society. In spite of the destructive power of evil, it is indeed encouraging that there are many courageous and committed people who work for establishing communities based on human values.

The Zoroastrian motto is to "do in holiness anything you will." Gentlemanliness is their basic characteristic which encourages them to do good, not evil for evil. This approach was clearly seen not only in their religious life but also in their social life and business transactions. So, they were considered as trustworthy people. Their morality was basically an ethics of moderation; they tried to avoid both the extremes as in the case of Buddhism. Buddha, after going through the enjoyment of all possible pleasures and severe austere life, finally, realized that only the middle path would give a person complete liberation from suffering. Zoroastrians did not consider austerity, self sacrifice and celibacy as values. Unlike the Charvakas or the Epicureans they did not indulge in enjoyment of pleasures for the sake of enjoyment, but they encouraged people to make use of the things which are good for a peaceful and happy life. Loving one's enemy is not a great value for them, because an enemy is the follower of Lie; hence has to be punished. The basic approach in Zoroastrian ethics is that Ahura Mazda is good and righteous; so, his followers are called to be good and righteous.

Endnotes

[1] Zoroastrianism is also called Mazdahyasnian religion, fire worshippers, Parsee religion, etc. Because of religious persecution by the Muslim rulers in Persia, a number of Zoroastrians migrated to India, the present-day Gujarat in the year 716. English education, Political patronage (British) and openness to adapt to the new cultural context made them a prosperous community. The descendants of these Zoroastrians in India are called Parsees because they came from Persia/Parse.

[2] The name Zoroaster, which was popularized by the Europeans, is the Latinized form of *Zarathustra*, the Persian name of the prophet. In this paper we will use the name Zoroaster. Zarathustra was the main character in the famous work of Frederich

Nietzsche, *Thus Spoke Zarathustra*. Though there is no conclusive agreement with regard to the date of Zoroaster among the scholars, the date 628 - 551 is a commonly accepted time period.

[3] Zoroaster was born into a society which was mainly divided into three, i.e., chiefs and priests, warriors, and husbandmen and cattle breeders. *Mithra* and *Varuna* were the gods of the first class, so too there were other gods. Also refer the Sacred Books of the East vol. XLVII E. W. West (trans) Pahlavi Texts part V, (Delhi: Motilal Banarsidas, 1965), 28-30.

[4] Moses (14-13 century BCE) liberated the Israelites from the Egyptian slavery and established a well-organized community based on covenantal relationship between Yahweh and the people. Moses, through the Ten Commandments emphasized belief in one God.

[5] *Exodus* 20.1-3. "Anyone who sacrifices to other gods will be put under the curse of destruction." Ex. 22.19.

[6] The Persian king Cyrus conquered Babylon in 538 B C and allowed the Jews who were in captivity since 587 B C to go back to their country and build a temple for their God. Many of the Jews stayed back, got integrated into the culture. II *Chronicles* 36: 22-23; *Ezra* 1: 2-4.

[7] "Thus, from the moment that the Jews first made contact with the Iranians they took over the typical Zoroastrian doctrine of an individual after life in which rewards are to be enjoyed and punishments endured. This Zoroastrian hope gained ever surer ground during the intertestametary period, and by the time of Christ it was upheld by the Pharisees, whose very name some scholars have interpreted as meaning 'Persian', that is, the sect most open to Persian influence. So, too, the idea of a bodily resurrection at the end of time was probably original to Zoroastrianism, however it arose among the Jews, for the seeds of the later eschatology are already present in the *Gathas*." R. C. Zaehner, *The Dawn and Twilight of Zoroastrianism* (Oxford: Phoenix Press), 58.

[8] Moses is considered the father of prophets in the Old Testament, *Deuteronomy* 18:5,18 and their representative because he spoke with God, *Dt* 34:10-12, *Numbers* 12:6-8.

[9] Dr. Spiegal, *Avesta and Genesis*, as quoted by Manilal C. Parekh, in *The Gospel of Zoroaster* (Rajkot: Bhagwat-Dharma Mission House, 1939),.90-91.

[10] Manilal C. Parekh, *The Gospel of Zoroaster* (Rajkot: Bhagwat-Dharma Mission House, 1939)86.

[11] *Yasna* is one of the three sections in the sacred scriptures of the Zoroastrians known as *Zend Avesta* or *Avesta*. The other two are Yashts and *Vendidad*. *Gathas* are the sections believed to be composed by Zoroaster himself but later inserted into the

larger part of the scripture *Yasna*. The translation of the *Yasna* we refer to in this paper is from the *Sacred Books of the East*, edited by Max Muller and published by Motilal Banarsidas, Delhi: 1965.

[12] James Darmesteter (trans), *The Sacred Books of the East*, Vol. IV (Delhi: Motilal Banarsidas, 1965), *The Zend Avesta*, Vendidad Part I, 45,46,218.

[13] Y. 43.8. Ignatius Loyola in his *Spiritual Exercises* (second week) presents a meditation on two standards, *i.e.* one of Christ (representing good) and the other of Lucifer (representing evil). *The Spiritual Exercises of Saint Ignatius* (trans) George E. Ganss, S. J., (Gujarat: Gujarat Sahitya Prakash, 1992), 65.

[14] Mills L. H. (trans), *The Sacred Books of the East*, Vol. XXXI (Delhi: Motilal Banarsidas, 1965), *The Zend Avesta*, 134-135. References to *Yasna* in this paper are from Mill's translation unless otherwise mentioned.

[15] Woodward, Mark R. (ed.) *Religions of the World* (New Jersey: Prentice hall, 1998), 243.

[16] The Wise Lord Ahura Mazda created both the Holy Spirit and the Evil Spirit but the Holy Spirit chose to be good and the evil spirit chose to be wicked. *Yasna* 47. 2-4. Though Mazda is the supreme Lord, He is not the cause of evil in this world. According to this understanding the origin of evil can be traced back to the freedom of choice both in the case of the primeval spirits and in the case of human beings. In Christian theology angels and the first parents sinned by exercising the freedom given to them which gave rise to evil in this world.

[17] "Hear ye then with your ears; see ye the bright flames with the (eye) better mind. It is for a decision as to religions, man and man, each individually for himself. Before the great effort of the cause, awake ye (all) to our teaching." Y. 30.2.

[18] Mircea Eliade, *A History of Religious Ideas* Vol. I (London: University of Chicago Press, 1978) 310.

[19] Joseph Campbell, *The Masks of God: Occidental Mythology* (New York: Viking, 1964), 198, 199.

[20] The book of Esther in the Old Testament acknowledges the high moral standards of the Medes and Persians. *Esther* 1.19.

[21] Mensching Gustav, *Structures and Patterns of Religion,* (trans) by Hans F. Klimkeit (Delhi: Motilal Banarsidas, 1976), 24.

[22] Ignatius Loyola, *The Spiritual Exercises,* no. 23: Principle and Foundation (trans) George E. Ganss, S.J. (Gujarat: Gujarat Sahitya Prakash, 1993), 32.

[23] *Haoma* represents the ritual drunken orgies of the traditional religions and invading tribes in ancient Persia. It is also used in ritual sacrifice and prepared from a holy plant that grows on the mountains Y. 10.4 and is considered as one of the immortals Y. 8.9; 9.1,2.

Spirituality of Ahimsa
- A Jaina Perspective

Priyadarshana Jain

'Ours is a world of nuclear giants and ethical infants. We know more about war than we know about peace, more about killing than we know about living.'

- Omar N Bradley

Jainism is a way of life and admonishes its followers to take to a non-violent, awakened, compassionate and enlightened way of living in all walks of life. It is an out and out spiritual way of living which springs from the thoughtfulness and experience of the inner, pure, divine self. The Tirthankara Arhats and other Jinas practiced the same, perfected it, liberated themselves from the wheel of transmigration and accomplished the perfect spiritual state through the practice of ahimsa, self-restraint and the supreme austerities. Besides serving spirituality, the core values of Jainism address all issues that concern mankind at any given time be it sociological, psychological and environmental. Lord Mahavira was the 24th Tirthankara who lived 2600 years ago and was preceded by a legacy of 23 Tirthankaras who were spiritual scientists and taught not just by precept but by practice, demonstrating the noble way of non-violent, enlightened, spiritual living. All the Jina images in the beautiful temples in India and abroad are more or less alike, silently giving the supreme spiritual message to all creatures, 'to come unto one-self and discover one-self.' Thus the Gods of the Jains are not creator Gods but pure Paramatmans (*param-ātmans* i.e., supreme souls) who have manifested and accomplished their pure spiritual potential and become self-sovereign (Siddha, Buddha, Mukta)[1] through the practice of Ahimsa. The greatest of their teachings is Ahimsa which has extensive implications, psychological, social, environmental and above all spiritual. An evaluation of the dimensions of Ahimsa is important for spiritual development on one hand and its application is crucial for the well being of all stakeholders.

Emphasis on spirituality of Ahimsa

Tirthankara Mahavira emphasized on spirituality and spiritual way of living as the *summum-bonum* of life. It is from this insight that the great principle of Ahimsa emerged which is the basis of Jaina ethics. This principle of Ahimsa is an ancient one, and of great relevance today. The Jaina ethics which is the heart of Jainism promotes an eco-friendly, non-violent, compassionate, awakened and spiritual way of living. This is not based on any dogma or blind faith but is grounded in reason and rationality with a great concern for all micro and macro life forms. This uniqueness of Jainism makes this philosophy universally relevant[2]. There is no substance, be it living or non-living without qualities and modifications. There are six substances in the Universe which are comprehended through their characteristics and modes.[3] The soul too is a living entity characterized by infinite attributes viz., knowledge, vision, power, etc. which are obscured and distorted due to perversion, lack of right understanding of the nature of the self, and hence the soul is found in the defiled state of bondage.[4] This ignorance of the self is violence related to the self which needs to be checked first and foremost. It is from this ignorance and perversion that all other kinds of violence spring and so today we have the New Spirituality in the form of human rights, animal rights, environmental rights, sustainable development, etc crying for attention so that man may exact his behavior and save the beautiful planet.

Albert Einstein remarked that science can denature plutonium but it cannot denature the evil in the heart of man. Science coupled with spirituality is the need of the hour. Jainism is one of the oldest living religions, which establishes that all life is connected and mutual co-existence is the mantra for universal peace and harmony on one hand and for sustainable development on the other. The scriptures reveal that there is a deep inter-relationship between man and man as well as man and the environment at large. Jainism has paved the path of spiritual progress through discrimination between right and wrong, purity of thought, word and deed, compassion for the meek creatures, concern for the environment and above all self-restraint for victory of the self. Since ages it has advocated that self-restraint is the key to equitable and sustainable development and the practice of these basic vows is the formula for an eco-friendly life style. 'Scientific vision is to know the reality and spiritual mission is living the reality to combat the global crisis.'

Perfection of spirituality of Ahimsa

The enlightened, omniscient Tirthankaras have described the different levels and kinds of the self and revealed that there are 8.4 million kinds of *jiva yonis* (birth places)[5] where infinite living beings transmigrate in the four-fold existences (*gatis*) due to lack of right understanding of the self (deep spirituality) and taking to different kinds of psychic (*bhāva himsa*) and physical violence (*dravya himsa*). Hence the path of liberation constitutes the right understanding of the self which encompasses heightened consciousness and awareness of the self first and in its light being considerate of all kinds of life forms be it the one-two-three-four or five sensed, micro or macro beings; or not hurting, abusing, insulting, injuring, killing, wounding, ill-treating, exploiting, neglecting, manipulating, disregarding and being cruel to any life form in thought, word and deed. Looking upon all life forms as one's own-self, one refrains from all kinds of *himsa*, thus protecting one-self and being instrumental in the well-being of the other. Without harming oneself, none can harm another being. Violence when inflicted externally may or may not affect the other, but it surely harms one's own-self. Thus Ahimsa springs from a deep and profound spirituality and is an outcome of this deep realization of the true self. Spirituality is thus the lifeline of Ahimsa and the latter is regarded as the supreme virtue. All other virtues are secondary and are elaborations of this cardinal virtue.

There can be no spirituality without Ahimsa and the vice versa too holds true. To be spiritual internally is to be non-violent by thought, word and deed externally. The vow of Ahimsa is all-comprehensive and extolled for the welfare of one and all. The violent acts committed due to carelessness amount to violence; and non-violence is a vigilant attitude of the awakened spirit. Even when one is not causing injury to any creature externally but if he is unawakened spiritually, violence of the self is taking place. When one is spiritually awakened, and one appears to be taking to some violent activity externally due to the fruition of past karma, there is no punishment for such an act in the universal order of cause and effect. As the person is spiritually alert and wise, and understands the reality of the self, knowing that he is only a knower and a seer and not a doer and enjoyer of the mundane activities, he is said to be non-violent. Not just Ahimsa but it is this spirituality of Ahimsa that enables one to realize and release the self from all karmic bondage. External Ahimsa of other creatures in the absence of spiritual awakening is the cause of bondage of auspicious karma, but it is the spirituality of Ahimsa that sets the soul free of all fetters.

Ahimsa should be of the self first in the form of (i) self-realization/ right perception of the self, (ii) right knowledge of the self, (iii) shifting one's mind from all attachments to the observer within (*jnāta-drshta*) - i.e., moving from the *rāgadhara* to the *jnānadhara*, (iv) giving up all *rāga* (attachment) and *dvēsha* (aversion), *mōha* (delusion) and *kashāya* (4-fold passions and the 9-fold quasi passions) and trying to be in a state of enlightenment even though bonded by karmas. As one thinks, so does one become. When one understands and sees oneself as the potentially liberated, pure soul, beyond body, senses, and attachments and meditates on that latent divinity, one transcends all violence and material cuffs. This is the fruit of the observance of the spirituality of Ahimsa. Only when the spirituality of Ahimsa is perfected, one becomes an Arhat. It is only the Arhats who are spiritual and non-violent in the perfect sense of the term. Hence of the 1008 epithets of the Arhats and Siddhas, Vitaraga (i.e., without an iota of raga) sum up the spiritual and non-violent personality of Godhood. As they are absorbed in deep spirituality, and are without raga, they are not the creators, administrators or destroyers of the world. As they are enjoying the gift of spirituality and their non-violent nature, they are the role models of all spiritual seekers. And those who try to emulate the perfected personalities are the Shramanas devoted the contemplation of the self. Such spiritual practitioners of today are Gods in the making. Though very minuscule in number it is they who are practising the spirituality of Ahimsa and inspiring the vast multitudes to transcend from materialism to spirituality. One who cares for his pure godlike self alone can take to spirituality of Ahimsa, and over a progression of births eventually perfect it and accomplish the spiritual, non-violent state.

Thus a true renunciate is one who understands the nature of the soul and is spiritually awakened. His renunciation and detachment of worldly things and affairs is for a higher devotion and spiritual absorption. Only then he can be committed to the path of complete non-violence, come what may. Even in the face of death, he remains committed to the experience of the pure soul through the practice of Ahimsa and other vows viz., *Satya* (truthfulness), *Astēya* (non-stealing), *Bramhacarya* (chastity) and above all *Aparigraha* (non-possession/non-attachment). A householder who has faith in the right Gods, Gurus, and Dharma and has knowledge of the nine *tattvas* exerts in right conduct although partially and the first step towards this begins with the renunciation of intentional violence (*sankalpi himsa*)[6]. An aspirant, who seeks self-realization and victory over the self, takes care not to indulge in the transgressions of the prescribed vows. Inflicting cruelty to animals and human beings, torturing or terrorizing them, physical assaults to animals and humans, consumption of wine and flesh, hunting, deforestation, exploitation, corruption, inhuman behavior, unfair business practices, attack upon weaker people and nations, child labor, atrocities on women, racial discrimination, ill-treating prisoners, mass violence, suicide etc amount to violation of the vow of Ahimsa.[7] The ascetics follow the great vow of Ahimsa along with other vows completely whereas a householder follows it partially trying to balance his spiritual life and worldly life.

'Nothing is higher than Mount Meru and more expansive than the sky, so also know that no Dharma is equal to Ahimsa in this world,' reveals the *Saman Suttam*. This doctrine of Ahimsa forms the crux of Jaina ethics and provides a sustainable solution to the spiritual, mental, physical, social and environmental problems faced by modern man. The violations of spiritual living and violence attract great heaps of negative energy called karmas and the intrinsic nature of the soul gets veiled by such karmas and causes it to wander and suffer in the four-fold existence. The universal law of karma works automatically and a belief in this universal law inspires one to be spiritual and non-violent to the extent possible. The exhaustive and profound karma theory is propounded not to terrorize the bondage beings but is so revealed to enable the worthy souls to realize their latent divine potential through spiritual and compassionate living.

Two facets of the same coin

Spirituality and Ahimsa are two facets of the same coin. If spirituality is astute wisdom of one's consciousness, then absorption of the self, in the self, for the self, by the self is non-violence related to one's own-self. When one is awakened and self-realized then one is careful in all one's dealings. And then one looks upon all others as pure, godlike selves and does not injure them by thought, word or deed – then is the application of non-violence. One exerts wisely and compassionately, with all life forms irrespective of caste, creed, religion, gender, nationality, etc. Such a person sees the underlying unity of all existence and becomes a responsible pilgrim, who is secure in his wisdom and fearless of tomorrow. Thus spirituality of Ahimsa blossoms from wisdom and awareness. Hence it is said, 'first awareness, then compassion.'[8] There is only one way (of spirituality and non-violence) for all those who are enlightened and there are many mundane ways for all those who are ignorant, remarks Srimad Rajchandra.[9] Those who are spiritually awakened are definitely non-violent and those who are non-violent are indeed truly spiritual. One cannot subsist without the other.

Uniqueness of Jaina spirituality

Jainism is not a mere religion; it is a way of life. For, to be religious conveys an institutional connotation whereas to be spiritual connotes personal practice/sadhana and personal empowerment through the realization of the supreme reality thereby fulfilling the deepest motivations and impetus of life. As a result, spirituality has come to have largely positive connotation, while religion has been viewed more negatively. Spirituality is much more than going to a temple or a church and agreeing or disagreeing with institutional doctrines. Unlike in other traditions where spirituality is discussed as a relation with God or some higher force, in Jainism it connotes realizing one's pure potential and the infinite treasures latent in the confines of the self and manifesting it. Unless the divine, spiritual state is manifested, the soul continues to transmigrate and suffer and this is violence (*himsa*) of the self and suffering for the self.

To be absorbed in the pure soul is supreme Ahimsa (non-violence), to understand the soul rightly is *Anekāntavada* (non-absolutism) and to practise supreme detachment is *Aparigraha* (non-attachment). These are the three fundamental principles of Jainism and a fine blend of these is the crux of spirituality. All three have to be holistically examined and applied for spiritual evolution. Also, the three jewels (*ratna-traya*) revealed by all the omniscient emphatically, summarize the depth and extant of the unfathomable spirituality of ahimsa. The path of liberation constitutes of these three jewels viz., *samyak-darshan* (right perception of the pure soul), *samyak-jnana* (right knowledge of the pure soul) and *samyak charitra* (self-absorption) and they have to be understood from the real and practical view points; if not, one falls short of spiritual advancement and remains entangled in the whirlpool of transmigration even though he may be moral, virtuous, righteous and noble in all his dealings. The word '*samyak*' in the three jewels refers to mystical spirituality and ahimsa finds a place in the third jewel. Only on deeper examination and reflection one can understand that ahimsa is an essential and fundamental aspect of spirituality as realized, experienced and revealed by the all-knowing enlightened, spiritual personalities called Tirthankaras, Arhats, Jinas.

From the real or spiritual point of view *samyak-darshan* is the right perception of the pure soul, *samyak-jnana* is the right knowledge of oneself and *samyak charitra* is being oneself. The soul is a knower and a seer and not a doer or enjoyer of anything other than its own nature. The nature (dharma) of all living and non-living substances cannot exist out of it. So to be in one's own nature of living and enabling others to realize and abide in one's own spiritual self is the great spiritual message of the motto of 'live and let live.' From the practical point of view, faith in the spiritual personalities (Arhats and Siddhas) who have accomplished the perfect spiritual state through the practice of Ahimsa is *samyak-darshan*, knowledge of reality through the *tattvas*   (preaching of the omniscients) is samyak-jnana and complete or partial observance of Ahimsa and other vows is *samyak-charitra*. Thus we see that the practice of Ahimsa holds substantial value only when it is preceded by right understanding of the self and reality. The gods, gurus and scriptures are mere torch bearers, the kindly light guiding one and all to one's own self, which is godlike, divine, pure, blemishless, self-sovereign, self-born, eternal, transcendent as well as immanent, beyond sense perception, characterized by infinite knowledge, vision, bliss and power.

Basis for spirituality of Ahimsa

Lord Mahavira reveals that most living beings do not know from where they come[10] and what their purpose in life is! They spend their time nurturing the instincts of food, fear, pleasure and possessions and consider it to be true living. They flow with the worldly current and consider it to be right. But when one meets an awakened soul or studies the deep secrets of enlightenment through scriptural study applying the tools of Jaina logic viz., *syadvada* and *anekantavada*, one is transformed through spiritual insight. Such a person is addressed as an *ātmavādi* (believer in spirituality/the concept of soul)[11]. Secondly he also realizes that he is an eternal living being and has existed since time immemorial and shall exist in different existences (*gatis*) even after the body is relinquished until he is liberated. Such a person is called a *lōkavādi*[12] i.e., believer in the concept of rebirth. Thirdly he realizes that he transmigrates in these existences (8.4 million life forms) only because of his deeds (karmas) and that he alone is responsible for all the state of affairs in any given lifetime. Such a person is said to be the believer in the concept of karma (*kammavādi*)[13] which is the universal law of cause and effect. Fourthly he comprehends that all karmic attraction takes place due to some activity or the other and it is these activities of the mind, body and speech (*kriya*) that keep him away from the eternal spiritual self. Such a person is called *kriyavādi*[14] (believer in the concept of actions and its fruits). He then gets truly connected to his true spiritual nature and then the rectification of all sins, vices, defilements (*doshas*) begins in the form of abstinence, renunciation, asceticism, self-discipline and restraint, austerities, penance, meditation, detachment, devotion, selfless service, etc. Thus spirituality skillfully crafts a person to be humane, divine, responsible, non-violent, truthful, detached, virtuous and noble all at the same time.

Understanding spirituality of Ahimsa through Jaina metaphysics

There are two basic substances in the universe viz., living and the non-living. In Jaina metaphysics they are termed as *jiva* and *ajiva*.[15] The Sthananga Sutra reveals that there is one soul (*ege ayaa*)[16] and the Dashavaikalika Sutra says that there are infinite jivas (*anega jiva*).[17] Without the tool of Anekantavada (Nayavada and Syadvada included) one cannot rightly comprehend the nature of reality[18] and the real meaning of these two statements which seem to be contradictory. And without the comprehension of reality the real practice of spirituality of Ahimsa does not commence. Hence along with Ahimsa and *Aparigraha*, *Anekanta* is equally important for the understanding of Spirituality. '*Ege ayaa*' means all living beings are qualitatively (spiritually) one and 'anega jiva' means that we are quantitatively infinite. All living beings are of the same kind and himsa of another is verily the himsa of the self, reveals the Acharanga Sutra. The association of the *jiva* and *ajiva* is called *asrava* (karmic influx) which leads to *bandha* (bondage of soul and non-soul) and is the cause of transmigration (*samsara*); and their disassociation is termed as nirvana or moksha. And spirituality (*adhyatma*) through the practice of Ahimsa is the one that brings about this consequence of complete disassociation. This is done through *samvara* (stoppage of karmic influx) and *nirjara* (annihilation of all non-soul/foreign matter called karmas). Thus spirituality includes all those exercises, be it religious or spiritual which will bring about complete *samvara* and *nirjara*. If the soul ignorantly takes to religious exercises without self-actualization, the above outcome is never possible. One may acquire good karma and a temporary or a prolonged stay in the heavens depending on the quality of karmas (punya and papa) but never moksha which is a state of no-karma. Every soul has to attain that liberated state here and now through spirituality of Ahimsa in order to live happily ever after in that state. And that state is beyond description; words fail us as it is a subject of experience and not explanation. One who enjoys that spiritual state while embodied is called an Arhat and when he enjoys that state in a disembodied state, he is called a Siddha. Jainism reveals that this perfected state is the birthright of every jiva and one can channelize one's free will in the right direction and realize that state. Thus channelizing one's potential in the direction of the pure, divine self is spirituality and the fruit of it is Ahimsa (a complete *vitaraga* state devoid of attachment, delusion, karma, and suffering).

Application of spirituality of Ahimsa

In the Jaina tradition we can see the application of this deep spirituality in all walks of life be it their rituals of worship, fasting or food habits: 1) When one observes the art and architecture of the Jina images in the Jain temples one will see the deep spirituality reflected in the Tirthankara images. There will be no priest who will communicate to the Lord on our behalf. One invokes the Lord within taking clues from the perfected souls. 2) The Jain festivals of Paryushan, Dasa lakshan, Mahavira Janma Kalyanak, Akshay Tritiya, etc. too reflect the spiritual fervor. 3) The Jain monks and nuns walk barefoot through the length and breadth of India disseminating the teachings of the Tirthankaras through their life inspiring one and all to excel in spirituality through Ahimsa. 4) The belief that one is responsible for all actions and consequences, one exerts with utmost care, minimizing all violence, passions, etc to the extent possible. The protection of the inner pure self is the supreme state of Ahimsa and compassion. It is from this compassion that the Jains ought to take to philanthropic activities without attaching their ego (*karta bhāva*) to the noble activities. 5) The Jain fasting and food habits too exhibit their care for the self and all life forms of life. The very ardent Jains fast from sunset to sunrise all their life and take to periodical fasting, salt-less diet (ayambil, etc.). The reason for this is that when the body is emaciated by right comprehension, the atman is definitely thickened by spirituality; and this is done in repeated births in order to eventually disassociate oneself from the karman body which is the cause of the earthly body. Many Jains in the West are taking to Vegan way of living due to the violence involved in the dairy industry. 6) The Jains are admonished not to take to those trades and professions which involve cruelty to animals and are directly or indirectly responsible for environmental degradation and exploitation of the resources. 7) The Jains wish for *samadhi maran* through the spiritual observance of *Sallekhana*. As the Jains believe in the eternity of life they live and die for spirituality through the observance of Ahimsa in all its dimensions in order to be emancipated.

In olden times there were knives and swords, and only a part of the body was cut, then came the pistols and guns which killed individuals, following this came the atom bombs which destroyed a city or two, but today man has developed the nuclear weapons of mass destruction and the entire world shudders to think of the use of nuclear weapons and missiles. The problem today is not of guided missiles but misguided men, hence the need for the *vrata* (disciplined life of vows) culture and spiritual non-violence. The Acharanga Sutra says that there can be one weapon more powerful than the other, but the weapon of self-restraint (and non-violence) is the supreme one.[19]

As all wars must end in peace, all violence must end with non-violence, so also all materialism and suffering can end only with spiritual awakening. The need of the hour is protection and preservation of the pure self and the environment at large and this is possible when every individual, society and nation realizes the significance of the eternal spiritual value and lives accompanied with it. Thus through inter faith dialogue and faith in the culture of non-violence, humanity and spirituality can blossom and one can realize the higher truths of life and make life meaningful and the earth a better place to live.

Lifeline of Spirituality

Spirituality is the nourishment of the
inherent divinity within through Ahimsa.

Ahimsa is the lifeline of Spirituality.
Ahimsa is much more than non-injury.

Ahimsa is profound spirituality
and the heart of all religious practices.

Ahimsa is the very own nature of the pure soul.
It is a perfect state of the pure soul.

Ahimsa is that which enables one to evolve spiritually.

Ahimsa is supreme Dharma.
[That Dharma is supreme which comprises of Ahimsa,
Sañyama (self-restraint) and Tapa (austerity)][20].

Endnotes

[1] Uttaradhyayana Sutra 29.1, Editor Madhukara Muni, Jinagama Granthamala No. 19, Agama Prakashan Samiti, Byavara, First Edition, 1984.

[2] Priyadarshana Jain, "The Unique and Universal Dimensions in Jainism," *Satya Nilayam*, Vol. 27, No. 2, 2014.

[3] Umasvati (Author), Nathmal Tatia (Translator) *That which is-Tattvartha Sutra*, Yale University Press, 2010. Chapter 5.

[4] Uttaradhyayana Sutra, Chapter 32; Samayasara,Chapter 1, Editor Madhukara Muni, Jinagama Granthamala No. 19, Agama Prakashan Samiti, Byavara, First Edition, 1984.

[5] Avashyaka Sutra, 84 lakh jiva yoni lesson.

[6] A Source book in Jaina Philosophy, by Devendra Muni Shastri, Sri Tarak Guru Jain Granthalaya; 1st ed edition (1983).

[7] Jainism and the New Spirituality, by Vastupal Parikh.

[8] Dashavaikalika Sutra, Chapter 4, Concord Grover, 1983.

[9] Vacanamruta, Letters of Srimad Rajchandra.

[10] Acharanga Sutra, Chapter 1.1.

[11] Ibid Chapter 1.1.

[12] Ibid Chapter 1.1.

[13] Ibid Chapter 1.1.

[14] Ibid Chapter 1.1.

[15] Tattavartha Sutra, Chapter 5; Uttaradhyayana Sutra, Chapter 36.

[16] Sthananga Sutra 1.1.

[17] Dashavaikalika Sutra, Chapter 4.

[18] Bhagavati Sutra, Chapter 7, 2.

[19] Acharanga Sutra, Chapter 1, Ed by Madhukar Muni.

[20] Dashavaikalika Sutra 1.1, (trans) K.C.Lalwani, Motilal Banarsidas, 1973, 1.

The Engaging Spirituality of Fethullah Gülen: A Christian Appreciation

Victor Edwin SJ

Honouring a *co-pilgrim*

It is a privilege for me to write for the *Festschrift* that is to be published in honour of the Jesuit scholar-priest Sebastian Painadath. He is recognized and appreciated for his weighty theological essays in national and international journals, his lectures in centres of theology and his seminars on themes related to theology and interreligious dialogue. On the one hand, his scholarly and erudite essays stimulate exchanges on theological dimensions of dialogue. On the other hand, his life at Sameeksha points to another, equally important, dimension of dialogue—that is dialogue: *the dialogue of life*. The many contacts, both intellectual and social, that he has developed over the years with people of other religious traditions stand as a witness to his dialogical pilgrimage. Through his written word and life lived in the spirit of dialogue, Sebastian Painadath has made a huge contribution to interfaith relations in India.

While knowledge and thoroughness mark his scholarly work, the respect that Sebastian Painadath has for people of other faith traditions is a remarkable aspect of his life. His ability to engage with others spiritually underpins the academic-intellectual dimension of his life and his dialogical contacts with people. He humbly considers himself as a *spiritual co-pilgrim* with others.

This essay is a small tribute to his dialogical efforts.

Fethullah Gülen: Service to one's fellow human beings

As a student of Christian-Muslim relations I am fascinated by a number of Christians and Muslims who engage with others peacefully and give witness to their respective faiths by loving and serving others. One can identify many such people in history. Fethullah Gülen is one such outstanding figure in today's Muslim world. He engages passionately and creatively to give witness to his faith by engaging with all by breaking many walls of prejudice, thus building strong bridges of enduring friendship with others.

Gülen calls upon Muslims to find fulfilment in their life by serving others, especially the poor. He has initiated a vast civilisational project of dialogue by calling upon people from different intellectual and lifestyles in Turkey and elsewhere to interact with each other and to think anew for peace and reconciliation in the world.[1] Gülen lives a spirituality of action. In the post 9/11 world, where conflicts in many parts of the world directly affect people, Gülen's efforts for peace, justice and reconciliation are precious. His emphasis on serving one's fellow human beings, especially the poor, is particularly praiseworthy.

Fethullah Gülen—vision and mission: Initiating civilizations to work for a peaceful world

Fethullah Gülen was born on 27 April 1941 in a village in Eastern Turkey. During his schooling, he received a thorough training in Islamic religious sciences. He also acquired a wide and deep knowledge of language, history, philosophy, and literature. He received the state licence to be a preacher at the age of 18. In Turkey's secular arrangement, the Government certifies and licences preachers and imams.[2] While most preachers focused on religious matters and texts, Gülen has spoken and written prolifically about a variety of subjects, including the Qur'an and science, social justice, human rights, economics, education, parenthood, and parents' rights, in addition to many other, more standard, 'religious' subjects, such as the interpretation of the Qur'an and the sayings of the Prophet Muhammad.[3] In his preaching, it is obvious that Gülen neither confines himself to traditional teaching nor blames governments for the misery of people. Though he avoids confrontational strategies, he has never hesitated to speak on behalf of the poor.[4] He advocates a compassionate and brotherly form of Islam. He emphasises the inner spirituality and keeps away from the aggressive forms of Islam.[5] Many Muslims perceive Gülen as a traditional Islamic scholar (*alim*), while many others consider him a modern Sufi.[6] However, critics hold a different opinion: He is neither a Sufi nor an *alim*, they claim, but a propagandist.[7]

Whatever opinion people might have about him, one thing is noticeable: Gülen has grown to be an authoritative mainstream Turkish Muslim scholar, opinion leader and educational activist who supports interfaith and intercultural dialogue, democracy, human rights, and spirituality, and opposes violence and turning religion into a political theology. Gülen promotes the cooperation of civilizations toward a peaceful world.[8] He was cited as the tenth among 500 of the most important persons in the contemporary Muslim world.[9] In 2008, he was also voted "The world's top public intellectual" in an online poll jointly conducted by *Foreign Policy* and *Prospects* magazines.[10] He continues to teach, write and inspire many thousands of Muslims and people of other religious traditions. He has inspired a global movement that stresses reconciliation, tolerance and respecting everyone as they are at a time in which the modern age is encountering Islam and Muslim cultures around the world when the relations between civilizations are becoming strained.[11] It is interesting to note that some writers in the West call him the 'Muslim Gandhi'.[12]

A just, equitable and peaceful dialoguing world

Gülen envisions a *just, equitable* and *peaceful* world. He presents a new kind of Islamic intellectualism and altruism, coupled with a deeper sense of activism and spirituality to realise this vision here and now, in this world. He upholds moral and ethical values derived from the Qur'an and the traditions of the Prophet, and through his own words and deeds he spreads value-based education and people oriented-spirituality.[13]

This vision is underpinned by his theological belief on the beginning and end of this created world. These views provide the setting for his concentration on his vision for the present. His Islamically-grounded eschatology envisions humans of different religious and ideological commitments cooperating and working together to promote harmony and peace within human society and the natural world in anticipation of the future end of the cosmos and start of the hereafter.[14] In order to fulfil this vision and mission he emphasises the following core values.

The greatest value of human beings: Capacity to give witness to God

Human beings are superior merely because they are human beings. The greatest value of human beings is their capacity to give witness to God and interpret the universe. As witnesses, they mirror of certain aspects of God and are reflectors of the divine book of the universe. If there is no human person in this universe, the universe cannot be known.[15] He writes: "Humans, the greatest mirror of the names, attributes and deeds of God, are a shining mirror, a marvellous fruit of life, a source for the whole universe, a sea that appears to be a tiny drop, a sun formed as a humble seed, a great melody in spite of their insignificant physical positions, and the source for existence all contained within a small body. Humans carry a holy secret that makes them equal to the entire universe with all their wealth of character; a wealth that can be developed to excellence".[16] He visualises that if a close relationship between the human self and the attributes of God prevails and if Muslims commit themselves selflessly and honestly to human dignity, they can hope to regain the lost glory of the Muslim civilization.[17] He is convinced that where politics and military have failed, spirituality can succeed in bringing people together for peace and unity. This spirituality, Gülen firmly believes, gives birth to dialogue.

His conviction that if Muslims commit themselves to human dignity they can regain the lost glory of human Muslim civilization requires our attention. It should be observed that his conviction is in contrast to many Islamist thinkers, who would argue that Muslims have lost their glory because they have strayed away from pristine Islam. Their antidote to this malady is to forbid all what they consider 'un-Islamic' practices (often Sufi-related practices) and return to their understanding of the practice of the Companions of the Prophet, or a strictly literalist understanding of the Qur'an and the Sunna. These groups of Muslims focus on a literal reading of the past, neglecting the present and the future. On the other hand, Gülen seem to take into account of the progress of the world and to identify 'human dignity' as something that Muslim believers should take into serious account. Thus, he not only focuses on the future but also seeks a common ground between followers of other religions or of no religion. 'Human dignity' is certainly a common ground where all people can be united.

In the past, Christians emphasized that as long as a person adheres to 'eternal truth' he/she has certain rights. Thus, the human person was considered as the object of Truth. However, through the many events of their tumultuous history, they learnt that a human person cannot be reduced to an object in relation with 'Truth'. Rather, the human person will remain a subject. He/she has the freedom to make choices. One can choose a religion, leave one's own old religion and adopt a new religion. Neither the government nor the religious authorities can interfere with such decisions, that are made according to one's conscience. Any coercion in this regard will go against the dignity of the person. Thus, in Christian reflection on religious freedom 'human dignity' earned its central place. Christian friends who work with the followers of Gülen will appreciate a common ground between Christians and Muslims inspired by Gülen in the dignity of human person.

Gülen's human-centric approach

Gülen bases the human-centric approach of his life and mission on his conviction that the diversity of all that exists is in the design and will of God. "For Gülen, diversity of race, religion, nation, and life-way was intended by God and should be accepted and valued as a route to understanding. Diversity requires us to learn how to live together, which, in turn, necessitates, dialogue. According to Gülen, the response to diversity through positive engagement and dialogue is one of the major goals that the Divine will has set for humankind.[18]

Gülen's emphasis on diversity is endearing. Certainly, his inspiration is Islamic and precisely Qur'anic. Many Muslim scholars do emphasize that one of the fundamental principles of the Qur'an is that an individual is at liberty to adopt whatever religion he/she likes. Commenting on the following verse: "whoever wills - let him believe; and whoever wills - let him disbelieve" (Al-Kahf: 29), Muslim scholars confirm that the Qur'an recognises that it is neither possible for all people to observe one religion and one lifestyle, nor is it in concordance with the Divine expediency. They also quote that in Islam "There is no compulsion in religion" (Al-Baqarah: 256) and conclude their reflection with another Quranic verse: "For you is your religion, and for me is my religion" (Al-Kafirun: 6).[19]

However, this conviction of Muslims will be scrutinised by Christians and others in the light of what is happening in many Muslim countries. Christians and many other minorities are either killed or driven away if they refuse to adopt Islam—as, for instance, in parts of Syria and Iraq presently controlled by the ISIS. The intolerance shown towards Christians, Hindus, Sikhs and Shii Muslims in Pakistan certainly questions the interpretation that respects diversity and right to choose one's religion. The many efforts to establish a so-called Shari'a-based state in different parts of the world challenge the argument in favour of respect for diversity given by Muslim scholars like Gülen. It should be said that the voice of people like Gülen and others who emphasise diversity at the heart of Islam needs to be recognised and amplified. It has the authenticity and power to challenge intolerance and fanaticism born of narrow-mindedness.

Having discussed the core values that energise Gülen's mission, let us now move to recognise and affirm the basic principle of 'here and now' that characterises his action plan.

'Here and now': Serving others

It would be profitable to clarify some terms and their theological meaning in order to understand Gülen's emphasis on 'here and now'. Two Islamic concepts beg our attention. They are: *Al-Alamin* and *ad Dunia*. *Al-Alamin* denotes the whole spiritual and material cosmos. *Ad Dunia* refers to the present temporal world. In Islamic eschatology, the Resurrection (*Ma'ad*) is centred on the final state of *ad Dunia* and how this final state of *adDunia* involves the fulfilment of the whole *al-Alamin*. While Gülen holds the traditional Sunni Muslim views of resurrection, judgement and afterlife, he realizes that those teachings impact life here and now. 'Here and now' is the span of time and space granted by God for humans to fulfil their role of being God's vicegerents or representatives, on the earth and their relationships with one another before the ultimate dissolution of *al Alamin*. One manifestation of that vicegerents is the movement known as *Hizmet*.[20]

The fruit: Hizmet movement

"*Hizmet*" [literally 'service'] for Gülen implies that a person devotes his or her life to Islam, serving for the benefit of others, which is beneficial for life after death. Gülen always asks himself if he might do more for God. Death is always present in his preaching to his followers, and the fear of Judgement Day is the motivation for hard work.[21]

The overarching concept of Gülen's vision and mission is *hizmet*. The principles *gaye-i hayal* (the purpose of one's life), *diğergamlik* (altruism / selflessness), *başkast için yaşama* (living for others), *mes'uliyet duygusu* (sense of personal responsibility), and *adanmişlik ruhu* (spirit of devotion) define his life and work. The schools, student hostels, dialogue foundations, and universities run by the followers of Gülen witness to his Gülen's inspiration and his followers' commitment to strengthen the pluralistic world and to serve all people without discrimination.

Gaye i Hayal (the purpose of one's life)

A survey conducted by a Business School in the USA shows that people who extend their life beyond narrow personal circles experience the joy of life. They reach out to others in love, in sharing and in cooperation. The results of the survey also indicated that those who reach out to others have specific goals in life. They have clear directives in their lives. Their lives are purpose driven.[22] Gülen describes a person with purpose in life as one who embraces everything and everyone with compassion. He writes:

> A person of ideals is, first of all, a hero of love, who loves God, the Almighty Creator, devotedly and feels a deep interest in the whole of creation under the wings of that love, who embraces everything and everybody with compassion, filled with an attachment to the country and people; they care for children as the buds of the future, they advise the young to become people of ideals, given them high aims and targets; they honour the old with whole-hearted regard and esteem, develop bridges over the abysses to connect and unite different sections of society, and exert all their efforts to polish thoroughly whatever may already exist of harmony between people.[23]

What about one who has neither ideals nor goals in life? One could say that a purposeless life is like a boat without rudder. One cannot set sail on a rudderless boat. A rudderless boat is destined to drift and perish on the seas. For Gülen, life that is not motivated by higher principles will degenerate. He writes:

> Human generations can preserve their well-being only if they have high ideals and goals. Those who do not have goals eventually turn into walking cadavers. Every being in Nature can be fruitful, productive and benefit other beings only if it preserves its well-being. Similarly, a human can preserve his or her well-being only with high ideals, goals and his or her constant struggle and action to achieve those goals. Just like inactive materials that gradually corrode, a human generation without ideals and goals, and hence inactive, is destined to be dispersed.[24]

Gülen's principle of *gaye-i hayal* is founded on traditional Islamic teachings. Traditional Islamic teachings suggest that one's will, and carnal self are in constant struggle with each other. While the former instructs people to do what is beneficial to the self and to fellow humans, the latter instructs the person to do whatever is pleasurable and whatever satisfies his or her desires. Hence, the latter feeds selfishness. *Gaye-i hayal* is seen as an instrument that can prevent a person's mental capabilities from being captured by his or her carnal self.[25] This concept makes one to live for others.

As a true leader, Gülen has, in word and deed, put on record that he works with all people of goodwill towards world peace as his *gaye-i hayal*. This vision and mission of his life is put into action by him and his followers in their educational work, imbued with values such as dialogue, tolerance and altruism.

Diğergamlik (Altruism / Selflessness) and *Başkast Için Yaşama* (Living for others)

Gülen emphasises that selflessness and dedication to live for others are essential for anyone who commits himself/herself to serve others. Emphasising the importance of selflessness, he writes: "Just like a tree can grow in direct proportion to the strength of its roots, man can improve himself and elevate spiritually in proportion to his ability to avoid selfishness and thinking of self-interest."[26] Selflessness empowers one to face all the storms of life. He writes: "They struggle with disasters befalling society, stand up to 'storms', hurry to put off 'fire', and are always on the alert for possible shocks."[27]

A person who has a specific purpose in life rooted in selflessness will be able to tackle society's most burdensome problems. Such individuals, according to Gülen, should come together for collective action. This can revive societies and usher in a new era of peace and justice. Gülen emphasises collective action. He recognises that it is simply impossible to struggle against ills of the society alone. Working together with many people of goodwill can help synergise each individual and give a needed momentum for the work at hand.

Gülen reminds us that avoiding sin is not enough; rather, engaging to help create a more humane world is required. Salvation means not only to be 'saved from' sinful activities, but also to be engaged actively in the improvement of the world. According to Gülen, moral consciousness toward other cultures can be raised only through participating in action. In a way, becoming morally upright person is possible only through morally informed conduct.[28]

Mes'uliyet Duygusu (Sense of personal responsibility)

Gülen derives this principle of the sense of personal responsibility from the Qur'anic belief that every individual is accountable for his commissions as well as omissions.[29] He writes:

> For me, the worldly life is only a small part of the life that has started in the realm of souls and will continue indefinitely either in Heaven or in Hell in the afterlife. And since one's afterlife is shaped by it, the worldly life is of the utmost importance. Therefore, the worldly life should be used in order to earn the afterlife and to please the One who has bestowed it. The way to do so is to seek to please God, and, as an inseparable dimension of it, to serve immediate family members, society, country, and all of humanity accordingly. This service is our right and sharing it with others is our duty.[30]

Individually-mobilised people can gather to form collectively-mobilised groups that can put this vision into action through education and other cultural activities that seek to further dialogue and to work for tolerance and understanding.

Adanmişlik Ruhu and Gönül İnsani (Spirit of devotion and person of heart)

Gülen emphasises that the person who has a proper purpose in life, who has a deep desire to live for others and whose life is marked with selflessness and a sense of responsibility should also learn to live in complete dedication to the service of humanity and seeking to please God in doing so. *Gönül İnsani* is a person dedicated to serving humanity and God. Gülen invites his listeners to live a life of such dedication. He transmits Islamic tenets in a way that everyone can see a role for himself and herself in building a compassionate society, where all human beings can co-exist with one another for greater causes based on sacrifice and altruism.[31]

In conclusion, it should be said that 'engaging with others' is the critical component of Gülen's civilisational project of building peace in the world. The foundation of such a project stands firmly on the Qur'an and the Sunnah, the very sources of Islam. Rootedness in the Islamic sources and openness to pluralistic values makes his offer attractive to both Muslims and people of other religions.

If religious sources are the foundation of his project, the pillars that hold the edifice of Hizmet are his commitment to the dignity and the freedom of human persons and his dedication to diversity among peoples. This human-centric approach and respect for the pluralistic world has many takers, not only among Muslims, but also among people of other faith traditions. Friends and well-wishers of Gülen are not only Muslims but are also from other religious traditions. This approach offers a broader base for bringing people together. Other key components of his spirituality like 'here and now' and 'service to the needy', revive and strengthen the motivation for living for others. Gülen's spirituality is essentially an 'other-oriented' spirituality and is based on his theological and anthropological commitments.

It is not only important, but also essential, that Christians engage with the followers of Hizmet movement. In order to establish a *just, equitable* and *peaceful* world, one has to engage all people of goodwill across borders of religion and culture. The platform for such engagement is to promote human rights and human dignity.

Endnotes

[1] M. E. Ergene, *An Analysis of the Gülen Movement: Tradition Witnessing the Modern Age* (New Jersey: Tughra Books, 2011), 14.

[2] W. Wagner, *Beginnings and Endings: Fethullah Gulen's vision for Today's world*[(New York: Blue Dome, 2013), 6.

[3] M. Kalyoncu, *A Civilian Response to Ethno-Religious Conflict: The Gülen Movement in Southeast Turkey*(New Jersey, Tughra Books, 2011), 2.

[4] M. A. Khan, *The Vision and Impact of Fethullah Gülen* (New York: Blue Dome, 2011), viii.

[5] M. A. Khan, *The Vision and Impact of Fethullah Gülen* (New York: Blue Dome, 2011), xi.

[6] T. Michel, "Sufism and Modernity in the Thought of Fethullah Gülen," *The Muslim World* 95, no.3 (July 2005): 341-358.

[7] Z. Saritoprak, "Fethullah Gulen: A Sufi in his Own Way," *Turkish Islam and the Secular State: The Gülen Movement*. M. H. Yavuz and J.L. Esposito (eds.), (New York: Syracuse University Press, 2003), 167.

[8] Journalists and Writers Foundation, *Understanding Fethullah Gülen* (Istanbul: JWF, not dated (but certainly after 2010)], 7.

[9] A. Schleifler, *The 500 Most Influential Muslims* (Amman: Royal Islamic Strategic Study Center, 2012), 34.

[10] M. A. Khan, *The Vision and Impact of Fethullah Gülen* (New York: Blue Dome, 2011), vii.

[11] M. E. Ergene, *An Analysis of the Gülen Movement: Tradition Witnessing the Modern Age* (New Jersey: Tughra Books, 2011), x.

[12] M. Scheel, "A Communitarian Imperative: Fethullah Gülen's Model of Modern Turkey," *The Fountain*, Issue 61, January – February 2008.

[13] M. A. Khan, *The Vision and Impact of Fethullah Gülen* (New York: Blue Dome, 2011), viii.

[14] W. Wagner, *Beginnings and Endings: Fethullah Gülen's vision for Today's world* (New York: Blue Dome, 2013), x.

[15] B. Jill Carroll, *A Dialogue of Civilizations: Gülen's Islamic Ideals and Humanistic Discourse* (New Jersey: The Gulen Institute & Tughra Books, 2011), 15-16.

[16] F. Gülen, *Towards a Global Civilization of Love and Tolerance* (New Jersey: The Light Inc., 2004), 112.

[17] M. A. Khan, *The Vision and Impact of Fethullah Gülen* (New York: Blue Dome, 2011), xiii.

[18] F. Sleap and O. Sener, *Gulen on Dialogue* (London: Centre for Hizmet Studies, 2014), 9.

[19] From Prof. A. Wasey's address to Christian and Muslim scholars at the Golden jubilee celebration of the PISAI, Rome.

[20] W. Wagner, *Beginnings and Endings: Fethullah Gulen's vision for Today's world*(New York: Blue Dome, 2013), xi.

[21] B. Agai, "The Gulen Movement's Islamic Ethics of Education," Turkish Islam and the Secular State: The Gulen Movement. M. H. Yavuz and J.L. Esposito (eds.), (New York: Syracuse University Press, 2003), 59.

[22] From the retreat notes of Fr Thomas V Kunnunkal SJ.

[23] M.F. Gulen, The Statue of Our Souls(New Jersey: The Light Inc., 2005), 125.

[24] M.F. Gulen, "Idealsiz Nesiller" (Generations without Ideals), in *Buhranlar Anaforunda Insan* (Izmir: Nil Yayinlarim, 1998), 85; cited in M. Kalyoncu, *A Civilian Response to Ethno-Religious Conflict: The Gülen Movement in Southeast Turkey* New Jersey, Tughra Books, 2011, 20.

[25] M. Kalyoncu, *A Civilian Response to Ethno-Religious Conflict: The Gülen Movement in Southeast Turkey* New Jersey, Tughra Books, 2011, 21.

[26] F. Gulen, "Ruh'un Zareri," *Sizinti* (July 1983): 383; cited in M. Kalyoncu, *A Civilian Response to Ethno-Religious Conflict: The Gülen Movement in Southeast Turkey* New Jersey, Tughra Books, 2011, 24.

[27] F. Gulen, Ölçii veya Yoldaki Işiklar(Istanbul: Nil Yayinlari, 1985) 208; cited in M. Kalyoncu, *A Civilian Response to Ethno-Religious Conflict: The Gülen Movement in Southeast Turkey* New Jersey, Tughra Books, 2011, 24.

[28] M. H. Yavuz, "The Gulen Movement: The Turkish Puritans," M. H. Yavuz and J.L. Esposito (eds.), (New York: Syracuse University Press, 2003), 26-27.

[29] Qur'an 2:56, 22:7, 6:36.

[30] F. Gulen, Yeni Türkiye 15 (1997): 668; cited in M. Kalyoncu, *A Civilian Response to Ethno-Religious Conflict: The Gülen Movement in Southeast Turkey* (New Jersey, Tughra Books, 2011), 28.

[31] M. A. Khan, *The Vision and Impact of Fethullah Gülen* (New York: Blue Dome, 2011), 103.

Part-3
... moving as spiritual co-pilgrims ...

My Experiences in Interreligious Dialogue

Georg Evers

When I was asked to contribute to the Festschrift for Sebastian Painadath, I felt honoured and challenged at the same time. During my years at the Asia Desk of the Institute of Missiology, *Missio* in Aachen, I have met Sebastian Painadath in Germany and also in India at many conferences dealing with interreligious encounter and dialogue. Whereas I myself am more a "generalist" in the ways of interreligious dialogue, having been engaged in dialogue with various religions, Sebastian Painadath struck me as one who in the encounter with Hinduism, and here especially with the Bhagavad Gita, had found the central theme of his life-work as a Christian theologian in India and abroad in Germany, where he has given courses in meditation and spirituality to many people over many years. A few years back, it was my privilege to write a short biographical essay presenting Sebastian Painadath's contribution to interreligious dialogue and spirituality for the journal "*Forum Weltkirche.*"[1] Collecting the material to write this article, gave me the opportunity to delve deeper into the work of Sebastian Painadath and to detect his unique way and contribution to a Christian spirituality nourished by the encounter with Hindu traditions, which he brought into interplay with Christian spiritual and mystic traditions, especially with the Gospel of John and the writings and ideas of the German mystic Meister Eckhart.

As topic for my contribution to the Festschrift of Sebastian Painadath I have chosen the title "My experiences in Interreligious Dialogue". Looking back at the many years of working as theologian in various settings and countries I found that engagement in interreligious dialogue has been the main focus and central theme of my life-work. This was brought home to me, for instance when I myself was honoured with a Festschrift on my 70th birthday. The editors had chosen as title "*Viele Wege – ein Ziel, Herausforderungen im Dialog der Religionen und Kulturen*"[2] (*Many Ways – One Goal, Challenges in the Encounter with Religions and Cultures*) which characterizes my life-long occupation in dialogue with members of different religions in various parts of the world. Having been born into a Catholic family during the time of the Nazi dictatorship, I experienced from early childhood that being a Christian meant to stand against the ruling powers of the day. The conservative upbringing in a stoutly Catholic family did not exactly qualify me to develop an open attitude towards different religious traditions, just to the contrary, during my youth and my activities in the Catholic youth movement "Neudeutschland" I was strongly convinced that the form of Catholicism prevalent during the pontificate of Pius XII was exactly the form of religion and spirituality which God had intended to be lived by all humankind. In my capacity as leader of the local group of the Catholic youth movement in my home town, I was responsible for organizing a mission exhibition in 1955. For the inspiration and help to present the missionary situation in Africa in the exhibition, we were helped by the White Fathers of Africa who had a study centre in Heerenberg close to my home town of Emmerich. My main motif of entering the Society of Jesus a year later was to become a missionary, preferably in Africa. During my training in philosophy, which was taught at that time in Latin, I learned the apologetic method used in the then obligatory disputations in which we students were trained to detect the faults in the argumentation of our opponents and thus defeat their arguments. By no way, were we advised or trained to listen to the opinion of our opponents, nor to appreciate the good and valid points in their argumentation. The training we received thus was far from enabling us to enter into dialogue with differing opinions and positions, but on the contrary, we were taught the apologetical way to defend our position as the only true and valid one (*sententia unica vera*).

Encounter with Buddhism, Shintoism and new religions in Japan

When I was sent by my superiors as future missionary not to Africa, which would have been my choice, but to Japan, which I accepted in holy obedience, I became exposed to a completely alien, at first rather incomprehensible, but at the same time fascinating cultural, religious and highly aesthetical tradition. Learning the Japanese language was a useful opening in trying to understand my new environment. The encounter with the Japanese way of thinking was somewhat of a cultural choice. My training in scholastic philosophy and its insistence on logical argumentation, run completely counter to the Japanese way of avoiding stringent logical expressions which do not leave room for interpretation, but insist on the exclusive principle of non-contradiction, leaving only the options of "either – or" with the exclusion of a "third" option. There is a Japanese expression: "You are arguing logically," which is not meant to congratulate you that you are expressing your ideas clearly and succinctly, but on the contrary, it expresses the disgust and uneasiness of the person addressed who has the feeling of being fenced in into a logical cage which leaves no escape. During the two years of language school in the Japanese language, I had the opportunity to delve deeper into Japanese and Asian cultural traditions. A great help was the seminal book of Hajime Nakamura: *Ways of Thinking of Eastern Peoples*[3] which gave a good introduction into Asian philosophical, ethical and religious traditions. A good introduction into Buddhism I received by attending the lectures by Heinrich Dumoulin, Professor for Religions at Sophia University, who had just published his books on the history of Zen-Buddhism. The theological courses at the theological faculty of Sophia University, however, were a disappointment. The new ideas with regard to mission, theology of religions and interreligious dialogue developed in the documents of Vatican II had not yet reached our professors, when I was studying theology during the years 1965-1969 in Tokyo. Looking back, it still surprises me, that while we were studying in Japan, a country where Christianity is a very small minority of just around 1% of the population, we were not taught any course in mission theology nor in the theology of religions. There was, after all, the example of Fr. Enomiya-Lassalle who was a pioneer in Christian-Buddhist dialogue, and who tried to find new ways of Christian meditation by including essential elements from the Zen-Tradition. But he was something of a prophet in the wilderness, suspected of syncretism, and only much later, recognised as a meditation master.

During my theological studies at Sophia University, one of the central problems which I experienced was the question what kind of mission the tiny Church in Japan could exercise in a country with many old and new religious traditions. The phenomena of the many "New Religions" which were active and very much successful in winning adherents, made me reflect on the reasons, why the proclamation of the message of Christianity reached only so few people. When I visited the centres of Rissho-Kosei-Kai in Tokyo and the centre of Tenri-Kyo in Nara, I was impressed by the ways these New Religions were able to respond to the spiritual and material needs of the people who came to them in listening to their problems in small groups and pointing out how they could improve on their karma situation with certain rituals and with religious and ethical guidelines. In contrast, the catechetical methods used by the Catholic Church appeared to me as too academic and not responding to the spiritual needs of the potential new members. My exposures to the world of the normal Japanese workers in the factories, which I had made by taking part in work-camps for theology students in working part-time during summer vacations in factories in Sapporo and Osaka, had convinced me, that no normal Japanese worker would be willing or able to participate in the two-years courses in catechetical lessons, made obligatory before receiving baptism in the Catholic Church. Some of my theoretical problems regarding mission and dialogue I dealt with when I wrote my Master's Thesis on the topic of "The Problem of the Theology of Non-Christian Religions."[4] In this thesis I gave an overview on the discussion on the topic by European theologians such as K. Rahner, R. Schlette, J. Heislbetz, J. Daniélou, Y. Congar, treating only European theologians with the only exception of Raimundo Panikkar who with his Indian background was the only Asian voice. After finishing my master studies in theology, I did my doctoral studies in Münster under the guidance of Karl Rahner whose theological ideas on the role of Non-Christian religions and the concept of anonymous Christians had influenced me very much. In the years preceding Vatican II, European theologians had been reflecting theoretically on the possibility of salvation for members on non-Christian religions. Theologians like Karl Rahner had shown that relying on the theological axiom of the universal salvific will of God (1 Tim 2:4-6) and the social aspect of salvation, non-Christian religions can be understood as "legitimate religions", prior to an existential encounter with the Christian message. Rahner's theory of "anonymous Christians" tried to show within the parameter of traditional Catholic theology a new approach to the non-Christian religions, opening new vistas for encounter and dialogue. These new insights into the potential salvific character of the other religions, however, were developed by theologians who did not have any experience of actual dialogue with any of the members of the other religions, and thus were basing their arguments solely on purely theoretical theological reflections.

In my doctoral thesis: "*Mission - Nichtchristliche Religionen - Weltliche Welt*"[5] (*Mission – Non-Christian Religions – Worldly World*) I returned to the subject of the theology of religions and interreligious dialogue, enlarged by including the developments in mission theology and in the theology of the world dealing with the problem of secularization. In my research again I examined only the work of European theologians and the documents of Vatican II. After all, Asian theologians had not been involved in developing the new insights of Vatican II with regard to the other religions, as expressed in the seminal document "Declaration on the Relationship of the Church to Non-Christian Religions" (*Nostra Aetate*) and on Religious Freedom. References to Asia's religious traditions in drafting the document "Nostra Aetate" were introduced only by foreign missionaries working in Asian countries, such as Josef Neuner with regard to Hinduism and Heinrich Dumoulin with regard to Buddhism.

Dialogue with Jews and Muslims in Germany

My first experiences in actual interreligious dialogue I made when working in a centre for ecumenical and interreligious encounter, the Hedwig-Dransfeld-Haus in Bendorf near Coblence, during the period 1973-1979. Every year the centre organized a Jewish-Christian Bible Study Week which brought together Rabbis, rabbinical students with Christian priests, pastors, theology students and other interested people to study together biblical texts in the original Hebrew and translated in other languages. During the study week the participants lived together, ate together while respecting the dietary rules of Kashrut, and praying together by celebrating Sabbath and the Christian liturgy, inviting each other to participate to the degree their tradition allowed. The centre also organized Christian-Muslim encounters, normally centred on a common theme. Again, the dietary rules were respected, whereas the participation in each other ritual and liturgical prayers mostly consisted in being present at the services of the others, but not actively participating. Another form of dialogical encounter where the conferences, organized within the initiative of "Jews, Christian and Muslims in Europe" (JCM), which annually brought together rabbinical students, Christian students of theology and young Muslims to deal with historical periods and persons of Jewish, Christian and Muslim tradition. These conferences dealt e.g. with the work and life of "Maimonides-Thomas Aquinas-Al Ghazzali" having lived and worked together in the 13th century, or with the contributions by "Leo Baeck-Karl Barth-Muhammed Abdouh" for the 19th-20th century. For me the encounter with Judaism as a living religion with its liturgical richness and its own specific way of interpreting Holy Scripture was a deep experience which brought home to me, that the connection with our Jewish roots remains an essential element in understanding Jesus' teaching and role. It was the encounter with the root of our Christian tradition which opened for me new vistas on understanding deeper the person and the work of Jesus of Nazareth whom we Christians proclaim as the Messiah, whereas the Jews are still expecting his coming in the future. That Jews were willing to come to Germany, the country which was responsible for the Shoah, was an expression of good-will and reconciliation much appreciated and dear.

The encounter with Islam was of a different kind. The Muslim participants in the dialogue with Christians, or with Jews and Christians together, presented their understanding of God's revelation to humankind by focussing on Muhammad, as the "Seal of all Prophets" who received the last and fulfilling revelation from the archangel Gabriel written down in the Quran. The Muslims recognise Jews and Christians as "people of the book", that is, as communities which have received God's revelation, but only partially, and who have distorted some parts of the revelation they have received. As a Christian theologian I realized that the Muslims were acting exactly towards Jews and Christians, as the Christians had done with regard to the Jews. After all, Christian theologians, e.g. Saint Augustine, have accused the Jews that they were in possession of Holy Scriptures containing God's revelation, which the Jews, however, had not understood correctly. Christian theologians were of the opinion that the Jews were thus the "book-keepers" of God's revelation which the Christians in the light of the New Testament's revelation were able to understand fully, whereas the Jews remained in darkness. The Muslims took a very similar superior position in that they saw themselves in possession of the fullness of God's revelation and invited Jews and Christians alike to overcome the shortcomings in their understanding of revelation and to open themselves to the fullness of revelation, only and completely found in the Quran. Luckily there were other Muslims, mostly from the mystical Sufi-tradition, who were more open to a genuine dialogue in respecting the other as he understood himself.

The seven years of having been engaged in dialogue with Jews and Muslims gave me a deeper understanding of the different stages and phases which can be observed in the process of dialogue with other religious traditions over a longer period of time. Most people who are entering into dialogue for the first time are coming with certain preconceived ideas about the "other" religion, which in the course of dialogue they gradually overcome. This stage can be called: "*overcoming prejudice*". The following phase is characterised by the "*exchange of information*", that is the listening to the presentation of the other religion by one of its adherents. For this phase it is characteristic that the representatives of a given religion present the ideal side of their religious tradition, by avoiding to mention the weak points and historical mistakes. The real dialogue begins with the third phase, the "*exchange and discussion of the information received*" in which clarification can happen and misunderstandings can be cleared up. During this phase it is important that the partners in dialogue are not only discussing their various religious traditions, but also pray, live, eat and play with one another. This exchange on the human level helps to understand the other better in his daily living. The following phase can be called "*the phase of experienced communalities*". The participants start to realize that they as "peoples of the book" have many points in common with regard to their liturgy, doctrinal points and ethical guidelines. In continuing in dialogue over a longer period, the last "*phase of experiencing communalities while being aware of remaining differences*" will be reached. In this phase the participants are aware that there is much which they have in common, but at the time, they become conscious of the remaining differences which all mutually should respect. Thus, dialogue will not lead to syncretism, but to the experience of "*communality by respecting remaining diversity.*"

The experience of dialogue changed my theological outlook. I had to realize that Rahner's theology to call members of other religions "anonymous Christians" was not at all helpful when entering into actual dialogue. The "bona fides" to adhere to their own religious tradition which Rahner attributed to members of other religions, became endangered in the moment when they entered into dialogue and thus were exposed to an encounter with the Christian message. When I was asked to contribute to a Festschrift for Karl Rahner's 75th birthday by recalling my experiences with his theology, I used it to describe the deficiencies of the thesis of "anonymous Christians" I had experienced in the actual dialogue.[6]

Observer of interreligious dialogue by Asian theologians and the FABC

From 1979 till 2001 I worked as head of the Asia Desk at the Missiological Institute Missio in Aachen. With my colleagues, who were following theological developments in Africa, Latin America and Oceania, I had the chance to observe the new theological insights presented by the "Theologians from the Third World". In our journal "Theology in Context" we presented seminal articles and books and reported on important theological conferences with the aim to make known the new theological insights and methods the theologians in the "Younger Churches" – a condescending term which was used at the time by those from the "Older and Established Churches" – were developing. For me it was fascinating to be privileged to observe how bishops and theologians in the Asian Churches were responding to the new ideas of Vatican II and how they tried to apply them to their own specific situations. The general theological awakening within the Asian Churches after Vatican II led to the development of distinct Asian ways of doing theology and prominently included new reflections on the theology of religions and the necessity of entering into dialogue with the members of other faiths. Asian Christian theologians are convinced that the Asian Churches with their experience of living as minorities in the religiously pluralistic world of Asia, are called in a special way to make a contribution towards the theology of religions. For them the central problem in reflecting on the other religions is not the relation of Christianity to these traditions, but the question of the place of Christianity within the religiously pluralistic world of Asia. This means a significant change in the perspective and the approach to the other religions.[7] Interreligious dialogue is for Asian theologians more than simply a particular problem among other theological problems, because they see in dialogue with other religions something of a heuristic principle to develop a genuinely Asian theology. At the first Plenary Assembly of the FABC in Taipei in 1974 the Final Statement says: "In dialogue with these religions, we will find ways of expressing our own Christian faith. The great religious traditions can shed light on the truths of the Gospel. They can help us understand the riches of our own faith."

Asian theologians are convinced that they are called in a special way to develop new approaches to the other religions. The traditional answers given by the early Church Fathers and the Magisterium were developed in an age and in circumstances which cannot be compared with the situation the Asian theologians find themselves in. After all, the early Church Fathers were not so much dealing with the feeble Greek and Roman religions, but more with the philosophical and Gnostic traditions challenging the Christian faith. In Asia, Christianity is facing the great religions of Buddhism, Hinduism and Islam in an encounter which is totally different from the situation in which the Church Fathers and later the Magisterium developed their theological responses to the other religions. Asian theologians are convinced to be facing a new situation which calls for new theological approaches and answers. In this situation, they see themselves in a unique position and challenged to do pioneering work for the good of the universal Church. To describe this different approach to the other religious traditions Asian theologians speak of a double loyalty or a double allegiance. As Christian theologians they accept the Bible, the Church Fathers, the documents of Ecumenical Councils and the teaching of the Magisterium as sources and guidelines in their theologising. As Christian theologians with Asian roots, they respect the religious traditions and holy scriptures of other Asian religions as parts of their own cultural and religious heritage which demand their loyalty and allegiance as well.[9] After all they are convinced that the Holy Spirit has been and still is working beyond the boundaries of Christianity and the Church. From the beginning, Asian theologians were convinced that interreligious dialogue must take into account the totality of the Asian situation, that it cannot be reduced to the sphere of religious expressions alone, but must take up as well the social problems of today's Asia, a continent marked by poverty, exploitation, excessive population growth. "Since the religions, as the Church, are set at the service of the world, interreligious dialogue cannot be confined to the religious sphere but must embrace all dimensions of life: economic, socio-political, cultural and religious. It is in their common commitment to the fuller life of the human community that they discover their complementarity and the urgency and the relevance of dialogue at all levels, socio-economic and intellectual as well as spiritual, among the common people in daily life as among scholars and people with deep religious experience."[10]

My connection with the work of the newly founded "Theological Advisory Commission" of the FABC – later renamed "Office of Theological Concerns" (OTC) – started in 1987 when I was invited to participate in the conference on interreligious dialogue held in Singapore. The outcome of this conference was a paper *"Theses on Interreligious Dialogue"* (TAC).[11] From then on, I took part in the yearly meetings of the TAC/OTC for nearly 10 years during which I changed from the status of being an "observer" to become a "resource person". The other connection with the FABC was my participation in several of the "Bishops' Institutes on Religious Affairs" (BIRA) which were held in different Asian countries. The series of the BIRA seminars centred on the relationship of Christianity with the different religious traditions of Buddhism, Hinduism, Islam, Daoism and Confucianism and on general common topics within these traditions. Already the First General Assembly of the FABC in Taipei in 1974 spoke of a triple dialogue, with Asian cultures, with the poor, and with the religions of Asia as the central task for the Asian minority Churches. As regards the dialogue with the great religious traditions of the Asian peoples, the assembly stated: "In this dialogue we accept the Asian religions as significant and positive elements in the economy of God's design of salvation. In them we recognise and respect profound spiritual and ethical meanings and values. Over many centuries they have been the treasury of the religious experience of our ancestors, from which our contemporaries do not cease to draw light and strength. They have been (and continue to be) the authentic expression of the noblest longings of their hearts, and the home of their contemplation and prayer. They have helped to give shape to the histories and cultures of our nations."[12]

This positive appreciation of the religious heritage of Asian peoples is not a conclusion arrived at by theological reflection and debate, but an attitude and conviction born out of direct and existential living contact with the followers of these religions. Rather than a theological issue to be tackled by experts in the field of religious studies and theology, religious pluralism is a lived reality for all the minority Churches in Asia. This constitutes the specific character of the approach to dialogue by Christians in Asia and by the FABC and distinguishes it from the theological discussion within the theological tradition of Europe or other Churches. The Asian Churches are aware that within the universal Church theirs is the task to address the urgent task to give new theological answers to the challenge of living within the orbit of the great religious traditions.[13]

Asian Theology of religions and dialogue: criticised by Rome

The attempts by Asian theologians to develop a specific Asian theological approach to respond to the challenges of the religiously, culturally and socially pluralistic situation in the Asian Churches met with criticism by the Magisterium, especially the Congregation for the Doctrine of the Faith in Rome. Its then prefect Cardinal Joseph Ratzinger made it very clear that the symbiosis of Judaism, Greek philosophy and Roman judiciary thought which had shaped the transition of Jewish Christians into the state legitimated religion of Christianity in the first 4th century was not only a historical fact but a theological reality which was providential and binding for all times. Therefore, Asian theologians were not allowed to repeat this historical and providential process achieved by the early Church Fathers in their attempts to bring into interplay the biblical Jewish-Christian tradition with their own religious and cultural traditions. The Sri Lankan theologian Tissa Balasuriya contributed to the debate in a publication proposing a "De-Routing and Re-Routing of Christian Theology"[14] in which he pleaded to give Asian theologians the freedom to repeat what the early Church Fathers had done in developing their theology in discourse with Greek philosophical traditions, by doing the same by making use of Asian religious and cultural traditions.[15] In 1989 the Congregation for the Doctrine of the Faith issued a *Letter on some aspects of Christian meditation*[16] in which it warned that some Eastern forms of meditation are erroneous, because they are in danger of leading into syncretism. These warnings clearly were aimed at attempts to make use of methods of Eastern forms of meditation in Christian meditation within the Asian Churches. At the same time the Congregation warned against the use of a "negative theology" common in Asian ways of doing theology, which it accuses to "transcend every affirmation seeking to express what God is and denies that the things of his world can offer traces of the infinity of God.[17]" The *Letter* of the Congregation met with astonishment and disappointment within the Asian Churches whose representatives complained that the negative criticism by the Roman authorities was misdirected, uninformed and therefore not doing justice to the contribution by the Asian Churches to Christian spirituality.

Much more damaging, however, was the declaration "*Dominus Jesus, On the Unicity and Salvific Universality of Jesus Christ and the Church*" published on August 6, 2000. The declaration de facto removed the foundation for any interreligious dialogue with other religions when it stated that theologically relevant "faith", as response to divine revelation, can only be found in the Catholic Church, whereas in the other religious traditions there is only "belief", that is "the sum of experience and thought that constitutes the human treasure of wisdom and aspiration", basically void of any "theological relevance."[18] In the Institute of Missiology Missio I was responsible for the open letter we published in response to the Declaration *Dominus Jesus* which was republished by several theological journals in Asia and Europe. In this response we pointed out that the

Roman declaration was not only harming theological development in the Asian Churches but had negative repercussions in the secular and political realm as well undermining the credibility of the Asian Churches' stance on dialogue and exchange with other religious traditions. Our open letter warned against a new "rites controversy", because the Roman authorities did not respect the legitimacy of plurality in theological reflection. The letter concluded with a plea: "There is an urgent need to find new ways to safeguard the freedom of theological research in response to the different cultural, religious and socio-economic contexts and at the same time to respect the duty of the magisterium to critically evaluate the results of this theological reflection in order to preserve the unity in concordance with the faith tradition within the world Church". Later I contributed to a special issue of the journal *Jeevadhara* which was edited by Sebastian Painadath. I contributed an article entitled, *"Recognise the Creativity of the Local Churches."*[19] The contribution by Sebastian Painadath concluded with the words: "We Christians in Asia do not convert confessional statements into metaphysical definitions. We do not declare *our* faith experience as absolute norm for others. We like to be constantly alert to what the Spirit is telling us through the Christian community, and through other religions as well, through the poor of Asia and through the secular movements too. We realise that to be disciples of Jesus we have to be fellow-pilgrims with believers of other religions on this continent of rich spiritual heritage and manifold religious experiences."[20]

The need to continue dialogue in spite of fundamentalist and communalist tendencies

For more than 20 years I have been contributing an annual column "Trends and Developments in Interreligious Dialogue" to the journal *"Studies in Interreligious Dialogue"* in which I try to report on actual developments in the relationship between the different religions. Over the years there has been much positive development in the field of dialogue and cooperation among the religions. Of late, the negative influence of fundamentalist tendencies in some religions has grown and threatens to destroy the trust and cooperation between different religions. Looking into the situation of several Asian countries today, we have to admit that there are many trends which are working against harmony and good relations among the different religious groups. Fundamentalist and communalist forces are active in countries like Indonesia, Pakistan, India, and the Near East and engage in the persecution of religious minorities. Sometimes these adverse tendencies are so strong that advocating the necessity of continuing the dialogue might look rather naïve, inappropriate or even outright impossible. On the other hand, the theological insights gained in the field of the theology of religions, that God's universal will of salvation is working in all religions and that the Spirit is active beyond the boundaries of Christianity and the Christian Churches are not refuted when radical elements in certain religions start Holy Wars and other kind of religiously motivated violence. The *Theological Advisory Commission* of the FABC has stated clearly:

"The obligation to enter into dialogue is in no way reduced because the other religious believers do not show an equal interest in dialogue, because dialogue is not simply an attempt at coexistence among religions, but a demand on the Church of its very life as mission. The interest and strength that come from such an awareness enable the Church not only to dialogue individually with each religion, but to render the service of unity by facilitating the encounter and collaboration among religions."[21] These general theological insights make clear that the obligation to be ready for dialogue rests on solid theological foundations. In conclusion I would like to express that I feel bound to honour this lasting obligation to stay in dialogue with other religious traditions, in spite of all obstacles. In this task I feel myself in companionship with Sebastian Painadath whose commitment to dialogue I have described in my biographical essay on him thus: "Sebastian Painadath, due to his biography, his studies and continuously working in the field of dialogue, has the special quality to act in a singular way as mediator between Eastern and Western spirituality. The continuously changing situation in the world where religious minorities are threatened by persecution, calls for people who have relevant experience in the living-together in peace and harmony of people of different faiths and convictions. Sebastian Painadath is one of these rare personalities who are able and knowledgeable to act as mediator and practical teacher, that people of different faiths and ideologies overcome their differences and are empowered to live in peace and harmony."[22]

Endnotes

[1] Cf. G. Evers, Sebastian Painadath, Theologe aus Indien, in: *Forum* Weltkirche 127 (2008), No.2, 28-31.

[2] L. Bertsch/M.Evers/M. Moerschbacher, Viele Wege – ein Ziel. Herausforderungen im Dialog der Religionen und Kulturen, Herder Verlag, Freiburg 2006.

[3] Hajime Nakamura, *Ways of Thinking of Eastern Peoples*, India, China, Tibet, Japan, Honolulu, East-Western Press, 1964.

[4] G. Evers, Die Problematik der Theologie der Nichtchristlichen Religionen, unpublished manuscript, Tokyo 1968.

[5] Cf. G. Evers, Mission- Nichtchristliche Religionen – Weltliche Welt, Aschendorff Verlag, Münster 1974; Italian translation: Storia e Salvezza, Missione – Religioni non-Christiani – Mondo Secularizzato, Bologna 1976.

[6] G. Evers, Die „anonymen Christen" und der Dialog mit den Juden, in: Wagnis Theologie. Erfahrungen mit der Theologie Karl Rahners, H. Vorgrimler (hg), Herder Verlag, Freiburg 1979, 524-539.

[7] The specific approach of the Asian Churches is formulated by the *Theological Advisory Commission* of the FABC (now: *Office for Theological Concerns*): "In the course of the last thousand years the Church has encountered and dialogued with various peoples, cultures and religions, with varying levels of success. Today, however, especially in Asia, in the context of the Great Religions, which are in a process of revival and renewal, the Church is aware of a markedly different situation. We do not ask any longer about the relationship of the Church to other cultures and religions. We are rather searching for the place and role of the Church in a religiously and culturally pluralistic world." Cf. J. Gnanapiragasam/F. Wilfred (eds.), Being Church in Asia, Theological Advisory Commission Documents, Manila 1991,9.

[8] Cf. Felix Wilfred, *Dialogue gasping for breath?* Towards new frontiers in interreligious dialogue, in: Vidyajyoti 51 (1987) 10, 449-466.

[9] Cf. FABC I, Taipei 1974, *Final Document*, No. 13-14, in: *For All the Peoples of Asia*, FABC Documents 1970-1991, G.B. Rosales/C.G. Arévalo (eds.), Manila 1992, 23.

[10] *For All the Peoples of Asia*, op.cit. Vol. I, No. 120.

[11] Theses on Interreligious Dialogue, in: Being Church in Asia, Theological Advisory Commission Documents (1986-1992), J. Gnanapiragasam/F. Wilfred (eds.), Manila 1992, 9.

[12] *For All the Peoples of Asia*, FABC Documents 1970-1991, G.B. Rosales/C.G. Arévalo (eds.), Manila 1992, 14.

[13] Cf. G. Evers, The Specific Contribution of Asian Theologians Towards a Theology of Religion, in: V. Tirimanna (ed.), Harvesting from the Asian Soil, Towards an Asian Theology, Bangalore 2011, 67-80.

[14] T. Balasuriya, Right Relations. De-Routing and Re-Routing of Christian Theology, Logos Vol. 30, Nos. 3-4, Colombo 1991.

[15] Ironically, this publication escaped the notice of the Congregation for the Doctrine of the Faith, which later took offence to an earlier publication by Tissa Balasuriya, namely Mary and Human Liberation (Logos 29, Nos. 1-2, Colombo 1990, which led to his excommunication in January 1997.

[16] Congregation for the Doctrine of the Faith, Letter to the Bishops of the Catholic Church on some Aspects of Christian Meditation, October 15, 1989.

[17] Ibidem, no. 12.

[18] Cf. Declaration of the Congregation for the Doctrine of the Faith, "Dominus Jesus." On the Unicity and Salvific Universality of Jesus Christ and the Church, Rome, August 6, 2000, no. 7.

[19] Cf. G. Evers, Recognise the Creativity of the Local Churches, in: *Jeevadhara,* Vol. XXXI, No. 183, 187-192.

[20] Cf. S. Painadath, Dominus Jesus: Rewritten, in: *Jeevadhara,* Vol. XXXI, No. 183, 248.

[21] *Being Church in Asia*, Theological Advisory Commission Documents (1986-1991), J. Gnanapiragasam/F. Wilfred (eds.), Manila 1994, *Theses on Interreligious Dialogue*, No. 2, 14.

[22] Cf. G. Evers, Sebastian Painadath SJ, *Theologe aus Indien,* in: Forum Weltkirche 127 (2008), No.2, 31.

Towards an Integral
and Interreligious Spirituality:

On Following a Spiritual Path between
Christianity, Zen and Sri Aurobindo

Christian Hackbarth-Johnson

B orn in 1964, I belong to a generation whose spiritual quest had already been naturally shaped as an interreligious one. Growing up as a Lutheran in Catholic Southern Bavaria, closely related to the Church as the son of sacristans, I was eventually awakened to spirituality by LSD. When I started to discover the world in the early 1980s, it was the later phase of the 1968 movement: a mix of hippie romanticism, punk music, the emergence of the Green Party and the city streets filled with Rajneesh's so-called neo-sannyasis and other "youth cults", as they were derogatively called by the media and Church experts. My conventional Christian childhood mindset was first opened up by the motley, politically dynamic *Kirchentag*-movement in Germany (a biannual national Church convention organized by lay people with usually about 100.000 attendants); then, by early contemplative experiences in the ecumenical community of Taizé, but soon severely shaken by those extraordinary experiences of expanding inner consciousness by the psychedelic drugs. For three years I ventured on the path of the "*paradis artificiel*" (Charles Baudelaire), of "*moksha medicine*" (Aldous Huxley), not knowing anything about spirituality but intrigued by those experiences. After having gone through the psychedelic dark nights, adolescent despairs, with John Lennon's mantra "All I want is the truth" in my mind, an inner guidance put me on a better path. A sequence of spiritual books, beginning with Allan Kardec's "The Spirits' Book", John C. Lilly's "The Center of the Cyclone", and culminating in Paramahamsa Yogananda's "Autobiography of a Yogi" radically opened my mind to spirituality. I stopped taking chemicals and plants and wanted to go a yogic or spiritual journey. Intuitively I thought that the world of spiritual experience found in Yogananda's book must also be present in Christianity. Having been born into this religion, I figured out that the most natural way to begin with would be to study theology, thus becoming better acquainted with my own tradition and at the same time focusing on the relationship between Christianity and Hinduism.

On the first day at the university, a woman who had just come back from India sat next to me. We struck up a conversation, and on the following day she brought me a book written by Henri Le Saux/Swami Abhishiktānanda, the German edition of "Guru and Disciple"[1]. In the first semester, I had my first Yoga lessons at the Catholic university parish in Tübingen. In the second, I enrolled in Hans Küng's seminar on interreligious dialogue, where I gave a report on Raimon Panikkar. I listened to lectures by the indologist Heinrich von Stietencorn, and started to learn Sanskrit in addition to Greek and Hebrew. In the third semester, I "fell into Zen"[2] on meeting Michael von Brück, a Lutheran theologian, disciple of Fr. Bede Griffiths, and teacher of Yoga and Zen, who had returned from a five-year stay in India to do research and teach in Tübingen at the Institute of Ecumenical Research of Prof. Küng in 1985. Besides his academic teaching he taught us Zen and Yoga. I became his ardent student. When 10 years later he proposed to me to write my doctoral thesis on Swami Abhishiktānanda, it was quite apt. But first I focused enthusiastically on Zen.

Falling into Zen

When, much later, I reflected on my early experiences with drugs, I came to think that, on the one hand, they were a sort of integration of early spiritual experience of humankind still practiced in native shamanic cultures, such as those in the Americas, and, on the other hand, they were undertaken most unskillfully, destroying the little mental structure I was beginning to develop in adolescence. So it seemed fitting to me that I fell into the highly structured spiritual, very strict practice of Zen. But as with LSD, Zen focuses on transcending the mental plane, with the difference, however, that it goes at it by means of intense meditation. At my first sesshin, after a period of single-pointed concentration, my consciousness suddenly opened. I was flooded with love and had a clear direct understanding of spiritual things. It was somehow similar to a high LSD experience only more real, more existential and brought about by meditative effort. After about two hours, thoughts had taken over again and I found myself in deep distress and suffering, similar to what one would call a horror trip. This changed after awhile, and the mental plane was stabilized again.

In the following years, I lived from sesshin to sesshin, trying to get back to that wonderful state of consciousness. In each sesshin, there was a little experience between long periods of intense internal suffering, which also brought about a psychosomatic disease over the years. It was just enough to keep me going but I was trying too hard. There was too much egocentric motivation. I wanted to show the teacher how good I was - a lot of callowness. This was quite normal, of course as I was young. Knowledge came slowly, very slowly. I found that what was needed is not just transcendence, but also structure, or the acceptance of structure and the acceptance of life in all its many dimensions. The birds of the spirit cannot sit on a tree with weak branches. Teaching[3] helped, as well as reading[4] and becoming a husband and father.[5] To sum it up: the development of an "integral spirituality"[6] was needed.

Christianity, mystical and interreligious

All this time it was very clear to me that the search for mystical experience was the essence of religion, of any religion. I studied the Bible. I studied theology from this angle. Liturgy became alive as a symbolic expression of this experience. However, working as a Church-intern for two and a half years, I wondered increasingly whether or not traditional Christian language was still a language understandable by modern people. As a liturgist I could affiliate myself with it. With some hermeneutical loops and a historical view in mind I could say and justify anything that was required, but I also did not feel fully comfortable. When worshipping, the words one utters should come from the heart. It must be a language that one can identify with. I could understand it and it spoke to me to some extent, but would it also speak to those who did not grow up with it? The solution for me was inter-religiosity, a kind of amplification for expressing what is meant by using different spiritual languages, as I had learned it from Fr. Bede on my first journey to India in 1988.[7] And, of course, silence cultivated by the practice of Yoga and Zen. Teaching Zen and Yoga gave me more freedom of expression than preaching in a church. It was more direct and, for the most part, non-verbal. However, the experiment of trying to bring Zen and Yoga into the parish failed. Although there were positive responses, not everybody in the Church shared my interreligious mystical inclinations. Judging my attitude to be too interreligious, the Church authorities of the Lutheran Church of Bavaria did not consider me appropriate for pastorship. I was denied ordination. Instead, I was given the chance to work for three years on the doctoral thesis on Swami Abhishiktānanda.[8] Focusing on the relationship of identity and spiritual experience, I analyzed Abhishiktānanda's dual religious identity as a Hindu-Christian monk following the meandering of his spiritual pilgrimage until his awakening experience in 1973 in Rishikesh. This experience swept away the rest of the doubts which had tormented him for 25 years, especially in the first half up to the years of Vatican II.[9] In the aftermath of the experience he could say:

The more I go, the less able I would be to present Christ in a way which could still be *considered* as 'Christian'. I can start with 'Christ' only if my approach is 'notional', by ideas. For Christ is first an 'idea' which comes to me from outside. Even more after my 'beyond life/death' experience of 14.7., I can only aim at awakening people to what 'they are'. Anything about God or the Word in any religion, which is not based on the deep I-experience, is bound to be simply 'notion', not existential. From that awakening to self comes the awakening to God – and we discover marvelously that Christ is simply this awakening on a degree of purity rarely if ever reached by man.

Yet I am interested in no *christo-logy* at all. I have so little interest in a Word of God which will awaken man within history ... The 'Word of God' comes from my/to *my* own 'present'; it is that awakening which is my self-awareness. What I discover above all in Christ is 'I AM'. I sometimes said jokingly that my next book's cover design would be an 'atomic mushroom'. There remains only the Ah! of the Kena Upanishad. Christ's experience in the Jordan – Son/Abba – is a wonderful Semitic equivalent of , 'Tat tvam asi'/ 'aham brahmasmi'. Of course I can make use of Christ experience to lead Christians to an 'I AM' experience, yet it is this I AM experience which really matters. Christ is this very mystery 'that I AM', and in this experience and existential knowledge all christology has disintegrated. It is taking to the end the revelation that we are 'sons of God'.

There is only One Son. Each of his manifestations is both *one* and *unique*. So what would be the meaning of a 'Christianity-coloured' awakening? In the process of awakening all this coloration cannot but disappear (the atomic mushroom). If at all I had to give a message, it would be the message of 'Wake up, arise, remain aware,' of the Katha Upanishad. The coloration might vary according to the audience, but the essential goes beyond. The discovery of Christ's I AM is the ruin of any Christic theology, for all notions are burnt within the fire of experience. Perhaps I am a little too Cartesian, as a good Frenchman, and perhaps others might find a way out of the atomic mushroom. I feel too much, more and more, the blazing fire of this I AM, in which all notions about Christ's personality, ontology, history, etc. have disappeared. And I find his real mystery shining in every awakening man, in every mythos...

The only message I could give now is too much burning to be given except with people whom the Spirit might send near me, as he did in the case of Marc. So you realize the dilemma in which I find myself, whenever I am asked to speak on Christian interiority and contemplation…"[10]

"Again, if my message could really pass, it would be free from any ‚notion 'except just by way of ‚excipient'. The Christ I might present will be simply the I AM of my (every) deep heart, who can show himself in the dancing Shiva or the amorous Krishna! And the Kingdom is precisely this discovery… of the 'inside' of the Grail! (…) The awakening is a total explosion. No Church will recognize its Christ or itself afterwards. And precisely for that (reason), no one likes the 'atomic mushroom'!"[11]

Abhishiktānanda's experience confirmed to him what he had intuited before,[12] that the Advaitic experience was identical with the God experience of Jesus Christ. The uniqueness of Christ could at best be seen in that this experience had been manifest in Christ in an unsurpassably pure form. But the I AM of his experience is principally the same as the I AM of every human being. On the other hand, Abhishiktānanda was aware that this message was unacceptable to the greater majority of Christians as it implied that all secondary identification, all Christian coloring had to be let go off. Abhishiktānanda's theological standpoint could be termed a unitive pluralism, the unitive principle being the trans religious mystical experience of the identity of Being (I AM), or a pluralism by transcendence,[13] meaning that the reality experienced in mystical experience is transcendent to anyone form but also is contained in the form.

Once more this kind of pluralist mystical theology was not acceptable to the Bavarian Church authorities.[14] After the completion of the thesis, I had to continue as self-employed, trying to do what I would have done in the Church freelance. I eventually have found the label of "integral and interreligious spirituality" for it. Things developed slowly, but there was always enough to live on. Since 2005, I occasionally travel to India for seminars, during which I try to introduce people to an interreligious spirituality by way of Abhishiktānanda's life, visiting places which were important for him as well as other spiritual places and ashrams, Hindu, Christian and more trans-religious ones.[15]

Towards an integral and interreligious spirituality

Two generations after Abhishiktānanda, most of us no longer seem to have those inner struggles with which he was afflicted for 25 years[16] whether or not one can be a Christian and practice Vedanta, Zen or Yoga at the same time. Theologians found a way out of the atomic mushroom.[17] Christians can be as inclusivistic or even pluralistic as Hindus or Buddhists, whether in India or in the West. For many an interreligious approach to spirituality seems almost natural today. Yoga and Zen have become an integral part of Christian spirituality in the West, or I may say, of a global spirituality. This is good news.

But the whole outlook on spirituality has also changed towards a more integral approach. The traditional religions were founded on the revelation of a spiritual reality far off from the physicality, animality and earth-bound mentality of the general human being. In St. John, Jesus says that his "The Kingdom is not of this world" (18: 36). Abhishiktānanda's spiritual ideal was acosmic; he was always aiming at the beyond. Indian religions were all focused on the release from the cycle of birth and rebirth. Transcending mind and life were the aim of religion while earthly life was characterized by suffering, sickness, finitude, it was seen as a vale of doom, a prison of the soul, a place of decision about one's eternal fate, etc.[18]

The modern mind, however, has a more positive attitude towards earth life than most religions which were formed in a pre-modern, mythical culture where the focus on God or the Absolute, religion and the afterlife was the governing force of life. The change came largely through scientific knowledge and its technological adaptations. Reason took over after religion which though spoke of God and love, had proven to be the cause of discord and war, and religious claims were debunked to be inconsistent with scientific truth. Moreover, science and technology seemed to be more successful at making the earth a better place to live in than religions had been.[19] More and more the mind of the global humanity turned from God and the afterlife to life on earth. Religion slowly took up the challenge. Modern Christian theology, which I studied at the university, largely concurred with this turn of attention toward the world and its needs (e.g. Protestant Liberal Theology, Dialectical Theology, Bultmann's "existential interpretation", Vatican II's aggiornamento, Liberation Theology). But there was nearly no spirituality in it like what I had found in Eastern traditions. My own spiritual outlook was thus deeply influenced by the traditional teachings of the East aiming at enlightenment in order to be free from karma, the ascetic ideal, even if it was the version of the non-dualist traditions (Vedānta and Mahāyāna Buddhism), while I was living a modern life. The usual context of the spiritual quest in the West today is a lay structure; teachers conduct workshops in meditation centers or at local on-going education organizations. Traditions like Zen originate in monasteries or ashrams where the whole life is oriented toward spiritual dynamism. Here, after a Zen sesshin (e.g. 7 days of intense monastic practice in silence with about 8 hours of meditation daily) I come back to a life that is focused on other concerns like earning money, taking care of the family etc. The task and difficulty I felt was the integration of spirituality and worldly life. After the first enthusiastic years, there was an increasing discrepancy between the traditional spiritual ideals which I had and life.

Sri Aurobindo's integral yoga

The change came with reading Sri Aurobindo. In his spiritual philosophy I found the leap in Indian spirituality towards a positive evaluation of the world.[20] The Integral Yoga he discovered comprises all the spiritual experiences of the "old yogas" (as he likes to name them) but views them in a different context. Its spiritual ideal is not liberation from the cycle of rebirth, but the transformation of life on earth.[21] Spiritual practice therefore has two objectives: one is the evolution of the soul towards perfection in manifesting the Divine (and not just realizing its Divine nature as such), and the other is contributing to the evolution of life on earth (a collective evolutionary goal to which the evolution of the individual soul contributes). Both evolutions are interconnected movements in the manifestation of the Divine as creation or manifestation culminating in a Divine Life on earth. Souls are not just born in the body to find the fastest way out again, but to have experiences and learn from them, also to learn how to be in the material form and manifest an ever-increasing capacity to manifest spirit in matter. In this way they bring forth the evolution.

Most helpful for my own spiritual practice und for understanding it were the recorded talks with Sri Aurobindo and his Letters on Yoga.[22, 23] In these Sri Aurobindo is very open about his own spiritual practice and experiences[24] as well as about the difficulties of the path, explaining the intricacies of the sādhana in a rational, human, and often humorous way.[25] I obtained a better understanding of the difficulties of the path and the importance of being on the path, and I came to realize that without these one would not become stronger. I learned from him that the higher one climbs, the greater the fallbacks can be. Therefore it is much more important to establish calm and peace in the mind than to have experiences at any cost. Experiences would come when the system is ready for it. Experiences open up the mind for new vistas; but in order to reach a higher level and get established there, the system needs to undergo the necessary transformations in the mental, vital and physical being. Sri Aurobindo emphasizes the approach of the mind and the heart. Stillness of the mind is reached by focusing on the Divine, preferably in the heart and/or head centre. The opening of the heart center awakens the psychic being, which gives a direct connection to the Divine within. The opening of the head center aims at opening the mind toward the Divine *śakti* above the head. It is the soul's aspiration which calls down the Divine Force into the mind, and from the mind to work its way down to the vital and the physical being. In this way, he says, the dynamics of the sādhana are much more secure than starting with the physical and working one's way up. In any practice one is asked to focus on the Divine; it is never a matter of method or technique.[26]

Zen and the form of Yoga I have been practicing[27] aim at stilling the mind with a strong emphasis on the body and the breath. Focusing on the body and the breath is the main means to still the mind. From the physical one proceeds to the pranic level. For this a mental focus on the region below the navel, called *hara* (Japanese for stomach), is used in Zen.[28] More advanced practices are the mental practice of *koans* (in Rinzai Zen; The Zen stories used in meditation which display an aspect of awakening) aiming at a sudden, often dramatic awakening, and the "silent illumination" practice through "just sitting" (*shikantaza*) without any special focus (in Soto Zen), being just there with all else, in the non-duality of emptiness and form. Zen, as is well known, highlights "sudden awakening". The Southern Chan school in China with its "sudden approach" developed in distinction to the Northern School with its "gradual approach". The Rinzai style of sitting with its focus on *satori* (awakening) experience through intense sitting and the practice of Koan mainly in group retreats with a Zen master or teacher produced severe *enlightenment stress* leading, as mentioned above, to a psychosomatic illness. When one thinks that enlightenment is just around the corner, right at hand, then one asks, of course: Why doesn't it come right now? Later I discovered the seemingly milder Soto approach, which does not focus on satori but on "silent illumination" through extended "just sitting" (*shikantaza*), just being there in the present moment and letting things unfold. Soto master Dogen (1200-1251) says that awakening develops over a long time, but when it is there, it is sudden and full.[29] Dogen also emphasizes that enlightenment is already there (in the form of "original enlightenment"), but in the beginner it shows itself as, for example, pain in the legs. Practice is the unfolding of this original enlightenment. Today I see that the problem I had was mainly due to my limited understanding and the egocentric manner in which I undertook the practice. In the early years I did not read or reflect much on the teaching. I just practiced it. Today I know that it is very helpful to study the teachings of the tradition one follows and the others, too. All the great Zen masters did this. And today there is the fullness of the spiritual traditions at hand. So much to study and get knowledge from! Of course, practice is more important than study. But to have a good mental understanding is very helpful and part of the integrality of sādhana. Sri Aurobindo's extensive written works displaying a broad and in-depth understanding of spirituality and life and their interconnection; his intellectuality, and the appreciation of all human achievements, were an eye-opener.

> "Sudden enlightenment" means that enlightenment is already there as the "original face"; it is not something which can be produced by practice. This is illustrated by many Zen stories. Mazu Daoyi (709-788) was practicing intensive zazen in his hermitage. His master, Nanyue Huairang (677-744), sat next to his hut making noise by rubbing a brick on a stone. Mazu, disturbed in his meditation, came out and asked what he was doing there. The master said that he was rubbing the brick to make a mirror out of it. Mazu questioned: How can you make a mirror by rubbing a brick? The master retorted: How can you become a Buddha by practicing zazen? Mazu experienced a sudden awakening.

The above story illustrates the famous poem of Huineng (638-713) in which he says that in emptiness (śūnyatā) there is no mirror on which dust can settle. It is an answer to the poem of Shenxiu (505-706) which says that the mind is like a mirror which constantly needs to be wiped clean in order to reflect reality properly.[30] The awakening is an awakening to the ultimate reality which is already there. The true nature is always there and practice is just an unfolding. The 20th century Zen master Shunryu Suzuki (in his classic *Zen Mind Beginner's Mind*) says that all problems in Zen derive from wanting to achieve something. What is to get rid of is the egocentricity in the practice. The pure Zen practice is just sitting, just being, with all that is there, in non-duality or suchness. The enlightenment stress I experienced earlier was due to my psychological structure. It was my own ignorance, youth, inexperience that was responsible, not Zen as such. I didn't know yet that the meaning of the talk of "sudden awakening" is that there is no need to force oneself to climb from level to level towards the goal, but that you can relax in the present moment as there is nothing to be reached, it is there already. [31] It is, in order to use another language, the causal state in which all immanence has its roots, the non-dual state, in which nirvāṇa and saṁsāra, form and emptiness, being and non-being are one and the same. So "sudden enlightenment" in a way is related to the concept of grace and of calling down the Divine śakti by the aspiration of the psychic being in Sri Aurobindo's yoga. But in Sri Aurobindo there is a more balanced understanding of the whole process, and there is the view of the evolutionary transformation of mind, life and matter through spiritual sādhana.

The integrality of spiritual practice is especially highlighted in Sri Aurobindo's synthesis of Karma, Jñāna and Bhakti Yoga, which correspond to the mental faculties of will, knowledge and emotion. All planes and parts of the being have to be included and developed and seen in their interconnectedness. Karma Yoga is important as a means to bring the Power down the decisive component towards integrality. The world has to be integrated to one's spiritual practice. No integrality without Karma Yoga, working. Thus practice is in and with the world. Jñāna Yoga is important to expand the mind and the vision. And Bhakti Yoga integrates the emotional part of our being. All three Yogas contribute to the Yoga of Self-Perfection towards a Divine Life on earth which is the eschatological horizon of Sri Aurobindo's Integral Yoga. The aim is not just realizing one's true nature but transforming one´s life. The ascent is combined with the descent of the Force (Christian language would call this grace). This process is not to be approached under coercion, but with a sense of harmony. Too much activity (coming from egocentricity) would disharmonize the process. The process is itself started by the movement of the Divine Spirit and Force to manifest itself by evolution. This integral perfection is brought about by a progressive surrendering to the Divine Force which is active in all life, in all spheres and in all details. All the levels and details have their integral necessity with respect to the whole, and their relative autonomy and freedom as well. But all these are everywhere and at all times they are a manifestation of the Divine, held by the Divine will. In meditation one may focus on the heart centre as the seat of the psychic being, or on the head-centre to widen the mind and transcend it into *Overmind*. You cultivate this relation and have the faith and the expectation that it deepens and deepens ever more. The evolutionary process is as well a collective as an individual one. It goes via the individual but aims at the collective. The incarnated soul works on her own perfection as part of the manifestation of the Divine in matter. Manifesting the highest level of consciousness in conscious beings must be the rationale of the process of manifestation.[32]

Interestingly Sri Aurobindo places love higher than knowledge, and correspondingly the personal aspect of the Divine higher than the impersonal. In Buddhism one is used to an impersonal language, so one tends to throw out the personal aspect altogether.[33] For a Zen practitioner Sri Aurobindo's high appreciation of the personal aspect of the Divine was therefore quite challenging. But can one love an impersonal Divine? Can a person originate from a non-person? The non-personal aspect, he says in the part on *The Yoga of Divine Love* in his *Synthesis of Yoga*, is an aspect of the Divine person which takes on the śūnyatā and nirguṇa garment in order to lead the devotee beyond any notion towards an absolute *Beyond*. But behind it is the īśvara aspect leading back into the manifestation of that beyond in the whole of creation, in the endless potentiality (śūnyatā) as well as in the tiniest transitory manifestation governing the evolution of each and all. The final jñāna or gnosis does not dissolve the personality of the soul; a certain kind of individuality continues. The ego has to go, but a Divine personality is gained, which keeps its individuality in harmony with the whole. Thus the ideal is not a static oneness, but the harmony of the one in the many.[34]

Ken Wilber's integral spirituality

Building upon the evolutionary spiritual philosophy of Sri Aurobindo (among others), Ken Wilber has recently drawn up a modern integral spirituality which sees more levels of evolution before the Supermind.[35] He takes up, of course, the focus on spiritual reality, seeing the world and its many levels and dimensions as integral parts of the divine project of evolution. Scientific knowledge and progress, therefore, are also seen as integral parts of the whole. Spirituality, the experience and knowledge of the ultimate reality, is thus *One*, allegedly a very important line of development, but there are others too (kinesthetic, moral, cognitive, emotional, aesthetic, etc.[36]) All those lines undergo development of structural stages of consciousness - magical, mythic, rational, pluralistic, holistic. So the different lines or parts of the being have their own evolutions through the different stages, meaning, for example, one can have access to higher spiritual states but still be emotionally, cognitively or morally on a mythic-conventional level. Integrality is a level or stage beyond those mentioned, still mental but open to the spiritual states of consciousness. Wilber's formula of progress is: "transcend and include". The integral structure of consciousness transcends rationality, but also integrates it, just like it integrates the former mythical and magical structures. Integrality sees the nature and value of all the structures and all dimensions of the being. Its basis thus is pluralism and holism, but it has a greater scope of freedom, on the one hand, and most importantly a more or less experiential (and also theoretical) knowledge of the spiritual states on the other, which Wilber divides into four structures: psychic, subtle, causal, and non-dual.[37]

Religion is grounded in the spiritual experience. This experience or the variety of possible spiritual experiences was historically received in a mythical and preliminary rational structure.[38] The role of religion in an evolutionary, integral structure of consciousness is that it acts like a conveyor belt.[39] Religions can pick up people in all the former kinds of consciousness structures and lead them on towards the next ones. Meditation is a central practice as it fosters a process of interiorisation, making that which was identified as subject into an object, thus revealing a progressively deeper and more integral level of subjectivity, with the mystical stages being realized as a truer and more encompassing self, and finally the Divine as the ultimate Self, the Self of all.

Ken Wilber and the Integral Institute which he founded have developed an Integral Life Practice, translating the high dynamic mysticism of Sri Aurobindo's spiritual philosophy into the mental scope of the information age accessible to many people today with the intention of providing means to take the next step on the ladder of evolution. It is an integral and interreligious[40] spirituality which builds upon the fullness of humanity's spiritual heritage in dialogue with its traditions, as well as with scientific knowledge and other contemporary lines of making sense of life on earth. It sees value and meaning in all traditions (religious, humanist, spiritual) resuming its threads in the further evolutional weaving towards the Kingdom of God as Divine Life on earth. We are all partners on this path, enriching each other dialogically with what we have found out and will further find out. If there is an evolution of human consciousness then, all of that will contribute to it.

Endnotes

[1] *Das Feuer der Weisheit. Ein Benediktiner verbindet den lebendigen christlichen Glauben mit dem reichen spirituellen Erbe Indiens*, Bern/München/Wien (O.W. Barth Verlag) 1979 (transl. Martin Kämpchen). *Guru and Disciple: an Encounter with Sri Gnanananda, a Contemporary Spiritual Master*, rev. ed., Delhi (ISPCK) 1990 (1974; orig. French ed. 1970).

[2] This is a formulation of Fr. AMA Samy (SJ), who once asked me, "How did you fall into Zen?"

[3] In 1993, Michael von Brück asked me to teach introductory sesshins which I started the year after.

[4] In the first years I did not read much on Zen or Buddhism. When I did I found it very helpful. Although the Zen school defines itself as a "transmission outside the scriptures" the great Zen masters were all very educated people who had studied a mass of scriptures. Of course reading and knowing the scriptures is secondary to meditation.

[5] I was married and became a father of a daughter in 1995, a second one came in 2001.

[6] See below.

[7] On this journey I had been deeply impressed by Fr. Bede's liturgies and preaching which marked my self-image as a pastor-to-be.

[8] Christian Hackbarth-Johnson, *Interreligiöse Existenz. Spirituelle Erfahrung und Identität bei Henri Le Saux* (O.S.B)/Swami Abhishiktānanda (1910-1973). Frankfurt et al. (Peter Lang) 2003.

[9] See the following quote from a letter written on Feb 9, 1967 summarizing the identity synthesis he had reached then:

[10] James Stuart, Swami Abhishiktananda. *His life told through his letters.* ISPCK rev. ed. 1995, p. 310f (letter to Murray Rogers, 2.9.1973), corrected from the French original. Ibid: p. 317 (letter to Murray Rogers, 4.10.1973).

[11] See esp. the diary entry of Feb 2, 1973. But similar thoughts can be traced back until the 1950s.

[12] André Couture talks in the context of Le Saux of a "relativism of transcendence" ("relativisme du dépassement"), which takes the different religious traditions serious, "by daring to follow them to their last point where they call for conversion and seem to transcend themselves from inside." See André Couture, Altérité et religions dans l'expérience de Dom Henri Le Saux, in Chemins de dialogue, Revue bisannuelle, Marseille (L'Institut de Science et de Théologie des Religions de Marseille) No. 2 (1993), S. 28. See also the chapter "Pluralismus und Transreligiosität" in Hackbarth-Johnson, op. cit., p. 484-500, esp. p. 495.

[13] When I explained what I was working on, the person responsible asked: "And what do you believe?" When I answered that this is what I believe in, too, her decision was made. The Church Council took about one and a half years to decide on my case. Of course, it felt bad to be rejected, my worst fears of standing alone without an institutional and financial net came true. But it was also a relief not to have to work within the narrow boundaries of an institution, having to speak a certain language, etc. Today I have a more integral view of the necessity of institutions than at that time. Maybe I would be able to fight the case more conciliatorily.

[14] Sri Aurobindo Ashram and Auroville, Krishnamurti Society.

[15] As documented in his spiritual diary, see Abhishiktananda, Ascent to the Depth of the Heart. The Spiritual Diary (1948-1973) of Swami Abhishiktananda (Dom H. Le Saux). A selection, edited with introduction and notes, by Raimon Panikkar. English translation by David Fleming and James Stuart. ISPCK, Delhi²1998.

[16] Like for example Fr. Sebastian Painadath. See his books: *The Spiritual Journey. Towards an Indian-Christian Spirituality.* ISPCK, Delhi 2012; and also: *We are Co-Pilgrims. Towards a Culture of Inter-religious Harmony.* ISPCK, 2nd rev. ed. Delhi 2012.

[17] For example, in a text like the Buddhist Mahāsatipatthāna Sutta, the physical body was seen as a sack of skin filled with disgusting stuff like urine, blood, slime etc., which will die and get cremated or rot and will be eaten by dogs and worms. Of course, meditating the body like this was supposed to counteract a naïve identification with the body, to also see the body as something that perishes; it was supposed to help orienting the mind towards the spiritual truth.

[18] See for example the statement of Steve Jobs, that an engineer does more for the good of mankind than all the prophets and gurus together. (I couldn't find the quote which I read in an Indian newspaper shortly after the passing away of the founder of Apple).

[19] Before him Swami Vivekananda already reinterpreted Advaita Vedantic philosophy to include social work.

[20] This clearly goes beyond the non-dual traditions like Zen or Tantra which see nirvāGa and saAsāra as one reality, as their goal is still mainly the overcoming of the cycle of rebirth.

[21] A. B. Purani, Evening Talks with Sri Aurobindo, Pondicherry (Sri Aurobindo Ashram Trust) 1982; Nirodbaran, Talks with Sri Aurobindo (2 Vol), Pondicherry (Sri Aurobindo Ashram) 2001; Nirodbaran, 12 Years with Sri Aurobindo, Pondicherry (Sri Aurobindo Ashram) 1988; Sri Aurobindo, Letters on Yoga (3 Vol), Pondicherry (Sri Aurobindo Ashram) [3]1970; Nirodbaran's Correspondence with Sri Aurobindo. The complete set (2 Vol), Puducherry (Sri Aurobindo Ashram) [3]2012; Sri Aurobindo to Dilip (4 Vol), Pune (Harikrishna Mandir) 2003-2011.

[22] Especially in the recorded talks he displayed a high esteem for any human achievement.

[23] See the collection in Sri Aurobindo, On Himself, Pondicherry (Sri Aurobindo Ashram) 1972.

[24] See Nirodbaran, Sri Aurobindo's Humour, Pondicherry (Sri Aurobindo Ashram) 2006; Dilip Kumar Roy, Sri Aurobindo came to me, Pune (Harikrishna Mandir) 2004 (1952).

[25] In a little section of the book "More lights on Yoga" Sri Aurobindo gives an answer to a disciple's question about whether it is harmful to switch between concentration on the heart and on the crown cakra. And he says, it is fine to switch, but the important thing is wherever you concentrate you do not concentrate on the heart or the space above the head, but wherever you concentrate, you concentrate on the Divine. For me this was extremely illuminating: it is not the technicality of the practice which is important, but to be focused on the Divine!

[26] The Yoga tradition I have been studying is the late style of Sri T. Krishnamacharya, taught by his son Sri Desikachar (Chennai). My teacher is R. Sriram, whose teacher was Sri Desikachar.

[27] Sri Aurobindo helped me to expand the range of focuses. All the centers had already started to become active by themselves, but I had tried to suppress them. Also helpful was to understand the centers in their correlation to the physical, vital and mental being, and the differentiation in outer and inner physical, vital and mental.

[28] See Shobogenzo, Genjokoan.

[29] Shenxiu is the representative of the gradual school of Chinese Zen, Huineng of the sudden school. Huinengs lineage was the one which gained acceptance and exists until today.

[30] One can see a homeomorphic equivalence in the Christian debate about grace and works. The sudden approach in Zen builds upon the givenness and nonproductability

of Buddha nature or enlightenment. The rationale of Luther's *sola gratia* is also that it is given, one cannot make it.

[31] Sri Aurobindo's evolutionary eschatology gives new vistas for the Christian belief in resurrection, an eschatological fulfilment in a manifested body. Beyond its exegetical and mythical background, the Biblical talk of resurrection may have its intuitive roots in the evolutional drive towards supramentalization of the physical which Sri Aurobindo foresaw as an evolutionary possibility and which his and the Mother's yogic sādhana was aiming at. There are close relations to the evolutionary theology of Pierre Teilhard de Chardin. (See Amal Kiran, Teilhard de Chardin and our Time, Waterfor CT (The Integral Life Foundation) 2000).

[32] Of course, in popular Buddhism anywhere as well as in Mahayana Buddhism the personal aspect is practically very much reintegrated in the worship of Buddhas und Bodhisattvas who are there to help us on our way to Buddhahood.

[33] The experience and philosophy of non-duality in Zen (and in Tantrism) certainly is related to Sri Aurobindo's vision while in the context of Buddhism one would not talk about the person as a reality. But the philosophy and experience of pratītya samutpāda, or dependent origination, is also a kind of seeing the person as part of a greater movement which can be reinterpreted in an evolutionary context. In many respects Sri Aurobindo's spiritual philosophy throws new light on traditional Christian beliefs which in modernity seem to have lost its foothold. The theologoumenon of resurrection was already mentioned. One may add the dynamic monotheism of the Trinity, the Father as ground of being, the Son as manifestation, and the Holy Spirit as the creative and unifying agent, expressed in Sri Aurobindo in a modern language of spiritual philosophy free from the mythical language of antiquity and brought back to the reality of spiritual experience.

[34] Ken Wilber, *Integral Spirituality. A Startling New Role for Religion in the Modern and Postmodern World,* Boston MA, (Integral Books) 2006.

[35] See Wilber, Integral Spirituality, 58ff.

[36] Sri Aurobindo discriminates the following stages: illumined mind, intuitive mind, Overmind, Supermind.

[37] Spiritual states can be experienced in any structure of consciousness and is interpreted in their respective notional scopes.

[38] Ken Wilber, Integral Spirituality, Ch. 9.

[39] It can also be transreligious in its form.

Dialogue between Christianity and Hinduism

Martin Kämpchen

Dialogue has become a fashionable word in recent times. We consider it progressive to discuss the need for the dialogue of religions and cultures and how to become competent for dialogue. It is generally accepted that interaction between human beings, especially between human beings of different origins, lead to a positive result and are for that reason desirable. This conviction is part of our European-Christian Enlightenment tradition. It naively assumes that people who know each other face-to-face are likely to develop sympathy for each other.

But is the opposite not possible as well? Namely, people who get in touch with each other and know each other's views thus create the opportunity for dissent and conflict, perhaps even violence. Obviously, more is needed for dialogue than just a coming together and speaking with each other. This additional feature is called "good intention," or the a priori positive inclination towards each other, the willingness to listen, the expectation of enrichment and the hope for a personal meeting of minds. Unless good intention exists, dialogue is impossible. This positive inclination towards each other is an occidental heritage. It is a reflection and a consequence of the Christian command to love one's neighbour. It embraces whoever happens to be near; that is, potentially is includes everybody.

Dialogue reveals a Christian-Enlightenment optimism. It claims that conversation pays off *because* and *although* men are different. Conversation is useful in order to discover differences and liberate ourselves from illusions. It is useful because we expect that beyond those difference lies something which unites us and which we are able to discover in our conversations. Whatever we may have in common does not nullify these differences. However, our Christian optimism demands that the common features are given more weight reducing the perceived differences to insignificance. How to term this common bond beyond all differences? The Human Factor, the Divine in Man, the Holy Spirit, the *atman* or divine soul in every man?

Dialogue makes sense only when this common feature residing in all men can be activated and made constructive use of. This means that the first condition for dialogue is that dialogue is the encounter of two partners who share equal rights, i.e. who are equal because God has equally endowed them with that common heritage. No cultural or religious superiority can be expressed, not even in innuendoes or by uttering obsolete clichés. A constant watch over our language, also body language, is needed to avoid slipping into our clichés of superiority. This means that Christians must not encounter Hindus with a sense of superiority; neither should Hindus show superiority towards Christians. Both religions harbour an inherent element of superiority. The claim that Christianity is the only religion capable of salvation is countered by the Hindu claim that Hinduism embraces all religions and therefore other religions have nothing new or different to offer.

This claim of uniqueness of one's own religion is psychologically easy to understand. In the Old Testament we encounter a jealous God who is venerated by a jealously loyal devotee. Neither God nor the devotee wish to accept somebody equal beside them. God reveals himself as God when he emerges victorious from the competition with other gods. This kind of tribalism is inherent in the psyche of all of us. Distinguishing between different tribes, social groups and economic strata is natural with us. I believe that only enormous efforts can free us from it. This freedom defines perhaps the quality of saints.

We transfer this group mentality from our human society to God. Divine revelation of the various religions expresses itself through languages which are man-made and shaped by history. They speak to us from a particular historical context into our contemporary context. God is shown as a God who does not tolerate other gods beside him. The path towards the realization that there cannot be but *one* God, only *one* Divine Being that reveals Himself/Herself/Itself in each religion – this path is long and needs prayer, contemplation, dialogue and above all the renunciation of selfishness.

The practical situation of dialogue

Let us consider the practical situation of dialogue between the Christian Churches and Hinduism developing mainly in India. Since the Second Vatican Council the Catholic Church has endeavoured to enter into dialogue with members of those religions whose communities dwell near Christians. In India, Christians constitute a minority of 2.6 %. Their neighbours are mostly Hindus and Muslims. The life of Christians in India is characterized by their awareness that they belong to a minority group. Therefore, their psychological situation is fundamentally different from the situation of Christians in most parts of Europe. A minority group craves for a clear and strong profile which can be recognized from outside. Those who enter into dialogue, however, need to be careful and sensitive with their identity. It should be maintained without making a show of it.

The dialogue between religious communities, especially between Christians and Hindus, is strongly influenced by the *history* of their interaction. After 1500, Portuguese Christians entered India as traders and conquerors who were later followed by colonizers. Missionaries of various countries soon entered India. They were motivated by a desire to convert and "save souls" and began this process by condemning

Hindu beliefs and practices as the work of the devil, sometimes even stooping to violence. This practice has wounded the Hindu psyche which has not healed until today. Even now the aversion of Hindu fundamentalists is based on the conversion methods of the Christian Churches. Contemporary Christianity in India must accept and manage these accusations and counteract them by reinventing itself theologically, culturally and socially. It needs to find a strong *Indian* identity. It took several centuries until it was accepted that Hinduism is a religion with an elaborate philosophy, an exciting and intricate mythology, and noble scriptures. They can indeed be the material from which one builds a Christian Indian identity.

There are basically three separate levels of dialogue operative between Christianity and Hinduism.

1. *The official dialogue.* – In a context carefully set up in advance members of the two religions, mostly "official" members like priests, teachers of religion etc., come together in order to discuss a subject which has been decided upon before. These members are known to be interested in interacting with members of the other religion. They are willing to learn and to achieve a consensus. In India, Christian dialogue centres have been established by the Churches which foster such kind of dialogue. A good number of enlightened and faithful Christians and Hindus attend these meetings. Conversations guided generally by theologians are followed by joint meditations and prayers. They are meant to deepen the intellectual consensus reached during these conversations and continue the atmosphere of togetherness.

2. *The academic dialogue.* – Theology and Religious Studies must lay the foundation on which dialogue can build. They must identify and analyse what is common and what is different in Christianity and Hinduism. They must analyse how far a Christian can accept the teachings and practices of Hinduism. This level of dialogue derives its value from the study of the Holy Scriptures and the traditions

of world religions. It is less geared towards immediate contact with members of other religions. Here human contact is restricted to the meeting of scholars at conferences and in universities. Their scholarly work is meant to instruct priests and educated laymen about the comparability of their own religion with other religions. It demonstrates how Christians can live their faith within the context of other religions and about the possibilities and limitations of interaction with other religions.

3. *Dialogue in daily life.* – The essential level of dialogue is the dialogue of everyday life. Here dialogue comes into its own. The two previous levels are of a preparatory nature. Everyday life with its hundreds of spontaneous encounters and unpredictable, unplanned situations is the actual field of dialogue. It is a challenge to find and maintain a wise balance between practising one's own religion and accepting, or even feeling and showing a real empathy for the believers of other religions. People who are in contact with members of other religions without tacitly or overtly, in conversation or in action professing one's own religion, cannot be said to engage in a dialogue. Neither can persons who impose their religion upon others without granting them a chance to profess their own religion, engage in a dialogue.

In the last two decades the barriers of ignorance and ill will between Hindus and Christians have become lower. The prejudices and the reservations towards Christians have fortunately become less. This is due to education, urbanisation and due to a less aggressive and more sensitive Christian missionary activity, and due to a wider scope of Christians and Hindus meeting socially. The enormous prestige of Christian educational institutions and Christian hospitals has helped to improve the image of Indian Christianity.

There is also no denying that the efforts by Christians to enter into dialogue with Hindus and to reduce the prejudices against them have multiplied. The intellectuals among Indian Christians, even to some extent among the clerics and bishops and especially within the monastic orders, have accepted that they have to enter into dialogue with Hindus and find a greater proximity to them. The bishops and the monastic orders have built institutes with the aim to initiate a formal dialogue; courses and seminars on Hinduism are being held. Members of Christian orders visit and stay in Hindu Ashrams as guests in order to acquaint themselves with their religious life. The openness of Western youth towards Hindu spirituality has had a positive effect on many educated Indian Christians.

Especially the āshram has become important as a space where Christians and Hindus meet for spiritual encounters and exchanges. An ashram is comparable to a Christian monastery, but it has its special features. A *guru* gathers his or her disciples together and leads them towards a spiritual life. Within the atmosphere of a community life the guru can teach mainly through an exemplary life, by propounding the scriptures and celebrating the daily rituals. Ashram life is characterised by a spontaneous and charismatic community life around the master. The disciples are either monks tied to monastic vows, or they live a family life and visit the ashram regularly. This kind of ashram life in Indian Christianity, characterised by spontaneity and a deeply personal guru-disciple relationship, was first imitated by European missionaries, although its flexibility had little in common with a Christian monastic life-style. They are the pioneers of the Christian Ashram Movement which has attracted countless European guests, and which meanwhile has become popular among Indian Christian communities. External forms of life are adapted to the Hindu ashram life, while the prayer life remains committed to Jesus Christ. Ashram life remains one of the important instruments of interreligious dialogue and of Christian inculturation in India today, although the appealing newness of ashram life has worn off.

Obstructions to dialogue

There are, however, certain reservations to dialogue both from the Christian and from the Hindu side. Some Hindu groups consider dialogue as a new method of converting them to Christianity and they approach Christian offers with suspicion. Hindu theologians consider a dialogue between their religion and Christianity (or any other religion) as of little use. They are convinced that, by entering into dialogue, they cannot learn anything new for their own faith life. They insist that Hinduism already contains everything that any religion teaches. Hence Christianity is, essentially, not different from Hinduism. Why, then, engage in dialogue?

Many Christians hesitate to enter into dialogue and into the project of inculturating their Christian way of life according to Indian-Hindu habits and values because of a fear of syncretism. Basically, they doubt that Hindus can have a genuine religious experience without the experience of Jesus Christ. Their suspicion is that Hindus do not go beyond the veneration of stone figures, animal sacrifice and pantheism. They are unwilling to respect the high ethical and spiritual aspirations of many Hindu believers.

Unfortunately, the relatively peaceful atmosphere of religious cooperation and harmony that prevailed in India so far has been disturbed since about two decades by Hindu fundamentalism. This was made possible by right-wing political parties that gained in strength and were able to turn many innocent minds against Christianity. Their dominant reason to reject Christianity is Christian missionary activity which, according to these groups, diminish the pride of Hindus in their own religion.

Principles and aims of dialogue

One virulent question is: Where does inculturation come to an end and syncretism begin? In other words, how far can Indian Christians proceed with their attempts at inculturating themselves into Hindu ways of life without harming their Christian faith? Syncretism comes into its own when Christians indiscriminately mingle and accept Hindu and Christian elements side by side without careful evaluation and without combining these elements in a meaningful whole. I here present a number of *principles* of Hindu-Christian dialogue, derived from my own experience, which aim at giving a more comprehensive response to this vital issue.

1. Not everyone is competent to engage in religious dialogue. Basically, those of us who are ready for dialogue in other spheres of life – in the family, at the working place, in school or College, in social groups and amidst minorities of any kind – are also equipped to have dialogue on the religious level.

2. Dialogue is possible and meaningful only when *whole* persons address themselves to *whole* persons. By that I mean that dialogue must engage persons on all levels of their humanity. Their strengths and weaknesses, their idiosyncrasies and peculiar difficulties all flow into the process of dialogue. Those of us who are engaged in dialogue are never merely the representatives of a certain religion or religious group. Essentially, we engage in dialogue as individuals. This means that dialogue is shaped by the particular human situation which the dialogue partners face at the time. Such a situation can inspire dialogue, but it may also weigh it down. Dialogue not only reflects the religious teaching of the dialogue partners, but it also, and perhaps more seriously so, reflects the personality and life history of individual religious believers.

3. Dialogue must accept the risk that we transform ourselves in its process. For example, it is quite possible that we begin to view our religion in a different light and accordingly change our thoughts, habits and perspectives. Persons who engage in dialogue are supposed to be mature in their religious belief and present a viewpoint which reflects a mature, lived faith. However, that does not mean that they are hardened and inflexible. We must accept this risk of transformation as an opportunity and a positive result of dialogue, rather than as a peril. We must allow ourselves to deepen our faith life through dialogue and receive new ways of experiencing our faith.

4. Interreligious dialogue forever goes beyond the accepted theological positions of each religion. Dialogue is prophetic and experimental; typically, it develops a dynamism which is spontaneous and intuitive and thus has the propensity to disregard systematic and dogmatic teaching and conventional habits. Persons in dialogue may encounter a transformative experience to such an extent that they, at least for the time being, totally inhabit the position of the partner in dialogue. This may happen "ecstatically", that is in the sudden rush of joy of experiencing a deep communion with people of other faiths.

5. By its very nature and intent, religious dialogue prefers to find similarity and harmony between religions. It downplays the differences and the controversies dividing them. For the time being these divisions may even be ignored. The aim is forever to transcend the divisions and find strategies for peaceful co-existence and co-operation in as many spheres as possible.

After we have formulated some principles of dialogue, we can now approach the *aims of dialogue* more easily. Some of them are:

1. To try to understand and accept the partner in dialogue in his/her otherness. We must seek a wise balance between appreciating this otherness and maintaining a critical distance from it. We should not cultivate a possessive and monopolizing attitude towards the other and his/her religion, robbing him/her of his/her identity. Equally, every attempt by the other to monopolize us must be warded off.

2. To become aware of the sensitive issues and vulnerability which the other struggles with. These areas should then be avoided as much as humanly possible and justifiable. Our aim should be to find and define a common "emotional field" with a matching language that does not offend. I am surprised to realize that often a harmonious understanding between religious groups fails only because of the use of insensitive language, while the real issues could have been resolved.

3. To foster understanding between religious groups by getting personally acquainted with as many individuals from the other group as possible. Many conflicts between religions are superficial and do not touch any religious content at all. Rather, they reflect the otherness of cultures, regions, professions, educational standards and emphases, family environments and language conventions. Personal friendships and good will can reduce and resolve such conflicts clearing the way to the deeper religious content.

4. To reduce and abandon the hesitation and reserve towards living together and co-operating with people of other faiths in all spheres of life.

The experience of God's mystery in dialogue

Dialogue first of all is meant to celebrate a common belief in God. Dialogue gathers together the community of believers, of men and women who confess to God's greatness and consciously employ this communality for the spread of peace and justice and love. It is meant as a visible and powerful sign in a world characterised by a lack of faith and by injustice.

By associating with non-Christian communities for some length of time, we become aware of the fact that they worship their God or their gods with the same fervour and dedication as we Christians do, and, indeed, sometimes with greater fervour and dedication. Dialogue professes the general aim to learn about the experiences and realizations of other religions and in this way to find a new depth and breadth in our own Christian religion. As has been stated often, we discover what we are by associating with the other. In India, Christians habitually live in close contact with Hindus. As a result, Christians feel the psychological urge to set themselves apart. However, such an identity must never be cultivated for its own sake, i.e. for selfish reasons. Rather, Indian Christians should emphasize their identity in order to discover a new depth and maturity in their religion. This may also mean that Christians absorb certain elements from Hinduism or other religions and integrate them into their Christian faith life. Christian tradition, as any tradition, remains alive and vibrant only when it continues to develop and grow. It must be involved in a constant process of self-doubt and self-discovery. Accordingly, Christians in India must fruitfully balance out two seemingly contradictory goals: On the one hand, to maintain an identity apart from the identity of Hindus; on the other hand, to learn from Hindus for the sake of a renewal of their own faith.

Christian theology has reflected a great deal about other religions. It has formulated several versions of a Theology of non-Christian Religions, starting with the proposal initiated by Karl Rahner that Hindus (and members of other religions) are "anonymous Christians". Vatican Council theologians suggested that Christianity "fulfils" the other religions which are, so-to-say, "pre-Christian." These were theological crutches which shied away from formulating a genuine *pluralism* of religions. Dialogue cannot but assume such a genuine pluralism. At the very least Christians must *at the time of dialoguing* take Hinduism as seriously as they take their own faith. If they do not do so, they cannot accept and treat their partners in dialogue as full and equal partners.

Personally, I cannot but take the faith of the Hindu and tribal friends in India with whom I have spent decades of close association, as seriously as I do mine.

There is, however, another, still more profound reason for accepting the plurality of religions while engaged in dialogue. The theological thinking of the last few decades has been filled with a variety of "negative theologies." They evoke visions of a "dark God" who cannot be experienced by the senses nor defined by words. God remains enveloped in "mystery." The consequence for Christians engaged in dialogue is compelling: The *relationship* between the God or the gods of Hinduism and the God of Christians is equally shrouded in mystery and cannot be defined. Hindu scriptures have described the mysterious nature of God in a variety of ways. The eternal verities cannot be formulated by Hindu theologians in any other way but by paradoxical evocations. Scripture postulates that God and his activity in the world is *anirvachaneeya*; that is "beyond the expression of thoughts and words." Ultimately, all relationships between religions and between the faithful members of these religions touch upon the mystery of God's inexpressible nature. A joint reverent respect, pervading all true religions and sincere believers, of the inexpressible nature of God constitutes the essence of dialogue.

Let me mention two observations as a result of my many decades of experience in dialogue: First, it is indeed easier to interact and maintain a harmonious relationship with people of our own faith. Many basic things in life need not be mentioned to a co-religionist. Many issues on the level of ideas and ideals and in practical life need not be mentioned because they are "understood."

Second, it is indeed more difficult to interact with people of other religions because this kind of tacit understanding is absent. However, an inspired communion of two people of different religions can spontaneously evolve to such heights of intimacy that these differences become practically void. Then the simple communion of these two people before God is all that exists. The one is hardly aware of the religion of the other; the one is totally focused on the other as a beloved person (not as a member of another religion).

The dynamics of interpersonal relationships will deal with religious beliefs in different ways. It is hard to define what should still be accepted as "Christian." I should think that as long as Jesus Christ remains in the centre of our faith life, everything seems to be "allowed." However, no rationally unambiguous law can be established in a field which in the final analysis is ruled by the mystery that is God.

The Mystique of Dialogue:
The Pathway to Spirit-Power
for a Liberative Struggle

Jojo M. Fung SJ

The experience of more than two decades of journeying with the indigenous peoples of Lakota the Apache in US, the Semai of Perak and the Murut of Malaysia, the Boctoc and Ifugao of the Philippines, the Karen and Lahu of northern Thailand and the Kayah and Kayan of Myanmar has been most enriching. These peoples have taught me the most valuable lesson that interaction and participation in their rituals entail recognizing the mystique of the intercultural, interreligious dialogue.

In the first section, I will explain a more contextual version of interreligious experience of which involves a time of *discipline* under the immediate tutorship of a reputable shaman or by the spirit-guide of primordial or deceased shamans. In the second section, I will offer a more contextual reflection on the fourfold dialogue as enjoined by the Asian Bishops in the light of my interreligious experience. This reflection calls for a greater recognition of the mystique in our dialogue with indigenous peoples which I will explain in the third section. Finally, my reflection on my interreligious experience convinces me that dialogue must be about empowering indigenous peoples to access and actualize the spirit power for the liberative struggle against the neocolonial imperialism that spawns the globalization of neo-liberal capitalism.

Discipling as integral to dialogue

Indigenous shamanism is one of the many religious traditions in Asia that predates Christianity and offers a unique and valid process of *discipling* under the guidance of a *guru* in the person of the shaman. Christianity has its own course of initiation and the Catholic Church has her own rite of initiation, but the process of *discipling* in indigenous shamanism is markedly different.

Indigenous shamanism, with its age-old beliefs and practices, stemming from the ancient civilization of the indigenous peoples, offers various ways of initiation.[1] What I term as a *baptism* into the deep mysteries of life offers such a pathway into the actual experience of shamanism in a village of the Murut community called Bantul in Sabah, East Malaysia. This *baptism* into the deep mysteries of life calls for a humbling of oneself to take one's place as an uninitiated and begin what can be a lifelong filial relationship with the master. The aspirant is normally driven by a certain passion to come and live with a community-acclaimed master-shaman in the rural village, and learn at his feet. When the master-shaman deems the aspirant suitable, he exercises the sole discretion to present the selected aspirant to the spirit-world for approval and admission to apprenticeship. This period of apprenticeship is informal, ranging from daily conversations, doing daily chores together with the master-shaman, unto the actual ritual celebration.

This informal rural school begins from the initial stage of dipping in the waters of shamanism, known to the initiated among the Muruts as "*na rio*" (taking a bath). Upon the completion of the initial phase, the initiated enter a more advanced level of immersion in which the master-shaman guides the initiated in calling the different spirits for different purposes that range from healing of the sick to deliverance of those possessed by evil spirits in order to improve the wellbeing of the community and the harmonious relationship between the human world and the spirit-world that guards over the Murut, the river, the forests and the land. Thereafter the learning of the initiated comes under the tutorship of the guiding spirits. Up until the last stage, the initiated comes under the guidance of the master-shaman who *disciples* the initiated through daily conversations and a series of rituals. These rituals are occasions for the master-shaman to dictate more incantations offered by the spirit-guide to the initiated. The master-shaman will instruct the initiated on intended purposes of the incantations and the kind of occasions when such incantations can be used by the initiated.

Certain evenings, during the season of the full moon, the initiated has to live with the master-shaman alone, in a hut, away from the community, so that the master-shaman introduces him to the family of spirits that the master-shaman is in touch with. With such a face-to-face introduction, the initiated recognizes the spirit-guide(s) assigned to him, besides the names that are given him earlier. Gradually, the master-shaman initiates the apprentice into the art of "summoning" and "communicating" with the spirit-guides and the initiated enters into a more familial relationship with the family of spirits.

When the master-shaman passes on, the initiated becomes the medium of communication with the family of spirits and continues to mediate the power of the spirits for the general wellbeing of the indigenous communities and their struggle for dignity and livelihood. Gradually with the exercise of the powers of the family of spirits, the disciple-shaman is acclaimed as the community shaman and thereafter, over time, even as an acclaimed shaman of the indigenous peoples in a given region.

This whole process, from the stage of a newly initiated to a "newly qualified" shaman, who acts as an intermediary between the communities and the spirit-world, is strewn with "a soteriological nucleus not yet assimilated into Christian consciousness" and yet "an Asian theology of liberation lies hidden there" and the "recovery of an ancient revelation is indeed a new creation."[2] In other words, the immersion has convinced me that God reveals through indigenous shamanism its salvific value. This immersion further convinced me that God saves the indigenous peoples of the primal religions (soteriology) through their sincere worship and practices.

Reflecting on my own process of *discipling* and the subsequent *baptism* into the deep mysteries of life in the light of the double experiences of Pieris, my own process has been a call to accompany these indigenous poor of Asia, unleash the soteriological power of their shamanic beliefs through the celebration of their shamanic rituals.[3] Indigenous shamanism is a source of liberative power not just for indigenous peoples but the teeming masses who suffer from the shocking scandal of crushing poverty and all forms of oppressive marginalization. Not unlike other religiosity of the poor, indigenous religiosity has the liberative power to set free a world caught up in a model of unsustainable development that relentlessly exploits both the natural and human resources based on the motifs of greed and dominance.

In indigenous religiosity lies a germinal liberation theology of sustainability. This liberation theology empowers the religious poor and enables them to supplant the logic of global capitalism by the logic of sustainable livelihood and dignity where the earth's resources are enough for all. This sufficiency is based on a just relationship with fellow humans and a harmonious relation between humans and the earth.

Dialogue with indigenous communities

Pope John Paul II, in his 1991 encyclical, *Redemptoris Missio* (56-57) highlighted the importance of "the dialogue of life" which includes three additional related aspects: cooperation in social concerns, theological exchange and sharing of religious experience. In the context of my experience of interacting with the indigenous peoples, this dialogue of life calls for the dialogue of accompaniment, of sharing religious experience and liberative struggle (*Redemptoris Missio*, 59).

Dialogue of accompaniment

The shamans believe that accompaniment is *from within* - they live in the midst of the village communities and guide the communities through ritual celebrations so that they have an inner mystical experience of the sacred power of the sacred spirits. Through communal prayers, chants and dance, the shamans enter into the sacred presence of God. In trance, the shamans enter an intimate and mystical experience of God who descends and missions them to act on God's behalf as salvific intermediaries.

Like Moses who guided the indigenous tribes across the wilderness, Red Sea and desert to the promised land, acting as their intermediary for manna and quail (Ex 16: 1-36) and water (EX17:1-7), and further revelation from God (EX 24: 18; 33: 1-35) on the relationship of Israel with Yahweh, so too the shamans who accompany the indigenous communities constantly seek God in ritual celebrations and act on God's counsels for the good of their communities. The intimate experience of the God of the shamans in ritual celebrations resonates with Jesus' experiences of the theophanic-Abba at his baptism, transfiguration, and at the hour of his anguish before the arrest (Jn. 12: 28-30; Lk. 22: 43-44).

Only such recurrent intimate mystical experiences of God empower the shamans to guide the indigenous communities out of all forms of addiction, evil desires and especially greed. In this way, the marginal indigenous communities will be delivered from the burden of poverty and offered the joy of sustainable livelihood with dignity, justice and peace.

In this dialogue, the shamans delight in the accompaniment of the Church that encourages them to establish a network of shamans so that they feel strengthened as a community of like-minded indigenous women and men specialists, be they healers, elders, exorcists, prophets, ritual performers or teachers. The presence of the Church during the process of accompaniment lends moral support to the gathering of shamans.

The presence of the Church legitimizes the shamanic traditions as the loci of God's salvation and revelation (Eilers 1997, 212), since

Craffert (2008, 296) unequivocally postulates that the shamans are types of the Galilean shamanic figure, Jesus of Nazareth.[4] The presence of the Church acknowledges and affirms their revelatory and salvific significance in the economy of God's plan of salvation. As envisaged by Fr. Jean-Pierre Oxibar, the empowering presence and protection of the Church ensures the "full flourishing" of these shamanic traditions.[5]

On the other hand, the Church is in a position to resolve the many dilemmas which the shamans face with regard to the religious practices of their shamanic rituals. A case in point is the lack of full attendance by the family members at the rites under the care of each shaman. The absence of the family members prohibits the shamans to perform the rites, calls into question the efficacy of the ritual celebration and thus undermines the shamans' authority, even exposing the shamans to traumatic experiences such as sickness and madness.

Dialogue of religious experience

The nature of this dialogue enjoins the Church of Asia to put out into the deep by taking a plunge into the ritual celebrations so as to take delight in the sacred presence of the mystic Owner and absolute Being, *Taj Hti Ta Tau*. This dialogue of religious experiences enables the Church to understand the importance of entering into the inner world of the mystical experience of the shamans (Fung 2014, 10). This will enable the Church to understand and appreciate the richness therein and thus be disposed to receive the revelation of God who is at work in their rites.[6]

With the indigenous shamans, this dialogue of religious experiences is not always discursive and therefore academic, but rather conversational, celebratory and therefore experiential. Upon the invitation of the shamans, there will be opportunities to attend and participate in the ritual celebrations presided over by the shamans, be it listening to the chants as observers or taking part in communal dancing as participants in order to experience spirit-possession by the God-who-descends (*ruach elohim*). Such spirit-possession will enable the Church to get an inner experience of the mystical experience of the shamans. This inner experience complements what is observed from the outside. It is important for the Church to have both the observational experience from the outside and celebratory experience from the inside to attain the desired complementarity of human and mystical experiences.

This dialogue of religious experiences will enable the Church of Asia to increasingly understand the inscrutable omnipresence of the Pentecostal Spirit.[7] The Spirit shattered a mono-ecclesial Jewish community and poured it forth into the Greco-Roman milieu. This universalization of the Creative Spirit, alluded to in the multi-glossarial phenomenon of Pentecost (Acts 2: 1-13), is a multi-religio-cultural manifestation and presence well attested by the shamans, the religious sages and the Church of Asia involved in this dialogue of religious experiences.

The multi-religio-cultural manifestation paves the way for the Church to enter into a gradual understanding of the alternative ways by which the shamans and the indigenous communities express their religious experience and how they articulate their understanding of God, their experience of being possessed by the Spirit (spirit-possession), and the liberative-salvific mission of this God. This articulation is more of a conversational sharing, either on a one-on-one basis or in a small group that involves recognition and clarification of what each dialogue partner is saying in the multiple rounds of personal sharing.

What appears to be a personal sharing is indeed an ongoing verbalized reflection on their mystical experiences of the shamanic ritual celebrations. In participating in this conversation, the Church is able to receive the revelation of God in and through the shamanic traditions. The Creative Spirit is already at work, purifying, elevating the current understanding and completing the experience with a new awareness so that the "elements of truth, of grace and goodness" that are not only "in the minds and hearts" of indigenous shamans and communities but also in "the rites and customs" of indigenous peoples being "'healed, elevated, and completed" by God's Spirit (AG no. 9, LG, no.17).

In this dialogical process, the Church is able to perceive, intuit and understand how God's Spirit is revealing from within the shamans' inner or mystical experiences. It is important for the Church to understand the verbalization of their shamanic spirituality – the uniqueness of their God (*Theos*) who descends in Spirit invisible to the human eyes but "experienceable" in their human heart as the divine touch and mystical spark. The Church needs to experience and understand how the shamans are overshadowed by the Creative Spirit (*Pneuma*) and hence spirit-possessed, and how this God (*Soter*) saves their people in the life-struggles as marginal communities.

In fact, what the Church witnesses in the shamans' communal prayer, chant and dance is the living local indigenous *theo*logy, *pneuma*tology and *soter*iology arising from within the communities of believers and shamans of the primal religions. The *arising* and *blossoming* of a local indigenous *theo*logy, *pneuma*tology and *soter*iology point to a Creative Spirit, breezing like the Spirit and blowing where the Spirit pleases (Jn 3: 8), operating in and out of the ecclesiastical structures, never totally monopolized or domesticated, always empowering, liberating and saving God's marginal peoples.

As the intermediary of God in the dialogue, the Church is invited to affirm and supplement what is needed to enrich the shamans' verbalized understanding and liberate their local theologies from any undue shadow of unethical influences. Finally, as the co-pilgrim, the Church is enjoined to "lift up" (as opposed to suppress and denigrate, cf. Jn. 8: 28; 12: 32) the local indigenous theologies and communicate them in a language intelligible to the outside world so as to challenge and enrich the local, regional and global Church and society.[8]

Dialogue of liberative struggle

Enkindled by the shamanic God-experiences, empowered by the indigenous theology, pneumatology and soteriology, motivated by the indigenous spirituality, both the dialogue partners are poised for actions – a praxis involving the liberative struggle of the indigenous communities in partnership with other stakeholders in the civil and political society, always in collaboration with the local councils and interfaith networks at the local and national levels.

It is a communal struggle for land to ensure a sustainable livelihood with greater security and dignity in their villages. It is a struggle that invokes the Divine in a communal interfaith prayer service for the recreation of sacred space and in the collective rite of sacralizing the forests, the sources of water for irrigational purposes, the rice grains before planting, the fields for planting, etc., in the ancestral homeland of these indigenous communities. Finally, it is a struggle against encroachment by developers and annexation by the hegemonic nation-states and against a neo-liberal economy that violates the dignity and security of the marginal communities.

As a dialogue partner, the Church of Asia is enjoined by the indigenous shamans to engage in a liberative struggle with the indigenous shamans and their peoples at different levels. At the socio-cultural level, dialogic reverence calls for respect of the otherness of their identity as the cultural and religious *other*, so that the indigenous peoples are not totally assimilated or annihilated by the dominant cultures. When it comes to the ecclesial level, it is a liberative struggle for greater democratic space to articulate their indigenous *theo*logies and practice their shamanic *spirit*ualities that call for the sacred sustainability of the earth and all life forms therein. Finally, at the local-regional-global structural level, it is the liberative struggle for freedom from the oppressive idolatry of global capitalism (see section 4 below).

The Church of Asia has much to gain from the dialogue with indigenous shamans to become a more inculturated Church among the indigenous peoples. In this dialogue, the Church will learn to behold the shamans with dialogic reverence, emulate their model of accompaniment, honor their mystical experiences of God, and engage in the liberative struggle of indigenous peoples for greater sacred sustainability of their livelihood in their ancestral homeland.

The mystique of dialogue

The experience of dialogue with indigenous peoples always brings us into the realm of the spirit-world of the divine assembly of Yahweh and the gods (Dt 10:17; Ps 29:1, Ps 82:1) that is inclusive of all those who have gone before us, from the biblical patriarchs, judges, kings, prophets, to Jesus, Mary, the saints, apostles, martyrs, congregational founders and foundresses of religious orders, our genealogical fore-grandparents and parents. This spirit world is more than a memory but a living presence and divine spirit-power that suffuse the human world and consciousness.

The experience of the mystery and power of the spirit-world is a felt-presence among the indigenous elders, healers, sages and shamans. When the mystery of the spirit- world is embraced with openness of the heart and mind, this felt sense is acquired after recurrent experiences of the lived indigenous spirituality mediated in a unique way through their seasonal ritual celebration like the annual water-spirit-ritual. This lived spirituality is best described as an embodied sense of an everyday mysticism (Rahner 1967, 87-88; Egan 1998,76-77).[9] This mystical sense of the spirit presence and power is akin to Rahner's insight, "For the experience meant here is the experience of eternity" (Ibid.) because the suffusing sacredness, in all its infinite expansiveness, is experienced in our midst as plausible. This mystical sense is the lived mindfulness of the eclipse and a compenetration of the *anthropos*, the *cosmos* and the spirit-world, in this open and multiversal space of God's creation. It is a recurrent yet perpetual mindfulness that "*they are here with us, with power, accessible for our everyday resistance and liberative struggle.*" It is this mystical sense that is akin to the Ignatian mystique of "*seeing all things in God and all God in all things,*"[10] always thankful for God's presence in everyone and everything in creation.[11]

This mystical sense of the compenetrative presenting of the spirit-world enables the everyday mystics of indigenous communities to explain that the humans actually live suspended in a relational web of interdependency and interrelations that is suffused with sacredness and mystery.[12] In this cosmic relational web, the mystic alerts us that *"everything is sacred and rituals make everything sacred"* due to suffusing and sacralizing presence of the spirit-world.[13]

This mystical sense enables us to appropriate the mystical cosmology and anthropology in a mystical age (Coyle 2013; Touti 1997)[14] with the paradigmatic shift in consciousness that we are *homo spiritus* and *homo shamanicus* (Fung 2014).[15] In other words, we are spirit-body with a mindfulness of the everyday presence and power of the spirit-world. The Great Creative Spirit, ancestral and nature spirits, alert us and communicate with us through the discernible signs, like dreams, call of birds and animals and local and regional events, like drought, climate change, superstorm and polar vortex. At the same time, the spirit-world seeks the human agency in the activity of suffusing, sacralizing, sensitizing and sustaining the *cosmos* and *anthropos*.

Gaining access for actualization

The *homo spiritus/shamanicus* lives in the Ignatian sense of being (Pieris 2008, 187) as a "discerning person" (*anthropos diatritikos*) who is "perpetually mindful or watchful of God working in all things and at all times."[16] In other words, they live in a mindful mystical sense that facilitates the connection and communication with the cosmic spirit-power. In this one-spirit-ness, the *homo spiritus/shamanicus* senses and discerns the communication from the spirit- world. Once discerned and understood, the *homo spiritus/shamanicus* becomes the mediatory conduit of the spirit-power and thus actualizes the power in confronting the local onslaughts of the postcolonial, imperial and globalized corporate hegemony of global (neo-liberal & state) capitalism and imperialism. These local onslaughts are meted out by the demonstrable hegemonic forces of the corporate cartel-controlled by the Eight Families who operate the Horsemen, the international banks, with colossal influence over the Conference of Foreign Relations, the Gulf Cooperation Council, the Royal Institute of International Affairs, the G7/G8 and G22, UN, World Bank, World Trade Organization and International Monetary Fund, etc. (Kanyandago 2008, 461; Wickeri 2008, 466).[17]

The menace has to be confronted with mounting multi-sectoral and leveled countercultural movements of local-regional-global solidarity with the excluded populace of the world. Such subaltern movements need to wed the religio-cultural sensibilities and wisdom with the cosmic-divine power of the creation-wide spirit-world. This is the confluence that the *homo spiritus/shamanicus* readily gains access to and actualizes the cosmic power for reversing the hegemony of cartelism, spawned by neo-colonial-liberal capitalism and military imperialism. This access to the inter-generational and creation-wide spirit-power is a growing consciousness among the indigenous communities who are negotiating these onslaughts. With the gradual globalization of this *mindful access*, this consciousness becomes a ready access to the actualization of the spirit-power. The conjoining of spirit-power with the human spirit makes possible the eruption of the insurrectional power (Baliber 2001, 18; Soguk 2007, 296-299)[18] of the subaltern movements for the concerted contestation (Wilfred 2004, 86)[19] against the systemic and despotic dark forces (*mammon*, Luke 16: 13) that perpetuate the neoliberal, imperial and military hegemony (Freedman 1995, Henderson 2005).[20]

The same contestation calls upon the *homo spiritus/shamanicus* to engage in the fourfold activities of God's Creative Spirit: (i) suffusing the *cosmos* and *anthropos* with God's sacred presence and power so that humankinds relate to God's creation with reverence and sensitivity; (ii) sacralizing the *cosmos* and *anthropos* through the power of the spirit-world, especially through ritual celebrations so that everything and everyone is made sacred; (iii) sensitizing the rest of humankind to the need for developing and globalizing the mindfulness that gains ready access to the power of the spirit-world and actualize that spirit power for the concerted efforts of contestation, that reverses the onslaughts at the local, regional and global levels ; (iv) sustaining the *cosmos* and *anthropos* with the sacred presence and power of the spirit-world so that creation manifests the eternal glory and splendor of the God's Creative Spirit.

This theological reflection on my interreligious experience of the dialogue of life with the religio-cultural traditions of the indigenous peoples is more than a verbal engagement. It is an embodied dialogue between humans who are body-spirits. The humans (*homo spiritus/ shamanicus*) live in a web of relations with the spirit-world. The discipled *homo spiritus/shamanicus* exercises the capacity to access and actualize the sacred power of the spirit-world in the various sites of contestation orchestrated by the super/supra hegemons around the world. This actualization also facilitates the fourfold activities of God's creative spirit through the *homo spiritus/shamanicus* so that God and God's reign pervade in creation. In this way the mystique of dialogue from an indigenous perspective of Asia is to bring about the total sacralization of creation so that God is in all, through all and all in all.

Endnotes

[1] Among the indigenous communities of the Areuna and Taulipang in South America, "the shamanic novitiate was reported to last from ten to twenty years" (Sullivan 1988, 395). For detail, see Lawrence E. Sullivan, Chapter 7, "Specialists" in *Icanchus' Drum: An Orientation to Meaning in South American Religions* (New York and London: MacMillan Publishing Company and Collier Macmillan Publishers, 1988), 386-465.

[2] Aloysius Pieris, "Toward An Asian Theology of Liberation: Toward a Definition of the Religio-cultural Dimension," in *An Asian Theology of Liberation* (New York: Orbis Books, 1992) 71.

[3] See Jojo M. Fung, *Garing The Legend: A Decorated Hero A Renowned Shaman*. Sabah Museum. Kota Kinabalu, Sabah: Percetakan Kolombong Ria, 2006.

[4] Eilers, Franz-Josef, ed. *For All the Peoples of Asia. Vol. II. Federation of Asian Bishops' Conferences Documents from 1992 to 1996* (Quezon City, Philippines: Claretian Publications, 1997.

[5] The Lahu regarded Jean-Pierre Oxibar (1898-1964), a Betharram priest, as a prophet, a liberator and protector of the Lahu who "rejoiced in such indigenous traditions as being those of a people who, like his own Basques, could become Christians but still express their joy of life through the ways of their ancestors.

[6] Participation in the shamanic rituals draws its assurance and inspiration from the Asian Bishops who state, "In Asia, the dialogue of prayer and spirituality is highly valued. Prayer together, in ways congruent with the faith of those who take part, is an occasion for Christians and followers of other faiths to appreciate better the

spiritual riches which each group possesses, as well as to grow in respect for one another as fellow pilgrims on the path through life. Human solidarity is deepened when people approach the divine as one human family" [FIRA IV (Pattaya): 8].

[7] The Asian Bishops state the same conviction that "Christians believe that God's saving will is at work, in different ways, in all religions. It has been recognized since the time of the apostolic Church and stated clearly again by the Second Vatican Council (cf. GS. 22; LG. 16).

[8] The Asian Bishops have declared that "each local church, each people's history, each people's culture, meanings and values, each people's traditions are taken up, not diminished or destroyed, but celebrated and renewed, purified if need be, and fulfilled ... in the life of the Spirit." [IMC (Manila): 15].

[9] See Karl Rahner "Reflections on the Experience of Grace," *Theological Investigations III*, trans. Karl H. and Boniface Kruger, OFM (Baltimore, MD: Helicon Press, 1967.

[10] Cf. *Contemplatio ad Amorem*, Sp. Ex. 230-234.

[11] In the October 4, 2010 report on Ecumenism and Interreligious Dialogue, Fr. Nicolas Aldofo, SJ, Superior General of the Society of Jesus, remarked that "of course, in our encounter with others, our Ignatian tradition trains us to use methods which are discerning, contemplative, and grateful for God's presence alive in everyone and everything."

[12] This mystery, as quantum physics suggests, is characterized by complementarity, complexification, probability, profundity, synchronicity, unpredictability and even a profound sense of direction. See Diarmuid O' Murchu, *In the Beginning Was the Spirit: Science, Religion, and Indigenous Spirituality* (Maryknoll, New York: Orbis Books, 2012), 46, 72, 73.

[13] As for understanding God as creative activity, see Jürgen Moltmann (1985, xii; O' Murchu 2012, 138) who used the phrase "God the Holy Spirit...is *in* all created things" and this God, in the postulation of Gordon D. Kaufmann (2004, xi, 48) "is an activity rather than a person" for "God is our name for the creativity in nature" and "the creativity in nature is God enough" (2008, 142, 284).

[14] See Frank X. Tuoti, *The Dawn of the Mystical Age: An Invitation to Enlightenment* (New York: The Crossroad Publishing Co., 1997) and Kathleen Coyle, "Theology and the New Cosmology: A Quantum Leap in Theological and Spiritual Insight," *EAPR*, Vol. 50, no. 2 (2013), 189-205.

[15] See Jojo M. Fung, SJ, "Sacred Time For A Sacred Sojourn In The Mystical Age," *Ignis*, Vol. XLII, 4 (2013/ 14), 7-32

[16] See Aloysius Pieris, "Spirituality as Mindfulness: The Biblical and Buddhist Versions, in Patrick Gnanapragasam and Elisabeth Schüssler Fiorenza, *Negotiating Borders: Theological Explorations in a Global Era* (Delhi: ISPCK, 2008), 185-198.

[17] See Thomas J. Volgy, Kristin Kanthak, Derrick V. Frazier, and Robert Stewart Ingersoll, "The G7, International Terrorism, and Domestic Politics: Modeling Policy Cohesion in Response to Systemic Disturbances." *International Interactions* 30 (2004), 191-209.

[18] See Etienne Balibar, "Outlines of Topography of Cruelty: Citizenship and Civility in the Era of a Global Violence," *Constellations* 8, no. 1 (2001), 15-29.

[19] Felix Wilfred believes that "the hope for tomorrow lies in the resistance today," see his article, "Searching for David's Sling: Tapping the Local Resources for Hope," *Concilium* (2004:5), 85-95.

[20] See Dean Henderson, *Big Oil & Their Bankers in the Persian Gulf: Four Horsemen, Eight Families & Their Global Intelligence, Narcotics & Terror Network, The Grateful Unrich: Revolution in 50 Countries*, USA Bridger Publishing House, 2005.

With the Eyes of a Friend

Henry Pattarumadathil SJ

This is not an article on any topic connected with inter-religious dialogue, nor a scientific paper with footnotes and explanations. Rather, it is a short narrative, semi autobiographical in nature, recalling some of my memories and experiences from my forty-year long relationship with Sebastian Painadath. My purpose is to share with readers how he and the inter-religious mission of Sameeksha have influenced me in my life as a Christian, a Jesuit and a Bible teacher. Three different phases of my life are touched on below. From each phase I relate an event or two highlighting its impact on my journey of faith.

Jyothis, Kaloor

It was in 1983 that I met Sebastian Painadath for the first time. In those days he used to conduct Bible classes at Jyothis, the Jesuit community in Kaloor. My eldest sister, who is a religious, regularly attended them. One day she requested me to accompany her to the class. I was not at all interested, nevertheless, I joined her for a Saturday afternoon session. I had heard quite a lot about him from my sister, but I had never seen him in person. He appeared on the stage wearing brown pants and a saffron kurtha, and greeted us with a warm and charming smile.

A map of Palestine had been spread out on a board. He took a piece of chalk, drew a pyramid shape diagram on the board and began his class. His presentation of Jesus against the socio-religious background of

Palestine excited me tremendously. He divided the pyramid into three horizontal columns, each representing a stratum of Jewish society. In the upper stratum he wrote the term *śudha-vargam* ('the pure ones'), assigning that column to the religious elite of Jesus' time (the chief priests, Sadducees, Pharisees and the scribes) who claimed themselves pure and blessed and who thanked God everyday for their God given superior status. In the second column the Samaritans were marked, with the title *śankara-vargam* ('the mixed ones'). Though originally they were Jews, they had lost their purity by entering into marital relationship with Assyrians and other non-Israelites. The third column represented the lower stratum of society with the label *aśudha-vargam* ('the impure ones'). People with different diseases, people who carried out impure jobs, the tax collectors, prostitutes and so on were mentioned in this column. The so called 'pure ones' of the upper stratum despised these people and interpreted their physical, social, religious and cultural misery as signs of a curse from God.

Having given a detailed explanation of all these groups and their position in the society, Painadath posed some challenging questions: Where do we place Jesus in this diagram? With whom did he associate himself during his life? Why did the religious authorities plot against him? I, who was a first year degree student, had not thought much about a Jesus who was a friend of tax collectors and sinners, who enjoyed the company of women, who boldly challenged the unjust and inhuman laws and rituals of the Jewish religion. He summarized his portrayal of Jesus with a verse from Sri Vayalar Ramavarma, a Malayalam poet: *"Snēhikayilla njān nōvumātmāvine snēhichidāthoru thathva śāstratheyum"* (I will not embrace any philosophy that does not embrace a wounded soul).

Then on every second and fourth Saturday I walked to Jyothis for Bible classes, sometimes even without my sister. Some of my friends from the parish also joined me later for these fortnightly treats. Under the influence of these classes I wrote my first Biblical article, with the title *Chunkakārum Pāpikalum* (The tax collectors and sinners) and published it in a manuscript magazine. Let me append an aside here. At present I teach the New Testament at the Pontifical Biblical Institute, Rome. In literary criticism, we use the term *inclusio*, when we observe a similar structure or verse or idea that functions like a frame at the beginning and end of a section of text. I see my Jesuit life as a journey within such an *inclusio*, started at Jyothis on those Saturdays of 1983 and continuing at the Biblical Institute today. In this journey Sebastian Painadath has played and is playing an extremely significant role. With great joy and gratitude let me continue my narrative.

I was fortunate to be a member of the Catholic Youth Movement (CYM) in our parish. We used to organize various study circles, and get involved in different socio-cultural issues. Our contact with Sebastian Painadath in the Bible class opened up new horizons for our young and dynamic minds. We became frequent visitors at Jyothis and spent hours and hours with him discussing a variety of topics. Such discussion forums gradually led us to active social involvement. For example, in 1984 when the traditional fishermen of Kerala called a strike against the exploitation by the mechanized boat-owners and their political patrons, we too organized, under his inspiration, protest marches and public meetings in support of them. I remember he arranged a personal meeting for us with the leaders of the fishermen's struggle. They inspired us with their commitment to the cause of the poor and their courage to take a stand on justice. Let me affix another aside here. Seven years later, in 1991, I was assigned to do my regency in being with the fishermen of Calicut, and I felt so thrilled to meet these people again and work with them.

Even now, my old friends from the parish recall those days with great nostalgia. Many of them recognize that the guidance and training that they had received those years gave them a positive and optimistic outlook on life. And for me, my contact with Sebastian Painadath and Jyothis, prompted me to take a new turn in my life's journey; it showed me the way to the Society of Jesus!

Sameeksha

After eight years of formation in different institutions of the Society, in 1993, I was sent to Sameeksha to pursue my theology studies. Sebastian Painadath was the director of Sameeksha and the director of studies of the RTC (Regional Theology Centre). Thus I got the opportunity as a Jesuit to live in the same community with him. Later, from 2001 to 2003 and from 2007 to 2012 we were together there. These years of my life at Sameeksha with him and others helped me appreciate the faith-experience of others, and treat the people of other religious traditions with great respect.

I am sure that most of the readers of this article are familiar with Sameeksha and its mission, but let me add a few lines about it and the theological formation we received there. In the second half of the 1980's, dangerous traits of religious fundamentalism began to stir up animosity between people of different religions in Kerala, and threaten the celebrated religious harmony of Kerala society. In response to it, the Jesuits of Kerala through the inspiration of people like Sebastian Painadath contemplated the creation of a 'common space' where people of different religious traditions could meet together and share their faith-experience. Sameeksha, Centre for Indian Spirituality, on the banks of the river Periyar in Kalady, was the fruit of that collective search and discernment. It was founded in 1987 with a view to promoting inter-religious dialogue. The Society of Jesus entrusted the leadership of this noble mission to Sebastian Painadath, appointing him as its director.

Though some people call Sameeksha an *ashram*, I like to qualify it as a 'home for all.' He together with Bro. Varkey Mampilly SJ has made it truly a home for all. I have heard people lauding Sameeksha for its simple life style, warm reception, informal settings, prayerful atmosphere, friendly neighbourhood, fresh air, evergreen ambience, shady trees, magnificent river-view and of course, its healthy vegetarian food. People from different walks of life come to Sameeksha to pray, to study, to relax, etc. Indeed, it is a home for all irrespective of religion, caste, rite, colour, gender, profession, ethnicity, etc. While explaining the meaning and aim of Sameeksha, Painadath usually quotes a verse from Yajurveda (36:18): *"Mitrasya chakshushā sameekshāmahē"* (let us look at each other with the eyes of a friend). Indeed, Sameeksha does invite and inspire us to look at each other with the eyes of a friend!

Now, a word about the theology centre is in order. If theological quest is to be authentic and profound, it should be rooted in one's own culture and context, should be learned through life-experiences, and should be articulated in one's own mother tongue. This was the conviction that made Jesuits in South Asia, three decades ago, to open regional centres to train their theology students. When the Kerala Jesuits decided to initiate such a formation programme, Sameeksha, with its intercultural and interreligious milieu, was spotted as the ideal place for it. Thus, in 1988 Kerala Regional Theology Centre (RTC) was born on the Sameeksha campus with Joe Thayil SJ as the Superior and Sebastian Painadath, the director of studies. As mentioned above I came here as a theology student in 1993.

My life and theology studies in the RTC offered me more clarity about my vocation and mission. The whole village where Sameeksha is located functioned as our 'formation centre'. The villagers made us welcome in their houses. We had plenty of opportunities to interact with people - with young and old, with men and women, with Hindus and Muslims – to take part in their joys and struggles, to listen to their stories of faith and frustrations. We were only too delighted to realize that the people took pride in being our *co-formators*. Together with the Bible and Christian theological literature, we also read and meditated the scriptures of other religions. Under the guidance of Sebastian Painadath we participated in inter-religious prayer services and dialogue sessions. Needless to say that such inter-religious and socio-political exposures helped us to go beyond the rigid boundaries of religious exclusivism and theological dogmatism, deepen our faith convictions and cherish our Christian identity.

My first phase of Sameeksha life came to an end in 1996, with my ordination to priesthood. Later, after my higher studies in Bible I came back to Sameeksha in 2001, as a teacher at the RTC and an animator of AICUF, an organization of the university students. But I had to leave Sameeksha again in 2003, when I went for further studies. Again, I got another golden opportunity to live in Sameeksha with him from 2007 to 2012.

I would like to conclude this short narrative by writing a brief note on an inter-religious living programme that we designed and conducted as a team for the youth at Sameeksha during the last phase of my stay there. It was called *sahayātri samgamam* (gathering of co-travelers).

To experience the beauty and richness of various religious beliefs, to develop openness towards other faith traditions, to listen, understand and appreciate the faith experience of others, to share with others one's own consolations and desolations in the journey of faith - these were some of the main objectives of the *sahayātri sangamam*. In each group about twenty-five to thirty youth, belonging to various religious traditions participated. Every *sahayātri sangamam*, which normally lasted for three days, was a unique experience. The frank and open sharing of the young people, their unbiased and unreserved dealings with others, their authentic expressions of prayer, etc. helped me to realize that an inter-religious openness makes one deeper and more genuine in one's own spirituality. I remember the feedback given by a Muslim girl at the end of one such *sangamam*: "Father, if we continue living the spirit that we have shared here, how meaningful our life and faith will become. I feel that I am going away from here as a better Muslim, more compassionate and more loving." I can quote many more such hope promoting expressions by the participants!

I have shared a few things in this semi autobiographical narrative showing how Sebastian Painadath and Sameeksha helped me and others to experience the genuine profundity of our own faith as well as that of other religious traditions. The greatest contribution of his mission, in my opinion, has been the 'inter-religious space' that he has helped hundreds of people to develop in their heart. He has liberated many people, especially the youth, from the destructive fundamentalist religious ideologies. He has instilled tremendous optimism in many minds. He has lent a helping hand to many souls to come closer to the Divine! He is still continuing that mission relentlessly.

Part-4
... epilogue ...

My Pilgrimage on the Landscape of Religions

Sebastian Painadath SJ

Diversity is beauty- this has been an abiding insight all through my life. I perceive beauty-in-diversity not only in the cultural spheres of human creativity, like languages, art forms, literature, ideologies, etc., but also on the sacred landscape of religions with their scriptures, symbols, sages, myths and mystics. I do not remember how and when this insight became a guiding principle in my life, but I know that this has shaped my way of thinking and dealings. The Vedic axiom *ēkam sat viprāh bahudhāh vadanti* (Reality / Truth is ONE, those who perceive it speak of it in diverse ways, Rig Veda, 1.164.46) and the Catholic principle *Deus semper major* (God is ever beyond) shaped my theology and spirituality all these years. Any sort of absolute claim in relation to religion and the consequent fundamentalism disturb me for these do not promote a culture of harmony and peace in humanity. For me the principle of inter-religious harmony means respecting the diversity of religions and recognizing the unity in spirituality. The distinction between spirituality and religion has been a basic premise in my theological reflection.

E.P. Mathew and Xavier Tharamel, my good friends and confreres, asked me to look back on my spiritual pilgrimage on the landscape of religions and share some significant experiences and insights. There is an inborn reticence in me when asked to speak of personal experiences. Being aware of this I attempt to share some reflections on my spiritual journey.

Every human person is shaped by the family in which one is born. I was born in a family which had a Hindu intellectual heritage. My maternal grandfather was born a Hindu in a Namboothiri (Kerala Brahmin) family. His parents with the children came over to Catholic faith in 1893. At that time my grandfather was only 6 years old. He was given the traditional Sanskrit education and later he became Professor of Sanskrit at two Catholic colleges, first at Trichy and later at Trichur in South India. His father and he himself were known in the literary circles in Kerala for their poems and literary studies.

As a child I was brought up in my mother's ancestral home under the patronage of my grandfather. He used to keep me on his lap and chant Sanskrit hymns which created a resonance deep in my psyche. He was firm in the Catholic faith but kept up several elements of the Hindu family heritage. The integration of these two religious experiences seems to have meant much for me in the early formation of my mind-set. Till his death in 1967 he has been a decisive influence in my spiritual life.

Some of the teachers who impressed me during the school years were Hindus. I was touched by their deep personal God-experience, their concern for the students and their commitment to the country that emerged with great dreams in the early years of independence. With all this a passionate love for the spiritual heritage of India has been instilled in me right from the childhood days.

In the long years of Jesuit formation, I got initiated to the sources of Christian spirituality as well as to those of the Indian spiritual traditions. The sages of India and of the Church spoke to my heart. In their deep mystical experiences, I sensed the spiritual convergence of world religions: mysticism is the depth dimension of spirituality and hence the real meeting point of religions. Swami Abhishiktananda´s writings opened new theological perspectives. At the age of 18 the Bhagavad Gita entered my life and became a *vade mecum* all these years. In the triadic structure of bhakti-jnana-karma I discovered a paradigm for an integrated Indian-Christian spirituality.

In the second year of my theological education at the University of Innsbruck Prof. Nicholas Kehl SJ asked me to study Carl Albrecht´s research volume *Psychologie des mystischen Bewusstseins* and present a seminar paper on the stages of the inner spiritual journey. This book gave me a lot of clarity on the inner structure of mystical experience that unfolds the spiritual undercurrents of religions. With this scheme I read the mystical writings of the Upanishadic sages, Meister Eckhart, Bhagavad Gita and John´s Gospel. It seemed that I got a key to interpret spiritual classics of the East and West in my later publications.

For the doctoral dissertation at the University of Tübingen under the guidance of Prof. Walter Kasper I took the theme: Towards a Theology of Prayer in the Light of the Pneumatology of Paul Tillich. The great German-American Protestant Theologian Tillich gave me wide theological perspectives to develop a *systematic* way of reflecting on Christian faith in dialogue with other religions and secular sciences. For Tillich the *dynamics of faith* is a spiritual force that gives the *courage to be*; the particular, religion-bound articulations of faith are to be understood in the universal *Spirit*-generated horizon of humanity´s spiritual evolution. In this process how does *prayer* with its *mystical* dimension fit in? – this was my exploration (*Dynamics of Prayer*, Towards a Theology of Prayer in the Light of the Paul Tillich´s Theology of the Spirit, Asian Trading Corporation, Bangalore, 1980).

During my student years in Europe (1970-78) I came in contact with several German families. Often, I stayed in their homes and journeyed with them in their spiritual search. This was the turbulent times of early seventies. I realized that the so-called crisis of faith in Europe was actually a crisis of traditional Christian religiosity, but at the same time the awakening of a mystic-prophetic spirituality in dialogue with world religions and secular sciences.

After my doctoral studies I returned to India in 1978. For eight years I worked at *Jyothis Jesuit Centre for Religion and Culture* at Cochin, Kerala. During these years I got acquainted with several Hindu friends and families, sages and movements, which confirmed my conviction: at the depth-level we all meet spiritually. As the coordinator of the training programmes of the Xavier Board of Higher Education I conducted a lot of seminars for teachers in various Colleges on themes of inter-religious dialogue, Christian spirituality and biblical faith experience. I found that the spiritual quest that I sensed in Europe was waking up in the intellectuals of Kerala too, who were critically looking for a liberative spirituality beyond religions.

During these years I studied intensely some of the spiritual classics of India and the writings of the great sages; I made a pilgrimage through the auspicious places of the Himalayas and visited several āśhrams. All that made me realize that the communication of spirituality has credibility only if it is nourished by an alternate way of life. I was inspired by the āśhram tradition of India and impressed by the initiatives of Abhishiktananda, Bede Griffiths and Vandana to experiment with another way of consecrated life. I am especially grateful to Bede Griffiths for guiding me during these years of search for authenticity.

In 1985 I shared with my Provincial and some of the Jesuit confreres the vision of creating a *space* where seekers of different religions would feel accepted and respected. This was enthusiastically received, and every support was assured by the Jesuit Province of Kerala. In 1986 a formal *society* under the name "Centre for Indian Spirituality" was registered as the legal holder of the new initiative under the auspices of the Jesuit Province. The Province bought a four-acre land at Kalady, on the banks of the Poorna river. It was a grace that we could start this new project of inter-religious harmony in the village blessed by the birth of the great

Sankaracharya. It was a greater grace that the Province gave me Brother Varkey Mampilly SJ as companion to give shape to this new venture. Both of us started working on the project in mid-1986.

Sameeksha, Centre for Indian Spirituality, gradually took shape in an āśram setting incorporating the sublime values of Indian and Christian spiritual heritage: simplicity of life-style, closeness to local people, harmony with nature, an atmosphere of silence and study, and above all genuine hospitality to seekers of different religions and cultures. The meditation hall built according to the specifications of the classical Kerala temple-architecture has four doors open in four directions, welcoming seekers from everywhere; an oil lamp is burning at the centre, symbolizing the divine presence, and four Holy Books – *Bhagavad Gita, Bible, Dhammapada and Quran* – are kept around it as guides to the luminous divine centre. Just outside the meditation hall one can sit on the banks of the Poorna river and get attuned to the silent stream of water. Adjacent to the meditation hall there is a labyrinth inviting seekers to a walking meditation dwelling on the process of one´s life-journey. The library has a good collection of books on inter-religious dialogue and Indian-Christian spirituality. The seminar hall built in Kerala style is designed as the *Hall of Religions* (*Samanvaya*). There is accommodation in simple huts for about 30 people. The kitchen supplies simple vegetarian food of the Kerala cuisine. The āśhram campus is full of nutmeg trees and banana plants giving a lush green ambience. "Learn from the trees: what grows makes no noise!" – one reads on a display board under the trees.

Over the years Sameeksha has become a place where people of different religions and cultures feel at home. I cannot speak of big projects running at this centre. Our concern all these years has been mainly to promote a culture of inter-religious harmony. In view of this we have been organizing inter-religious meditation sessions and *satsangs*, study of the classics of different religions, retreats based on the Bible, Bhagavad Gita, Upanishads and Sufi mystics, seminars on issues related to dialogue, ecology and social justice, a certificate programme of theological formation of the laity, life orientation programmes and counseling for adolescents, involvement in the acute issues of migrant labourers and some social uplift projects for the poor of the locality. Spiritual seekers from all over India and from other countries do come and spend a few days here for silent retreat and focused study. Those who have been thus acquainted with Sameeksha say that their stay in this ashram opened their minds to the mystery of the Divine vibrating in all human hearts, through all religions. A lot of warm friendship between persons of diverse religions emerged through these spiritual encounters; this is actually the base and goal of a culture of inter-religious harmony. Genuine inter-religious dialogue takes place where hearts meet in spiritual communion. True harmony evolves where the religious otherness of the other is respected. Genuine spirituality unfolds where there is openness to the *Spirit that blows where it wills* (S. Painadath SJ, "Sameeksha, Harmony of the Spirit", in: *The Yearbook of the Society of Jesus*, 2011, 116-118).

Considering the personnel competence and the resourceful library of the Centre, Sameeksha has been recognized by the Mahatma Gandhi State University as a Research Centre in Philosophy. With this we have been able to organize a few National Research Seminars on philosophical questions underlying inter-religious encounter. Quite a few books and several articles have been published by the Jesuit staff of the Centre on themes related to inter-religious dialogue and spirituality. The regular seminars on every second Saturday of the month exploring the dimensions of spirituality-beyond-religions –*dharmasameeksha* – are attended by 40-60 participants from different religions. The message that evolves through these sessions is that a humanizing spirituality is the common concern of world religions. All scriptures and sages invite us to explore the infinite horizons of the liberative movement of the divine Spirit. The moment one gets stuck in what is achieved religious fundamentalism gathers momentum; when one is constantly on the move spirituality becomes vibrant. With believers of different religions, we are *spiritual co-pilgrims.*

Some of the basic theological perceptions which shape my understanding of inter-religious harmony are the following:

1. **Intuition and Mind**: The axiom of the Upanishadic sages, *manasastu parā buddhih* (beyond the mind is the buddhi) is a key to interpret the inner spiritual process. The Greek philosophers and early Church Fathers do speak of *nous* as the intuitive eye in us. Mind is the discursive faculty; nous / buddhi is the intuitive faculty. Mind objectifies everything, including the Divine, while through buddhi one enters into the mystery of the subject and experiences the deep oneness with the Divine. Mind pursues the logic of reality; buddhi explores the mystique of reality. Mind analyses the diversity of things and renders information; buddhi intuits the unity of reality and makes transformation possible. Mind senses the structures and qualities of things, while buddhi perceives the universal inter-connectedness. Mind swings between the past and the future; buddhi is always present to the present moment (*nunc aeternum*). Nous is the door to the heart, the inner organ of enlightenment (Origen), the eye of faith (*oculus fidei*, Augustine), the inner eye of mystical vision (Dionysius), the spark of the soul (*Seelenfünklein*, Meister Eckhart). We make spiritual experiences with the *nous*, but we reflect on them with the mind. Faith as response to divine grace takes place at the level of the *nous*, theological reflection evolves at the mental level. (S. Painadath SJ, *Spiritual Co-pilgrims*, Claretian Publications, Quezon City, 2014, pp. 20-37)

2. **Spirituality and Religion**: Through the nous / buddhi one wakes to spirituality; through the mind faith is expressed with religious symbols. Spirituality, as the term indicates, is the experience of the Spirit (*pneuma*), the lived awareness of the unity between human self (*ātma*) and the divine Self (*Ātma*). Religion is an expression of spirituality, an articulation of being gripped by the Divine, a symbolic manifestation of one´s relatedness to God. Spirituality is openness to the *Beyond* (*parāt param, semper major*); religion is the form (*rūpa*) of adherence to a concrete symbol of the Divine. Spirituality is the inner dynamics (*bhāva*) of awakening to the Divine, religion is the symbolic way of

expressing spirituality. Spirituality is the point of mystical unification; religion is the pole of creative diversification. At the level of spirituality there are converging lines of experience; at the level of religion there are divergent forms of expression (S. Painadath SJ, *Spiritual Co-pilgrims*, Claretian Publication, Quezon City, 2014, 117-124).

3. Unity and Diversity: A significant insight of the Indian sages is that of harmony (*samanvaya*, Brahma Sutras 1.2). Harmony is neither the suppression of diversity nor a naïve postulate of unity. Harmony acknowledges diversity in unity and explores unity in diversity. Harmony respects the diversity of religions as divine grace and at the same time perceives the underlying unity in spirituality as a divine invitation. Diversity is beauty – this is what we experience in nature: no two trees are exactly alike; on a tree no two leaves are exactly the same. If diversity is beauty in nature, it is true of culture too: so many languages, customs, styles of art, and forms of dance; there is a rich diversity in philosophical reflections, scientific explorations and political ideologies. Diversity in cultural forms speaks for the creativity of the human spirit. Diversity of religions unfolds in different ways the unfathomable mystery of the relationship between the human and the Divine. As the FABC stated in its Plenary Assembly, 1974, "For us in Asia the various religions have been the doorway to God, for they have shaped our history, and our way of thinking. God has drawn our people to himself through them" (Nr.12, 14).

Diversity of religions can be truly respected only if they are seen in the unity of spirituality, ie. as manifestations of the *one* divine Spirit. A few simple imageries help me to clarify the meaning of harmony: (i) In a musical programme there are different instruments, each contributing its unique sound vibration. But in the process of the concert there is perfect harmony. One does not lose one's identity but realizes the identity in the dynamic process of symphony. (ii) In a classical dance each posture has its significance; every step has its rhythm. In the process of the dance the dancer pours herself into the dance: the dancer and the dance form a dynamic unity. There is perfect harmony between the diversity of forms (*rūpa*) and the unity in the aesthetic experience (*bhāva*) (iii) The human body is made up of so many limbs and organs, each having its function. The one vital energy flows through them all and forms a dynamic and living unity. The eye does not become the leg; the heart does not function as the brain. There is perfect harmony among the various parts of the body. (4) Look at a tree: immense diversity and yet a deep unity. Spirituality is like the one flow of vital sap that enlivens the entire tree; religions are like the branches with which the tree grows in different directions. (5) Modern physics speaks of the dynamic nature of reality. There is nothing static as such. From the core of the atom unto the orbit of the galaxies everything is in movement, everything is a becoming. Matter is energy; reality is vibration. Energy is the universal dynamics, matter unfolds in diverse forms. Respect the rich diversity of religions and explore the dynamic unity in spirituality – this is how I formulate the abiding principle of a culture of transformative harmony (S. Painadath SJ, *Spiritual Co-pilgrims*, Claretian Publication, Quezon City, 2014, 153-176).

4. **Uniqueness and Universality**: Each religion is unique, yet each religion has a universal message for the entire humanity. Every religion articulates in a specific manner the relentless quest of human beings for salvation and reveals a particular dimension of the ineffable divine mystery. Hence every religion has to be respected in its uniqueness with its universal salvific message. Yet all religions are inter-connected: every religion is related to every other religion in the universal process of the spiritual evolution of humanity. The history of humanity can be understood theologically as the process of the dialectics between human quest and divine revelation. The spiritual evolution of humanity takes place through the ongoing dialogue between the Divine and the human. "Inter-religious dialogue seeks to discover, clarify and understand better the signs of the age-long dialogue which God maintains with humanity." (John Paul II, Rome, 13.11.1992). In this process of divine-human dialogue there are *peak moments* in which the divine undercurrents surface with intensity, the divine Word finds a powerful articulation, the

divine Spirit explodes the stagnated structures. In such *kairos* moments a prophet emerges, or a sage appears, a salvific event happens, or an enlightened person emerges. The divine breakthrough is accepted in faith by a small community and is registered in a Holy Book. Every religion has its origin in such a *kairos* moment of the divine-human dialogue communicated either through a person or through a community. In the universal process of divine self-revelation religions are therefore inter-related. No religion is an isolated phenomenon. No religion, in as much as it is limited by time and space, can unfold the fullness of the divine mystery. The finite cannot fully comprehend the Infinite! No religion can declare itself to be the absolute religion. This does not mean looking at religion as something *relative*, but assessing it as relational: every religion is related to every other. Each religion is understood better in dialogue with the others. Just as I become truly *I* by encountering the *thou*, a Christian grows in the self-realization of being a Christian by encountering a Hindu or a Buddhist, and *vice versa*. Dialogue of religions leads me not to the loss of my Christian identity, but to the rediscovery of my true Christian identity: faith grows through dialogue. "God would like the developing history of humanity to be a pilgrimage in which we *accompany one another* towards the transcendent goal which he sets for us" (John Paul II, Assisi, 27.10.1986).

5. Faith and Mission: It is with this universal perspective that I try to look at the person and event of Jesus the Christ. "The divine Logos became flesh" – this is the basis of Christian faith. Incarnation means that God accepts the brokenness of the human predicament (*sarx, flesh*) and makes the limitation of human existence as the language of his self-revelation. The Infinite pours itself out in the confinement of the finitude (*kenosis*). God says *yes* to our body, to our world, to our history. Hence, we need to accept the finite with all its limitedness as the medium of divine self-giving. What God has relativised, we shall not absolutise! Faith in God´s self-giving in Jesus Christ is therefore an invitation to respect the fragmentary character of divine self-revelation in different times of the spiritual evolution of humanity. As Christians we have access to the understanding of divine revelation in history only through Jesus Christ: He is "the way, the truth, the life and the light," through which we discern the salvific presence of the Divine in cultures and religions. But our faith in Christ cannot be a judgment on God's self-revelation communicated in other religions. We cannot project Christ against other religions (Karl Barth); we can explore *the length and breadth, the height and depth* of the mystery of Christ in dialogue with other religions (Paul Tillich). In the light of the revelation of the divine mystery in the sages, scriptures and symbols of other religions we discover the deeper dimensions of the unfathomable mystery of Christ. Then we realize that God is greater than all religions and the salvific plan revealed in Christ embraces the entire spiritual evolution of humanity.

With this openness we share our Christ experience with believers of other religions. That Jesus the Son of God is the face of God turned towards humanity, that Jesus the Son of Man proclaimed the Kingdom of God with the values of love and compassion, that through the death and resurrection of Jesus God reconciled the world to himself, that the Spirit of Christ recreates this world to a new creation, that we are called to be collaborators of this salvific work – these are central elements of Christian faith; these we share with the sisters and brothers of other religions. We get inspired through their revelatory experiences too. Dialogue is the new language of mission. In fact, terms like *evangelization, proclamation* and even *mission* have to be avoided, for they smack of the domineering tendency of the colonial past. A simple term in resonance with the spirit of the Gospels would be *sharing of Christ experience* with others. We share it in a way that is in tune with the praxis of Jesus, with the willingness to wash the feet of the other, and not to lord authority over the others. (John, 13:14; Mk. 10:42) With believers of different religions we are *spiritual co-pilgrims.* On this pilgrim route we share with others what Jesus Christ means to us and how he is a liberating presence within human hearts. In this pilgrim process we remain ever alert to the movements of the divine Spirit that brings about the Kingdom of

God in all realms of human life (S. Painadath SJ, *Spiritual Co-pilgrims*, Claretian Publication, Quezon City, 2014, 153-176).

6. Mystic and Prophet. The basic dynamics of spirituality consists in the dialectics between the mystical and prophetic dimensions. Every religion has a mystical sensitivity and a prophetic vitality. The mystic awakens the believers to the mystery of the Divine and the prophet alerts them to the demands of the Spirit. The mystic emerges out of a contemplative awareness of the divine Light present in all, and the prophet comes out of an encounter with the divine Word in the struggles of history. Mystic is a seer, prophet is a listener; mystic insists on transcending all names and forms towards the ineffable mystery of the Divine; prophet demands the concern for justice in response to the all-embracing presence of divine Spirit. At the origin of all great religions there has been an integration of mystical introspection and prophetic commitment. But in the course their evolution one or the other dimension is weakened. Through inter-religious dialogue the mystical dimension is awakened the prophetic potential is activated. Through contemplative-mystical pursuits one realizes that one is called to participate in the divine nature; through active prophetic involvement one commits oneself to the divine work of bringing about justice, peace and eco-wellbeing. Action out of contemplation is the fruit of an integrated spirituality that unfolds through inter-religious dialogue (S. Painadath SJ, *Spiritual Co-pilgrims*, Claretian Publication, Quezon City, 2014, 125-153).

7. God and the Divine: Mystics of all religions make a consistent distinction between God and the Divine, between saguna-Iśwara and nirguna-Brahman (Upanishads), between der Gott and die Gottheit (Meister Eckhart). Mind needs personified names and forms to relate to God; but the divine reality is beyond names and forms; it is ineffable mystery, pure presence, vibration of Love. The basic terms used in religions to refer to the Divine point to this divine dynamism: Ruah (Judaism), Spirit (Christianity), Brahman / Atman (Hinduism), Śunyata (Buddhism), Al-lah / Rahim (Islam). Some of the universal symbols of the Divine like light, love, life, word, dance and fountain too refer to the vibrant nature of the divine presence. We can sense this divine dynamism only with the intuitive faculty of the buddhi / nous, not with the mind. Mind is oriented to duality; buddhi / nous perceives unity. With the enlightenment of the nous in divine Light we wake to the divine presence as vibration within the heart, and further we sense the creative movements of the divine Spirit in the entire cosmos. Through contemplative introspection we realise that we are called to resonate with this divine vibration; the human soul is created to get attuned to the divine Spirit. Deep in our heart we realise that we are divine. This mystical perception is the deepest meeting point of all religions (S. Painadath SJ, You are divine, ISPCK, Delhi, 2018, 77-118).

8. **Convergence and Divergence**. World religions seem to converge on five basic spiritual insights: (i) The Divine is an unfathomable mystery (ii) The Divine is Spirit, vibrant energy of Love that enlivens our life, and Light that enlightens our paths. (iii) We are called to resonate with the divine dynamism, to get united with the Divine, to participate in the divine nature. (iv) We should be able to perceive the divine dynamism in all things, and all things in the Divine. (v) Mercy and justice are the fruits of spirituality. Though these perceptions of spirituality are found in every religion, the language and symbol used to describe them may be conditioned by the cultural background of each religion. Every believer has to be true to her / his faith-experience in interpreting them. What is experienced at the *heart* level with the intuitive faculty (*buddhi / nous*) has to be expressed at the *head* level with the discursive faculty of the mind. This is where religion emerges with the divergent patterns. As long as we are bodily entities, social beings with an inter-personal orientation, we need to reflect on spiritual experience and communicate it to others. Here the limitation of language inevitably comes in and consequently the limitedness of every religion is felt. Existential exigencies of human existence are not something to be suppressed, but to be enriched through inter-personal encounters. This is where dialogue of religions becomes an imperative. "By dialogue we let God be present in our midst, for

as we open ourselves in dialogue to one another, we open ourselves to God" (John Paul II, Madras, 05.02.1986).

9. Search and Respect: The diverse forms of religion have to be respected; at the same time the converging lines of spirituality have to be explored. Respect for diversity of religions is needed for three reasons: (i) Every human person endowed with freedom and creativity responds to the Divine in a uniquely personal way. (ii) The divine Spirit works in human hearts in ways which we cannot predetermine. (iii) Religious symbols evolve out of a concrete culture, which is conditioned by many spatio-temporal factors. One has to explore the deep unity in spirituality too for three reasons: (i) There is one divine reality, which as ineffable mystery transcends all human perceptions and at the same is immanent in every human endeavor. (ii) There is only one humanity in spite of all cultural differences and geographical distances. (iii) There is only one divine plan of salvation that embraces the entire humanity. This deep unity eludes our full grasp, and hence we are all seekers.

These are some of the theological perspectives which grew in me over the years through personal friendship with followers of other religions, through my study, reflection and meditation, and through the dialogue seminars which I have been offering in India, Europe and the Far East in the last 40 years. I am convinced that the deeper we grow in Christ-experience the more open we become to the presence of the Spirit in other religions, and the more we respect the other religions the stronger our faith in Christ becomes. (S. Painadath SJ / Sr. Rose Pudukadan, *Christ-Consciousness*, ISPCK, Delhi, 2018, 65-82). We shall not elevate Jesus Christ above the process of history, for through incarnation he made our history into God's *history*. "Without in any way relativizing our faith in Jesus Christ or dispensing with a critical evaluation of religious experiences, we are called upon to grasp the deeper truth and meaning of the mystery of Christ in relation to the universal history of God's self-revelation." This is the demand put on Jesuits by the 34th

General Congregation of the Society of Jesus, 1995 (*Our Mission and Inter-religious Dialogue, 7*). It is a fascinating experience to enter upon a spiritual pilgrimage with sisters and brothers of other religions in alertness to the divine Spirit *that blows where it wills.*

Books and Articles of
Sebastian Painadath SJ
(The titles of books are in bold)

1962

1."സ്നേഹത്തിന്റെ അപ്പസ്തോലൻ" (Apostle of Love) *Satyadeepam,* Cochin 18 April 1962, pp.10, 11.

1964

2. "കന്യകാമറിയവും സഭൈക്യവും" (Ecumenism and Mary) *Satyadeepam,* Cochin, 14 November. 1964, pp.9, 11.

1965

3. **കേരളസഭ നാളെ, ദൈവശാസ്ത്രപരമായ ചില വിചിന്തനങ്ങൾ** (Kerala Church Tomorrow) Ed:John Arakkal / S. Painadath, Aloor, BLM, 1965. pp. 150.

4. "സുവിശേഷത്തിന്റെ വെളിച്ചത്തിൽ ഒരു കുരിശിന്റെ വഴി " (Way of the Cross in the Light of the Gospels) *Satyadeepam,* Cochin, 16 June, 1965 p.2.

1966

5. "ജീവിതപ്രശ്നങ്ങൾ" (Life problems) *Satyadeepam,* Cochin, 12 January 1966, p.2.

6. "ക്രിസ്തു – ആത്മീയവീഥിയിലെ കേന്ദ്രബി" (Christ at the Centre of Spiritual Path) *Satyadeepam,* Cochin,09.March 1966, p.1, 7.

1967

7. "പ്രാർത്ഥനാജീവിതം കൗൺസിലിന്റെ കാഴ്ച്ചപ്പാടിൽ" (Prayer in the Light of the Council) *Satyadeepam*,Cochin, 08.November 1967, pp.1.10.

8. "തൊഴിൽ - ക്രിസ്തുവുമായി ഒരേറ്റുമുട്ടൽ" (Labour in Encounter with Christ) *Satyadeepam,* Cochin,10.May 1967, pp.1, 2.

1968

9. "പ്രാർത്ഥനാജീവിതം നവമായ കാഴ്ചപ്പാടിൽ" (Prayer, a New Approach) *Satyadeepam,* Cochin, 03.April 1968, pp.1.10.

10. "വിശ്വാസദൗത്യം ഇന്നത്തെ ലോകത്തിൽ" (Faith in Today's World) *Satyadeepam,* Cochin, I. 24 July, 1968pp.1.4, II 31 July, 1968 pp.3.4.

11. "ലോകസമാധാനത്തിനു തിരുസിംഹാസനത്തിന്റെ സംഭാവന" (Holy See and World Peace) *Satyadeepam,* Cochin,10.July. 1968, pp.3.10.

12. "ഒരു ക്ഷേമരാഷ്ട്രം കെട്ടിപ്പടുക്കാൻ രംഗത്തിറങ്ങുക" (Christians and National Welfare) *Satyadeepam,*Cochin, 14 August. 1968, pp.4.11.

1971

13. "നാളത്തെ ദൈവവിജ്ഞാനീയം" (The Future of Theology) *Deepika,* Kottayam, June 27, 1971, p.3.

1972

14. "Christology and the Spiritual Heritage of Mankind", *Jeevadhara,* Kottayam, May, 1972, pp.230-240.

15. "ക്രിസ്തുവിജ്ഞാനീയവും മനുഷ്യകുലത്തിന്റെ ആത്മീയസമ്പത്തും" (Christology and the Spiritual Heritage ofMankind), *Jeevadhara,* Kottayam, June, 1972, pp.276-285.

1977

16. "Kraft aus der Stille", *Maria und Martha,* Rottenburg, Oktober 1977, pp.15-17.

1978

17. "പുതിയ മാർപാപ്പയുടെ ജീവിതപശ്ചാത്തലം" (The Background of the New Pope), *Mathrubhumi Daily*, Cochin,20. October 1978, p.5.

18. "സഭകളുടെ ഭാരതീയവത്കരണം " (The Indianisation of the Church), *Mathrubhumi Daily*, Cochin, 24.Dec. 1978, p.4.

1979

19. "ഭാരതീയവത്കരണത്തെപ്പറ്റി" (On the Indianisation of the Church) *Mathrubhumi Daily*, Cochin, 28.01.1978, p.4.

20. "മാനവവിമോചനം ക്രൈസ്തവസാഹിത്യസേവനത്തിന് വെല്ലുവിളി" (Human liberation) *Dynamic Action*, Tiruvalla, July 1979, pp.20-22.

21. "ജറുസലേം മൂന്നു ലോകമതങ്ങളുടെ വിശുദ്ധനഗരം" (Jerusalem the Holy City of three Religions), *Mathrubhumi Weekly*, Calicut, 15. April 1979, pp.15-21.

22. "യോഗസ്ഥ: കുരു കർമ്മാണി" (Action out of Contemplation) *Talent*, Cochin, January 1979, pp.32-40.

23. "ഭാരതത്തിന്റെ ആദ്ധ്യാത്മികപൈതൃകം" (The Spiritual Heritage of India), *Talent*, Cochin, December 1979,pp. 588-594.

24. "കരയുന്ന ദൈവം, വളരുന്ന ദൈവം" (The Weeping and Growing God) *Kerala Times*, 25. 12.1979, p. 3, 5.

1980

25. "Towards Inter-religious Understanding," *Bulletin of the Peace Studies Institute*, Manchester College, October, 1980, pp.12-13.

26. "വിലയ്ക്കു വാങ്ങാം" (On Corruption), *Talent*, Cochin, November 1980, pp.539-546.

27. "ഹാൻസ് ക്യുാംഗ്" (On Hans Küng) *Satyadeepam*, Cochin, 23. 01. 1980, pp.3,4.

1981

28. **Dynamics of Prayer, Towards a Theology of Prayer in the Light of the Pneumatology of Paul Tillich, Bangalore: Asian Trading Corporation, 1981, pp.390.**

29. "മണ്ണിനെ പ്രേമിച്ച ദൈവം" (God Loved the Earth), *Talent*, Cochin, March 1981, pp.89-96.

1982

30. "The Idea of a Salvific Community in the Bhagavad Gita", *Jeevadhara*, Kottayam, 1982, pp.305-311.

31. "Die Bhagavad Gita, Ein indischer Weg zu Gott und zur Gotteserfahrung", *Geist und Leben,* München, 1982, pp.288-293.

32. "ഗീതാസാധന" (Retreat with the Gita) *Mathavum Chintayum*, Alwaye, 1982, pp.601-610

33. "അത്ഭുതങ്ങൾ നവസൃഷ്ടിയുടെ ആദ്യചലനങ്ങൾ" (Miracles as New Creation) *Talent*, Cochin, June1982, pp. 266-274

34. "ഐശ്വരപ്രേമത്തിൽ വളരുന്ന സമൂഹം–ഗീതയിലെ സാമൂഹികദർശനം" (Community in Divine Love according to the Gita), *Jeevadhara*, Kottayam, 1982, pp.293-302.

35. "മതാന്തര ആത്മബന്ധം" (Inter-religious Relations) *Talent*, Cochin, December 1982, pp.586-592.

36. "വിദ്യാലയങ്ങളിലേയ്ക്കു വീണ്ടും"(On Education) Mathrubhumi Daily, Cochin, 17.06. 1982, p. 8.

1983

37. "Umkehr in der Kirche am Beispiel Indiens", *Katechetische Blätter*, München, 1983, pp.114-117.

38. "Der leidende Gott", *Katechetische Blätter*, München, 1983, pp. 920-922.

39. "Begegnung mit der östlichen Mystik", *Katechetische Blätter*, München, 1983, pp.926-929.

40. "മിസ്റ്റിക്കും പ്രവാചകനും സമന്വയത്തിലേക്ക്" (Integration of Mystic and Prophet), *Jeevadhara*, Kottayam, October 1983, pp.347-355.

41. "നേർച്ചക്കാഴ്ചകൾ" (Ritual Offerings) *Talent*, Cochin, November, 1983, pp.521-529.

1984

42. "Das Geist-getragene Gebet, Ansätze für eine systematische Theologie des Gebetes im Rahmen der Pneumatologie Paul Tillichs", *Schriften der Akademie Hofgeismar*, 1984, Nr. 210, pp.16-37.

43. "Der Weg zum Ganz-werden", *Missio-Pastoral*, Aachen, 1984, pp.23-4.

44. "Der leidende Gott" *Missio-Pastoral*, Aachen, 1984 pp.49-51.

45. "Katholische Ashram-Bewegung in Indien," *Katholische Mission*, Bonn, 2/1984, pp.41-42.

46. "മതം മാനവവിമോചനത്തിന്" (Religion for Liberation) *Jeevadhara*, Kottayam, October 1984, pp.349-372.

47. "യേശുവിന്റെ ഊട്ടുമേശപ്രസ്ഥാനം" (Table Fellowship of Jesus), *Kerala Times*, Cochin, 19.04.1984, pp.3, 5.

48. "യേശുവിന്റെ നാടും നമ്മുടെ നാടും" (The Socio-cultural Background of Jesus) *Talent*, Cochin, (a series of five articles), August – December, 1984, 49.

49. "ഈ ഭൂമി ഈശ്വരന്റെ കർമ്മഭൂമി" (This Earth the Work-space of God), *Satyadeepam*, Cochin, 18.04. 1984. p.13.

50. "ദാർശനികർക്കു വഴികാട്ടിയ കാൾ റാണർ" (Karl Rahner) *Malayala Manorama*, Kottayam, 03. 04. 1984, p.4.

1985

51. "Spirituality for Human Liberation", *Ignis Studies*, Anand, 1985, pp. 22-26.

52. "Unterwegs mit den Religionen Indiens", Ed: Paul Imhof, *Karl Rahner, Bilder eines Lebens*, Freiburg: Herder, 1985, pp.153-154.

53. "വിമോചനം, സിദ്ധിയും സാധനയും യോഹന്നാന്റെ അനുഭൂതിയിൽ" (Liberation in John´s Gospel) *Jeevadhara*, Kottayam, April, 1985, pp. 94-101.

54. "ഭഗവദ്ഗീതയും സമഗ്രവിമോചനവും" (Gita and Integral Liberation-I) *Jeevadhara*, Kottayam, October 1985, pp.356-368.

55. "ഭഗവദ്ഗീതയും സമഗ്രവിമോചനവും" (Gita and Integral Liberation-II) *Jeevadhara*, Kottayam, December, 1985, pp.403-410.

1986

56. "Bhagavad Gita´s Vision of Liberative Action", Ed. Paul Puthenangady, *Towards an Indian Theology of Liberation*, Bangalore: NBCLC, 1986, pp.49-65.

57. "ആർഷസംസ്കാരത്തിന്റെ ആത്മാവിനെ തേടി" (John Paul II in Search of the Soul of India), *Jeevadhara*, Kottayam, October 1986, pp.334-344.

1987

58. "Towards an Inter-religious Hermeneutics", *Word and Worship*, Bangalore, 1987, pp.83-90.

59. "Leib als Sprache des Gebets", *Weltweit*, Nürnberg, 3/1987, 19-29.

60. "Christus in uns", *Christ in der Gegenwart*, Freiburg, 1987, Nr. 47. p.22.

61. "ശ്രീനാരായണദർശനത്തിലെ വിമോചനദൈവശാസ്ത്രം" (Liberation Theology in Narayana Guru´s View) *Mathrubhumi Daily*, Cochin, 07. September, 1987, p.4.

62. (The Liberation Theology in Narayana Guru) *Jeevadhara*, Kottayam, October, 1987, 401-404.

63. "ദൈവദശകം–ഒരു സർവ്വമതപ്രാർത്ഥന" (An Inter-religious Prayer) *Jeevadhara*, Kottayam, October, 1987, pp.405-410.

64. "ക്രിസ്തുമസ്, മതസമന്വയത്തിന്റെ തിരുനാൾ" (Christmas the Festival of Inter-religious Harmony), *Mathrubhumi Daily*, Cochin, 25. December 1987, p.4.

65. നവചേതന (Leaflets for Bible Classes in Colleges) Ed: S.Painadath SJ, Cochin, Jyothis, 1982-88, pp.264.

1988

66. "Contemplation and Liberative Action", *Vidyajyoti*, Delhi, 1988, pp.210-223.

67. "Bhagavad Gita and the Ignatian Ideal", *Ignis*, Anand, 1988, pp. 59-66.

68. "Mukti – der hinduistische Befreiungsbegriff und seine Bedeutung für eine indische Theologie der Befreiung", Ed: Felix Wilfred, *Verlass den Tempel*, Freiburg: Herder, 1988, pp.51-68.

69. "വേദനിക്കുന്ന ദൈവം" (Suffering God), *Mathrubhumi Daily*, Cochin, 1. April 1988, p.4.

70. "മതാന്തരസഹവർത്തിത്വം ഭാരതത്തിൽ" (Inter-religious Coexistence in India) *Jeevadhara*, Kottayam, June 1988, 187-195.

71. "ഭഗവദ്ഗീതയിലെ വിമോചനദൈവശാസ്ത്രം" (Liberation Theology in the Bhagavad Gita) *Ora*, Aleppey, January 1988, pp.5-10.

1989

72. "Priestly Spirituality", *Apostolic Union*, Pune, Vol. 35, September 1989, pp.1-6.

73. "Tischgemeinschaft Jesu", *Christ in der Gegenwart*, Freiburg, 26. March, 1989, Nr. 13, p.110.

74. „Das Fünklein in uns", *Christ in der Gegenwart*, Freiburg, 19. November 1989, Nr. 47, p.411.

75. "Gott wird im Menschen geboren", *Christ in der Gegenwart*, Freiburg, December 1989, Nr. 53, p.437.

76. "ക്രിസ്ത്വനുഭൂതിക്ക് ഒരു അദ്വൈതഭാഷ്യം" (An Advaitic Understanding of Christ-consciousness) *Jeevadhara*, Kottayam, October 1989, pp. 296-309.

1990

77. "Quest for Spiritual Masters, Some Theological Comments on the Roman Letter on Christian Meditation", *Vidyajyoti*, Delhi, 1990, pp. 387-399.

78. "Westliches Christentum und östliche Meditation", *Katholische Mission*, Bonn, Mai, 1990, pp. 93-95.

79. "Was nützt der Dialog mit Hindus?", *Weltweit*, Nürnberg, Nr. 3. pp.16-19.

80. "സന്മനസ്സുള്ളവർക്കു ശാന്തി" (Peace to the People of Goodwill), *Mathrubhumi Christmas Supplement*, Cochin, 25. December 1990, pp. 29-30.

81. "സുവിശേഷവത്കരണവും സംസ്കാരസമന്വയവും" (Evangelization and Inculturation) *Mathavum Chintayum*, Alwaye, 1990, pp.581-587.

82. "ദൈവരാജ്യം–സാകല്യവിമോചനത്തിന്റെ പ്രക്രിയ" (Kingdom of God and Integral Liberation) *Jeevadhara*, Kottayam, February, 1990, pp. 159-166.

83. "മതാന്തരസംവേദനം ക്രൈസ്തവദർശനത്തിൽ" (Inter-religious Dialogue in Christian Perspective) *Jeevadhara*, Kottayam, February, 1990, pp.325-346.

1991

84. "Dynamics of a Culture of Dialogue", Ed: T.K. John, *Bread and Breath, Festschrift for Samuel Rayan SJ*, Anand: GSP, 1991, pp.279-291.

85. "Nachwort: Die Bhagavad Gita und christliche Spiritualität ", Ed: Peter Schreiner, *Bhagavad Gita, Wege und Weisungen*, Zürich: Benziger, 1991, pp.189-225.

86. "God is beyond all Religions" , Ed: A. Pushparajan, *Pilgrims of Dialogue, Festschrift for Albert Nambiaparambil CMI*, Thodupuzha: Sangam, 1991, pp.217-223.

87. "Towards an Indian Christian Spirituality in the Context of Religious Pluralism", *Indian Journal of Spirituality*, Bangalore, 1991, pp.299-311.

88. "Atmabodha, the Challenge of Indian Spiritual Heritage to Christian Theological Reflection", Ed: Kuncheria Pathil, *Religious Pluralism*, Delhi: ISPCK, 1991, 45-63.

89. "Spirituality, Christian and Secular", *Kristujyoti*, Bangalore, December, 1991, 10-20.

90. "Der mitleidende, mitgestaltende Gott", *Christ in der Gegenwart*, Freiburg, 24.11.1991, Nr. 47, p.420.

91. "സ്വർഗ്ഗസ്ഥനായ പിതാവേ... എന്ന പ്രാർത്ഥനയ്ക്ക് പുതിയൊരു ഭാഷ്യം" (A New Understanding of the Prayer, *Our Father*) *Jeevadhara*, Kottayam, February, 1991, pp.136-143.

1992

92. "യേശു വ്യക്തിയും ശക്തിയും" (Jesus Person and Power), Kottayam: Yatra, 1992, pp.202.

93. *"Mukti*- the Hindu Notion of Liberation", Ed: Dan Cohn-Sherok, *World Religions and Human Liberation*, New York: Orbis, 1992, 63-78.

94. "Das Heil wird in uns geboren", (Gedicht über Theosis), *Missionsandacht-Heft*, Missio, München, 1992, p.14-15.

95. "മനുഷ്യനാണ് ദേവാലയം" (The Human Person is the Temple of God) *Mathrubhumi Daily*. Cochin, 13. December, 1992, p.4.

96. "ക്രിസ്തുമസിന്റെ അർത്ഥതലങ്ങൾ" (The Meaning of Christmas) *Mathrubhumi Daily*, Cochin, 25 December 1992, p.4.

97. "ലോകോന്മുഖമായ ആദ്ധ്യാത്മികത" (World-affirming Spirituality) *Bodhi*, Calicut, Nr. 14, 1992, pp.7-12.

98. "ഭഗവദ്ഗീതയുടെ വിപ്ലവാത്മകദർശനം" (The Revolutionary Perspective of Bhagavad Gita), *Jeevadhara*, Kottayam, 1992, pp.268-280.

99. "യേശുവിന്റെ വ്യക്തിത്വവും പ്രബോധനങ്ങളും" (The Person and Message of Jesus) *Jeevadhara*, Kottayam,1992, pp.196-217.

1993

100. "Towards an Indian Christian Spirituality in the Context of Religious Pluralism, Ed: Dominic Veliath/ *Towards an Indian Christian Spirituality in a Pluralistic Context*, Bangalore: Dharmaram, 1993, pp.3-15.

101. "Ost begegnet West, Kultur- und Religionsverständnis", *Werkmappe Weltkirche*, Missio-Wien, Nr. 90, 1993, pp.22-23.

102. Leibhaftes, mystisches und kosmisches Beten", *Werkmappe Weltkirche*, Missio-Wien, Nr. 90, 1993, pp.24-29.

103. "Lernt vom Baum, eine indische Deutung der Trinität", *Werkmappe Weltkirche*, Missio-Wien, Nr. 90, 1993, p.30.

104."സന്യാസം ഭാരതീയദർശനത്തിൽ" (Consecrated Life in Indian Tradition), *Mathavum Chintayum*, Alwaye, 1993, pp.524-536.

105. "കുരിശിന്റെ പാഠം" (Lesson from the Cross) *Mathrubhumi Daily*, Cochin, 09.04. 1993, p.4.

106. "സമന്വയത്തിന്റെ സംസ്കാരം ക്രൈസ്തവദർശനത്തിൽ" (Culture of Harmony in Christian Faith) *Jeevadhara*, Kottayam, 1993, pp. 301-312.

107."ഭക്തി ഭഗവദ്ഗീതയിൽ" (Bhakti in Bhagavad Gita) *Jeevadhara*, Kottayam, 1993, pp.385-391.

108. "ദൈവരാജ്യത്തിന്റെ അർത്ഥവും പ്രസക്തിയും" (The Meaning of the Kingdom of God) *Jeevajwala*, Cochin, 1993, pp.7-8.

1994

109."Paul Tillich's Theology of Prayer, An Indian Perspective", Ed: Raymond Bulman / Frederick J. Parrella, *Paul Tillich, A Catholic Assessment*, Minnesota: Glazier, 1994, pp.218-241.

110."Ashrams, A Movement of Spiritual Integration", *Concilium*, 4/1994, pp.36-46. (Translation in five languages).

111. "Theology of Inter-faith Dialogue", *Information on Human Development*, FABC, Manila, July 1994, pp.3-5.

112. "Counter-Cultural Perspectives for Kerala", Ed: EMS Namuthiripad, *Keralam, International Congress on Kerala Studies*, Vol. II, Trivandrum: AKG Centre, 1994, pp.144-146.

113. "Das Wort, die Stille, den Mystiker wachrufen, den Propheten beleben", *Christ in der Gegenwart*, Freiburg, 1994, Nr. 16, pp.134-135.

114. "Maria Lichtmess", *Christ in der Gegenwart*, Freiburg, 1994, Nr. 6, p.46.

115. "മതാന്തരസംവേദനം മാനവവിമോചനത്തിന്" (Inter-religious Dialogue for Human Liberation) *Jeevadhara*, Kottayam, 1994, pp.346-356.

116."യേശുവിന്റെ മനുഷ്യദർശനം" (The Human Vision of Jesus) *Assisi*, Palai, December 1994, pp.8-10.

117. "മതം മാനവവിമോചനത്തിന്" (Religion for Human Liberation) Ed: T. Bhaskaran, ശ്രീനാരായണഗുരുവും മതസൗഹാർദ്ദവും Trivandrum: Sree Narayana Study Centre, Keral University, 1994, pp. 134-146

118. "ഭഗവദ്ഗീതയിലെ വിമോചനദർശനം" (The Liberative Vision of the Bhagavad Gita) *Mathavum Chintayum*, Alwaye, December 1994, pp. 233-241.

119. "നാളത്തേയ്ക്ക് ഒരു ആദ്ധ്യാത്മികത" (Spirituality for Tomorrow) *Ora*, Aleppey, December 1994, pp.24, 26.

1995

120. "Awaken the Mystic in the Church", *Vidyajyoti*, Delhi, 1995, 815-22.

121. "Meister Eckhart" , Ed: Vandana, *Sabda Sakti, Sangam*, Bangalore: Asian Trading Corporation, 1995, 277-281.

122. "Christian Youth for Communal Harmony", *The Examiner*, Bombay, 25. November, 1995, pp.11-12.

123. "Move to the Frontiers", On GC 34 of Jesuits, *Jivan*, Anand, April, 1995, p.13.

124. "Auf der Grenze die Mitte, Erfahrungen bei der Generalkongregation der Jesuiten", *Christ in der Gegenwart*, Freiburg, 1995, Nr. 21, pp.172-173.

125. "Verwandlung des Leibes, Gedanken zum eucharistischen Geheimnis", *Christ in der Gegenwart*, Freiburg, 1995, Nr. 28, p.206-207.

126. "ക്രൈസ്തവ ആദ്ധ്യാത്മികതയുടെ മതേതരഭാവം" (The Secular Dimension of Christian Spirituality), *Jeevadhara*, Kottayam, 1995, pp. 422-430.

127. "സമഗ്രതയുറ്റ സുവിശേഷവത്കരണം" (The Integral Sharing of the Gospel) *Satyadeepam*, Cochin, 05.07.1995, pp.1, 6.

1996

128. "The Vulnerable God", *Jeevadhara*, Kottayam, 1996, pp.230-238.

129. "*Coincidentia Oppositorum*, Nicholas de Cusa in Search of the Harmony of Religions", *FABC Papers*, Hongkong, Nr. 76 pp.26-30/ *Vidyajyoti*, Delhi, 1996, pp. 455-60.

130. "The Spiritual Dynamics of Dialogue", *Vidyajyoti*, Delhi, 1996, pp. 813-24.

131. "Life in Spiritual Freedom, Sannyasa in the Bhagavad Gita", *In Christo*, Nagpur, July 1996, pp.1-11.

132. "Den Mystiker beleben – den Propheten wachrufen, Zur Begegnung östlicher und westlicher Spiritualität", *Ordensnachrichten*, Wien, 5/1996, pp.20-30.

133. "Der Geist weht wo er will. West begegnet östlichem Christentum und hinduistischer Spiritualität, *Zeichen unter den Völkern*, Missio-München, 1996, pp.71- 74.

134. "Zwischen Amt und Charisma, Wie religiöse Erfahrungen fruchtbar werden", *Christ in der Gegenwart*, Freiburg, 1996, Nr. 23, pp.189-190.

135."മതവിശ്വാസികൾ സഹതീർത്ഥാടകർ" (Believers as Spiritual Pilgrims), Ed: J. Thachil, ദാർശനിക സ്മൃതി Thannirmukkam: Mankuzhikary Trust, 1996, pp.85-90.

136. ജോൺപോൾ മാർപ്പാപ്പ, മതസമന്വയത്തിന്റെ പ്രവാചകൻ" (John Paul II, Prophet of Inter-religious Harmony) *Jeevadhara*, Kottayam, 1996, pp.369-379.

137. "വിഭിന്നമതസ്ഥർ സഹതീർത്ഥാടകർ" (Spiritual Co-pilgrims), *Deepika*, Kottayam, 16.11.1996, p.4.

1997

138. "The Father of Jesus is Mother. A Meditation on the Symbols of the Gospel according to John", *Jeevadhara*, Kottayam, 1997, pp.204-11.

139. "Theological Perspectives of FABC on Inter-religious Dialogue", *Jeevadhara*, Kottayam, 1997, pp. 272-88. / *FABC-OEIA Bulletin*, Bangkok, December, 1997, pp. 6-9.

140. "The Meaning and Scope of Religious Pluralism", *Jeevadhara*, Kottayam, 1997, pp.353-361.

141."Contemplation and the Future of Mission in Asia" *Indian Missiological Review*, Gauhatti, September, 1997, pp.114-22.

142. "The Inter-personal and Trans-personal Dimensions of Asian Spirituality", *FABC Papers*, Hongkong, 1997, Nr. 83, pp.8-15.

143. "La Rencontre spirituelle de l'Orient et de l'Occident in Jules Monchanin", *FAC-CREDIC, Institut d'Histoire du Christianisme*, Lyon, 1997, Nr.3, pp.337-344.

144. "Despertar la Mistica en la Iglesia", *Selectione de Teologia*, Barcelona, 1997, pp.211-216.

145. "Aus dem Widerspruch, Kreuz und Auferstehung als Quellen christlichen Lebens", *Christ in der Gegenwart*, Freiburg, 1997, Nr. 13, pp.109-110.

146. "Leib als Sprache des Gebets, Sonnengebetsgebärde für Religionsunterricht", Ed: Ursula Heinemann, *Unterrichtswerk für kath. Religionslehre an Realschulen*, Stuttgart: Bibelwerk, 1997, pp.65-66.

147. "ആത്മസാക്ഷാത്കാരം നൽകുന്ന യേശു" (Jesus and Self-realisation) *Jeevadhara*, Kottayam, June 1997, pp.190-198.

148. "കർമ്മഭൂമിയിലേക്കുണരുക", (Move to the Active Field), Ed: Janakeeyam, വിശപ്പിന്റെ ആത്മീയ മാനങ്ങൾ Punaloor: Sarovara,1997, pp.115-119.

1998

149. "The Inter-personal and Trans-personal Dimensions of Asian Spirituality", *FABC Papers*, Hongkong, 1998, Nr. 83, pp.8-15.

150. "Hermeneutics in Indian Theology", *Vidyajyoti*, Delhi, May, 1998, 303-14.

151. "Bhagavad Gita's Contribution to the Future of India", *Jnanadeepa*, Pune, 1998, 19-30.

152. "Christ, Church and the Diversity of Religions", *Jeevadhara*, Kottayam, 1998, 161-92.

153. "Cross and Resurrection", *Vidyajyoti*, Delhi, March, 1998, pp. 141-143.

154. "An Asian Paradigm for the Integration of Spirituality", *Information on Human Development*, FABC, Manila, July-August, 1998, pp.8-11.

155. "Ecosophy, Lessons from India's Spiritual Heritage", Ed: J. Mattam, *Ecological Concerns, An Indian Christian Perspective*, Bangalore: NBCLC, 1998, pp.92-103.

156. "Hin zu einer Kultur des interreligiösen Dialogs", Ed: J. Röser, *Christsein 2001*, Freiburg: Herder, 1998, pp.204-06.

157. "Östliche Mystik und Christentum", *Jahresbuch der Diözese Gurk*, Klagenfurt, 1998, pp.85-87.

158. "Why should we be afraid of Mystics?", *The New Leader*, Madras, December, 1998, pp.39-40.

159. "Ich war immer unterwegs, Über Priester-sein heute", *Christ in der Gegenwart*, Freiburg, 1998, p.230.

160. "Ich und der Vater sind eins, Die mütterliche Dimension in Jesu Abba-Anrede", *Die Mitarbeiterin*, Düsseldorf, 1998, pp.20-22.

161. Den Mystiker beleben, den Propheten wachrufen, *Werkmappe Weltkirche*, Missio-Wien, Nr. 108, 1998, pp.14-17.

162. "Hinduismus und Christentum", *Denken und Glauben*, Graz, 1998, Nr. 97, pp.20-21.

163. "ക്രൈസ്തവരും ഇതരമതങ്ങളും" (Christians and other Religions) *Prabudhakeralam*, Trichur, Part I, May 1998, pp.180-182; Part II, June 1998, pp.215-218.

164. "മൈസ്റ്റർ എക്കാർട്ട്, ക്രിസ്തുമതത്തിലെ അദ്വൈതാചാര്യൻ" (Meister Eckhart, Advaita in Christianity), *Prabudhakeralam*, Trichur, September,1998, pp.331-333.

165. "ആത്മീയതയിൽ സമന്വയം" (Harmony in Spirituality), *Jeevadhara*, Kottayam, June, 1998, pp.213-219.

166. "തനിമ തേടുന്ന കേരളസഭ" (Kerala Church Seeking Identity) *Jeevadhara*, Kottayam, October, 1998, pp.329-343.

167. "പൗരസ്ത്യ തിരുസംഘത്തിന്റെ മാർഗ്ഗരേഖ – ഒരു ദൈവശാസ്ത്രവി ശകലനം" (The Document of the Decastery for Oriental Churches, A Theological Response), *Vachanadhara*, Cochin, October 1998, pp. 23-34.

1999

168. "Hindu Rites of Passage and Christian Sacraments", *The Way*, London, 1999, pp.131-140.

169. "The Understanding of Christ in the Indian Renaissance", *Jeevadhara*, Kottayam, 1999, pp.165-187.

170. "The Liberative Spirituality of the Bhagavad Gita", *Jnanadeepa*, Pune, 1999, pp.27-33.

171. "Ashrams – Movements of Spiritual Integration", *Ashram Aikya Newletter*, Bangalore, April, 1999, pp.6-15.

172. "We are Co-pilgrims, A Christian Understanding of Inter-religious Harmony", Ed: Albert Nambiaparambil, *Footprints of Dialogue*, Cochin: WCRP, 1999, pp.72-74.

173. "Im Bild vom Baum", *Christ in der Gegenwart*, Freiburg, 1999, Nr. 33, p.270.

174. "Ströme lebendigen Wassers, Symbole der Mütterlichkeit in der Abba-Erfahrung Jesu", *Die Mitarbeiterin*, Düsseldorf, 1999, Nr. 1, pp. 20-22.

175. "മതസൗഹാർദ്ദത്തിന്റെ സംസ്കാരം– കേരളസഭ ഒരു ആത്മപരിശോധന യ്ക്ക് തയ്യാറാകുമോ?" (A Culture of Interreligious Harmony, Towards a Self-examination in the Kerala Church), *Satyadeepam*, Cochin, 24.02.1999, p.5.

176. "വിവേകം – സാധനാപഥത്തിലെ ദിശാബോധം" (Discernment in Spiritual Life) *Prabudhakeralam*, Trichur, 1999, Part I. pp.237-238; Part II pp.264-266; Part III pp.308-310.

177. "മതങ്ങളിലെ വൈവിധ്യം, ആത്മീയതയിലെ ഏകത്വം" (Diversity in Religions, Unity in Spirituality) *Mathrubhumi Supplement*, December, 25.1999 pp.14-15.

178. "വിവിധ മതസ്ഥരോടൊത്തു മൂന്നാം സഹസ്രാ�’ദത്തിലേക്ക്" (With the Religious other to the Third Millennium) *Jeevadhara*, Kottayam, October 1999, pp.341-350.

179. "കേരളത്തിലെ മതസംസ്കാരം" (The Religious Culture of Kerala) Ed: Scaria Zacharia, 500 വർഷത്തെ കേരളം, Kottayam: Current Books, 1999, pp.44-49.

180. "ക്രിസ്തുമതത്തിനപ്പുറം ക്രിസ്തുവിനെ തേടുക" (Seek Christ beyond Christianity) *Assisi*, Palai, December 1999, pp.13-13.

181. "മതസമന്വയത്തിന്റെ സംസ്കാരം" (A Culture of Inter-religious Harmony) *Satyadeepam*, 8. December 1999, pp.5,11.

182. "മണ്ണിനെ പ്രേമിച്ച ദൈവം" (The God who Loved the Earth) *Satyadeepam*, 22. December, 1999, pp.3,4.

2000

183. *Das Sonnengebet, Ein Übungsbuch zum Tagesbeginn*, München: Kösel, 2000, pp.136.

184. **എസ് കാപ്പൻ, ഇരുപത്തൊന്നാം നൂറ്റാണ്ടിന് ഒരു പ്രതിസംസ്കൃതി,** (Towards a Counter Culture) Ed: and Tran: S. Painadath SJ, Kottayam Yatra, 2000, pp 160.

185. "Ecosophy: An Indispensable Step towards the Civilization of Love. Lessons from India´s Spiritual Heritage", Ed: Thomas Paul, *Civilization of Love*, Delhi: Media House, 2000, pp.77-95.

186. "Ashram Initiatives in the Church in India" , Ed: Paul Puthenangady, *The Church in India after the All India Seminar 1969*, Bangalore: Kristujyoti / NBCLC, 2000, pp.133-156.

187. "The Eucharist as Sacrament of the Earth", Ed: Francis Gonsalves, *Body, Bread, Blood, Eucharist Perspectives from the Indian Church*, Delhi: ISPCK, 2000, pp.133-46.

188. "Dem Geist Raum geben. Zu einer Spiritualität im Dialog der Religionen", *Forum –Weltkirche*, Freiburg, 2000, pp.14-17.

189. "Lebendige Quelle oder abgestandenes Wasser? Messfeier mit dem Rücken zum Volk in Indien! ", *Publik-Forum*, Frankfurt, 25. August, 2000, Nr. 16, pp.43-44.

190. "Gott als Subjekt unseres Seins", *Katechetische Blätter*, München, September, 2000, pp.357-359.

191. "Gebet und Meditation. Perspektiven eines indischen Theologen", Ed: Ulrich Willers, *Beten, Sprache des Glaubens, Seele des Gottesdienstes. Fundamentaltheologische und liturgiewissenschafltiche Aspekte,* Tübingen: Francke, 2000, pp.103-113.

192. "Gott ist größer als alle Religionen", *Publik Forum*, Frankfurt, 20. Oktober, 2000, pp.30-32.

193. "Aus der gleichen Quelle, Einheit in der Spiritualität", *Werkmappe Weltkirche*, Missio-Wien, March, 2000, pp.20-21.

194. "Vom Aufgang der Sonne, Frühschicht mit Elementen aus Indien", Ed: Klaus Vellguth / H. Heidemanns, *Gott feiern in der einen neuen Welt*, Aachen: Missio, 2000, pp.8-15.

195. "പ്രകൃതി നമ്മുടെ ശരീരമാണ്." (Nature is our Body) *Mukharekha*, Aleppey, June, 2000, pp.6-9.

196. "കുർബ്ബാന ജനജീവിതത്തിന്റെ കൂദാശ" (Eucharist as the Sacrament of People´s Life) *Satyadeepam*, Cochin, 26. July 2000, pp.1,6.

197. "മതങ്ങൾക്കപ്പുറം ആത്മീയതയിലേക്ക്" (Spirituality beyond Religions) *Assisi*, Palai, September 2000, pp.6-9.

198. "നാളത്തെ ആദ്ധ്യാത്മികത" (The Future of Spirituality) *Prabudhakeralam*, Trichur, October 2000, pp.407-410.

199. "വിശ്വാസാനുഭൂതിയും വിശാലദർശനവും" (Faith Experience and Openness), *Jeevadhara*, Kottayam, October 2000, pp.341-347.

200. "മതസമന്വയത്തിന്റെ ദൈവശാസ്ത്രതത്ത്വങ്ങൾ" (The Theological Principles of Inter-religious Harmony), *Mathavum Chintayum*, Alwaye, September, 2000, pp. 47-55.

2001

201. "The Spiritual and Theological Perspectives of Ashrams", *Vidyajyoti*, Delhi, 2001, pp.214-228.

202. "We are Co-Pilgrims, A Christian Understanding of Interreligious Harmony", Ed: Albert Nambiaparambil, *Footprints of Dialogue Pilgrims*, Cochin: Chavara Centre, 2001, pp.72-74.

203. "Rooted and Related, A Meditation on Interreligious Harmony", *Word and Worship*, Bangalore-NBCLC, May, 2001, pp.149-153.

204. "Inter-religious Hermeneutics in Theology", *Third Millennium*, Rajkot, 4/2001, pp.6-21.

205. "The Spiritual Encounter of East and West", Ed: Santivanam, *Jules Monchanin as seen from East and West*, Delhi: ISPCK, 2001, pp.91-99.

206. "Peace in the Vedantic Age of Hinduism", *Jnanadeepa*, Pune, January, 2001, pp.5-13.

207. "*Dominus Jesus* Rewritten", *Jeevadhara*, Kottayam, May 2001, pp. 238-248.

208. "Dem betenden Geist Raum lassen", *Geist und Leben*, Würzburg, 3/2001, pp.161-66.

209. "Gottes Werden im Menschen. Theosis – eine vergessene Grunderfahrung der christlichen Spiritualität", *Christ in der Gegenwart*, Freiburg, 15/2001, pp.117-118.

210. "Meditation auf dem Weg des Dialogs", Ed: J. Lähnemann, *Spiritualitätund ethische Erziehung, Erbe und Herausforderung der Religionen*, Hamburg: EB Verlag, 2001, pp.202-206.

211. "Gott als Subjekt unseres Seins", *Werkmappe Weltkirche*, Missio, Wien, 123/2001, pp.8-9.

212. "മതസമന്വയത്തിന്റെ സംസ്കാരം കേരളത്തിൽ" (Culture of Inter-religious Harmony in Kerala) Ed: Vijay Issac, കെ.സി.ബി.സി. – ക്രിസ്തു ജയന്തി മഹാജൂബിലി സ്മാരകം, Cochin: POC, 2001, pp.285-290.

213. "കരുണയിൽ വിടരുന്ന വിശുദ്ധി" (Spirituality of Compassion) *Jeevadhara*, Kottayam, April, 2001, pp.103-118.

214. "സനാതനമൂല്യങ്ങൾ മൈസ്റ്റർ എക്കഹാർട്ടിന്റെ ദർശനത്തിൽ" (Eternal Values in Meister Eckhart) *Prabudhakeralam*, Trichur, October 2001, pp.399-401.

215. "മനുഷ്യനിലെ ദിവ്യതയെ ഉണർത്താൻ" (Awakening the Divinity in the Human) *Satyadeepam*, Cochin, 19. December, 2001, p.11.

216. "ഈസ്റ്റർ –ഭൂമിയുടെ ഉയിർപ്പുതിരുനാൾ" (Easter, the Resurrection of the Earth), *Chraistavakahalam*, Tiruvalla, April, 2001, pp.8-10.

217. "തീരം തേടുന്ന സഭ" (Church seeking Shores) *Jeevanum Velichavum*, Trivandrum, September-October, 2001, pp.47-49.

2002

218. *Der Geist reißt Mauern nieder, Die Erneuerung unseres Glaubens durch interreligiösen Dialog*, München: Kösel, 2002, pp.156.

219. *Sebastian Kappen: Jesus and Society*, Ed: S. Painadath SJ, Delhi: ISPCK, 2002, pp.200.

220. *Sebastian Kappen: Jesus and Culture*, Ed: S.Painadath SJ, Delhi: ISPCK, 2002, pp.190.

221. "Church´s Theology of Religions, A Historical Overview", Ed: Edmund Chia, *Dialogue, Resource Material for Catholics in Asia*, (Released from FABC- Office of Inter-religious and Ecumenical Affairs), Delhi: ISPCK, 2002, pp.93-144.

222. "FABC´s Theology of Dialogue", Ed: Edmund Chia, *Dialogue, Resource Material for Catholics in Asia*, (Released from FABC- Office of Inter-religious and Ecumenical Affairs), Delhi: ISPCK, 2002, pp.189-197.

223. "Towards a Culture of Dalogue in a Religiously Pluralistic Milieu", *The Living Word*, Alwaye, 2002, pp.211-21.

224. "The Spiritual Process according to the Bhagavad-Gita, A Christian Approach", Ed: A. Thottakara CMI, *Western Encounter with Indian Philosophy*, (Festschrift for Thomas Kadankavil CMI), Bangalore: Dharamaram, 2002, pp.127-137.

225. "Divinisation, the Unfolding of the Divine in the Human", Ed: L. Fernando, *Seeking New Horizons*,(Festschrift for Michel Amaladoss SJ) ISPCK, Delhi, 2002, pp.278-287.

226. "Church as the Continuation of the Table-Fellowship of Jesus", Ed: Rosario Rocha SJ / Kuruvila Pandikatt SJ, *Dreams and Visions*, (Essays in Honour of Kurien Kunnumpuram SJ) Pune: Jnanadeepa, 2002, pp. 71-91.

227. "The Spiritual and Theological Perspectives of Ashrams", Ed: Saccidananda Ashram, *A Commemorative Volume for Santivanam 50 Years*, Tiruchi: Santivanam, 2002, pp.6-19.

228. "Does the Gita advocate Violence?", *Jnanadeepa*, Pune, July 2002, pp.23-30.

229. "Spiritual Encounter of East and West, The Interpersonal and Transpersonal Streams of Spirituality", Ed: Tom Michel SJ, *Papers of the 15th International Congress of Jesuit Ecumenists*, Rome, Curia SJ, 2002, pp.5-12; Response by F.X. Clooney SJ, pp.13-17.

230. "Hat das Ordensleben eine Zukunft in der Kirche? *Ordenskorrespondenz*, Bamberg, 2002, 259-263 / *Ordensnachrichten*, Wien, 2002, Nr. 2: pp.44-49.

231. "Unser Christus fordert keine Leistungen", *Publik-Forum*, Frankfurt, 7/ 2002, p.60.

232. "വിശ്വധർമ്മസാരം" (Essence of Religions) *Prabudhakeralam*, Trichur, April, 2002, pp.155-157.

233. "മൗലികത വെടിഞ്ഞ് സമന്വയത്തിലേക്ക്" (Harmony beyond Religious Fundamentalism) *Matavaum Chintayum*, Alwaye, March 2002, pp. 61-70.

234. "പ്രവാചകചൈതന്യം മതങ്ങളിൽ" (Prophetic Spirit in Religions) *Assisi*, Palai, September 2002, pp.6-10.

235. "കേരളത്തിലെ മതമേഖലയിലെ സംഘർഷങ്ങൾ" (Tensions on the Religious Landscape of Kerala), *Jeevadhara*, Kottayam, November 2002, pp.309-319.

236. "ആദ്ധ്യാത്മികത, മൈസ്റ്റർ എക്ഹാർട്ടിന്റെ അനുഭൂതിയിൽ" (Spirituality according to Meister Eckhart), *Prabudhakeralam*, Trichur, October, 2002, pp.419-422.

237. "മതങ്ങളും കമ്പോളവത്കരിക്കപ്പെടുന്നു" (The Commercialisation of Religions) *Satyadeepam*, Ernakulam, 04. September, 2002, pp.7-8.

238. "മതവൈവിധ്യത്തിന്റെ ദൈവവിജ്ഞാനീയമാനങ്ങൾ" (The Dimensions of Religious Diversity) *Matavaum Chintayum*, Alwaye, October, 2002, pp.5-12.

239. "മനുഷ്യനിലെ ദിവ്യതയെ ഉണർത്താൻ" (Awakening the Divine in the Human) *Christavakahalam*, Tiruvalla, December, 2002, 4-6.

240. "സഹ്യന്റെ മകൾക്ക് ഒരു ചരമക്കുറിപ്പ്" (On the Eco-crisis of Periyar River), *Jalatharangam*, Alwaye, September 2002, pp.6-12.

2003

241. ***Solitude and Solidarity, Ashrams of Catholic Initiative***, **Delhi: ISPCK, 2003, pp.183.**

242. "What is happening to Kerala! ", *New Leader*, September 1-15, 2003, pp.10-11.

243. "An Indian Reading of the Gospel of John", *Word and Worship*, Bangalore, July-September, 2003, pp.148-163.

244. "I seek the Convergence between Theosis and Advaita", Ed: S.Painadath SJ, *Solitude and Solidarity*, Delhi: ISPCK, 2003, pp.53-56.

245. "The Spiritual and Theological Perspectives of Ashrams", Ed: S.Painadath SJ, *Solitude and Solidarity*, Delhi: ISPCK, 2003, pp.120-148.

246. "Catholic Ashrams in India, Priests and Nuns inculturating into Sannyasa", *Satyadeepam* (Engl), Cochin, 1-15, December, 2003, pp.3, 12.

247. „Das eine Wort und die vielen Heiligen Schriften", *Materialheft für Missionssonntag*, Missio-München, October, 2003, pp.5-7.

248. "Sich loslassen", (Fastenmeditation: Verwandlung), *Christ in der Gegenwart*, Freiburg, 11 / 2003, p.87.

249. "Sich niederlassen", (Fastenmeditation: Verwandlung), *Christ in der Gegenwart*, Freiburg, 12/ 2003, p.95.

250. "Einswerden" ", (Fastenmeditation: Verwandlung), *Christ in der Gegenwart*, Freiburg,13/ 2003, p.104.

251. "Neuwerden lassen", (Fastenmeditation: Verwandlung), *Christ in der Gegenwart*, Freiburg,14/ 2003, p.112.

252. "Gottes Geist in allem"", (Fastenmeditation: Verwandlung), *Christ in der Gegenwart*, Freiburg, 15 / 2003, p.120.

253. "Erfüllte Zeit", *Memo, Österreichische Rundfunk*, Wien, 20. April, 2003, pp.33-36.

254. "ക്രൈസ്തവാദ്ധ്യാത്മികതയും വേദാന്തദർശനവും" (Christian Faith and Vedanta), *Prabudhakeralam*, Trichur, October, 2003, pp.410-412.

255. "ആഴങ്ങൾ തേടുന്ന ആശ്രമാദ്ധ്യാത്മികത" (Ashram Spirituality Seeking Depth), Satyadeepam, Cochin, 3.12.2003, pp.5,12.

256. "ബെദ്ലെഹത്തെ മറന്നുപോയോ?" (Forgetting Bethlehem?) *Satyadeepam*, Cochin, 17. December, 2003, pp.3, 8.

257. "സർവ്വധർമ്മസാരം" (100 Weekly Meditation an Inter-religions Themes) *Satyadeepam*, Cochin, 2001-2003.

2004

258. *De Geest breekt Muren af, Vernieuwing van ons geloof door de interreligieuze dialoog* (Flemish Translation of *Der Geist reißt Mauern nieder*) **Gent: Carmelitana, 2004 pp.134.**

259. "An Asian Reading of the Gospel of John," *East Asian Pastoral Review*, Manila, Nr. 2, 2004, pp.176-190.

260. "The Integrated Spirituality of the Bhagavad Gita, A Contribution to Hindu Christian Dialogue", *Journal of Ecumenical Studies*, USA, Summer, 2004, pp.305-324.

261. "Integration through Spirituality according to the Bhagavad Gita", *Jnanadeepa*, Pune, July, 2004, pp.17-28.

262. "Towards a Culture of Interreligious Dialogue", Ed. Selvister Ponnumuthan, *Christian Contribution to Nation Building* (Commemorative Volume of the Centenary of Saint Thomas/Francis Xavier), Cochin: POC, 2004, pp.314-319.

263. "Verwurzelt sein", (Fastenmeditation: Baumsymbol), *Christ in der Gegenwart*, Freiburg, 9/ 200471.

264. "Getragen sein", (Fastenmeditation: Baumsymbol), *Christ in der Gegenwart*, Freiburg, 10/ 2004, p.80.

265. "Genährt werden", (Fastenmeditation: Baumsymbol) *Christ in der Gegenwart*, Freiburg,11/ 2004, p.87.

266. "Verwandelt werden", (Fastenmeditation: Baumsymbol) *Christ in der Gegenwart*, Freiburg, 12/ 2004, p.95.

267. "Verbunden sein", (Fastenmeditation: Baumsymbol) *Christ in der Gegenwart*, Freiburg, 13/ 2004, p.102.

268. "Gott als Subjekt des Betens", Ed.: Werner Schüßler/ Reimer, *Das Gebet als Grundakt des Glaubens*, Münster: LIT, 2004, pp.29-47.

269. "Sakrament der Erde, kosmische Eucharistie", *Christ in der Gegenwart*, Freiburg, March 2004, 8 / 2004, p.64.

270. "Das eine Wort und die vielen heiligen Schriften", *Christlich Pädagogische Blätter*, Wien, 2004, Nr. 4, pp.208-210.

271. "പരിസ്ഥിതിയുടെ ക്രൈസ്തവദർശനം" (The Christian View on Ecology), *Satyadeepam*, Cochin, May, 2004, pp.1,5.

272. "ലോകോന്മുഖമായ ആദ്ധ്യാത്മികത" (World - affirming Spirituality) *Jeevadhara*, Kottayam, October 2004, pp. 319-326.

273. "മതാനുഷ്ഠാനങ്ങളിലെ യാന്ത്രികതയും പ്രവാചകന്മാരുടെ പ്രതിഷേ ധവും" (Ritualism and the Protest of Prophets), *Prabudhakeralam*, Trichur, October 2004, pp.384-387.

274. "ആദ്ധ്യാത്മികത–മതാത്മകത" (Spirituality, Religiosity) *Assisi*, Palai, October-November, 2004, pp.11-13.

2005

275. "Diversity of Religions and Unity in Spirituality", Ed. Thomas D'Sa, *The Church in India in the Emerging Third Millennium*, Bangalore: NBCLC, 2005, pp.625-632.

276. "Harmony between the Mystical and the Prophetic Streams of Spirituality", *Third Millennium*, Rajkot, July-September, 2005, 7-18.

277. "Respect the Diversity of Religions, Recognize the Unity in Spirituality", *Word and Worship*, Bangalore, March-April, 2005, pp. 124-131.

278. "Inculturation of Life-Style" Ed. Saturnino Dias, *Rooting Faith in Asia –Source book for Inculturation*, (FABC Handbook), Bangalore: Claretians, 2005, pp.347-352.

279. "Diversity of Religions, Unity in Spirituality", Ed. L. Boeve, *Religious Experience and Contemporary Theological Epistemology*, Leuven: University Press, 2005, pp.141-151.

280. "Mysticism, the Depth Dimension of Spirituality", *Journal of Dharma*, Bangalore, 4/2005, pp.395-409.

281. "Der Weg in die Tiefe", (Fastenmeditationen zum Brunnensymbol), *Christ in der Gegenwart*, Freiburg, 7 / 2005, p.56.

282. "Der Vater als Quelle ", (Fastenmeditationen zum Brunnensymbol), *Christ in der Gegenwart*, Freiburg, 8 / 2005, p.63.

283. "Christus als Brunnen", (Fastenmeditationen zum Brunnensymbol), *Christ in der Gegenwart,* Freiburg, 9 / 2005, p.72.

284. "Geist als Strom", (Fastenmeditationen zum Brunnensymbol), *Christ in der Gegenwart,* Freiburg, 10 / 2005, p.80.

285. "Kinder Gottes sein, Mutter Gottes werden", (Fastenmeditationen zum Brunnensymbol), *Christ in der Gegenwart,* Freiburg, 11 / 2005, p.88.

286. "Dialog als die neue Sprache der Mission, *Forum Mission,* Luzern, 2005, pp.150-165

287. "In Indien geistig unterwegs sein, Was können wir von den Hindus lernen?", *Materialheft,* Missio-München, October, 2005, pp.9-11.

288. "ഫാ. ഷാക് ദുപൂയി, മതസമന്വയത്തിന്റെ ദൈവശാസ്ത്രജ്ഞൻ" (Jacques Dupuis, Theologian of Inter-religious Harmony) *Satyadeepam,* Cochin, 12.05.2005, pp.1. 6.

289. "മതാതീതക്രിസ്താനുഭവത്തിന്റെ ഭാരതീയ നീർച്ചാലുകൾ" (The Channels of Spirituality beyond Religions), *Satyadeepam,* Cochin, 23. November, 2005, pp.1,6.

290. "നവോത്ഥാനാചാര്യന്മാരുടെ ക്രിസ്തുദർശനം" (The Christ experience of the Reformers in India), Ed: Thomas Panikulam SJ: `mcXw I{InkvXp (The Christ that India perceived.) Palai: Jeevan Books, 2005, pp.122-140.

291. "ഭൂമിദർശനം വേദങ്ങളിലും ബൈബിളിലും" (The Theology of the Earth in the Vedas and in the Bible), *Prabudhakeralam,* Trichur, March 2005, pp.106-110.

292. "ഭാരതീയ വിദ്യാഭ്യാസമൂല്യങ്ങൾ " (The Educational Values of Traditional India) *Prabudhakeralam,* Trichur, October 2005, pp.408-411.

293. "ദൈവം മനുഷ്യനായത് മനുഷ്യനിലെ ദിവ്യതയെ ഉണർത്താൻ" (God became Human to Awaken the Divine in the Human), *Assisi,* Palai, December 2005, pp.9-11.

294. "സർവ്വമതപ്രാർത്ഥന" (100 Weekly Meditations with Universal Prayers) *Satyadeepam,* Cochin, 2003-2005.

2006

295. *The Spiritual Journey*, Delhi: ISPCK, 2006, pp.120.

296. *We are Co-Pilgrims*, Delhi: ISPCK, 2006, pp.122.

297. *Befreiung zum wahren Leben, 50 meditative Schritte der Selbsterkenntnis*, München: Kösel, 2006, 150.

298. *Co-Workers for your Joy, Festschrift in Honour of George Gispert Sauch SJ*, Ed: S. Painadath SJ / Leonard Fernando SJ, Delhi: ISPCK, 2006, pp.331.

299. പ്രാർത്ഥനാഞ്ജലി, മതസമന്വയത്തിന്റെ ഭാവഗീതങ്ങൾ (100 inter-Religious Prayers) Kalady: Sameeksha, 2006, pp.107.

300. മൂല്യബോധനപാഠകങ്ങൾ, അദ്ധ്യാപകസഹായി, ഭാഗം – 1 (Teachers' Manual for Value Education) Ed: Roy M. Thottam SJ / S. Painadath SJ, Cochin: Snehasena, 2006 pp.111.

301. "Awaken the Mystic, Alert the Prophet", Jeevadhara, Kottayam, Sept. 2006, 372-378.

302. "Credal Formula, End or Beginning? The Nicea-Constantinople Creed in the age of Dialogue initiated by Vatican II" , *Jeevadhara*, Kottayam, May, 2006, pp.211-220.

303. "Ecosophy: An Indian Paradigm of Eco-spirituality", *Jnanadeepa*, July 2006, 149-161.

304. "Towards the God beyond God – The Mystical Way of Meister Eckhart and the Vedantic Path of the Upanishads", Ed: S.Painadath SJ / L. Fernando SJ *Co-Worker for your Joy*, (Festschrift for Gispert Sauch SJ) Delhi: ISPCK/ Vidyajyoti, 2006, 284-311.

305. "The Integrated Spirituality of the Bhagavad Gita", *Dharma*, Pure Life Society, Kuala Lumpur, 2005, Part I: Nr. 1-2, pp.37-41; Part II: Nr. 3-4, pp.37-43.

306. "Integration through Spirituality according to the Bhagavad Gita", Ed: Kurien Kunnumpuram SJ, *Life in Abundance, Indian Christian Reflections on Spirituality*, Bombay: St. Paul´s, 2006, pp.22-32.

307. "A Culture of Competition or Compassion? Relevance of the Bhagavad Gita", Ed: Youth Geetha Conference, *Souvenir of the International Geetha Conference*, Kuala Lumpur: Geetha Ashram, 2006, pp.91-93.

308. "The Tree as our Spiritual Master", *Ashram Aikya Newsletter*, Bangalore, 2006, Nr. 47, pp.16-19.

309. "Erkenne, wer du bist, und werde, der du bist", *Christ in der Gegenwart*, Freiburg, 2006, Nr. 25, pp.205-06.

310. "Askese",(Fastenmeditationen über Grundtugenden), *Christ in der Gegenwart,* Freiburg, 10 / 2006, p.80.

311. "Achtsamkeit", (Fastenmeditationen über Grundtugenden), *Christ in der Gegenwart,* Freiburg, 11 / 2006, p.88.

312. "Vertrauen", (Fastenmeditationen über Grundtugenden), *Christ in der Gegenwart,* Freiburg, 12 / 2006, p.96.

313. "Barmherzigkeit", (Fastenmeditationen über Grundtugenden), *Christ in der Gegenwart,* Freiburg, 13 / 2006, p.104.

314. "Freude", (Fastenmeditationen über Grundtugenden), *Christ in der Gegenwart,* Freiburg, 14 / 2006, p.112.

315. "Der Geist reißt Mauern nieder. Erfahrungen des Dialogs aus Indien", *Forum-Weltkirche*, Freiburg, 2006, Nr. 4. 33-34.

316. "Versöhnung, der Weg zum Frieden", Geistlicher Impuls, *Jesuiten*, München, 2/ 2006, pp.22-23.

317. "Kulturelle Vielfalt ist Lebensqualität, Ein indischer Jesuit zum Dialog der Religionen", *Main Post*, Würzburg, 23.01.2006, p.2.

318. "Christen und Muslime wollen die Welt bekehren, Zu den Reaktionen auf die Mohammed-Karikaturen", *Main Post*. Würzburg, 08.03.2006, p.2.

319. "Een brug tussen Azie en Europa", Ed: Lucette Verboven, *Pelgrims Onderweg, Spirituele Ervaringen en Gesprekken*, Kessel-Lo: Pelckmans, 2006, pp.161-176.

320. "മിസ്റ്റിക്കിനെ ഉണർത്തൂ, പ്രവാചകനെ കേൾക്കൂ." (Awaken the Mystic, Alert the Prophet) *Jeevadhara*, Kottayam, August 2006, pp.351-357.

321. "ഗീതാസാധന" (A Retreat with the Gita), Series of six articles, *Prabudhakeralam*, Trichur, March-December 2006.

322. "ആഗോളവത്കരണത്തിന്റെ പ്രശ്നങ്ങളും ഗീതയുടെ പ്രതിവിധിയും" (The Crisis of Globalisation and the Response of the Gita) *Prabudhakeralam*, Trichur, October, 2006, pp.445-449.

323. "തിരുവോണം" (Tiru Onam, Festival of Harmony) *Deepanalam*, Palai, 31.08.2006, p.4.

2007

324. മൂല്യബോധനപാഠകങ്ങൾ, അദ്ധ്യാപക സഹായി, ഭാഗം – II (Teachers' Manual for Value Education) Ed: Roy M. Thottam SJ / S. Painadath SJ, Cochin: Snehasena, 2007 pp.96.

325. മൂല്യബോധനപാഠകങ്ങൾ, അദ്ധ്യാപക സഹായി, ഭാഗം – III (Teachers' Manual for Value Education) Ed: Roy M. Thottam SJ / S. Painadath SJ, Cochin: Snehasena, 2007 pp.120.

326. "Jesuit Spirituality and Inter-religious Harmony", Ed: Michel Amaladoss, For others, with others, Arrupe challenges Indian Jesuits, Anand: GSP, 2007, pp.179-202.

327. "The Bhagavad Gita´s Message of Hermony in an Inter-dependent World", *Jnanadeepa*, Pune, July 2007, 5-15.

328. "Towards a Paradigm for Inter-religious Harmony", Ed: Victor Edwin SJ, *Dialogue in a New Key*, Delhi: Jesuit Secretariat for Dialogue, 2007, pp.45-48.

329. "Respect Diversity, Recognise Unity", *Jeevadhara*, Kottayam, September, 2007, pp.452-456.

330. "The Integrated Spirituality of the Bhagavad Gita", *Dharma*, Pure Life Society, Kuala Lumpur, 2007, Part III, Nr. 1-2, pp.40-50.

331. "Diversity of Religions, Harmony in Spirituality, A Search with *Fides et Ratio*", Ed: Kuncheria Pathil CMI, *Indian Theology seeking New Horizons* (Festschrift for Constantine Manalel CMI), Bombay: St. Pauls, 2007, pp.138-144.

332. "A Story of Spiritual Search" , *Jivan*, Anand, May-June, 2007, p.19.

333. "The Three Cs of Jesuit Spirituality", Ed: Victor Edwin, *Dialogue in a New Key*, Delhi: JCSA, 2007, pp.49-51.

334. "Die Elemente im Gleichgewicht", (Fastenmeditationen zur Frage *Wer bin ich?*), *Christ in der Gegenwart*, Freiburg, 8 / 2007 p.64.

335. "Wer bin ich? ", (Fastenmeditationen zur Frage *Wer bin ich?*), *Christ in der Gegenwart*, Freiburg, 9 / 2007, p.72.

336. "Der Name Jesu", (Fastenmeditationen zur Frage *Wer bin ich?*), *Christ in der Gegenwart*, Freiburg, 10 / 2007, p.80.

337. "Nach innen horchen", (Fastenmeditationen zur Frage *Wer bin ich?*), *Christ in der Gegenwart*, Freiburg, 11 / 2007, p.87.

338. "Teile und genieße", (Fastenmeditationen zur Frage *Wer bin ich?*), *Christ in der Gegenwart*, Freiburg, 12 / 2007, p.95

339. "Achtung", *Missio-Magazin*, München, 2007, Nr. 5. pp.8-9.

340. "Das eine Wort und die vielen Schriften", Ed: Josef Sinkovits / Ulrich Winkler, *Weltkirche und Weltreligionen, Die Bilanz des II. Vat. Konzils 40 Jahre nach Nostra Aetate*, Innsbruck: Tyrolia, 2007, pp.247-256.

341. "Geben und Empfangen", *Missio Konkret*, München, 3 /2007, pp. 14-15.

342. "Ein Weg nach Innen", *Weltweit, Magazin der Jesuitenmission*, Nürnberg, June 2007, pp.12-14.

343. Die Erde ernährt uns, wenn wir sie ernähren, Jesuitenpater über den Umgang mit der Schöpfung, *Main Post*, Würzburg, 08.03.2007, p.2.

344. "Hinduismo" , Ed: Jose Garcia de Castro SJ, *Diccionario de Espiritualidad Ignaciana*, 2007, Vol.II, Malino: Sal Terrae, pp.939-942.

345. "സുവിശേഷം ലോകമതങ്ങളിൽ" (The Good News in World Religions) *Prabudhakeralam*, Trichur, October 2007, pp.445-448.

346. "ആത്മീയതയിലെ ഏകത്വം മതങ്ങളിലെ വൈവിധ്യം" (Unity in Spirituality, Diversity in Religions) *Manodarsanam*, Maradi, September-October, 2007, pp.45-46.

347. "കുർബ്ബാന ജനകീയമാകണം" (The Eucharist and the People) *Nazranideepam*, Thodupuzha, April 2007, pp.5-7.

348. "വർഗ്ഗീയതാചർച്ച മതകാഴ്ചപ്പാടിൽ" (Communalism from Religious Perspectives) Ed: E.J. Thomas SJ, വർഗ്ഗീയതയോ മതരാഷ്ട്രീയതയോ ? Pilathara, St. Joseph´s College, 2007, pp.19-42.

349. "ബ്രഹ്മബന്ധബ്, ഭാരതീയ ദൈവശാസ്ത്രത്തിന്റെ ഉപജ്ഞാതാവ്" (Brahmabandhab Upadyaya, the Initiator of Indian Theology), Satyadeepam, Cochin, 07. November 2007, pp. 5,12

350. "മരുഭൂമിയിലെ ഗർജ്ജിതം" (Reflection on a Poem) Ed: L. Kizhakedam, ദേവസ്മൃതി, പ്രൊഫ. പി.സി. ദേവസ്യയുടെജീവിതവും സംഭാവനകളും, Cochin: St. Paul´s, 2007, pp.29-34.

2008

351. *Wyzwolenie przez medytacje, 50 krokow do samopoznania,* (Polish translation of *Befreiung zumwahren Leben*) **Krakow: Wydawnictwo WAM, 2008, pp.150.**

352. *A Hindu-Catholic, Brahmabandhab Upadhyay's Significance for Indian Christian Theology*, Ed: S. Painadath SJ / Jacob Parappally MSFS, Bangalore: Asian Trading Corporation, 2008, pp.208.

353. "Towards an Inter-Scriptural Hermeneutics, Divinisation of the Human in the Bhagavad Gita and in the Gospel of John", *Word and Worship*, Bangalore, March-April, 2008, pp.112-125.

354. "Exploring Unity in Spirituality", Ed: Victor Edwin SJ / E. Daly SJ, *Journeying together in Faith* (Festschrift for Paul Jackson SJ), Anand: GSP, 2008, pp.99-102.

355. "Brahmabandhab Upadhyaya's Inspiration for Intra-religious Dialogue and Inculturation", Ed. S.Painadath SJ / J. Parappally MSFS, *A Hindu-Catholic, Brahmabandhab Upadhyaya's Significance for Indian Christian Theology*, Bangalore: Asian Trading Corporation, 2008, pp. 87-99.

356. "Nurture a Culture of Respect", *Jivan*, GSP, Anand, November-December, 2008, pp.15-16.

357. "We are Divine, Atmabodha and Theosis Converging in Indian Christian Spirituality", Ed: Jacob Kavunkal SVD, *Theological Explorations* (Festschrift for Joesef Neuner SJ), Delhi: ISPCK, 2008, pp.125-144.

358. "The Asian Heritage", Ed: Anthony Rogers, *Colloquium on Laity in the Church*, Manila, FABC-OHD, 2008, pp.187-191.

359. "The Inward Journey", Ed: Anthony Rogers, *Colloquium on Laity in the Church*, Manila, FABC-OHD, 2008, pp.193-200.

360. "Der leidende Gott, der neugestaltende Gott, Gottes Sein ist im Werden", Ed: Wilhelm Küsters / T.Meurer, *Religion betrifft uns*, Aachen: Bergmoser + Höller, 2008, pp.21, 23, 26.

361. "Wir leben in einer begnadeten Zeit", Ed. Johannes Röser, *Mein Glaube in Bewegung*, Freiburg: Herder, 2008, 247-248.

362. "Kontemplation", *Kontemplation und Mystik*, Petersberg, 2008, Nr. 2, pp.3-15.

363. "Der Prozess der spirituellen Versenkung, Ein Replik zum Vortrag von S. Painadath", (vonGeorg Reider), *Kontemplation und Mystik*, Petersberg, Via Nova, 2/ 2008, pp.19-24.

364. "Eine Spiritualität für die Zukunft", *Wendekreis*, Luzern, 2008, Nr. 6. pp.13-14.

365. "Das neue Leben in Christus", (Fastenmeditationen über Vergöttlichung) *Christ in der Gegenwart*, Freiburg, 6 / 2008, p.72.

366. "Gott wird im Menschen geboren", (Fastenmeditationen über Vergöttlichung) *Christ in der Gegenwart*, Freiburg, 7 / 2008, p.80.

367. "Bild Gottes sein – Gleichnis Gottes werden", (Fastenmeditationen über Vergöttlichung) *Christ in der Gegenwart*, Freiburg, 8 / 2008, p.88.

368. "Christus als Subjekt unseres Seins", (Fastenmeditationen über Vergöttlichung) *Christ in der Gegenwart*, Freiburg, 9 / 2008, p.96.

369. "Vermählen, Verwandeln, Vereinen", (Fastenmeditationen über Vergöttlichung) *Christ in der Gegenwart*, Freiburg, 10 / 2008, p.116.

370. "Dialog als die neue Sprache der Mission", *Christlich Pädagogische Blätter*, Wien, 2008, Nr. 4. pp.236-238.

371. "Die Erde unser Leib: zu einer mystischen Spiritualität der Erde", Ed: Detlind Langer, *Gottesfreundschaft*, (Festschrift für Gotthard Fuchs), Stuttgart: Kohlhammer, 2008, pp.313-325.

372. "ആത്മാവിന്റെ അന്വേഷണം" (The Searching Soul) *Piravi*, Trivandrum, November 2008, pp.12-17.

373. "വിദ്യാഭ്യാസം വിവേകാനുപദർശനത്തിൽ" (Education in the Vision of Swami Vivekananda) *Vandevivekanandam*, Palghat, Vivekanandasamajam, 2008, pp.54-55.

374. "ക്രൈസ്തവസന്യാസത്തിന്റെ ഭാരതീയപശ്ചാത്തലം" (Christian Monasticiam and its Indian Background) *Jeevadhara*, Kottayam, October, 2008, pp.324-335.

375. "ധ്യാനത്തിന്റെ സാമൂഹിക ഊർജ്ജം" (The Social Potential of Meditation), *Sujeevitam*, Cochin, May, 2008, pp.10-12, 23.

376. "നാം സഹതീർത്ഥാടകർ" (100 Meditation on inter –religious harmany), *Satyadeepam*, Cochin, 2005-2008.

2009

377. *The Power of Silence, Fifty Meditations to Discover the Divine Space within you*, Delhi: ISPCK, 2009, pp.173.

378. "Sameeksha the Jesuit Inter-religious Ashram in Kerala", *Jivan*, Anand, September 2009, pp.4-9.

379. "Paulus – Zur Freiheit berufen", *Katechetische Blätter*. München, 2009, Nr. 4. pp.282-289.

380. "Den Einklang der Herzen entdecken", *Kontinente, Die Magazin der Missionsbenediktinnerinnen*, Sehlehdorf, July, 2009, pp.1-6.

381. "Die Harmonie der Herzen entdecken", Ed: Christoph Quarch, *Unsere Welt ist heilig, Auf dem Weg zu einer globalen Spiritualität*, Freiburg: Herder, 2009, pp.46-56.

382. "Vom Gesetz zu Christus", (Fastenmeditationen über Paulus) *Christ in der Gegenwart*, Freiburg, 9 /2009, p.96.

383. "Vom Fleisch zum Geist", (Fastenmeditationen über Paulus) *Christ in der Gegenwart*, Freiburg, 10/ 2009, p.116.

384. "Von Sklaverei zur Freiheit", (Fastenmeditationen über Paulus) *Christ in der Gegenwart*, Freiburg, 11 / 2009, p.124.

385. "Von der Furchtzur Liebe", (Fastenmeditationen über Paulus) *Christ in der Gegenwart*, Freiburg, 12 / 2009, p.132.

386. "Vom Tod zum Leben", (Fastenmeditationen über Paulus) *Christ in der Gegenwart*, Freiburg, 13 /2009, p.140.

387. "ഗാന്ധിജിയും ഫ്രാൻസീസും" (Gandhiji and Francis) *Assisi*, Palai, Ocobter 2009, pp.14-17.

388. "മനുഷ്യനിലെ ദിവ്യവത്കരണം" (Divinisation of the Human) Ed: Martin Kallungal, ക്രിസ്തീയ വിശുദ്ധി, നൂതനാഭിമുഖ്യങ്ങൾ, Cochin: Mar Luis Press, 2009, pp.140-148.

2010

389. *Wir alle sind Pilger, Gebete der Welt,* München: Kösel, 2010, **pp.135.**

390. "For a Culture of Respect", *Jivan,* Anand, November –December, 2010, p.9.

391. "The Asian Heritage", Ed: Anthony Rogers, *Laity in Public Life, Nurturing the Inner Being for a New Social Evangelization,* Manila: FABC-OHD, 2010, pp.187-191.

392. "The Inward Journey", Ed: Anthony Rogers, *Laity in Public Life, Nurturing the Inner Being for a New Social Evangelization,* FABC-OHD, Manila, 2010, pp.193-200.

393. "A Christian Reading of the Bhagavad Gita", *Jeevadhara,* Kottayam, 2010, pp.388- 398.

394. "ക്രൈസ്തവ ദർശനവും മാനവികതയും" (Christianity and Humanism) Ed: T. Bhaskaran, {io\m-cm-b-WKp-cphpw am\-hn-I-Xbpw, Varkala: Sivagiri, 2010, pp.221-228.

2011

395. *The Power of Silence, Fifty Meditations to Discover the Divine Space within you,* Manila: Claretian Publications, 2011, **pp.165.**

396. *Gott hat viele Namen, Spirituelle Erfahrungen, die unser Herz berühren,* Ed: Richard Rohr /Sebastian Painadath, Münsterschwarzach: **Vier-Türme-Verlag, 2011, pp.208.**

397. "Sameeksha, Harmony of the Spirit", *Yearbook of the Society of Jesus,* Rome, Jesuit Curia, 2011, pp.116-118 (in five languages).

398. "Respect for other religions in Hinduism", Ed: Josef Meili, *Forum Mission*, Kriens: Brunner Verlag, 2011, Nr. 7, pp.162-175.

399. "Gitasadhana – Retreat with the Bhagavad Gita", *Ignis*, Anand, 2011, Nr. 1, pp.22-29.

400. "Bhagavad Gita's Message of Harmony in a Globalised Word", *Gita Vani*, Singapore,Gita Society, 2011, pp145-155.

401. "An Indian Paradigm of Jesuit Spirituality", *Sparkles, Souvenir of 50 years, Kerala Jesuit Province*, Calicut, 2011, pp.73-74.

402. "Die Einkehr", (Fastenmeditationen mit Gebeten der Religionen), *Christ in der Gegenwart*, Freiburg, 11 / 2011, p.123.

403. "Die Geborgenheit", (Fastenmeditationen mit Gebeten der Religionen), *Christ in der Gegenwart*, Freiburg, 12 / 2011, p.132.

404. "Die Zuversicht", (Fastenmeditationen mit Gebeten der Religionen), *Christ in der Gegenwart*, Freiburg, 13 / 2011, p.140.

405. "Das Licht", (Fastenmeditationen mit Gebeten der Religionen), *Christ in der Gegenwart*, Freiburg, 14 / 2011, p.160.

406. "Die Liebe", (Fastenmeditationen mit Gebeten der Religionen), *Christ in der Gegenwart*, Freiburg, 15 / 2011, p.168.

407. "Die Sehnsucht nach Gott in der östlichen Mystik", Ed: Richard Rohr / S.Painadath, *Gott hat viele Namen, Spirituelle Erfahrungen, die unser Herz berühren*, Münsterschwarzach:,Vier Türme, 2011, pp.34-47.

408. "Persönlichen Gotteserfahrungen – Blicke über den Horizont", Ed: Richard Rohr / S.Painadath, *Gott hat viele Namen, Spirituelle Erfahrungen, die unser Herz berühren*, Münsterschwarzach: Vier Türme, 2011, pp.81-103.

409. "Der Prozess der spirituellen Versenkung", Ed: Richard Rohr / S.Painadath, *Gott hat viele Namen, Spirituelle Erfahrungen, die unser Herz berühren*, Münsterschwarzach: Vier Türme, 2011, pp.104-123.

410. "Kirche in einer pluralistischen Gesellschaft", Ed: Richard Rohr / S.Painadath, *Gott hat viele Namen, Spirituelle Erfahrungen, die unser Herz berühren*, Münsterschwarzach: Vier Türme, 2011, 144-152.

411. "Auf dem Weg zu einer Kultur der inter-religiösen Harmonie", Ed: Richard Rohr / S.Painadath, *Gott hat viele Namen, Spirituelle Erfahrungen, die unser Herz berühren*, Münsterschwarzach: Vier Türme, 2011, 153-156.

412. "Gott und Gotteserfahrung in der Bhagavad Gita", Ed: Richard Rohr / S.Painadath, *Gott hat viele Namen, Spirituelle Erfahrungen, die unser Herz berühren*, Münsterschwarzach: Vier Türme, 2011, 188-198.

413. "Höre, was der Geist den Kirchen sagt". Ed: Richard Rohr / S.Painadath, *Gott hat viele Namen, Spirituelle Erfahrungen, die unser Herz berühren*, Münsterschwarzach: Vier Türme, 2011, 200-201.

414. "Gottes Sein ist im Werden, " *Christ in der Gegenwart*, Freiburg, 25/2011, p.281.

415. "ക്രൈസ്തവ സന്ന്യാസത്തിന്റെ ഭാരതീയ വേരുകൾ" (The Indian Roots of Christian Monasticism) Ed: Sojan Paul Peekunnel, സ്നേഹം പെയ്തിറങ്ങുന്ന സന്യാസം , Thellakam: Vidyabhavan, 2011, pp.20-36.

416. "ഈശോസഭ മലസാർസഭയെ പിളർത്തിയോ വളർത്തിയോ?" (Have the Jesuits Divided or Nourished the Malabar Church?) *Kerala Jesuit*, Cochin, 2011, Nr. 86, pp.7-10.

417. "മിത്തുകളിലെ ദൈവാവിഷ്കാരം" (Revelation through Myths in Hinduism), *Jeevadhara*, Kottayam, 2011, pp.159-168.

418. "ഭാരതസംസ്കാര മുദ്രകൾ" (100 Weekly Meditations on Indian Culture), *Satyadeepam*, Cochin, 2008-2011.

2012

419. നാം സഹതീർത്ഥാടകർ, മതസമന്വയത്തിന്റെ ക്രൈസ്തവ ഭാഷ്യം (On the Theology of Inter-religions Harmony), Kottayam: Yatra, 2012. pp. 138, pp.159-168.

420. "Eco-spirituality in the Hindu Tradition", Oriens Journal, Shillong, 2012, Nr. 3, 61-76.

421. "Dialectics between Spirituality and Religion", *Jeevadhara*, Kottayam, September, 2012, pp. 333-352.

422. "Does the Gita advocate Violence?", Ed: Kurien Kunnumpuram SJ, *Blood and Tears, Interdisciplinary Studies on Religion and Violence*, Bombay: St. Paul´s, 2012 pp.37-47.

423. "Sharing Christ-experience in the Light of Asian Spiritualities", Ed. Joy Thomas SVD / V. Zacharias SVD, *New Evangelization, Asian Perspectives*, Bombay: St. Paul´s, 2012, pp.185-190.

424. "Im Namen Jesu", (Fastenmeditationen mit Jesus-Gebet) *Christ in der Gegenwart*, Freiburg, 9 /2012. p.96.

425. "Göttliche Energien", (Fastenmeditationen mit Jesus-Gebet) *Christ in der Gegenwart*, Freiburg, 10 / 2012, p.116.

426. "Der innere Raum des Jesusgebets", (Fastenmeditationen mit Jesus-Gebet) *Christ in der Gegenwart*, Freiburg, 11 / 2012. p.124.

427. "Der Prozess des Jesusgebets", (Fastenmeditationen mit Jesus-Gebet) *Christ in der Gegenwart*, Freiburg, 12 / 2012. p.131.

428. "Die Erfahrung des Jesusgebets", (Fastenmeditationen mit Jesus-Gebet) *Christ in der Gegenwart*, Freiburg, 13 / 2012. p.140.

429. "Geschichte des Jesusgebets", (Fastenmeditationen mit Jesus-Gebet) *Christ in der Gegenwart*, Freiburg, 14 / 2012. p.160.

430. "Die heilende Wirkung des Jesusgebets", (Fastenmeditationen mit Jesus-Gebet) *Christ in der Gegenwart*, Freiburg, 15 / 2012. p.168.

431. "സമീക്ഷയിലെ കാൽവയ്പ്പ് : മലയാളത്തിൽ ദൈവശാസ്ത്രം പ രിപ്പിക്കുന്ന രീതി " (Teaching Theology in Malayalam at Sameeksha) *Karunikan*, Cochin, 2012, pp.24-26.

432. "തനിമ തേടുന്ന ഭാരതസഭ" (Indian Church Seeking Identity) *Satyadeepam*, 4. January, 2012, pp.1, 6-7.

433. "മതവൈവിധ്യത്തെ ആദരിച്ച വലിയ മനസ്സ് " (On Cardinal Joseph Parecattil) *Deepika Week-end*, Kottayam, 24.03.2012, p.1.

2013

434. *Perception, an Interdisciplinary Exploration*, Ed: S. Painadath SJ / Sreekala M. Nair, Delhi: ISPCK, 2013, pp. 216.

435. *Die Kraft des Gebets*, Ed: Sebastian Painadath / Gerondissa Diodora, Anslem Grün, Münsterschwarzach: Vier-Türme-Verlag, 2013, pp.169.

436. നാളെയിലേയ്ക്കൊരു നീൾക്കാഴ്ച (Festschrift for Samuel Rayan SJ) Ed: P.K. Michel Tharakan/ S. Painadath SJ, Cochin : St. Pauls, 2013, pp. 334.

437. "Quest for Indian Theology, Preface, for the book", Ed: George Gispert-Sauch SJ, The Gospel and the Newspaper, Theological Queries digging the Indian Quarry, Delhi, ISPCK, 2013, pp.vii-x.

438. "Silence of the Heart to gain Spiritual Depth", *Jivan*, Anand, August, 2013, pp.5-9.

439. "Towards a Culture of Transformative Harmony", *Gandhi Marg*, New Delhi, April-June, 2013, pp.89-97.

440. "Towards Theo-centrism in Inter-religious Relations. Jouneying with Pope John Paul II", *Jeevadhara*, Kottayam, September, 2013, pp. 408-412.

441. "The Trans-mental Intuitive Perception. Insights from the Christian Mystical Heritage" Ed. S.Painadath SJ / Sreekala M. Nair, *Perception, An Interdisciplinary Exploration*, Delhi: ISPCK, 2013. pp.165-182.

442. "Gott mit uns", (Fastenmeditationen über Gott in uns) *Christ in der Gegenwart*, Freiburg, 7 / 2013, p.80.

443. "Gott unter uns", (Fastenmeditationen über Gott in uns) *Christ in der Gegenwart*, Freiburg, 8 / 2013, p.88.

444. "Gott für uns", (Fastenmeditationen über Gott in uns) *Christ in der Gegenwart*, Freiburg, 9 / 2013, p.108.

445. "Gott um uns", (Fastenmeditationen über Gott in uns) *Christ in der Gegenwart*, Freiburg, 10 / 2013, p.116.

446. "Gott bei uns"", (Fastenmeditationen über Gott in uns) *Christ in der Gegenwart*, Freiburg, 11 / 2013, p.124.

447. "Gott in uns", (Fastenmeditationen über Gott in uns) *Christ in der Gegenwart*, Freiburg, 12 / 2013, p.132.

448. "Gott durch uns", (Fastenmeditationen über Gott in uns) *Christ in der Gegenwart*, Freiburg, 13 / 2013, p.140.

449. "Spiritualität und Christologie" Ed: Klaus Krämer / Klaus Vellguth, *Weltkirchliche Spiritualität, Den Glauben neu erfahren*, (Festschrift zum 70-ten Geburtstag von Sebastian Painadath SJ, Reihe: *Theologie der einen Welt*), Freiburg: Herder, 2013, pp.159-166.

450. "Gebet- Meditation- Kontemplation: Was geschieht beim Beten?" Ed: Sebastian Painadath /Gerondissa Diodora / Anslem Grün, *Die Kraft des Gebets*, Münsterschwarzach: Vier TürmeVerlag, 2013, pp.17-26.

451. "Das mystische Gebet in der östlichen Religionen", Ed: Sebastian Painadath / Gerondissa Diodora / Anslem Grün, *Die Kraft des Gebets*, Münsterschwarzach: Vier Türme Verlag, 2013,, 65-82

452. "Neue Perspektiven für das Beten", Ed: Sebastian Painadath / Gerondissa Diodora / Anslem Grün (ed) *Die Kraft des Gebets*, Münsterschwarzach: Vier Türme Verlag, 2013, 143-147.

453. "Nachwort", 149-150 Ed: Sebastian Painadath / Gerondissa Diodora / Anslem Grün (ed) *Die Kraft des Gebets*, Münsterschwarzach: Vier Türme Verlag, 2013, pp.149-150.

454. "വിശ്വമാനവികത യേശുദർശനത്തിൽ" (Universal Humanism in Jesus´s Vision) *Jeevadhara*, Kottayam, August 2013, pp.322-330.

455. "വിവേകാനന്ദദർശനവും മാനവികതയും" (Vivekananda and Humanism), *Prabudhakeralam*, Trichur, October 2013, pp.83-85.

456. "ഋഷിതുല്യനായ സാമുവൽ രായൻ" (Samuel Rayan the Sage) Ed: Michel Tharakan / S. Painadath SJ, നാളെയിലേയ്ക്കൊരു നീൾക്കാഴ്ച, Cochin: St. Paul´s, 2013, pp.28-31.

457. "സാമുവൽ രായന്റെ ദൈവശാസ്ത്രദർശനം" (The Theology of Samuel Rayan) Ed: Michel Tharakan / S.Painadath SJ, നാളെയിലേയ്ക്കൊരു ന ീൾക്കാഴ്ച, Cochin: St. Paul´s, 2013, pp.32-41.

2014

458. *Das Herz in Schwingung bringen, Beten mit Mantras und Melodien*, (with **Rose Pudukadan**), **Münsterschwarzach: Vier-Türme-Verlag, 2014, pp.127.**

459. *Spiritual Co-Pilgrims, Towards a Christian Spirituality in Dialogue with Asian Religions*,**Manila: Claretian Publications, 2014, pp.259.**

460. "Jesuits and their Secular Spirituality", *Ignis*, Anand, Nr. 2-3, 2009, pp.58-60.

461. "Interreligious Relations in Civil Society", *Jeevadhara*, Kottayam, 2014, pp.55-67.

462. "In his Light we See Light", *New Leader*, Madras, October 16, 2014, pp.10-14.

463. "Die Mystik öffnet den Horizont", Ed. Klaus Bäuerle, *Gott einzig und vielfältig*, Würzburg: Echter Verlag, 2014, pp.261-270.

464. "Christuserfahrung", (Fastenmeditationen über *Evangelii Gaudium* von Pp. Franziskus), *Christ in der Gegenwart*, Freiburg, 10 / 2014, p.116.

465. "Geisterfahrung", (Fastenmeditationen über *Evangelii Gaudium* von Pp. Franziskus), *Christ in der Gegenwart*, Freiburg, 11 / 2014, p.124.

466. "Instinkt des Glaubens", (Fastenmeditationen über *Evangelii Gaudium* von Pp. Franziskus), *Christ in der Gegenwart*, Freiburg, 12 / 2014, p.132.

467. "Wirtschaft und die Armen", (Fastenmeditationen über *Evangelii Gaudium* von Pp. Franziskus), *Christ in der Gegenwart,* Freiburg, 13 / 2014, p.140.

468. "Was dient der Würde? ", (Fastenmeditationen über *Evangelii Gaudium* von Pp. Franziskus), *Christ in der Gegenwart,* Freiburg, 14 / 2014, p.160.

469. "Vielfalt der Kulturen", (Fastenmeditationen über *Evangelii Gaudium* von Pp. Franziskus), *Christ in der Gegenwart,* Freiburg, 15 / 2014, p.167.

470. "Türen zum Göttlichen", (Fastenmeditationen über *Evangelii Gaudium* von Pp. Franziskus), *Christ in der Gegenwart,* Freiburg, 16 / 2014, p.176.

471. "Das gewordene Christentum und die werdende Kirche", Ed: Wolf Notker, *Anselm Grün begegnen*, Festschrift für P. Anselm Grün, Vier Türme Verlag, Münsterschwarzach, 2014, pp.278-91.

472. "Kontemplation und Aktion nach der Bhagavad Gita", *Rundbrief der Gesellschaft der christlichen Mystik*, 2 /2014, 24-35.

473. "Spirituality and Christology", Ed. Klaus Krämer / Klaus Vellguth (ed), *Spirituality of the Universal Church*. Rediscovering Faith, Commemorative Volume marking the 70th Birthday of Sebastian Painadath SJ, Claretians, Quezon City, Philippines, 2014, 119-125.

474. "Die Mystik öffnet den Horizont", Ed: Kalus Bäuerle, *Gott einzig und vielfältig*, Würzburg, Echter Verlag, 2014, pp.261-270.

475. "സഭ അതിരുകളിലേക്ക് നീങ്ങിത്തുടങ്ങിയോ?" (Church Moving to Frontiers? On *Evangelii Gaudium*) *Satyadeepam*, Cochin, 27. November, 2014, pp.1, 17, 19.

476. "ഗീതാസാധന" (100 weekly Meditation on the Spirituality of th Bhagavad Gita) *Satyadeepam*,Cochin, 2011–2015.

2015

477. "The Transforming Power of Contemplative Silence", *Concilium*, 5/2015, pp.33-43.

478. "Jesus Prayer and Jesuit Spirituality", *Ignis*, 1/2015, pp.16-34.

479. "Flexible Communities of Spiritual Search", *Jeevadhara*, Kottayam, May 2015, pp.57-74.

480. "The Impact of Indian Thought on Samuel Rayan´s Theology", Ed: Kurien Kunnumpuram SJ, *The Vision of a New Church and a New Society*. A Scholarly Assessment of Dr. Samuel Rayan´s Contribution to Indian Christian Theology, New Delhi: Christian World Imprints, 2015, pp.350-360.

481. "GC 36 should think of Wider Jesuit Families", *Jivan*, Anand, Nov-Dec. 2015, pp.4-9.

482. "Rezeption des II. Vatikanischen Konzils in der indischen Ortskirche", *Weltkirch & Mission*, Sekretariat der Deutschen Bischofskonferenz, Bonn, 2015, pp.59-68.

483. "Vernetzt und verschieden", (Fastenmeditation I) *Christ in der Gegenwart*, Freiburg, 8/2015, p.87.

484. "Eine Spiritualität in den vielen Religionen", (Fastenmeditation II) *Christ in der Gegenwart*, Freiburg, 9/2015, p.107.

485. "Suche nach Gotteserfahrung – Die Wurzel des Baumes", (Fastenmeditation III) *Christ in der Gegenwart*, Freiburg, 10/2015, p.114.

486. "Der Kanal des Göttlichen", (Fastenmeditation IV) *Christ in der Gegenwart*, Freiburg, 11/2015, p.124.

487. "Was Gott relativiert hat, dürfen wir nicht verabsolutisieren", (Fastenmeditation V) *Christ in der Gegenwart*, Freiburg, 12/2015, p.132.

488. "Wir sind Mitpilgernde", (Fastenmeditation VI) *Christ in der Gegenwart*, Freiburg, 13/2015, p.140.

489. "Kritische Harmonie", (Fastenmeditation VII) *Christ in der Gegenwart*, Freiburg, 14/2015, p.160.

490. "Innere Pilgerreise in Achtsamkeit," *Missio-Konkret*, München, 4/2015, p.5-6.

491. "Wir sind Pilgernde", Christ in der Gegenwart, Freiburg, 33/2015, p.365.

2016

492. *Erkenne deine göttliche Natur, 55 Meditationen,* **Münsterschwarzach, Vier-Türme-Verlag, 2016, pp.160**

493. "Barmherzigkeit als gebärender Vorgang" (Fastenmeditation I), *Christ in der Gegenwart*, Freiburg, 7/2016, p.80.

494. "Jesus, das Antlitz der Barmherzigkeit" (Fastenmeditation II), *Christ in der Gegenwart,* Freiburg, 8/2016, p.86.

495. "Gottes Gegenwart ist Barmherzigkeit" (Fastenmeditation III), *Christ in der Gegenwart,* Freiburg, 9/2016, p.95.

496. "Kirche der Barmherzigkeit" (Fastenmeditation IV), *Christ in der Gegenwart*, Freiburg, 10/2016, p.116.

497. "Barmherzigkeit mit Gerechtigkeit" (Fastenmeditation V), *Christ in der Gegenwart*, Freiburg, 11/2016, p.124.

498. "Wie die goldene Regel" (Fastenmeditation VI), *Christ in der Gegenwart*, Freiburg, 12/2016, 132.

499. "Zu einer Kultur der Barmherzigkeit finden" (Fastenmeditation VII), *Christ in der Gegenwart*, Freiburg, 13/2016, 140.

500. "Der eine Geist und die vielen Religionen, " Ferment, Schweizer Pallottiner Zeitschrift, Gassau, 3/2016, p.40-43.

501. "Der Fluß, meine Meisterin, " Ed: Johannes Schleicher, *Niklaus von Flüe, Engel des Friedens auf Erden,* Münsterschwarzach, Vier-Türme Verlag, 2016, p.98-108.

502. "Vertiefung der christlichen Spiritualität durch Begegnung mit der Östlichen Mystik, " Ed: Christian Rutishauer / M. Hasenauer, *Mystiche Wege*, Münsterschwarzach, Vier-Türme Verlag, 2016, p.84-98.

2017

503. *Das Sonnengebet, Ein Übungsbuch zum Tagesbegin,* (Überarbeitete Ausgabe), **Münsterschwarzach, Vier-Türme Verlag, 2017, pp.84.**

504. "Der eine Geist und die vielen Religionen, Zur Theologie der interreligiösen Harmonie, " *Ökumenisches Forum, Journal for Ecumenical and Patristic Studies,* Theol. Fakultät, Graz, *37/38, 2017,* p.121-133.

505. "Christification, the Mystical Dimension of Indian Christology," Ed: PR John SJ, *Searching Christology through an Asian Optic*, Forum of South Asian Jesuit Theologians, Nr. 1.Delhi, ISPCK, 2017. pp.13-22.

506. "Stretch the Canvas and Extent your Tents," NBCLC in the area of inter-religious harmony, Ed: Annette Thottakara, *Towards a New Horizon*, Bangalore, NBCLC, 2017, pp.193-204

507. "Die Ursprache des Menschen, " *Christ in der Gegenwart*, Freiburg, 39/2017, p.427.

508. "Frieden ist die Botschaft aller Religionen", Franz-Thomas im Gespräch mit S.Painadath SJ, *Unsere Seelsorge*, Themenheft der Hauptabteilung Seelsorge, Münster, 2017, p.28-29.

2018

509. *You are divine, 100 Meditations on Theosis*, **Delhi, ISPCK, 2018, pp.237.**

510. *Christ-Consciousness, Contemplation with Jesus Prayer*, (with **Sr. Rose Pudukadan), Delhi, ISPCK, 2018, pp.146.**

511. *Das Herz in Schwingung bringen, Jesus-Gebet mit Mantras und Melodien*, (Durchgesehene Ausgabe), Münsterschwarzach, Vier-Türme Verlag, 2018 pp.128.

512. "Geistige Begegnung zwischen West und Ost, Meister Eckhart und die Upanishaden", *Kontemplation und Mystik*, Holzkirchen, 2/2018, p. 5-32.

513. "Know that You do not Know, the Dynamics of Theology," Ed: K. Henry Jose MSFS, *Becoming Human, Becoming Christ*, Festschrift for Jacob Parappally MSFS, Bangalore, ATC, 2018, pp.104-116.

514. "Brücken bauen: Über Religionen und Fluten hinweg", *Jesuiten Weltweit*, Nürnberg, 2018, 22-25.

515. "Die Fremde Gnade *Theosis*, " (Fastenmeditation 1) *Christ in der Gegenwart*, 7/2018, S. 80.

516. "Christus werden, " (Fastenmeditation 2) *Christ in der Gegenwart*, 8/2018, S. 88.

517. "In der Gegenwart des Geistes", (Fastenmeditation 3) *Christ in der Gegenwart*, 9/2018, S. 108.

518. "Die Flamme, die Quelle, das Licht, " (Fastenmeditation 4) *Christ in der Gegenwart*, 10/2018, S. 116.

519. "Theosis-Erfahrungen in Weltreligionen, " (Fastenmeditation 5) *Christ in der Gegenwart*, 11/2018, S. 124.

520. "Theosis im Alltag," (Fastenmeditation 6) *Christ in der Gegenwart*, 12/2018, S. 132.

Contributors

AMA Samy, SJ a is renowned Zen Master (Gen-Un-Ken). He is a Jesuit of Madurai Province and became the first Indian to have received the Dharma Seal of Enlightenment from a recognized Zen master. In 1972, he went to Japan to get trainded in Zen under Yamada Ko-Un Roshi. He began teaching Zen in the 1980s and, in 1996, established the Zen centre, Bodhi Zendo, at Perumalmalai, Kodaikanal, Tamil Nadu where he lives and teaches. He has numerous publications to his credit.

Dr. Anand Amaladass, SJ is Professor Emeritus from Sacred Heart College, Satya Nilayam Chennai. He is a visiting Professor to various Universities in Germany, Austria and other parts of Europe. He was founder-editor of *Satya Nilayam Chennai Journal of Intercultural Philosophy* for six years and co-editor of the *Journal of Hindu Christian Studies* for the last 20 years. He has numerous publications to his credit dealing with Indology, Christian themes in Indian Art and Intercultural encounters.

Dr. Aloysius Pieris, SJ is a Sri Lankan Jesuit priest and founder-director of the Tulana Research Center for Encounter and Dialogue. He is a renowned scholar in Buddhism and a reputed theologian. He has STL from the Pontifical Theological Faculty in Naples and a Th. D from Tilburg University. Aloysius Pieris has studied Pali and Sanskrit from the University of London and completed doctoral studies in Buddhist philosophy from the University of Sri Lanka. He has held academic positions in many theological centers. A prolific author, his books deal with Christian-Buddhist encounters and Asian theology of liberation.

Dr. Bettina Sharada Bäumer is an Austrian scholar of religion and a renowned Indologist, and one of the foremost expounders of Kashmir Saivism and a well-known figure in the field of inter-religious dialogue. She was awarded the Austrian Decoration for Science and Art by the Government of Austria in 2012 and Padma Shri by Government of India in 2015 for her contribution to Literature and Education. She pursued higher studies in Philosophy, Religion, Theology and Music at the Universities of Salzburg, Wien, Zurich, Rome and Munich. She did doctoral studies at the University of Munich and her thesis was, *Creation as Play: The concept of Lila in Hinduism, its Philosophical and Theological Significance.*

Dr. Christian Hackbarth-Johnson studied Protestant theology with emphasis on interreligious dialogue between Christianity and Asian religions in Tübingen, Vienna and Munich. He did doctoral studies at Ludwig-Maximilians-University Munich 1998-2002 with a doctoral thesis on "Spiritual experience and identity in the life of Henri Le Saux/Swami Abhishiktananda." He continues to work as independent theologian and spiritual teacher. He did specialized research project at the University of Salzburg on "The Biographical Location of Interreligious Processes". He has many publications to his credit.

Dr. Christian M. Rutishauser, SJ Provincial of Jesuits in Switzerland, is the former Program Director of the Lassalle-Haus, Centre for Spirituality, Interreligious Dialogue and Social Responsibility, Bad Schönbrunn (Switzerland). He has lectured on Jewish Studies in Munich, Freiburg, Rome, Jerusalem; member of the Swiss and German Episcopal Conference Commissions for Dialogue with Judaism. He has several publications to his credit.

Dr. Felix Wilfred is a renowned theologian. Born in Tamilnadu in 1948, he belongs to the Diocese of Kuzhithurai and currently is the Founder Director of Asian Centre of Cross-Cultural Studies, Panayur, Chennai. He was Professor of the School of Philosophy and Religion, University of Madras and was a member of the International Theological commission of the Vatican. He was the editor of *Concilium* and has numerous publications to his credit. As visiting professor, he has taught at the Universities of Nijmegen, Munster, Frankfurt am Main, Boston College and Ateneo de Manila. His researches and field studies today cut across many disciplines in humanities and social sciences.

Dr. Francis Xavier Clooney, SJ is a well-known scholar in the teachings of Hinduism. After receiving his doctorate in South Asian Languages and Civilizations at the University of Chicago in 1984, Clooney taught at Boston College until 2005, serving also as the Academic Director of the Oxford Centre for Hindu Studies. He is the Parkman Professor of Divinity and Professor of Comparative Theology at Harvard Divinity School. In 2010 Clooney became the Director of Harvard's Center for the Study of World Religions. That same year he was named a Fellow of the British Academy. He has been nominated as the winner of the John Courtney Murray Award in 2017 for his distinguished theological achievements.

Dr. Francis X. D'Sa, SJ is presently Emeritus Professor of Systematic Theology and Indian Religions (JDV, Pune), and Founder-Director of Institute for the Study of Religion, Pune. He had his studies at the Universities of Mumbai, Poona, Innsbruck and Vienna. He was Guest-Professor in different universities such as Innsbruck, Freiburg, Salzburg, Frankfurt/M, and occupied the Chair of Missionswissenschaft und Dialog der Religionen, University of Würzburg (2007-08). He has lectured extensively in the German speaking countries. Numerous are his publications in English and in German. In 2007 he was awarded *Doctor honoris causa* from the University of Frankfurt, Germany. He is a creative thinker and an acknowledged Panikkar-specialist.

Dr. George Gispert-Sauch, SJ is a Jesuit of Bombay Province of the Society of Jesus. A Spaniard by birth he came to India in 1949 and did specialized studies in Sanskrit and Pali and contributed much to the growth of intercultural explorations in theology. He began his teaching career in theology at St. Mary's College, Kurseong in 1964 and later on completed doctorate from *Institut Catholique de Paris*, France. He continued to teach in Vidyajyoti, Delhi till 2015. In the mid 1980s he delivered the Teape Lectures at the Divinity School of Cambridge. He has six books to his credit and has written more than 200 articles. At present he is in Vinayalaya, Bombay.

Dr. Henry Pattarumadathil, SJ holds a licentiate in Sacred Scripture from the Pontifical Biblical Institute and a doctorate in Biblical theology from the Pontifical Gregorian University, Rome. He taught Bible for many years at the Jesuit Regional Theology Centre, Kalady. Since 2011, he teaches at the Pontifical Biblical Institute, Rome.

Dr. Jojo M. Fung, SJ is a member of the Malaysia-Singapore Region of the Society of Jesus. He is an Assistant Professor of systematic theology at the Loyola School of Theology in Quezon City, Philippines. He also serves as the Coordinator of the Pastoral Renewal Program and Assistant to the director for Academic Affairs of East Asian Pastoral Institute, Manila. He has done specialization in Contextual Theology from the Association of Theological Colleges, Chicago. He has numerous articles and books to his credit and especially noteworthy are his publications in the field of Shamanic Theology.

Dr. Martin Kämpchen, writer, scholar and journalist, was born in Germany and continues to stay in India since 1973, mostly in Santinketan. He has translated Sri Ramakrishna and Rabindranath Tagore from Bengali to German, written on interreligious and intercultural dialogue, and is a contributor to *Frankfurter Allgemeine* on Indian culture. He works among Santal tribal villages since thirty years. Website: www.martin-kaempchen.com

Dr. Michael Amaladoss, SJ is a Jesuit from Tamil Nadu. A prolific writer and a reputed theologian, he began his teaching career at Vidya Jyoti, Delhi and later taught in many theological centers across the world. He has been an Assistant to the Superior General of the Jesuits and a Consultor to the Pontifical Council for Interreligious Dialogue and Pontifical Council for Culture. He is the founder-director of the

Institute of Dialogue with Cultures and Religions, a research institute affiliated to the University of Madras. He has published 31 books and some of his books have been translated into various languages.

Dr. Priyadarshana Jain is currently the Head of the Department of Jainology, University of Madras and also the Course coordinator for Prakrit Studies in Chennai. Besides Jainology she has been teaching Comparative Religion and Philosophy. She has lectured in UK, USA, and Thailand on projects related to Jainology and Interreligious dialogue. She has authored three books and translated original sources from Hindi/Prakrit to English.

Dr. Norbert Nagler, studied theology, German Literature and Comparative Religions at German universities. He holds a doctorate in theology. From 1991 to 1996 he worked as a diocesan coordinator of Missio, the International Catholic Organization of Missions. From 1996 to 2016 he was the director of the Formation Sector of *Missio*, Aachen. Since 2016 he works as the Project Manager of the Pastoral Department of the diocese of Hamburg for the Promotion of Missionary Consciousness. His special involvement is in the region of Mecklenburg.

Dr. Stephen Chundamthadam, SJ is the Director, Samanvaya Centre for Indian Studies, Kanjirapally, Kerala. He holds a Ph.D from the University of Madras. For several years Stephen taught courses on Indian Philosophy, Spirituality, World Religion, Yoga and Karate in Jnana-Deepa Vidyapeeth, Pune. He has done specialized training in Yoga and Karate.

Dr. Victor Edwin, SJ is director, Department of Islamic Studies at Vidya Jyoti College of Theology. Besides his studies in philosophy and science, he acquired an MA in theology (Delhi), M.Phil in Interfaith Relations from the University of Birmingham, MA in Islamic Studies from Aligrah Muslim University, and a PhD from Jamia Millia Islamia. He teaches in several Christian theological institutions and edits *Salaam*, the Journal of Islamic Studies Association and Coordinates Jesuit relations with Muslims in South Asia. He is dedicated to interfaith dialogue and promotes better relations with believers of other faiths. He has edited/ co-edited six books.

Dr. Xavier Tharamel, SJ has postgraduate degree in Philosophy, University of Madras, Christianity and Interreligious Relations, University of London, and a PhD on Raimon Panikkar's theology of religions from the University of Birmingham, UK. He has published articles and presented research papers at national and international seminars.

www.ingramcontent.com/pod-product-compliance
Lightning Source LLC
Chambersburg PA
CBHW060410030726
47495CB00003B/518